RISING STARS
COLLECTION

July 2015

August 2015

September 2015

October 2015

Carol Marinelli recently filled in a form where she was asked for her job title and was thrilled, after all these years, to be able to put down her answer as 'writer'.

Then it asked what Carol did for relaxation and, after chewing on her pen for a moment, Carol put down the truth—'writing'. The third question asked, 'What are your hobbies?' Well, not wanting to look obsessed or, worse still, boring, she crossed the fingers on her free hand and answered 'swimming and tennis'. But, given that the chlorine in the pool does terrible things to her highlights and the closest she's got to a tennis racket in the last couple of years is watching the Australian Open, I'm sure you can guess the real answer!

Published in Great Britain 2015
by Mills & Boon, an imprint of Harlequin (UK) Limited,
Eton House, 18-24 Paradise Road, Richmond, Surrey, TW9 1SR

ONE SUMMER NIGHT © 2015 Harlequin Books S.A.

An Indecent Proposition © 2012 Carol Marinelli
Beholden to the Throne © 2013 Carol Marinelli
Hers for One Night Only? © 2012 Carol Marinelli

ISBN: 978-0-263-25419-8

024-0715

Harlequin (UK) Limited's policy is to use papers that are natural, renewable and recyclable products and made from wood grown in sustainable forests. The logging and manufacturing processes conform to the legal environmental regulations of the country of origin.

Printed and bound in Spain
by CPI, Barcelona

An Indecent Proposition

CAROL MARINELLI

CHAPTER ONE

SHE looked forward to his calls far more than she should.

Charlotte knew that.

She should be distant, professional, polite when dealing with this powerful man—but the sound of his voice, the way he paused after her comment, the way she knew that he was smiling at something she had said made Charlotte's toes curl as she lay in her bed.

There had been several calls now. The first had started with Zander terse and abrupt. His Greek accent had been confusing for Charlotte, so much so that she'd actually thought it was her boss Nico in a bad mood. Her phone had rung at six a.m. and it had taken a moment to register that the caller was, in fact, the elusive property owner that she had been chasing on Nico's behalf. It was not one of his lawyers, or the sour PA she was more used to dealing with, but the very man himself.

'This is Zander,' he had snapped to her fuddled brain. 'I thought you wanted to speak with me—it would seem that I was mistaken.'

He had been about to ring off—clearly irritated that she hadn't instantly recognised him—but knowing how badly Nico would take it if she lost this point of contact, Charlotte had stammered out an apology. 'I'm s-sorry for the confusion. It's wonderful to have you return my call.' She hadn't added a sarcastic *finally* to her sentence, though she'd been tempted; instead, she'd glanced at her bedside clock. "It's just that it's six a.m. here.'

There had been a pause, a lengthy one, and though certainly not conciliatory his voice had been a touch less brusque when next he spoke. 'I thought it was eight. You are in Athens, no? Xanos?'

'London.' Charlotte had dragged herself up to sitting in bed.

'You are Charlotte Edwards? Nico Eliades's PA?'

'Yes, but I'm based in London.'

And then, most unexpectedly, came an apology.

'Forgive me. I am in Australia…I just assumed when I worked out the times that, like your boss, you would be in Greece. I will call you back during office hours.'

'There's no need,' Charlotte said hurriedly, not wanting to tell Nico the elusive Zander had finally called and that she had been too groggy to deal with it. 'Don't ring off—I'm up now. Well, not up…'

Oh, dear!

There was a long pause, from both parties. Charlotte cringed because, far from coming across as an efficient PA, she had made it clear she was lying in bed. Zander, well, his pause, followed by a light huskiness to his voice, made her blush further, and not because she was cringing. It was for other reasons entirely.

'Do you want to get a coffee?' he asked. 'I will call back.'

'No, I'm fine…' Charlotte lied, reaching for a pen, determined to be ready whatever figures he flung at her, to be poised and fully engaged. Even if she was desperate to go to the loo, to check on her mum, and, yes, grab a coffee, she would not show it. Then he spoke again and, on a cold London morning, somehow his voice seemed to caress her. Somehow the elusive billionaire spoke not at her but to her.

'Charlotte, I will call you back in five minutes. Go and get a coffee and bring it back to bed—and then we can talk.'

She was about to correct him, for only Nico called her Charlotte in her work. Ms Edwards kept things rather more formal—instilled immediate distance—but it seemed petty to correct Zander when she may have already appeared rude. Whether it sounded efficient or not, she answered with the truth.

'That would be lovely, Mr…?'

'Zander,' came his brief response before he promptly rang off.

This was how it had started.

Yes, she looked forward to his calls far more than she should—their early morning chats had become a routine. He would call at some ungodly hour, talk for a brief moment and then hang up; she would make coffee, bring it back to bed, wait for the ring of her work phone and then listen to his rich, deep voice. She would write down the messages to relay to Nico, dispense with work, and then *they* would talk.

Not much.

Just a little more than perhaps she should.

'So you don't actually work with Nico?' Zander had probed one Sunday night. The unexpected timing had surprised her, though, of course, Charlotte realised, it was Monday morning there. She was huddled under the sheets, the weather filthy outside, the sound of rain on the windows and his voice keeping her warm.

'I work for him.'

'But not alongside him.'

'I work from home,' Charlotte explained. 'Nico travels a lot and I organise things from this end.'

'And do you enjoy it?'

And she hesitated, not for long, just a brief second. 'I love it.'

Which she did, Charlotte told herself and then told herself again. It was a wonderful job, but that was all it was to her—a job rather than a passion, a means to an end rather than the career she had once loved. As a child, 'an international flight attendant' had been her unwavering response when asked what she wanted to be when she grew up. She had studied language at school, and beyond, had applied for and worked for her first airline of choice, been swiftly promoted through the ranks to become a lead attendant. How she longed to be in the air now with her first-class passengers, taking the flight crew their breakfast and lingering in the cockpit at forty thousand feet in the air as they flew towards dawn.

'Don't you miss the company?' he asked, and his question was so direct, so right on the mark she couldn't answer for a second, and stupidly there were tears in her eyes because, hell, yes, she missed company, missed so badly not just the flying but the social aspect too. 'Of course, it would be perfect,' Zander mused to the silence, 'if you have young children.'

'Oh, I don't have children,' she said without thinking, and there was a beat where she realised his question hadn't been so idle, that Zander was gauging her, and it made her feel warm. 'You?'

'Absolutely not. I'm far too irresponsible.' The way that he said it had Charlotte biting on her bottom lip. She chose not to tell him that she nursed her mother at home, and that Amanda's Alzheimer's was worsening. Chose not to tell him that, far from hard, working for Nico was the only work she could do. That being available all hours on the computer or phone, with the handsome wage Nico paid, meant that she could keep the promise her mother had begged for and look after her at home.

'So?' Zander did not let it rest. 'Do you miss the company?'

'Not at all.' She lied, because it was safer. Lied, because if she told him the truth she might just break down. So she told him about lunches with friends and cocktails on Friday, told him about the Charlotte she had once been when she had travelled the world for a living.

'I am reluctant to sell this land.' He turned the conversation back to work. 'Your boss is very insistent. He wants the jetty, of course, because then that entire stretch of cove would be his.'

She said nothing. She was not there for discussion, or for negotiation. Her job was to pass messages on to Nico.

'Have you seen it?' Zander asked. 'Have you been to Xanos?'

And here she could not stay silent, for she had been there, just for a day, and just the once, and she could see absolutely why her boss wanted a slice of it. 'I have and it's completely stunning.' It was—an exclusive, private retreat for the rich and famous. Nico had, for an extremely inflated price, bought from Zander an undeveloped house but, newly married and used to the best, he wanted more for his new wife and son. For weeks now his main focus had been on securing the neighbouring land; however, Zander was reluctant to sell.

'Did you put my lease option to him?'

'I did,' Charlotte said, 'but he's not interested. He really wants to speak with you himself.'

'I rather prefer speaking with you.'

He didn't go far, but it was far enough to have Charlotte blushing, the little hint that he enjoyed their conversations as much as she.

'I should get up,' Zander said.

'Oh.' And she closed her eyes for always he sounded

so *dressed*, so together, she had assumed him at a desk, but it made her toes curl to think he was lying in bed too. 'I thought you were at work.'

'I am,' he said, and she could feel his seductive smile even if she could not see it. 'I can work just as hard on my back.'

He did smile then, though she could not see it. He smiled because he heard her. Heard her inhale as she did now and then, not through her nose but with a catch in her throat. Over the last days it was a sound he had come to crave—so much so that he had dropped his date at her home last night rather than bring her to his, choosing the pleasure of Charlotte's voice to wake up to.

'You sound tired, you're in bed early.'

'I am.' And it was far easier to say she had been at a wedding the previous night than up at two a.m., chasing her mother through dark streets, trying to persuade her to come back to the house. It was easier by far to tell this glamorous, exotic man, whom she had never met, that her life was a little more fab than drab, to paint a picture, safe in the knowledge they would probably never meet. With Zander on the end of the phone, for a few precious moments she got to live the life she invented.

'Was it a good wedding?'

'It was lovely,' Charlotte replied, thinking of her boss's wedding a few weeks ago, which she had organised but not attended. 'It went off without a hitch.'

'Was it very formal? Did you wear a hat?' His voice was so low she had to concentrate to hear it, but in the nicest of ways. 'I did,' Charlotte said, and that was a complete and utter lie, for Nico's wedding had been tiny and informal, held on the beach of his bayside property on the Greek Island of Xanos, with just a couple of witnesses. Charlotte played her game, closed her eyes and imagined, escaped for a little while, safe in the knowledge she would never meet Zander. 'Though it was a bit windy in the photos. I was worried I might lose it…'

'And do you have plans for tomorrow?'

'Just out for lunch with friends,' Charlotte said, wishing badly it were true, but long lunches with girlfriends were a thing of the past now. Still, it was nice to lie here and dream, nicer still to be in bed talking to Zander and know he was doing the same. 'Okay. Tell your boss I am still considering things.' It was Zander who wrapped up the conversation, but at the same time he opened up her heart. 'He is lucky to have you.'

'Lucky?' Charlotte frowned into the phone.

'Were it not for how much I enjoy speaking with his PA, I would have turned him down.'

And even if Charlotte glowed inside, she reined it in, for her boss was Nico.

'You're not just stringing him along?'

'Charlotte…' His voice was very even, perhaps a little precise. 'I have better things to do with my time than string your boss along. I was ringing to refuse his offer that first day—it was you that made me reconsider.'

He rang off then, and Charlotte lay there, replaying the conversation in her mind, trying to tell herself she was being ridiculous. He was making conversation, that was all, flirting as he probably did with most women. For maybe the hundredth time she pulled over her laptop, her intention to find out all she could about him.

To see him.

But as she had so many times before, Charlotte stopped herself.

His voice, the way he said her name, the way sometimes he *asked* about her, the way he made her feel... she didn't want it to fade, didn't want to find out he was some overweight married man, flirting on the phone. Didn't want this feeling to end.

She dreamt of him, heard his deep, rich voice over and over, and actually awoke with a smile on her face. Getting up, Charlotte looked into the mirror. Her long, honey-blonde hair needed a serious trim, her baggy pyjamas were unfit for male eyes and all she looked was exhausted, nothing like the glamorous woman Zander thought she was. As Charlotte walked into her mother's bedroom, the smell of wet sheets had her close her eyes for a moment. She opened them to her mother's vacant stare.

'Morning, Mum.' As usual, Charlotte got no response, so she tried in her mother's native language, which she had reverted to almost completely now. *'Bonjour, maman.'* Still there was no response. 'Let's get you up for your shower.'

It was so much easier said than done. Charlotte was thumped on the side of her head, scratched on her arm, told to *'Casse-toi'*, and the screams from her mother as she washed her would, had the neighbours not known better, have had them calling the police, for it sounded as if Amanda was being attacked.

Still, it got done and even if Charlotte was still in her pyjamas, at least her mum was bathed, scented and dressed and finally sitting down in her chair in the lounge.

'We could go for a walk on the beach.' Her mother finally spoke, as Charlotte fed her a soft-boiled egg, mashed in with butter, in the hope of adding a few calories, for it wasn't just her mother's mind that was fading away. But even if her words sounded lucid, even if it sounded like a normal conversation, it was, of course, otherwise—they were miles from the beach. But it was her mother's favourite place and when she spoke of the beach, it was always in English, as if she were truly remembering times when she had taken Charlotte there as a child.

'We will,' Charlotte said. 'We could feed the seagulls, maybe?' And she saw her mother smile, saw her eyes and face light up, and even if they would never get to the beach again, would never feed the seagulls together again, her mother's smile was worth the fib.

And it was worth it, Charlotte told herself as she dragged herself through another week. Worth putting her life on hold to take care of her mother, although deep down she knew it couldn't go on much longer.

That *she* couldn't go on much longer.

But, then, like a lifeline came the call.

Mid-afternoon, and not at all his usual time, her heart leapt when she saw that it was Zander. She answered with a smile, anticipating the summer of his words, except his tone was brusque, businesslike.

'Could you pass on a message to Nico?'

'Of course.' She glanced at the clock and tried to work out the times. It must be four in the morning where Zander was.

'I am going to be in Xanos next week. I fly in late Sunday and my schedule is very full, but if you can arrange a meeting with your boss, I have a small window at eight a.m. on Monday. We are moving into the next stage of the development in the coming weeks. I want to discuss with him, before the purchase goes ahead, our plans for that area. He might not be so keen and I don't want him wasting my time later with petitions.'

'I'll let him know.' She waited, waited for the conversation to change as it always did, to slip back to where they spoke about them—but it didn't. Zander rang off and Charlotte rang Nico and relayed the message, but as she hung up, she felt like crying. Knew that once Zander met with Nico, her part in this would be over—that the brief escape his calls had bought would finally come to an end. When Nico rang a few moments later she had to force herself back into business mode.

'How good are you with Greek planning permission laws?'

'Are there such things?' She smiled into the phone, but it faded as Nico spoke on.

'Exactly. Anyway, I've got Paulo onto it, but I'm going to need you in Xanos next week.'

'Me?' Charlotte blinked and then wished she hadn't

for in that instant her mother wandered out to the hall; Charlotte walked briskly, catching Amanda as she fiddled with the catch on the front door.

'Do you really need me there?' It wasn't a no, but it was as close as she dared.

'I wouldn't ask otherwise. I'd like you to visit a couple of homes for me, go through some records…' Since Nico had found out he was adopted, Charlotte had been helping him to find his birth mother, but it had all been through telephone calls and online. She had chosen not to tell him about her problems with her own mother: PAs dealt with their boss's problems, not the other way around. He'd asked her to join him in Xanos a couple of months ago, but that had just been for a day. The carer she had hired had informed her on her return that her mother required too high a level of care. For any future trips Amanda would need to be cared for in a home. 'Is there a problem?' She knew he was frowning. Nico was not a man used to hearing the word 'no', and certainly not from his PA.

'Of course not.' Charlotte swallowed. 'I just need to sort out a few things at this end, but I'll do my best to be there on Monday.'

'Actually…' Nico sounded distracted. 'If you can get in earlier, perhaps the weekend, we can go over a few things. Book in at Ravels and ring me when you get here.'

'Sure,' Charlotte said to thin air, for Nico had already rung off. She had to speak to him when she saw him, had to somehow tell her formidable boss that travel was practically impossible. But what if he insisted? Charlotte closed her eyes at the prospect. She needed this job, needed the wage, needed the flexibility working from home provided—maybe she would have to factor in an occasional trip.

She already had a list of nursing homes drawn up. Charlotte had visited several, riddled with guilt each and every time, for her mother had, on her diagnosis, pleaded with Charlotte to never put her in a home. Now she rang them, asking if there were any respite beds available, her anxiety increasing as she worked her way through the list and each time the response was the same. Far more notice was required.

Finally she found one. A resident had died overnight, and there was a spot available. It felt wrong to be relieved, wrong to be packing up her mother's things, wrong to be driving a distressed Amanda to the place she dreaded most in the world.

'It's just for a few days, Mum.'

'Please…' Amanda sobbed. 'Please don't leave me. Please.'

'I have to go to work, Mum.' Charlotte was crying too. 'I promise, it's just for a little while.'

All it felt was wrong—to sit in the chair at the beauty parlour and be waxed and manicured, to have foils put in her thick blonde hair. Wrong to think of her mother sobbing in a home as she transformed herself back into the glamorous flight attendant Nico had hired.

But there was a flutter of excitement there too as

she pulled out her old wardrobe and packed in her efficient way.

And there was that pit-in-the-stomach thrill as she drove the familiar route to Heathrow airport, saw the jets coming in and heard the high-pitched roar as they took off.

And then, as she sat in her seat, as the plane lifted off the ground and up to the sky, as she looked at the flight attendant facing her and wished she could be her, there was that moment at take-off she would forever adore, the surreal moment where the plane seemed to quiet and you gathered your thoughts. And only then did it actually dawn on her.

She was going to meet Zander.

CHAPTER TWO

ATHENS had been as grey as London, but flying towards Xanos it was as if the clocks had been rewound to autumn. Certainly it would not be as warm as the summer, but the sky was as blue, as was the ocean, and Xanos lay stretched out in the distance, a vivid tapestry of greens and browns. The vineyards laced the mountains and the stunning hotel development stood on the foreshore, gorgeous buildings carved into the cliff side, glittering blue infinity pools that matched the blue jewel of the ocean. She could not wait to land, to sink her feet in the golden sands and to drink in Xanos.

The seaplane came in, not beside the small jetty her boss craved to own but to the newly built, rather more sophisticated one. A ramp made disembarking far easier than it had been the last time Charlotte had visited Xanos, and because anyone who stayed at Ravels must be someone, though she would have loved to, she was not expected to make the short walk from the jetty to the hotel. Instead, she was swallowed by a huge car and driven the short distance into the development, escorted to check in and told that her bags would be taken straight to her room.

Usually she was not intimated by grand surroundings. She had worked long enough with the airline and later with Nico to sample fine hotels and luxury travel, but, though she did her best not to show it, Charlotte found this hotel somewhat overwhelming. Some of the guests who moved through the foyer she recognised from the magazines she devoured. A huge elevator was situated beside a grand staircase, separated by a fountain. There were lavish floral displays at every turn, wealth and opulence in every view; it was hard to believe the hotel had just been in operation for a few short months.

Checking in went smoothly; there was a message from Paulo, Nico's lawyer in Greece, asking her to contact him, and Charlotte declined the receptionist's offer of a booking in the restaurant. She would rather eat alone in her room. Swipe card in hand, she wandered through the hotel, not quite brave enough to have a drink at the bar; instead, she headed for her room, bouncing on the huge king-sized bed and revelling for a guilty moment in the feeling that tonight she would not have to sleep with one ear open in case her mother awoke, that she had a little time to herself.

Still, she was here to work, so she rang Nico and got his voicemail. She told him she had arrived and then she rang Paulo too.

'I'm unable to get hold of Nico,' Paulo said. 'I want to speak with him before this meeting on Monday.'

'I've just left a message.'

'Well, if you do get hold of him, make sure he speaks with me. He says that he doesn't want me present on Monday, but I don't want him speaking with this developer without me—he's bad news.'

'Really?' Normally she would not pursue the conversation, would simply pass the message on, but she was far too interested in the elusive Zander, too curious about the voice she had heard on the end of the phone, to let the opportunity to know more pass by. 'Zander certainly seems inflexible, but...'

Paulo said something in Greek that Charlotte couldn't decipher and then he translated. 'It's a saying here on Xanos—this man is someone who would sell their own mother to the highest bidder. Nico needs to watch out—make sure you have him ring me.'

Paulo was always cautious, Charlotte told herself as she hung up the phone. It was his job to be cautious, she consoled herself. Anyway, she was spending far too much time thinking about a man she had never even met, a man she had spoken to only on the phone, but she didn't want him to be a man like the one Paulo was describing. She wanted him to be every bit as gorgeous as the one she had secretly imagined.

Charlotte stepped out onto the balcony; she could hear a couple from the suite beside her, though couldn't see them because of privacy walls, but their conversation was so exotic and glamorous it was heaven to eavesdrop while she looked out to the beach, to the azure water and gorgeous sands. For a moment she almost felt back in her old life, except there were no colleagues to meet up with, no one to explore the island with, no one to lie with her by the pool, as so often she had.

An uneasy feeling seemed to pool in her throat, tasting of bitterness and martyrdom—the food she had been fed by her mother throughout her childhood. And that was the very last thing she wanted.

She needed to think, really think about her future, and even if the neighboring conversation was intriguing, the beach beckoned more and Charlotte headed inside. She pulled on a simple shift dress, light cardigan and sandals, wanting to catch the last of the evening sun.

Still, even though she was miles from home, even though it was a relief to have a night to herself and the secret pleasure of finally coming face to face with Zander on Monday, as she walked along the golden sands of Xanos, her thoughts turned to her mum. Amanda would have loved it here. Their yearly holidays through Charlotte's childhood were perhaps her most treasured of memories, for it was the only time she had ever really seen her mother happy; the only time Amanda had seemed at peace instead of bitter about the career she had forgone and the lover who, when Amanda had found out she was pregnant, had spurned her instead of facing up to his responsibilities.

How could Charlotte do it to her—put her in a home because it made life easier? Even all these years on, Charlotte nursed guilt for her childish selfishness, for the way she had idolised her absent father, not aware of the sacrifices her mother had made. Oh, the rows and tears that had come from her brought a sting of shame today. But once a year they had cast it aside, walked along Camber Sands or Beachy Head and, without fail, her mother would buy an extra portion of fries each evening, a ten-minute indulgence where they'd feed the seagulls and laugh and whoop as the gathered birds went wild.

There was Nico.

She looked up from her dreams and saw reality: her boss skimming stones in the water. It caught her by surprise, why she could not fathom for Nico lived here now—just along from this stretch of beach was his private residence. Something about him made her start. There was purpose to him, not idle relaxation as his wrist flicked the smooth, flat stones but an anger almost. She carried on walking, though she considered turning around, pretending she hadn't seen him, for so dark were his features, so deep his concentration, she wondered if he and his wife Constantine had just had a row. Still, it would be worse if he saw her turning and thought she was ignoring him, and she did need to pass Paulo's message on so, pretending she had not noticed his dark mood, she walked purposefully towards him, smiling as she called his name.

'Nico!' she called. 'I've been trying to ring you...' And then he turned around and her breath held in her lungs as she realised that, though he looked like him, though it surely was him, somehow the man that had turned to her call was not Nico. She could not explain it; the only thing she could liken it to was, years ago, as a small child she had lost her mother in a department store and a few panicked minutes later had rushed towards the familiar beige coat and tugged on it, had looked up at her mum and recoiled as she'd realised that it was not her, that the eyes that frowned at her had not been her mother's. The feeling was back, was there in her chest now, as her familiar greeting was met with a stranger's stare. 'Sorry.' She walked backwards for a few steps. 'My mistake…'

She wanted to turn and run, it was her first instinct, she wanted to run, for her head was a mass of jumbled thoughts, but instead she walked quickly, desperate to get back to the hotel, to think, to talk to Nico, to find out just what the hell was going on.

'Slow down.' His footsteps were muffled by the sand, but still she heard them, could feel him as he drew closer, jumped with the shock of contact as his hand closed around her shoulder and spun her around. 'Why are you running?'

She turned to eyes that were black, blacker than Nico's, to a face that appeared in every detail to come from the same canvas as Nico's except the brush had been dipped in an ink that was darker; the hand that had created this masterpiece just a touch heavier than the one that had made the other. His hair was longer, his bone structure more severe, but it was his mouth that drew her eyes for a second, a mouth that was heavy and sensual, with beautifully white teeth that smiled a smile that contradicted the bore of his gaze.

'I made a mistake…' She was far too confused to think logically. 'I thought you were someone else.'

'You thought I was Nico?' This was so not how he had planned it. Zander knew he had taken a risk walking on the beach, but being cooped in the hotel was driving him crazy. At the last minute he had changed his plans and flown in early, but it had been a mistake, for already there was a buzz at the hotel. He had checked in under a different name, wanting to see how the hotel ran when the staff were unaware the owner was in residence, but the curious looks told him that Nico was a regular. From the way this woman had approached, the fact she had been trying to ring Nico, Zander knew he had only moments to act to prevent his cover being blown. He wanted his moment on Monday, wanted to see Nico's reaction at first hand, and now he had to convince this woman, this stranger, not to tell him. Somehow he had to win her trust quickly, which was no trouble at all for a man like Zander, who could have any woman eating out of his hand in a matter of moments.

He smiled but his heart was not in it, though surely not a soul on earth could tell, for he had for so long perfected his routine. He looked deep into her eyes and focused on the glittering blue and his hand that was still on her wrist held her more loosely now, but the pulse that leaped beneath his fingers told him that she was in shock and it raced again when next he spoke.

'I am Nico's twin.'

'Twin?' She almost laughed at the ridiculousness of

her response, for of course he was his twin, except she hadn't even known that Nico had one.

'I'm Zander.' And from her blush when he said his name, from the slight catch in her throat, he recognised her. His weekend retreat suddenly became a lot more interesting, a lot more pleasurable perhaps? 'You must be Charlotte.' He smiled and it was deadly; it was a smile that had the hairs on her neck rise in strange response, made her arm pull back from his fingers, from the left hand that had shot out to grab her, when Nico would have used his right. 'Finally we meet.'

'You're Zander.' Her eyes flew away from his intense gaze as she wrestled with mortification—for if their dealings had already been a touch inappropriate, they were far more so now. It had been her boss's twin that she had flirted with.

Oh, and they had been flirting!

'I didn't know Nico even had a twin...' She could not think with him looking at her, could not be in his space. She stepped back a little, moved her eyes from the intensity of his gaze, back to his mouth, but she could not concentrate by looking there, so she looked downwards—to clothes that could never be described as casual, for there was luxury in every thread. The silk and cashmere black jumper billowed in the wind to give a blatant outline of his chest, the charcoal grey linen trousers rested low on narrow hips—there was no escape from his beauty. Even as she searched lower she was met with naked feet, the olive of his skin a contrast to the pale sand, and she wanted to get away from him, wanted the beach to be empty, wanted to get back to the safety of her thoughts and a walk that was gentle and aimless, instead of the confrontation with him.

'Neither does Nico,' Zander said. 'On Monday I plan to surprise him.' He must have seen the flare of worry in her eyes, for he moved swiftly to assure her, 'I am hoping that the surprise will be a pleasant one...' He sensed her doubt, knew that her instinct was to flee, and he did not want her spoiling all he had planned, did not want her running to Nico with her tales, but also... He looked down at the pale cream shift dress and the long slender arm he had a moment ago been holding, then up to the face that was just as pleasing as the voice he had dealt with in recent times, to the blonde hair that the wind whipped around her face and, yes, he wanted time with her, wanted to *meet* the voice that had entranced him, for on Monday, when he had said his piece, when he had wreaked his revenge, for sure, Charlotte would want nothing to do with him.

'I can't believe this.' She was completely stunned. 'Does this mean Nico has found his...?' She stopped herself from asking further. It was certainly not her business to probe into her boss's private life, and Nico gave little away. He had told her, more than a year ago, his suspicions that he was, in fact, adopted, but only so that she could be of assistance in researching his history. Though Nico was actively looking for his birth mother, not once had he mentioned that he had a twin—and an identical one too. She knew she had to speak with him, to get away from Zander and speak with Nico, but there was something that needed to be addressed.

'You knew when you spoke to me.' Her voice was accusing, which was ridiculous perhaps for he owed her nothing, but somehow she felt betrayed. 'I should go back…' There were so many questions and she must not look to him for answers. She plastered on a smile, pretended she was not perturbed, and tried to walk nonchalantly away from him.

'Stay,' Zander said.

'I have things to prepare, I have work to do…'

'Surely you have questions?'

She did, so very many, but surely the answers should come from Nico. Perhaps Zander sensed where her loyalties lay, and in that moment the battle was on—he wanted her loyalty, wanted to take everything from his brother, and Charlotte seemed a very good place to start.

'Let us just enjoy the evening,' he said. 'There is no harm surely in walking. Perhaps we could have a seat at the beach café and watch the sunset.'

Would it be rude to refuse?

Would Nico scold her on Monday for snubbing his brother?

'Or…' he sensed an opening '…we could just walk?'

She gave a hesitant nod. Her guard firmly up, she walked tentatively alongside him, determined to say nothing that might compromise Nico until she was sure what was going on.

'Are you enjoying the hotel?' Zander asked, and she remembered he owned it, that the man beside her owned the very ground they were walking on. She knew then the true might of this man.

'It's wonderful.'

'He was a hard man to find.' It was Zander who broke the tense silence; it was he who spoke of his brother. '*His* name is the one that is different.'

She said nothing to that.

'You like your job?' Zander changed track.

'Of course.' He heard her terse response and could only admire her restraint, for surely she must have a thousand questions, but he watched as she kept them in. He wanted her to speak of his brother, so he paved the way and spoke first about himself.

'I love it here.' The words choked in his throat, for he could not loathe the place more, but when she glanced up at him, Zander made sure he was smiling. 'Always it was my dream to come back…' He looked at the luxurious properties he'd had carved into the cliffs and hills of Xanos and she followed his gaze.

'Where was your house?' She could not help but ask, wondered for a mad moment if it was the house Nico lived in now, but he motioned vaguely to the middle of the development. 'Where is the one you grew up in?'

'Where the hotel is.' He saw her tiny frown. 'It was unsalvageable.' He chose not to tell her it had been the first property he had had knocked down, that he had stood with the best champagne in his hand in his office in Australia, and cheered silently as the bulldozer had set to work. Knowing that his family home was being destroyed had been the only moment of pleasure Xanos had given him.

'You like the beach?'

He saw that she relaxed a little at the less loaded question. 'I love it,' Charlotte admitted. 'Not swimming or anything…' She smiled, a real smile, the first since she had realised who she was speaking to, and he watched her blue eyes brighten, her mouth spread, and he wanted to see more of the same. 'Just walking, thinking…' Her eyes roamed the horizon. 'Remembering…' He wondered what. Perhaps romantic walks with Nico before he'd taken a wife, but her voice broke into his thoughts. 'We always holidayed at the beach,' Charlotte said. 'When I was younger.'

He heard her pensive pause and let it be, had learnt so very well how to deal with women, how to get them to unbend, how to win their trust. There was none more skilled at it than he. So brilliant was his technique that it left every woman stunned and breathless when his true nature was revealed, when the man who had listened so intently, had supposedly cared, just dismissed all they had briefly shared.

He was at his dangerous best now, a small question here, an insightful observation there, and as they strolled with seemingly little purpose Charlotte spoke more easily. As a seagull ducked and swooped at a piece of paper, she laughed. Another bird joined it and then another, furious screeches of protest when there was no food to be found.

'Poor things.'

'Poor things?' Zander gave a wry laugh. 'I can ensure for my guests many things, but a seagull-free beach would be the icing on the cake.'

'I love them.' And she laughed and then, because it was safer than talking about Nico, she told him about her long-ago walks with her mother on their holidays, how they had fed the gulls, how it had been a great end to their days.

They walked, five, maybe ten minutes more. The beach café was serving cocktails but they walked past all that to a place more secluded, away from the sand of the beach to the rocky coves around it. Charlotte, calm beside him, was forced to concentrate more on her step than her words.

'How long have you worked for Nico?'

'Nearly two years now,' Charlotte said, and he saw her tense, saw that she sensed perhaps he was fishing, but he worked carefully around that.

'And before that?' He tried to guess at her age, mid-twenties he gauged, which was very young to be an assistant to a man like Nico Eliades, but he was quite sure his brother had not hired her purely for her business skills. 'Did you do business studies?'

'Oh, no...' She shook her head. 'I never intended to be a PA—I was a flight attendant. International.' She added. 'That's how I met him.'

It galled Zander, but he did not show it.

'On a flight?'

Charlotte nodded. 'I recognised him back at the hotel I was booked into—he was having trouble being understood. We were in Japan and, unusually for that hotel, the staff member he was dealing with spoke very poor English, so I stepped in.'

'You speak Japanese?'

She held her finger and thumb a tiny space a part. 'A little. And my mother's French, so I can get by there too. Oh, and I can speak a little… *Mía glóssa then íne poté arketí.*' He smiled as she told him in his own language that one language was never enough. 'I love learning languages, it's my hobby. I'm studying now… Anyway, Nico was having trouble changing his flight…' And Zander had to force himself to remember that it was Nico he was trying to find out about, for instead he wanted to know more about her. He wanted to know about her life before Nico and her love of languages, and it wasn't a ploy when he interrupted her to ask.

'What are you studying now?'

'Russian.' Charlotte rolled her eyes. 'Well, when I say studying, it's just on the Internet and I *make* myself watch the Russian news… Where was I?' she asked, and he blinked, because he was having trouble remembering where he was. He was forgetting the very reason that he was here. 'I helped Nico to sort out his flight and his follow-on accommodation and he said that he needed someone part time…' She gave a tight shrug. 'I was in no position to accept his offer, of course, I spent half my life 40,000 feet in the air, but we kept in touch and now and then I'd arrange him a flight or book a hotel. But when his PA resigned I'd just left the airline…' Nothing in her voice revealed the regret in her decision, she just paused for half a second before continuing. 'It sort of grew from there.'

And something was growing here too—how, she did not know, for her guard was up and she was determined to be businesslike, but there was something about his company that engaged her, something about the hand that reached out for her as she stepped over a rock pool that steadied her stance, just not her heart.

'I ought to get back.' Charlotte reclaimed the hand that was warmed by his brief touch. 'I have to make a phone call. To my mum,' she added, because, though it didn't quite fit with her polished party-girl image, she didn't want him to think she was racing back to tell Nico. 'You can use mine.' He pulled out a slim phone from his pocket and she was about to decline, to head back to the safety of her suite, to work out what on earth she should do, but the sky was so gold and her hand was still warm from his touch, and for reasons better left unexamined she did not want their walk to end.

'It's international…' Her voice petered out along with her excuses, because the cost of a phone call would hardly be a problem to him. 'Thank you.'

Politely he walked on ahead and took a seat on a rock by the water's edge as she spent a moment locating the number and being put through.

It was heartbreaking. The confusion in her mother's voice, the pleading with Charlotte to come and save her, to bring her home, had Charlotte biting back tears as a nurse came onto the phone.

'It might be better if you don't talk to her just before

bedtime,' the nurse gently suggested. 'It unsettles her for a couple of hours after she speaks with you.'

'So it's better that she thinks I've forgotten her?' Charlotte retorted, and then apologised. "I'm sorry to snap, I just…'

'It's so hard on you.' The nurse was incredibly kind. 'If she was here permanently it would be different, but she's only with us for a few days and the change of surroundings is so unsettling, it just disorientates her all the more when you call. Why don't you ring and speak with the staff to find out how she is?'

It took a moment after hanging up to compose herself enough to join Zander, but he must have seen the glimmer of tears in her eyes because after a moment he spoke.

'You're close to your mum?'

'I don't know,' Charlotte admitted, though she had never done so before, her head still spinning from the emotion of speaking with her mother. 'I don't know if we're close or just bound…' She took a deep breath. This was not the professional conversation she was supposed to be having with him, but surely she wasn't being indiscreet in speaking about herself. Surely it was safer than speaking about Nico. And on this particular evening, knowing her mother was scared and in tears and that there was nothing she could do about it, it was easy to talk. Not that she would reveal her mother's illness to him, for she had been badly burned doing so in the past—the look of horror on her boyfriend's face when she had invited him in one night and he had witnessed

the chaos that was her life, and another fledgling relationship that had ended before it had really begun when
she had told him of her plight. Charlotte had long since
learned where to stay quiet.

'She had me when she was older...' Charlotte said a
couple of moments later, soothed by the company and
the view, her ankles dangling in the water. The sky was
a glorious riot of orange. She had front row seats to a
show she loved, but this was surely the best one ever,
the colours so vivid, the ocean so majestic. 'I think at
first she wanted my dad to leave his wife...' She hadn't
really told anyone this, but it was so good to talk and
have someone answer. Too used to her own thoughts, it
was so nice to finally share a part of herself, though she
chose not to tell Zander everything, chose not to reveal
all of her plight. 'She was my father's mistress. He was
from London, which was why she moved there. I think
she thought if she had a baby that he'd...' Charlotte gave
a shrug. 'Well, it didn't work—he wanted a mistress,
not a mother. He didn't leave his wife, didn't come and
see us.' She gave a wry smile, for her mother had never
let her forget just how much she had given up for her
child. 'I always thought he'd come and live with us one
day.'

'Did your mum?'

'Not in the end. By the time I was at school she'd long
since given up.' Charlotte shook her head. 'She just got
more bitter. I always dreamt he'd come and find us. She
said that I lived with my head in the clouds...'

'Clearly you were intended to,' Zander said. 'Forty

thousand feet up in them.' And she smiled, because he had listened, really listened, and then the smile on her face faded, because she was looking at him and he was looking at her, and it was more than talking and sharing. There was more, and in that moment she knew it but forced herself to deny it, changed the conversation, for they could not sit staring endlessly, and if they did, for even a moment longer, he would kiss her. He would kiss lips that were waiting, would be accepting, but he did not move.

'What about you?' Her voice did not break the spell.

'I live with my feet on the ground,' Zander said.

'Your parents,' she asked. 'Do you still see your mother?' There was so much she wanted to know, so much Nico was desperate to find out, but, sitting there, it was not Nico she was asking Zander the questions for but herself. She wanted to know him, but it was her question that broke the moment, her words that ended the kiss that never was.

'I live in Australia,' he said, which wasn't really an answer. He turned away from her and looked out to sea, changed the subject along with the mood. 'The sunsets are spectacular here,' he said, because they were. Whatever he felt about Xanos, that much was at least true.

'The sun doesn't set,' she said. He turned again to look at her, but she did not return his gaze, just stared out into the distance. 'It's just an illusion. We're the ones moving.' Now she did turn, saw him frown and she smiled. 'It messed with my head a bit when I read it, but it's obvious really—given that the sun never moves.'

He looked back at the ocean, to another truth that was a lie, to a different way of thinking, and it messed with his head too.

'But, yes,' Charlotte said, 'it's very beautiful.'

And they sat in silence, with separate thoughts but more comfortably together. Usually when she looked to the sky she wanted to be up there, just not this evening, not this time, for now, in this moment, she was happy where she was. Then, when he stood and offered his hand, she took it, let him lead her back, and they walked ankle deep through the lapping water and she was glad to be beside him.

There was no moon and it was growing too dark for idle walking, but as they passed the beach café he did something she never thought he would. There were no fries at the upmarket beach café, but he bought two souvlakis, not for them. They stood on the beach as it grew colder and darker and fed the gulls, and she laughed like she hadn't in a very long time as the hungry, frantic birds swooped and swirled around. They headed back to the hotel and as he located discarded leather shoes and slipped them on his invitation was not unexpected. 'Let me take you to dinner.'

'I really…' She wanted to say yes to him, so badly she wanted it, but she had to speak with Nico first. It was with true regret that she declined. 'I'm actually rather tired. It's been a busy day, I might just get room service…'

He was skilled enough with women not to push.

An utter gentleman, he walked her back to the hotel foyer and even windswept and with the bottom of his trousers damp with sea water and sand, he was easily the best-dressed man there. There was an effortless elegance to him that needed neither shirt nor tie nor black credit card on show, he was easily the most beautiful. 'Nico is going to be stunned when he sees you.' Of that she was certain.

'Then tomorrow let's work out together how best to surprise him.' He saw her swallow, knew she was torn, and he moved to assure her. 'I did not want to tell him over the phone. I want to see his face when he realises we have found each other. Perhaps tomorrow you will say yes to joining me for dinner?'

The bar was in full swing; beautiful couples and stunning singles were everywhere, and a piano was playing a gentle invitation. He saw her eyes drift towards it, knew he could perhaps secure a drink, and then dinner, and then who knew? But he was far cleverer than that and now they were back in the hotel she was as wary as a kitten.

He took her hand and Charlotte jumped at the contact then shivered as he did the most old-fashioned thing: he picked it up and held her fingers to his lips and briefly kissed her hand.

It looked formal, it felt anything but. The weight of soft lips on her hand made her stomach curl, had her thoughts skittering, her world confused, for she had never had such an intense response to a man, to any man.

It had been a great relief in fact that, despite her boss's devastating good looks, he did absolutely nothing for her, or Charlotte for him. Even prior to his wedding there had been nothing, not a hint of flirting, yet here stood a man in Nico's image, and she wanted to sink to her knees. Everything around this man made her feel weak and confused. His black eyes lifted to her burning face, his lips dropped contact, but she could feel the warmth of them still on her skin and if he were to ask her for dinner again, she could only say yes.

'Enjoy the rest of your evening.'

He bade her goodnight, saw the battle between relief and disappointment flare in her eyes and how delicious it would be tomorrow, he consoled himself, how much sweeter for waiting.

Would she tell Nico?

He watched her walk away and could not quite decide, but he had done his best to prevent it, bar tying her to a bed...

His tongue rolled in his cheek at the very thought, moved to his lips, tasting where her flesh had been, and he resisted the urge to follow, to ask her again, for never did Zander ask twice; instead, he headed to the bar.

She walked across the foyer, willed herself not to turn around, but want was stronger and as she made it to the lifts she allowed herself one tiny peek, hoped against hope that he was walking behind her, that Zander would ask her again, or at least be heading to his room, but, no, he was heading to the bar. She saw the unaccompanied females perk up as he stepped in. He said something to a waiter and then briefly turned around and caught her looking.

God, but she wanted to run to him. To go to the bar and claim her prize.

It was safer, though, to be away from him.

She made it to her room and closed the door, even slid the security chain, not to keep him out but more to keep her in.

Away from him she could think, could take a shower and slip into a robe, could order room service and remember who was her boss.

Loyalty was everything to Charlotte and without the flexibility of this job she shuddered to think what she would do. She had to ring him, had to tell him what she now knew, and away from the intensity of Zander, normality was returning.

'Nico…' She bit back a hiss of frustration at the sound of his voicemail. 'It's Charlotte—I'm in Xanos and something rather unexpected has come up. Could you call me back, please?'

He did not.

Again, as the maids came for turn-down service, she tried her boss's number, sat on the balcony, huddled in her dressing gown, cold but grateful for it, watching the delicious water. She got Nico's voicemail again, turning in surprise when a maid came out and served her a small glass of Raki and bade her goodnight. She took a sip, grimacing at the taste but liking the burn and hoping it would help her rest. Hope was short-lived for glancing above she looked straight into the eyes of Zander. He stood, glass in hand, on a vast balcony at the top. His eyes homed in on her and she sat there, frozen, like a mouse beneath a hawk and she thought he might swoop down and claim her.

She retreated to her room, slid the glass door closed and dropped the catch, scared not of Zander but of herself, of the woman inside who was screaming to be let out.

'Nico, please…' She rang again, just before she headed to bed. She slept with her phone beside her and when it rang at seven, she willed it to be her boss, but the devil inside leapt with delight when she heard Zander's voice.

'How about breakfast?'

She moved to the window, peered out, and could see him on his balcony, just a towel around his waist.

'I'm not sure.' She was hesitant, not just because of what Nico might say, more because this was a man no woman could safely handle. Even from this distance his beauty was evident.

'On the beach,' he added, and still she did not respond. 'I will have them pack a hamper. It's up to you if you join me. I'll be there in half an hour.'

CHAPTER THREE

ZANDER walked along the golden beach of Xanos, but as scenic as the view was, as pleasant the water, his stomach churned with bile. Everywhere his gaze fell brought a fresh memory, spearing his scalp as if arrows were aimed at it.

Why had he bought the south of the island? Why had he invested so much time and money in a place he would rather forget?

He should have left well alone.

He looked towards the land, to the vast complex he had built, and he thought of the scaled model that was in his office in Australia. Usually he was hands on with his investments, but not this time. He had vowed never to return, yet here he was, and no matter how accurate the model, it was different seeing the real thing—seeing firsthand the houses that would soon be bulldozed to make way for a nightclub and more shops and restaurants. He looked to where Nico lived and knew it had once been their grandfather's home, that their mother had been raised there. How it hurt to be back on Xanos sand. Yes, it had been a magnificent investment. Perhaps only a local could ever have envisaged the true potential of the hidden side of Xanos—the humble fishing village that was just waiting to be transformed—yet for all the prestige and profit, for all the erasure of the landscape he hated, all this place had ever brought him was pain, and it was doing so now.

His head throbbed from lack of sleep and he turned his mind to tomorrow, to the long-awaited confrontation with his twin—and Zander wondered if he had blown it, for no doubt Charlotte would have rung her boss already. He should have stayed in his suite, should have spent the weekend in isolation. Yet, Zander mused as he walked, he had enjoyed spending time with Charlotte. He glanced up at the hotel. Used to staring at the model in his office, he easily worked out which was her room, thought of her in it and wondered if she was preparing to join him.

It had not been his intention to call her this morning, but he had thought of the day that stretched ahead, the wait that that would be interminable without diversion.

'Forget it,' he told himself, heading back to his suite, and to the shower. He would contact her later, take her to dinner—women were for the night-time, a reward for hard work, a balm for insomnia, not for spending the day with. Still, he was curious whether she had told Nico, which, he told himself, was the reason he had called her.

Charlotte approached, and she was nervous, dressed in shorts and a strappy vest, topped with the previous day's cardigan. Her eyes were bruised with lack of sleep courtesy of this very man. Another call to Nico had gone unanswered and, as gorgeous as the smile was as Zander turned to greet her, still she would set the ground rules.

'Morning.' She made herself say it. 'I'd prefer not to speak about Nico.'

'Of course not,' Zander said.

'I just don't feel comfortable…' She was honest with this. 'I haven't been able to contact him yet.'

'You don't have to explain yourself. I'm just glad that you joined me. Let's see what they have prepared.'

The hotel had put on a sumptuous breakfast and they sat on the deserted beach and she drank hot chocolate, while Zander chose coffee. They both ate yoghurt drizzled with passion fruit and then pastries, which Zander thought tasted somehow sweeter this morning.

'I love seeing new places.' Charlotte dug her toes into the sand, looked up at the sky and to the flash of a silver plane but again, with him beside her, she did not want to be up there.

'What do you miss most about travelling?' He followed her gaze.

'All of it really.' She gave a smile. 'Except the unpacking. I don't know, I love airports, the excitement. I love going to new places, exploring them. My friend Shirley and I…' She did not continue, for sometimes she choked a little when she thought of those times, and the hours between flights that had been spent so well.

'Have you looked around Xanos?'

'Not yet,' Charlotte said. 'Maybe later today.' He was such good company, such an intriguing man, because it was not he who pushed for information. Instead, Charlotte asked the questions for he fascinated her so. When asked, he told her about his hotel chain, about the casinos he owned, about his life on the other side of the world.

'You must have missed this, though,' Charlotte offered, turning to watch as he stared out to the Mediterranean, just as he had yesterday.

'Australia is hardly lacking in beaches,' Zander pointed out. 'I have an office and a property in Sydney that overlooks what is arguably the most beautiful harbour in the world.' If it sounded like a boast, it had not been intended as one. More, Zander was trying to convince himself. For how could he miss a place that had brought nothing but pain—a view, this view, that as a child and later as a teenager he had wept into.

It should be hard to fathom now, strong, independent, beyond wealthy, it should be impossible to recall with precision just how afraid and confused he had once been, but when he looked out to the ocean, to a small mound of rocks a few hundred metres out where the waves crashed and broke up, he could wipe away twenty years. He could feel the fear and the confusion, the bruises on his back and legs from his father's beating, the wrenching pain that came with true hunger and the bewilderment of being left behind—that a mother, his mother, might have left him to deal with this. It was painful to recall it even now.

Each minute that passed brought him a minute closer to his brother, to the twin his mother had chosen to take.

Each minute that passed brought him closer to the confrontation of which he had long dreamed, the moment where he would finally face the brother who had lived in the lap of luxury while he had eaten from bins, the brother who had had been given the velvet-glove treatment, while he had been ruled by a fist.

'Every beach is different though…' Charlotte's voice was softer than his thoughts. 'And this feels like a slice of heaven.'

Or hell.

'It was not all happy.' He heard his voice, heard his own words, and it stunned him into silence, for he never revealed anything and certainly he should not to the PA of his twin. And yet as she turned, as she did not speak, just moved her mouth into a wry smile, she offered not words but the space of her mind. She turned her attention fully to him, and for once he did not want to retreat. 'The memories are not all good.'

'But are there some good ones?'

And his mind shifted because, yes, there had been some. He looked back at the ocean, to the same mound of rocks, and recalled teenage boys jumping, he in the middle, egging each other on. He remembered waiting for the tourist buses before it had turned more sordid, when pretty young things would arrive and he could escape. He remembered then the happier bits, instead of later—when he had relied on his looks to secure a bed, had kissed older, drunk women, for it had meant breakfast the next day. And his mind turned to the market at the north of the island, to being chased for stealing fruit and then laughing with friends as they'd eaten. There had been no innocence in his youth, but there had been some fun.

'We would go to the market...' Again, he was stunned that he told her, yet it felt good to speak, to share with another. 'We were about twelve.' He told her of the thieving and she laughed, but not too much, for after all he had been hungry. And he told her too of the taverna that would fill with tourists at night, how he had always looked older... He did not tell her about the women, or scrabbling through the bins out the back for something to eat. He told her the better bits and smiled at the better bits, and then Zander surprised himself again.

'I will show you Xanos,' he offered. 'The real Xanos.'

She thought, because it was Zander, that she would be swallowed again by a huge limo, that the island of Xanos would be revealed to her through thick darkened glass, but instead he rang ahead and by the time they had made their way back, to her surprise and nervous delight two scooters had been delivered to the foyer of the hotel.

'I've never ridden a scooter...'

'I thought you liked exploring.'

'On foot,' Charlotte said, and then laughed. 'Or on camel.'

He smiled at the thought. 'Few tourists have ridden a scooter when they come here. You'll soon pick it up.'

She wanted him to change his mind, to offer to let her climb on his scooter, to coast the island nestled into his back, but never did he offer easy; instead, he pushed her out of her comfort zone. She was grateful for it, for after a few nervous goes she enjoyed the thrill of riding her little scooter, the absence of a helmet not the only rule that was broken. With Zander she felt as if she were flying the trapeze without a safety net. It was wild and dangerous, the thrill of the chase, cat and mouse, as he accelerated ahead of her and waited for her to catch up, then sped off, laughing again.

The only blot on her happiness was a phone that still had not rung, and as they parked their bikes in the marketplace and they walked into a taverna, she caught him looking as she checked her phone.

'It's up to you whether or not you tell him, Charlotte,' Zander said as they took a seat. 'I don't want to put pressure on you. I just had hoped to surprise him. I have long thought of the day that we see each other again.'

'He's my boss,' she attempted, and thankfully he did seem to understand.

'I have put you in an impossible situation,' Zander said. 'Really, I should have just stayed in my suite. I should be there now...' He looked into her eyes and the world seemed to stop. 'But then we would have missed out on our day, so I cannot regret it.'

Neither could she.

It seemed like for ever since she had been so self-indulgent, not just with the food or the views, but with the company and conversation, and though she did her utmost to remain distant, warned herself it was a distinct lack of male company in recent years that made Zander impress her so—that a couple of years ago, she could so easily have handled him—she knew that she was lying to herself. For in whatever life she might be living, in whatever circumstances they might meet, Zander would have consumed her on sight.

'Soon you will be back in London,' Zander said, 'and I will be back in Australia.' His words were a brutal reminder that all they had was measured in days, a warning—or was it permission he was giving her?—to just enjoy this, to be the glamorous party girl that he perceived she was. 'To our day,' he said, and raised his glass. How delicious the sparkling water tasted as it slid down her throat, how heady and exhilarating it was to be with him, but she felt her face redden when her phone rang. There was sweat beading on her lip, which probably wasn't the most attractive of looks, but she was not thinking of that as she picked up her phone and saw that finally Nico was returning her call.

'Excuse me a moment.' Charlotte stood. 'I might take this outside.'

He wanted to know what was discussed, he *needed* to know, so Zander had a word with the waiter and handed him a very nice tip, warning him to be discreet. The waiter then headed out to clear the tables.

Charlotte took a seat at a small table, and took a deep breath as she answered, nervous to tell Nico but knowing she had to, no matter what Zander might think, no matter the surprise she spoiled, Nico was her boss and somehow, despite the dizzying effect of Zander close by, she must keep her head and remember that fact.

'Charlotte, it's Constantine.' The sound of Nico's wife

caught her by surprise. 'Nico knows you've been trying to get hold of him—he asked me to ring you back.'

'I really need to speak with him.'

'His father's been taken ill,' Constantine explained, and then clarified. 'His adoptive father. You know things have been tense…' Charlotte was quiet as Constantine took a steadying breath. Tense was the understatement of the year, for since Nico had guessed that he had been adopted, the already fragile relationship with his father had been tested beyond its limits. His adoptive parents had not even attended the wedding, and Charlotte closed her eyes in sympathy as Constantine made things frighteningly clear. 'He's on the small hospital in Lathira, but Nico is having him flown now to the mainland as things are very serious. Nico will be at the meeting tomorrow, but for now he asks that you hold the fort. He wants you to arrange a seven a.m. flight from Athens—he really wants to attend the meeting—but then he will fly directly back.'

'The thing is…' Charlotte attempted, but she halted. She could hear the chimes of the hospital, their baby, Leo, was crying too, and now was not the time. How could she reveal something so personal, and not even to Nico himself? Perhaps Zander was right. The surprise would be more meaningful coming from his brother and surely Nico did not need any extra stress right now. 'Tell Nico everything is fine. Tell him that there is good news waiting for him when he gets to Xanos and give him my best wishes.'

'I will. I have to go now, Charlotte.'

She rang off the phone and sat silent for a moment, declined when a nice waiter offered to bring her drink outside. 'It's okay—I'll be back in a moment.'

So she was on her own with the secret.

She looked into the bar where Zander sat and, to his credit, he did not look over, was not trying to work out what she had said to his brother and to see if she had spoiled the surprise; instead, he chatted to the waiter as his glass was refilled and smiled as she walked back into the taverna.

'Do you want to eat lunch here?' She was incredibly grateful that he did not try to delve, did not ask what she had said to Nico, and she returned his smile, with one that came from the bottom of heart, for now she trusted him.

'That would be lovely.'

She trusted this beautiful man to do the right thing by her boss, and by her.

Believed in tomorrow as she sat down and Zander took her hand.

After all, she had no reason to think otherwise.

He ordered hot peppered calamari and for Zander it was good to be back, to sit at a table with money in his wallet, to look the owner in the eye when he came in and laugh as he called out something in Greek.

'What did he say?' Charlotte asked, wishing her Greek was better.

'"Alexandros, you were banned from here,"' Zander translated, and then she was treated to that stunning smile. 'Then he said, "Welcome back".'

'Alexandros?'

'As I was then.' He looked into eyes that were blue, eyes that held his, eyes that made him go on. 'After my father.'

'He's…' Charlotte swallowed, for this much Nico had told her. 'He's deceased?'

'He is.'

'And your mother?'

And the question that yesterday had been probing felt different now, more like natural conversation, but if he answered with truth, if she glimpsed his hate, she'd be gone. All Zander knew was that he did not want that, he wanted this day, so his answer was guarded instead. 'I've never known my mother.'

'Did you always know that you had a twin?'

'I thought Nico was off limits,' Zander said. 'Your rule.' He gave her a smile as he stood and put down some money for the bill. 'Come on, we can ride to the hills.'

It was a day that was, for both of them, different.

For later, as afternoon turned to evening, as they parked the scooters and walked high in the hills of Xanos, the air chilly now, he was not plotting revenge, or thinking about tomorrow. Instead, he was thinking beyond that to a place he had never been—could almost see her in his world.

'I have hotels and casinos across Australasia. I do a lot of travelling…' They stopped at a flat rock and she nodded when he suggested that they take a moment to relax. She sat on the rock, enjoying the view, not just of

Xanos but of a world he was painting for her. 'You've been to Singapore?'

'Not on my route.' Charlotte smiled.

'Then you have missed an amazing place. There is good shopping, amazing salons...' She gave a wry smile, for dressed in her work best, with her finger- and toenails painted and her roots freshly done, her eyebrows newly shaped, it was a natural assumption that this was how she lived. Despite the coolness, her cheeks reddened, for all the lies she had told, the weddings and cocktails and long lunches with friends that had never happened. 'Unlike your boss, I would want my PA to be around...' He saw a blush darken her cheeks as he gently explored what was becoming an option. A job that was a hundred per cent glamour. He could give her this every day, instead of it being a rare treat.

'I thought we weren't talking about Nico.'

'We're not,' Zander said, 'we're talking about work.'

'I'm very happy with what I do now.' She stood as if to catch her breath, but instead it was to bite down on a sudden urge to weep, for he was offering her the world, and how she wanted to say yes, to be the woman he thought she was—if only she could be.

'I would pay you more.' He wanted his way, he always got his way, and he would have it now.

'It's not about money!' Her voice came out shrill, too sharp, too strained to pretend she was not upset. She could barely manage to keep up the façade for a week, let alone permanently.

'I would look after you better than he,' Zander said,

and he meant it. For he *would* look after her and that would start now.

Zander *was* at his most potent. The walk in the hills that had seemingly so naturally unfolded had been absolutely contrived. This was a route he had trodden so many times in his youth. It was no convenient rock they had ambled towards—this was his stomping ground, here, where with women he had always got his way. The letters 'AK' were carved in the rock beneath the moss where her bottom had sat.

'Zander, I don't know if I've…' How could she say it, how could she tell him about her real and drab life? She had not set out to lie, but knew of course that she had. 'I think I've misled you…' She saw his face darken. And darken it did as he braced himself to hear that Nico was, as he surely had already known, far more than a boss. 'I haven't told you—'

'Don't,' he interrupted her, for he did not need to hear it. He did not need an angel, Zander reminded himself, he was here only to get revenge. 'You don't have to say anything.' And then he said something else, something that, despite the cool Xanos breeze, made her warm inside, had her sit back down when his hand took her wrist. 'Let us enjoy *our* day.' She wanted that, wanted so very much this escape. She did not want to cloud it, to spoil it, to bring reality in to this magical place. 'Maybe you'll think about my job offer later, maybe…'

'I…' How could she say that she wouldn't think about it when it was all she would ever think about, even if it could never be? She closed her eyes and entered the luxury of his offer, working for him, seeing more of him, and then as his lips dusted her mouth, they confirmed the full extent of the debauchery behind his proposition. Yet it did not offend, it was the most delicious sensation she had felt in years, his lips warmer than her cool ones, his mouth so much more in control than hers. All she did was feel it—feel the warm pulse of his flesh on hers. She relished the weight of a mouth that moved slowly, a mouth that warmed rapidly, and she took his breath into her and held it, and held it some more, and then breathed it back to him and now they were one. It was one kiss that both were sharing, for now her mouth moved on his, now she tasted him, and their kiss was a slow one, a warning, a heady warning that there was so much more to come.

When Zander kissed, it was always with intent, a means to an end, a temporary place where he'd prefer not to linger, and now, in a minute, his hand would wander. Soon, in a minute, he would press her back to lie on the mossy stone, but there were things in this kiss that he had never noticed before, that her eyelashes swept on his temple and that the tip of her tongue was like a balm that made him forget the hell.

Sex made him forget, he reminded himself, kissing her just a little bit harder, for surely that was where this must lead, but she seemed to want more of a taste of him and, yes, he actually liked her tongue's tentative exploration, liked the faint taste of their breaths mingled. Had it not been so delicious he would have taken her right there on the hillside, would have moved his hand from

A to B and then a moment later a little lower again—
would have worked the trusted formula that never failed.
Had their kiss not been so unusually pleasing, he would
have had her panties in his hand just about now, except
all they were doing were kissing, and he did not want
Charlotte bare-bottomed on a hill.

Oh, but he did, Zander thought as his mouth still
moved hers and his ardor deepened as, not on formula
but instinct, his hand moved beneath her waist to the
low rise of her shorts. He wanted his fingers to slip in
there, wanted where this could so, so easily lead, but he
did not want her embarrassment afterwards. He resisted
the lure of her zip and his fingers moved to the hemline,
dug into her tender inner thigh as he attempted a rapid
halt but it was she kissing him now, her tongue calling
the shots.

She hadn't been kissed in so very long, and never
more thoroughly than now—so expert his tongue, so
blissful his hands, so faint-making his scent, all she
wanted was to give in to the press of his mouth and
move backwards, to lie down under him, to relish the
bliss of his hands—hands that slid from her arm to her
waist. There was the faint brush of his thumb on her
nipple and the sound of foreign birdsong, and so easily
he took her away, so tenderly he removed each splin-
ter on her mind, each shackle to her heart that with one
kiss she forgot what she knew. With his kiss she lost the
hurt and forgot to be wary.

His hands were near her bottom and then moving
around to the front, the weight of him pinning her down,

then the bliss of his fingers pressing into her thighs, climbing and then resting and then slowly climbing again as her mouth beckoned him on and, with his kiss, it was hard to remember she was here to work, here as Nico's PA. Somehow, as his mouth dragged her under, as his kisses pressed her down to the mossy rock beneath, her mind fought its way to the surface, resisted delicious temptation and remembered the reason she was here.

'Nico!' He heard the word in his mouth and he almost spat it out, heard her say his twin's name as he kissed her, and as her head pulled back, so too did his.

'The name's Zander!' Black were the eyes that looked down at her, and the tone of his voice sent a chill through her.

'I meant...' Did he really think she had mistaken him, that in the throes of passion she had been thinking of Nico? 'I forgot that I'm supposed to be at work.' Surely she must have mistaken the ice in his voice and the anger in his eyes, for there was no trace of either now, just the familiar smile that warmed and a brief kiss to her lips as still he pressed on top of her that told her all was okay. 'I don't think I should be here.'

He actually agreed, for the mossy hillside was not where he wanted to sample Charlotte. He wanted her only in his bed now. He wanted her writhing and sobbing beneath him, wanted to ensure a future where it was *his* name she sobbed into Nico's mouth.

'Look.' She aimed for confidence in her voice, even

if she could not quite meet his eyes. 'That should never have happened...'

'That?' Zander said, and his fingers gently stroked, crept up, just a little, but enough to remind her where they'd been heading. 'Or this?' He was still lying over her; she could feel his erection pressed into her hip, could feel his fingers at the hem of her shorts, and she felt as if the devil was beckoning.

It would be so much easier to simply kiss that mouth back, to deliciously resume; but the ease of her response to him unnerved her—and not for a moment could he comprehend how out of character this was, that the polished, sophisticated, well-travelled woman was, in fact, a ghost from her past, not the Charlotte she had now become. Neither would he understand that even the Charlotte of old would never have found herself half-naked on a hillside, that only with him had this wanton woman emerged.

'None of it,' she attempted, except it died on her lips, because back in London her only regret would surely be halting things.

'Well, for what it's worth...' he kissed her cheek as he released her '...I'm glad that it did. Let's get you back.' It was Zander, slightly breathless as he stood, Zander who rearranged her clothes and then offered his hand. As she took it, she felt as if she was handing over her heart, felt for a giddy moment as if she'd found the one person who would take care of her. Damp night swirled in on Xanos, and her head was literally in the clouds as she walked down the hillside with him.

'What is that bird?' She could hear the same call that had danced in her mind as he had kissed her, its song following her now down the hillside and she craned her neck, her eyes scanning the trees to glimpse the bird that made the strange '*po-po*' call.

'It's the hoopoe bird,' Zander explained. 'You rarely see them, you just hear them, but they are beautiful birds. They'll be gone soon…'

Like you, Charlotte thought as they walked down the hillside, a rare beauty she had briefly glimpsed but could never hope to truly capture. She wanted to be back in his arms, wanted more of his kiss, but instead she held onto his hand as they walked and Zander talked.

'They head to the Canary Islands for the colder months.'

'It's a strange call.' She stood for a moment and listened, drank in the unfamiliar sound, wanted to remember the Xanos hillside for ever. 'So relaxing.'

'Not for the locals.' Zander interrupted her thoughts. 'They say when the hoopoe sings in the evening then soon there will be war. It's just superstition.' He smiled as her eyes widened. 'The island is full of it.' His hand was warm around hers, his smile reassuring. 'You like birds?'

'I guess,' Charlotte said as they reached their scooters. 'I think I like anything that can fly.'

They rode back to the hotel, and only as she climbed off the scooter in such gorgeous surroundings did she realise how grubby and unkempt the day had made her, but she felt as if she was wearing a ballgown as he offered his arm and they walked inside.

'We will meet for dinner,' Zander said, for he would not take no tonight. 'I'll call for you in an hour. What is your room number?' He was so direct, so all-assuming. Again she reminded herself that Nico was her boss. She had to somehow wrestle control back, for around Zander she had virtually none.

'I haven't said yes yet.'

Oh, you just did, Zander thought, for he could see her pulse leaping above her collarbone, could almost smell the want that was in the air.

'Fine,' Zander said, and as he had last night he made as if to leave it, even turned his back and went to walk away, so positive was he she would call him back, but he was caught off guard by her words.

'Perhaps I should offer to take you to dinner,' Charlotte said, and he turned his head. 'I am sure Nico would expect no less.'

She saw his eyes shutter, for a moment thought she might have offended him, but when she looked again he was smiling, and she must have imagined the flash of darkness.

'I'll meet you in the foyer,' Charlotte said, not sure she wanted this stunning man knocking at her hotel-room door, not sure at all that she could resist him.

'I'll look forward to it' was all that Zander said.

And so too would she.

She rang the nursing home and, as advised, spoke not to her mother but to the staff and was informed that

Amanda had settled in a little better, which should have reassured her, but she didn't quite believe it was true.

'If she does get upset,' Charlotte said, 'please remind her that this is just temporary, that I'll be home in a couple of days.'

It might bring comfort to Amanda, but it brought little to Charlotte. She truly didn't know if she missed her mum, if she even wanted to get back to her real life. There was guilt with the realisation, guilt that seemed to layer on guilt, but she quashed it. She was determined to just enjoy her time her on Xanos, to go back a better daughter for the temporary reprieve.

He was a reprieve, Charlotte told herself, a brief indulgence that she could handle, dinner and perhaps one more kiss.

As she undressed in the bathroom, slipped her freshly foiled hair into a hotel shower cap, she felt more like the old Charlotte than she ever had—felt like the jet-set woman she once had been, a woman who could handle a man like Zander Kargas.

It was bliss to sink into the bath, and more to step out of the bathroom and to see the pulled curtains, to resist the temptation to open them. It was heady and dizzy but she felt as if his eyes could burn through the fabric as she massaged her skin with oil, felt as if he was watching her as she dressed slowly.

For him.

Somehow he made the fantasy real.

Made her feel special enough to take that extra care.

She was used to doing her hair quickly, so she stood

in the marble bathroom and smoothed it out with her trusty straighteners, but it needed something more so she skilfully spun thick, heavy ringlets, over and over again, each one, Charlotte thought, for Zander. With each curl, she imagined his fingers through it later, and then told herself there could be none of that.

She told herself he was a guest of Nico's tonight, if only to help herself behave.

There wasn't really much decision as to what to wear. She had brought her faithful travel wardrobe of old, which consisted of a black evening dress, a touch slinky with spaghetti straps, and a small wrap, or another more demure dress, a soft brushed velvet in chocolate brown with a cowl neck.

She settled for the brown.

Hoped the demure cut of the dress might calm her but, even slipping it on, the sex in her mind brought the dress to life; the fabric seemed tighter around her bust and more clingy over her hips. Her eyes glittered in anticipation and her cheeks glowed at the very thought of Zander. She begged herself to reel it in. She had to keep her head for one night, one night only, for tomorrow the secret would be out. Tomorrow she could fall into his arms, as she now so badly wanted to.

She was dizzy with lust as she sprayed fragrance not just on her wrists and neck but the backs of her knees too. She imagined his mouth there on the tender flesh and she knew she must not, that tonight somehow she had to resist him, that tomorrow, after tomorrow, when he and Nico were reconciled, when things were more ordered, then she could think about them.

Except she could only think about him.

Could only shiver at the memory of his kiss.

It wasn't a date. It was *not* a date, she told herself, but it felt like it was as she glossed her lips and had one final check in the mirror.

Zander was absolutely potent and she had to keep her head tonight, had to see how things went with Nico and Zander before she did anything. She almost doubled up then, stunned at the possibilities her mind lurched to, for he made her feel rash, dizzy, to *want*.

Zander too smiled as he looked into the mirror.

Tonight would be such an unexpected treat.

He had enjoyed flirting with Charlotte on the phone, getting her to open up a little, and though last night he had more intended to loosen her tongue with fine wine, the stakes were raised now. He had not anticipated the rare beauty of her, that she might live up to the voice he had enjoyed these past weeks.

Now he wanted her.

Wanted her to sob *his* name into his brother's mouth. How sweet was delayed revenge, for he wanted everything his brother had and then some more, but the thought of her with another made him churn in a way he never had before. As he stared into the mirror he chose not to shave, just splashed on cologne. Then his thoughts were darker, his intent deeper, for he would leave Nico with nothing, as he had been left with nothing, and his mind was made up. It was not a cruel decision, Zander told himself as he headed down to meet her. He might be misleading her but soon she would come to understand.

Tonight he would have Charlotte in his bed.

Tomorrow she would be in his life.

CHAPTER FOUR

CHARLOTTE had worked long enough with Nico to know how he liked things, and what he expected from her when dealing with clients. She knew as she arrived before their arranged time that, despite the butterflies in her stomach, despite the thrill of an evening with Zander, she was, even if Nico was unaware, working for her boss tonight.

She did as Nico would expect of her—arriving in the foyer a full fifteen minutes early, she whiled the time away till Zander arrived looking into the boutique windows at the bags and purses with leather so soft they seemed to beg her to go in and stroke them. She wandered to the jeweller's, blinked at the most stunning of necklaces, thick with rubies and diamonds. She had possibly never seen anything so lovely.

'It would look good around your neck.'

She heard his words, heard his greeting, smelt the freshly washed male scent of him. It felt as if not the necklace but Zander was around her throat, for it was so tight as she turned to greet him.

Oh, he had once looked like Nico, but now, to

Charlotte, all he was was Zander. There could be no mistake ever again. It wasn't just that Zander's hair was a little longer, his strong jaw shadowed, his eyelids slightly heavier lidded, his skin a touch darker. With Zander she felt far from safe, for each parting meant a new greeting and each time the stakes seemed raised. She registered the flare of danger that ignited whenever he approached, acknowledged that he took her, without asking, completely out of her usual bounds. It was Sunday night in Xanos, the dress code smart casual, and Zander wore it incredibly well—black dinner trousers with a white fitted shirt that showed his toned body. His hair was tousled but gleaming yet there was an edge to him, something in the unshaven jaw and black gypsy eyes that set him apart, a statement made without words, something that warned he had never been and could never be tamed.

'Have you been waiting long?' Zander asked.

'Not at all,' she tried, even if it was a little late to do so, to sound professional, to make things clear, to draw a safe line. 'Anyway, you're my guest.'

'Had you been mine,' Zander pointed out as the *maître d'* suggested they take a seat at the bar and their table would be ready in a few moments, 'our table would have already been ready.'

Not used to waiting, especially in a hotel he owned, Zander did not actually mind, for instead of the clean white linen and neat order of the restaurant they were led to a dark sultry bar that was to be their holding pen. He had seen the designs, the finished product on the computer, had even been in here last night, but had not really appreciated it till now.

Zander suppressed a smile as she sat down, her bottom lower than her knees on the extremely low couches, revealing a stretch of thigh. It was not his fault, of course, that he sat just an inch too close, that the soft plush of the sofa rolled his body in just a little, till the fabric of his black trousers almost melted as it encountered her flesh. He felt her attempt a discreet wriggle away as she tried not to touch him, but there was nowhere to go.

'I'm sorry about this.' She tried a smile that was supposed to come out professional and businesslike, tried to pretend that it was Nico for whom the table was not waiting, because with him she could talk, could laugh and yet reveal nothing. 'The table shouldn't be much longer.'

'I'm more than happy to wait,' Zander said as their drinks were delivered.

As she sat too close to this dangerous image, this sexy version of her boss, Charlotte felt as if she was in some erotic dream, some wild, vivid dream, where she would be unable to look at Nico in the morning thinking of the terrible, reckless, depraved things she had done with his twin, for how could a mouth look so divine just biting into the lime of his gin? How could a finger look so sexy and dark and debauched as it stirred the ice though his drink?

There was no lack of manners, he was not being rude,

but it was sex and she knew it. He melted the ice with his finger as he was melting her now.

'Where were we?' Zander said, and she struggled to remember whatever it was she'd been saying, struggled to keep her head in the most oppressive environments.

'About to have dinner,' Charlotte said, her eyes pleading for the waiter, for the summons to their table, for she could feel the length of his thigh against hers, remembered the press of him on the Xanos hillside. She had been a fool to think she could handle this, that for a moment she could resist the potent force of him.

'And how was your day?'

'Fine.' It was she being the rude one. 'Pleasant, in fact.'

'We could eat here,' he offered, and her eyes darted from him to the bar. Sure enough, people were eating at the tables. 'Shall I suggest…?'

Thank God for the waiter who came and told them their table was ready. She almost wept with relief as she stood, pulled down her dress over her thighs, tried to rearrange not just her clothes but her mind into some semblance of decency as they walked though the restaurant to a beautifully laid table. The music in the background was so unobtrusive she was sure the entire room must be able to hear her heart.

The waiter informed them that it was too cool and windy tonight for the balcony table she had ordered, which was a regret for her cheeks were on fire.

'I didn't order champagne,' Zander said as they were seated and the waiter started to pour it.

'I did.' She sat and gave him a smile. 'If he was aware of who my guest was tonight, Nico would insist. Anyway, I thought it appropriate, given that tomorrow you finally meet.'

He wanted to be wining and dining Charlotte; he did not want to sit here with his brother's PA, drinking champagne his brother would pay for, eating food that he had bought. He wanted nothing from Nico—well, no charity anyway. He wanted to take from him rather than receive, but not by a flicker did he betray the dark thoughts. Instead, he turned his charm to high beam, knew he could not be resisted. In the glare at first she attempted to resist, but he watched her melt, watched her weaken, and he would have her tonight, Zander decided. She would walk into the meeting tomorrow with the bruises from his mouth on her neck. Better, Zander decided, when he had told his brother his feelings, he would leave the meeting with her, would take Charlotte as his.

His for a while, Zander thought, because that was all it ever was.

The menu had delicious offerings and, grateful for reprieve from his gaze, Charlotte pored over it. It was a mixture of traditional Greek with a contemporary twist.

'I'd like the dips.'

'We are in Xanos,' Zander said. 'Why not try the crab ravioli? There is none finer.'

'I'd like the dips,' Charlotte said, but she chose fish for her main and winced just a little as he ordered herbed milk-fed lamb. 'Are you looking forward to tomorrow?'

'I'm not thinking about tomorrow.' Zander replied. 'Instead, I am enjoying tonight.'

'But...' She tried to quash her frustration. Almost every conversation was off limits till he met with her boss, yet there was so much she wanted to know about him, so much she wanted to share with him.

'I'd far rather hear about you,' Zander said.

Except that was off limits too. She didn't want the fantasy to end with the drudgery of her real life served up at this sumptuous dinner table, didn't want to watch his black eyes glaze as she droned on about her problems.

'It's a beautiful hotel...' she said.

'You'd have seen a few in your travels,' Zander commented. 'But, yes, it is.' He looked over at her. 'Have you tried the spa?'

'I'm here to work,' Charlotte said, for she was conscientious, and though she had had more than a peek at the luxurious spa menu, she would never expect Nico to foot such a bill.

'I am very proud of it,' Zander said. 'With all my hotels, I try for something different yet somehow the same.'

Their starters were delivered. She took one look at his ravioli and, though the dips were the best she'd tasted, she couldn't help but wish she'd taken his advice.

'Here.' He cut off a large piece and she thought he would place it on her plate but it was Zander, so of course the fork, *his* fork, went straight towards her mouth. She opened a jaw that felt rigid, tried to tell herself to relax, to take the offering, but with him it was so loaded. She tasted the butter on her tongue and tried to remember to swallow, tried not to ponder how with Zander everything tasted of sex.

'Tastes good, yes?'

She nodded. It was all she could manage. She licked a trickle of butter that was on her lip and as she did so the smile he gave her told her their minds were thinking along the same lines. He watched her toying with her food and, rather than summon the waiter, he moved forward a little to pour her more wine, which gave him the excuse to press his knee in. To his satisfaction she leaped as if branded, and then put a hand over her glass too late, for the champagne met slender fingers and bubbled and fizzed.

He took her hand and wanted to suck each finger dry. Perhaps, from the tremble that shot through her body, he could have got away with it, but she thought him a gentleman, and for now he obliged, took a thick white napkin and wrapped it around her hand.

And not a drop more passed her lips, and though somehow she made it through the main course, the conversation was awkward. He knew she was on guard, knew she was wrestling, could feel her nerves as the dessert menu was presented, as the evening neared a close.

'I'm not sure if I'm hungry.' She wasn't hungry, but surely it was better to be here in the restaurant than saying goodnight, trying to resist his kiss. If he did kiss her again, which he would, she knew exactly where it might lead, so she stared at the dessert menu till it blurred out of focus.

'If you're having trouble choosing, we can get a couple,' Zander offered. 'We can *share*.'

'It's terribly warm,' Charlotte said. She was babbling a little, Zander realised. 'I won't be a moment.'

He did not want to be here, fed by his brother. He wanted Charlotte for himself, on his terms.

He walked and found her easily, tucked away on the balcony, staring out to the Mediterranean, the wind blowing her curls around her face, and he could see from her profile she was troubled.

She knew he was approaching and was scared to turn around in case she fell against him.

So hard she wrestled with her conscience as she stood there.

She did not fall into bed with men. There had been a couple of relationships—one that had ended almost as soon as it had begun when she had told him about her mother's illness and one that had meant a lot but had faded and died as her mother's illness had become more and more consuming, but it was Zander consuming her now.

Zander was the first man in ages she had responded to, the first man she had ever reacted to with such force, and tonight, in this hotel, with this beautiful, beautiful man, it was not the champagne that reduced her inhibitions but the vibe of him, the presence that seeped into her pores, into her brain, and made her giddy with lust and with promise. It made twenty-four hours seem an impossible delay.

She had left for some privacy, to gather her thoughts, to convince herself she could hold out till tomorrow, but there was almost relief when she heard the door and his footsteps coming up behind her.

She felt the lips on the back of her neck and it felt like salvation, and she closed her eyes because all she wanted was to feel the tease of his mouth. He kissed her very slowly, and she felt the scratch of his unshaven jaw as lips slid across her flesh. She could stop him at any moment, his kiss so slow, so light, she could brush him off and turn around and pretend perhaps that it had never happened, except she gripped harder to the balcony wall and did not turn around, for she did not want it to end.

He kissed her harder, as if to warn her perhaps, as if to tell her she could end it here, but she wanted him more than she wanted a neat conclusion.

She wanted the hands that snaked around and slid to her stomach, she wanted the bruise she was sure he was leaving because he kissed low on her neck, so deep she felt like crying, felt like turning her head right round to suck on his mouth, but still she stood there. She wanted, how she wanted, the slight pressure on his fingers, the push back into him that gave her a daring feel of what was waiting, his solid length pressing into her bottom.

'We could take dessert upstairs,' Zander said, for he wanted her in his room. He wanted every morsel now that went into her mouth, every sip, to come only from him, everything to be untainted by his brother.

'I shouldn't.' Still she could not face him, still she dared not open her eyes, because if she did, she must make decisions, and she struggled so hard to remember. 'I'm working.'

'Not now,' Zander said. 'You just clocked off.'

'Your brother—'

'Forget about him,' Zander said, for he must be dismissed from this moment. Zander must not for a second reveal the bitterness that was there or she would run.

'I don't want to regret this in the morning.' It was a plea almost, because around him she could not think.

'Why would you regret something so nice?'

'Because…' she attempted, except his fingers were at the back of her bra and nimbly, easily, through her dress he unhooked her, and she was dressed except she felt naked, exposed. Shamelessly it exhilarated her. What did this man do? He turned her round and he gave her his mouth. He wrapped her in the heat of his arms and cooled her with his tongue. He kissed her, but Charlotte could never, she realised, recall it afterwards as just a kiss, for it stroked and it soothed and it beat in her mouth and dragged at her skin and it was faint-making and delicious and did things to her body that no mere kiss ever could. Even wearing her high heels he was the taller, and their bodies meshed. He pulled her right in, he leant on the balcony so his body was a curve for hers to melt into—and readily she did.

He gave all to that kiss and Zander had kissed many,

many women. Had kissed through his youth to assure a bed that night, had kissed just to get dinner when his stomach had been hollow with hunger, had kissed just to survive, but never, not once, had a kiss tasted so good.

Her lipstick was gone, her inhibitions fading, her breasts pressed against him, he caressed her. His mouth adored her in a way that made her feel both reckless and safe.

He took her away with his kiss and then he brought her back with its absence. He handed her her bag, which told her he had come out to fetch her; he draped her in her wrap and covered the swell of nipples beneath her dress, looked into her blue eyes and told her, looked right into them and told her, 'You'll never regret this.'

And he lied.

CHAPTER FIVE

WHY she trusted him she did not know.

Why she so willingly let him lead her to his room was not something she could readily explain.

In the bathroom of his luxury suite, she attempted to scold herself—to tell herself she knew nothing about this man, that he was a client of her boss, that she had known him for just a couple of days.

Not a single lecture worked.

He was the brother of Nico, whom she trusted, but it came down to something rather more basic than that, for there was no man on earth who made her feel the way Zander had in the time they had spent together.

She had not laughed so freely in years, had not talked so readily to another soul—and as for his kiss...

As she rinsed her mouth and looked up into her glittering eyes in the mirror, lifted the hair and saw the bruise he had left, she was also deeply honest with herself—in their few hours of contact he had offered escape. Tonight she was the dress and the shoes and the woman who looked back in the mirror, a woman who *could* handle things, she told herself as she removed her unhooked bra through the arms of her dress.

It was not love she sought as she walked from the bathroom to the lounge of his suite, it was escape and Zander offered it in spades.

Dessert had been delivered as loosely promised.

Shot glasses filled with mousses and brûlées, tiny pastries and potent custards, and not for a second was she tempted, at least not by the table, for she walked to him and was pulled down to his lap, to a kiss that did not need now to be tamed.

It was not the real Charlotte that kissed him back, it was the Charlotte she wanted to be, perhaps the Charlotte he thought he had met on the beach, a woman who could handle such things, could take the roaming of his hands on her body, could give her all and remember not to love him tomorrow.

For Zander, unusually, there was much at stake.

Wrongly, he assumed she had been his brother's lover and it was imperative he win before they met.

How delicious the moan in her throat as she sat on his knee and kissed him.

Did he do this? he wanted to ask as he tore down her dress to the breasts he had undressed and suckled at her nipples.

Or this? he begged in his head and stood with her in his lap and pushed her to the bed with his mouth.

Or this? As he slid down her panties.

There was a rough edge to his kisses, an urgency to him that hadn't been there before, an anger almost, and she pulled back on the bed, confused at the change in him.

'Zander?'

And he looked up to blue eye that held his, and saw her eyes were darker when troubled. He wanted them pale, wanted her soothed, wanted their night, not the conquest.

Wanted her.

'I've been thinking of you for so long,' he offered by way of explanation for his urgency. 'For weeks. Forgive me if I got carried away.' And he watched as she blinked, still wary. 'When we spoke, when you were in London and I was in Australia, when you were in bed...' And she blinked again, for she had thought of him too. Unable to picture him then, still her mind had wandered, so much so that she could now understand his haste. 'We'll take things slowly.' He smiled his lethal smile, except this time he meant it—thought not of his brother or hate, only of her. 'We'll go back to the beginning. How did you lie?'

She did not understand his question.

'How did you lie in your bed when you spoke with me?' And she could not help but smile at the memory of a dream that had come true, and could now forgive his roughness.

'On my side.'

'Show me.' He rose from the bed and she watched the suited man slowly undress as she rolled to her side and pulled up the covers around her shoulders.

'You?' Charlotte asked, as he climbed back into bed.

'On my back,' Zander said, and something deep in her stomach tightened. 'So tell me.'

'What?'

'How is the weather?'

And she lay on her side and closed her eyes and imagined the rain on her window and the grey of her life and his voice in her ear, only this time it was better, for it was cool but not cold in Xanos, and this time he was beside her.

'What did you do today?' This time, as she spoke of her day, she didn't have to pretend, didn't have to make anything up, for it was all real.

'I went walking in the hills.'

'Alone?' Zander asked.

'No, not alone.'

'And did you enjoy it?' This time, when she retold her day, there was his hand on her waist, this time and for evermore she would lie in her bed in her room and remember the feel of him, gentler hands now exploring her body, the nuzzle of his mouth on her arms along her shoulders, a tender exploration of her breast. 'Did you enjoy being with him in the hills?'

'Very much.'

'What did the two of you do?'

'We just kissed,' Charlotte said, as he rolled her onto her back.

'Just?' Zander asked, his mouth moving down to her stomach.

'Better than just.'

'Better than this?' he asked, and his head moved lower.

Though determined as his quest was to rise above Nico, as he tasted her with his mouth, he forgot to hate. Charlotte lay there, eyes open to the ceiling, to what should feel strange and wrong and unfamiliar, except as his tongue explored and his lips teased, he knew what she wanted as only a lover could; he knew more than her as he pushed down hips that were resisting and demanded she come to his mouth. He kissed her till she bore no more reluctance, till she gave to his mouth a part of her that had once been subdued.

And then, when her body was quiet, he rose over her and kissed her again, kissed her slowly till she was waking, till she was again alive with greedy want, could attune to different sensations. She wanted to feel him, to hold him, to sheath him, for his fingers were now within her and she wanted the rest.

Her fingers were all thumbs at the feel of him, the hard strength that would soon be within her, but his fingers were far more skilled than hers.

He felt the restraint of the latex, felt her clumsy roll down and wanted, for the first time, to tell her not to bother, wanted to really feel the intimate skin that wet his fingers now. Wanted more for himself than was usual as for Zander touching was merely a means to an end, the part where he said and did the right things, worked a while for a brief reward. Yet here and now this did not feel like work.

He forgot to hate for the first time, for it had no place in this room.

He forgot he was here to prove something, to claim something, as his body pressed towards her. He forgot too that he was performing, because that was all sex ever was, and he meant what he said as his fingers moved from inside her, as his erection moved to that place. What he said he would not recall, what she heard was in Greek and not fully understood, but it was an intimate declaration that did not require translation.

It was the words of a man moving deep into a woman he wanted.

She thought he would glide into her, so wet and ready was she, but Zander in full arousal did not make for soft landings, he slammed into soft tissue and stretched her completely. It was more compulsive than tender, a basic rhythm that was exquisite, and he took her breath away and did not let her catch it. When she wanted more, there was more; when she thought there could not be more, she was again proven wrong. He was in her body, in her head and in her heart as he gave everything and simultaneously demanded everything from her. She had never known hands roam so hungrily, or a tongue and a breath in her ear, or the sheen of his back beneath her fingers. There were too many sensations for Charlotte to focus on, so she did not try, just moved with him and beyond herself, moved to a place that was waiting for them.

He moaned and it made her feel dizzy; he moved faster and she did too, and there was a hush then, a moment of stillness, no work needed now, just a wait for arrival, and it was now that he glided, and flew her away. She felt every beat and responded with her own; she heard every breath and tasted his moan, and as their bodies quieted she went back in her head, closed her eyes and attempted to reel in her heart.

It was too soon to love him.

They did not sleep for ages; they tried not to sleep. Zander could see the red numbers on the clock that ticked beside them, their hours left too few, not that she knew it. And here in his bed, with a woman beside him, for once he did not want to roll over, did not want to escape to sleep, or order from the bar, or envision tomorrow. For the first time he was comfortable in a place.

'What is it like?' She lay there and tried to fathom it, to comprehend how it must have been for him, and though she had said not to discuss things, it was way too late for that now. 'What is it like knowing that you have a twin and never having seen him?'

'I have seen him,' Zander said, for he was not sure if it was a memory or if it was the one photo he had found, but he had seen his brother, they had once been together. 'When we were babies…' He did not want to talk about it, did not need to explain it. He turned to his side and closed his eyes, but she turned too, her hand loose on his waist, her breath on his back. He held his breath for if he did not he would speak, would ask her to leave, for suddenly she felt too close.

'I mean…' Still she would not leave it, did not heed the silent warning to halt. 'What was it like, growing

up without him? What has it been like, knowing you
have an identical twin?'

And maybe there was weakness, for already it was tomorrow, already the day was here. Maybe it was sex that
made him soften, or maybe it was her voice that sounded
more tender than probing, or her hand that still stayed
on his waist, because he did not tell her to be silent, did
not respond in the way that he usually would have; instead, he lay in the silence as she patiently awaited his
response and he thought about it.

He actually thought about it and how best to describe
it.

'You look in the mirror each morning?' He was grateful that she did not answer with the obvious 'Yes', that
she let him be for another moment with his thoughts.
'Imagine looking and there is no reflection, knowing
there is a you that you cannot see.'

And he could explain it no better, and he did not try
to.

There was no point anyway.

Tomorrow, when she knew him, she might not want
him in her life.

CHAPTER SIX

WAKING up in a strange bed, a strange country, should have had Charlotte in a complete panic, but she did not feel as if it was a stranger who lay beside her.

She watched him sleep and admired his beauty, her body lazy but still in arousal from the feel of his solid weight beside her through the night. Now, with the sun slowly waking Xanos, she got to watch him in colour. His skin, pale in the predawn light, glowed a smooth olive in the sun, and she gazed at the full, sensuous mouth that had explored her so intimately, had to resist moving over to kiss those lips; instead, she lay on her side and admired, saw the shadows to his stomach lift and reveal an ebony snake of hair. How she wanted to move that sheet, to see all of him.

He must have felt her eyes on him because he woke to find her watching, woke to the day he had long been awaiting, but he did not want to get out of bed. He looked at Charlotte and he wanted to stay, he wanted to pull her towards him, to bury his head in her hair, to make love in the morning, except that would be too cruel, even by his standards, for he knew what was about to come.

He did not move so she did, slid over the bed and kissed him because she still trusted in last night, in all they had found. Even as his mouth resisted, she did not question why. Still she kissed him. And he let her. She kissed him and he found himself kissing her back till there was a reluctant return, a recall to last night, to remember the intimacy they had shared that had gone way beyond sex, and Zander recoiled from her as he remembered just how close he had come to confiding in her. He did what he always did in the morning—instead of lingering, he climbed out of bed.

'I have to get ready.'

She heard and felt his dismissal, despite his appropriate words, for the clock was already nearing seven.

'So do I.' She pulled on her dress, readied herself for the shameful lift ride in last night's clothes. She could face it if he said farewell with a smile or a kiss that told her there was still tonight.

Neither was forthcoming.

'Good luck for today.'

'I never rely on luck' came his curt response.

'When I see you, when I speak with Nico—'

'We never met,' Zander said, and Charlotte nodded, for it did make things easier with her boss.

He was nervous about meeting Nico, about seeing his twin after all these years, Charlotte told herself as she headed to her room, and she was nervous too as she dressed in a smart navy suit and because of the bruise wore her hair down. Then she headed to the meeting rooms she had booked. She did a slight double-take when Nico walked in, a crisper, more clean-cut version of the man she had been in bed with last night, and, yes, she felt guilt, not for the act but towards her boss.

'I'm sorry to hear about your father,' she offered. 'How is he?'

'Extremely unwell,' Nico responded. 'After this meeting, I must go directly to the hospital—I trust that has been arranged?'

'Of course,' Charlotte said. 'I've cancelled the rest of your week. Do you need me to clear things further?'

'Not at this stage.' There was a pause, a long one, and she knew she must fill it, must do the right thing by Nico, for after all he was her boss. Unable to look him in the face properly, she wished this morning was over, that the surprise was revealed and that Nico knew, and then she could see where that left her and Zander. 'Nico…' God, how much to tell him? 'About this meeting. I know how important getting this land is to you. The thing is—'

'In the scheme of things it is not that important,' Nico interrupted. 'I have not come away from my dying father about a piece of land. There's something I need to tell you.' Nico, as always, was direct. 'I was going to explain things to you, except my father got ill. Still, I should have warned you, for had you bumped into him you would have got a shock…' She froze as Nico spoke on. 'This meeting today could get very personal. I just want to prepare you. You see, when I found out I had been adopted, I also found out that I had a twin. Zander. The businessman you have been dealing with is actually Alexandros Kargas...'

Her face flew to Nico's, her mind torn in two as if it were paper as she tried not to reveal that she knew already, tried to fathom how Nico did.

'When did you find out?'

'Just recently. I had no idea that the landowner was him, of course, but now that I do, it makes sense.' Nico was grim. 'I think he is hoping to shock me.'

'To surprise you?' Charlotte forced a smile, but it died when Nico shook his head.

'Yes, though I don't think he's planning a pleasant one. Fortunately I am one step ahead of him. There is a lot of history, Charlotte, none of it relevant to you. Suffice it to say the difficulties in reaching him these past weeks, well, it has nothing to do with a piece of land—he has been baiting me.'

'Baiting you?'

But, of course, Nico did not have to explain things to her. 'I just want you to be prepared that there may be a confrontation this morning, that there will be raised voices. On no account are you to come in or panic and call for assistance. I am expecting trouble and I am prepared for it.' He headed into the meeting room and she was left with racing thoughts. Taking a seat at the desk outside, she placed her head in her hands, tried to work out from the last couple of days if what Nico was saying was true. She went over and over the conversations between Zander and her and wondered if he had been quizzing her, but all she had witnessed had been kindness. Surely Nico had got things wrong?

Paulo too?

They were wrong, she was sure of it. And when Zander walked towards the meeting room, Charlotte turned worried eyes to him, for had she not been in bed with him last night, had she not been held by him, had she not witnessed his tenderness first hand? But, then, every presumption Nico had uttered rang true, for the only word that could describe Zander's appearance this morning was savage. Charlotte saw him in a suit for the first time, exquisitely tailored in the darkest of greys. He might have been dressed for a funeral, his tie a slate grey and that jet hair slicked back; he still had not shaved and somehow it spelt insolence. Her eyes begged for reassurance when they met his, and she willed from him a brief smile, a wink, some private reference to last night, to the knowledge that it would all be okay, but instead her eyes met those of a stranger.

'Is he in?'

It was all he asked, all he wanted from her, and when she nodded he swept past her desk, gave one sharp knock on the door, and did not wait for Nico to respond. He opened the door and walked straight in, and all Charlotte glimpsed before the door closed was Nico standing straight to meet his twin for the first time.

Thank God Nico had warned her as to how she should react, for though there were no really raised voices, there was a brutality to the words that were muffled by the walls. Then there was a scrape of furniture that, had she not been told to ignore it, would have had Charlotte ringing her boss to ensure that all was okay.

And she waited for it to be so.

She waited for it to be the surprise reunion Zander had assured that it would be, except it appeared the meeting was to go down as Nico had feared.

The door opened. Zander went to march out and then harsh words were hurled from Nico, and there were no walls or door now to muffle his anger, no barrier to deflect the strength behind his words.

'I will not leave Xanos.' She had never heard her boss so angry. 'I will stay here as long as I choose. There is still much to find out.'

'I've told you all you need to know.' She saw Zander turn, his back so taut she saw the stretch of the fabric that struggled to contain muscles that had rippled beneath her fingers last night. She wanted to stop him, wanted to rush over, but she knew it was not her place, knew even then that she had been deceived, especially as Zander spoke on. 'There will never be a relationship. I do not have a brother, or a mother. You left me with him and now you return—'

'As if I had a choice!' Nico's shout matched Zander's but his hate did not, for Zander was so full of loathing Charlotte could almost taste it.

'You lived your rich, pampered life away from Xanos. Now you return like some grandiose prodigal son... But you are not wanted,' Zander said. 'You do not belong here. I will build that nightclub, so enjoy the noise of machinery, for it will be nothing compared to the music that will pound in your home night after night…'

'For what purpose?' Nico demanded.

'Misery.' Zander's answer was simple. 'Touch my things, encroach on my life and I will make it my business to ensure the rest of yours is miserable.'

But Nico still had questions.

'What do you know—' so badly he need closure '—about our mother? Do you know if she lives?'

'She is dead to me,' Zander said. 'She was dead to me the day she chose you. Go find her if you must, show her the son she saved.'

'She did not save me,' Nico shouted at his brother. 'She sold me!'

'No!' Zander's roar was absolute, for only Zander had lived his life, only Zander knew the hell of being the one left behind—and he'd have rather have been sold to the devil than be left a single day with that man who bore the title of father. 'She saved you—so bask in it, *brother*.' He sneered the word. 'But get the hell away from Xanos, and keep the hell away from me.'

She sat, more at stake than her boss must ever realise, and as Zander swept out she had to resist leaping to her feet. She wanted to demand what had gone wrong with his plans, why Nico was so furious, or was it Zander?

For Zander it should now be over. He had said all he had come to say, yet it did not sate his anger. Still there was a burn in his guts, a need for more. Adrenaline still flooded his muscles, had his heart pounding in his throat with such force he wanted to rip off his tie and tear at his shirt. He was furious that his twin had known, that Nico had stood and faced him as he'd walked in rather than recoil in shock. Insulted by Nico's outstretched hand, Zander had declined it; instead, he had told him exactly his feelings—that there would be no contact, that forgiveness would never be on the table. That his mother had chosen the golden one, had given Nico the chance of a privileged life and left Zander to survive for himself.

And he had.

Oh, he had.

He did not need anyone.

He had made it alone and would go on doing so.

Would destroy Nico if he tried to get close.

And, now that was over, all he wanted was to get out.

Away from the man who looked like him, away from the reflection that was now in his mirror.

Away from the son that his mother had chosen.

And then, as he strode out, when he would have preferred to hit, or to run, he saw her sitting there, saw the confusion in her eyes and the tremble to the mouth that last night had been his. And he did not want her for Nico, he wanted her for himself.

'Get your things.' He snapped his fingers to tell her his haste. He wanted her away, he wanted her upstairs, he wanted her on his bed, and he would forget what he had just seen, forget the brother that never would be, he would lose himself in her. But she just sat there.

'Get your things!' Zander said. 'You come with me.'

He did not understand her hesitation. He was offering her his world, offering more of what they had had last night. 'You work for me now,' he clarified, except Nico was walking out of his office and still Charlotte sat there.

'Charlotte has nothing to do with this,' Nico said.

'Except that she comes now with me,' Zander retorted, without looking at the man he loathed. 'Come now.' He gave her one more chance when he gave others none but, pale, she still sat there, her eyes moving from his to Nico and then back to him.

'I work for Nico.' Her voice was as pale as her face.

'My staff are loyal to me,' came his brother's voice, and Zander could not believe that she would choose him after the night they had shared. His mind was so black with loathing, so angry having lived a life of betrayal, that there was no chance of straight thinking.

'Really?' Zander shot back. 'Well, that's not how it seemed when her legs were wrapped around me last night.' It all came out in one caustic response. Zander watched her quail as the words spewed out, but really the words were not aimed at provoking her and he looked at Nico to relish his response. He wanted his brother to thump him; he wanted a fist because it was pain he could see, a bruise he could feel, hurt that could be measured. He wanted to fight but his brother just stood there, and, worse, Charlotte apologised for the one good thing on Xanos that had ever taken place.

'I'm sorry, Nico…' She could not have felt more betrayed, more humiliated, more ashamed—could so clearly see now how she had been used. She could not stand to look at Zander, so she looked at her boss instead. He was the man she should have been loyal to, the man who paid her wages. 'I'm so sorry, Nico.'

'No problem.' Nico was tough, and could be just as cutting as his brother, though the barb in his response, she knew, was not aimed at her. 'We're all allowed a mistake—yours just happened to be my brother.'

CHAPTER SEVEN

SHE lay curled up and wounded on the bed, too mortified to go out, dreading Nico's wrath, but far more than
that she was beyond hurt by what Zander had done.

The contempt, the disregard, how he had used her.

A knock at the door a short while later did not see
Charlotte moving. She did not care who it might be:
Nico to fire her or Zander, for what?

An apology wasn't going to fix this.

Instead, when the knock came again, she closed her
eyes at the sound of a woman's voice.

'Charlotte, it's me—Constantine.'

She could not be rude to Nico's wife. She had met
her a few times and Constantine had always been nice.
Beyond ashamed, Charlotte opened the door, and burst
into tears when the other woman wrapped her arms
around her.

'Nico told me what happened.'

'I'm so sorry,' Charlotte wept. 'I'm so ashamed…'

'For what?'

'For what I did.' Everything that had been so beautiful had been turned around and it all seemed sullied

and sordid now. 'I thought…I never thought he hated Nico. It was not about being disloyal.'

'Charlotte.' Constantine was kind. 'What happened between you and Zander is not Nico's business, or mine.'

'It has become that though,' Charlotte wept. 'I really thought…' But she could not divulge her dreams because they seemed so pathetic now, that with one look, with one kiss, he had whisked her away, had let her glimpse a world she did not know and now wished she never had.

'Is Nico going to fire me?'

'He wants to speak with you, he wants to know what was said, what Zander revealed. I doubt he could fire you for sleeping with someone.' Constantine gave a wry smile. 'My husband is many things, but he is never a hypocrite. He is cross,' she admitted, 'furious, but I think that is more aimed at his brother. As I pointed out to him when he told me what had happened, we were together the night we met—it was, in fact, my wedding night and Nico was not the groom…' Charlotte blinked at the admission from Nico's wife. 'I know how devastating they can be, how irresistible Nico was to me. I am not here to judge you, I just want to know you are okay.'

'I will be,' Charlotte said, for she was certainly not okay now. She tried to scan her future for a time when this would not hurt so much, but Zander had changed it for ever. 'If I had thought, for even a second, that he was not looking forward to meeting Nico… Why would he hate him? It's not as if Nico was raised by his parents. Nico was the one that was sold…'

'Roula, their mother, she was not stable…' Constantine paused. Charlotte could see the other woman was uncomfortable discussing this, for though Charlotte had been privy to certain information, emotion had always been left out, only names and facts had been given by Nico. 'Or that is what we have been told. She left the father and worked the streets… The Eliadeses desperately wanted a baby…' Constantine screwed her eyes closed, and it was clear that she hated discussing this. 'Alexandros, I mean Zander, was raised by his father. It would seem…' Charlotte closed *her* eyes as Constantine spoke on and she recalled Zander telling her that his time in Xanos had not all been happy. 'He was not a good man, he was a cruel man, in fact.'

'If that was the case, why would she leave Zander with him?'

'That is what we are trying to find out. There are so many questions, which is why we are searching for her. But Zander has run true to form, it would seem—like father, like son.'

Charlotte's eyes opened at the rare bitterness in Constantine's voice and though she was hurting, bleeding inside, even though she had nothing to base it on, something within her rose to defend him. 'You can't say that.'

'Oh, but I can,' Constantine flared. 'He has done nothing to prove otherwise. Cruel seems a very good word to describe him to me. He has bought up the homes on the island for a pittance and now, till he is ready to bulldoze them, he rents them out for a small fortune, at least it is a fortune to the locals. He's building a night-club and there is talk of a casino, yet he does not give the locals the work. He wants my husband and son to leave Xanos, and will do anything to engineer it, even ruin the rest of the island just to get his way.'

'It's business,' Charlotte attempted. 'Maybe when he has calmed down… It must have been unnerving to finally meet his twin.'

'He has no nerves to unnerve' was Constantine's swift response. Was that pity in her eyes as she looked at Charlotte? 'How can you defend him after what he just did to you? If it is only in business that he is cruel, what does that make you?'

Her words were like a slap and Charlotte retracted as if hit.

'I don't want him to hurt you further, Charlotte, but he will if you let him.'

'I won't give him the opportunity.' Of that she was sure, but still she knew her own mind, would not be si-lenced because it suited Constantine. 'But you're wrong, Constantine. If it comes down to like father like son, what does that make Nico?'

'He was not raised by him.'

'No, he was raised by a man who bought him, who lied even when confronted with the truth.' This much at least Charlotte knew and she watched Constantine's flushed, angry cheeks pale a little. 'Zander is not all bad,' Charlotte said. He couldn't be. He simply could not be, for she remembered them walking on the beach. He was the only man to touch her soul. She remembered their day and she remembered his smile and the rare sound of his laughter. In a second, as she sat on the bed wounded with hurt, her heart forced recall, told her that despite evidence to the contrary, their time together, their day, their night had surely not all been contrived, had not all been a lie. Her heart told her so.

'You need to be careful when dealing with him,' Constantine warned.

'I'm having no dealings with him,' Charlotte replied, and then realised what Constantine was saying. 'I still have a job?' She thought of her mother, of all the balls she was juggling back home, and when Constantine hesitated, the surge of hope faded, but Constantine took her hands.

'You have to do it, though. Nico needs you to stay here for a few days to go through his itinerary. He is heading back to the hospital soon to spend some time with his father, but though Zander has made things difficult, some things just can't be put on hold. He wants to see you downstairs in the restaurant for a meeting. He wants to up the search for his mother and, no matter what, he wants that land.'

'I can't face Zander.' Charlotte could not go out there—she simply could not go out there.

'But face him you must.' Constantine was resolute. It was her little family under attack from Zander after all and, as kind as she had been to Charlotte, on this there was no compromise. 'You work for Nico—don't forget that again.'

CHAPTER EIGHT

'Charlotte, please…'

Just when her heart could surely not be more torn, she answered the phone to the sobs of her mother. 'When are you coming to get me?'

Charlotte closed her eyes. 'I'm at work, Mum.'

'You said you'd never leave me.'

'I'm sorry about this.' A nurse came on the line. 'We have a residents' phone…'

'Mum's got my number in her diary.' Charlotte closed her eyes. 'Is she okay?'

'She's taking a little while to orientate, but most of the time she's fine. It's just every now and then she gets into a panic. It often happens with temporary residents. She'll settle in in a couple of days.'

And then it would be time to take her home. Charlotte thought of the battle that lay ahead, of the increased confusion that awaited, of the impossibility of it all, but she could not think of that now. Getting through the morning was proving a difficult enough task, let alone looking to the future.

'Can you put her back on to speak with me, please?'

Charlotte spoke with her mother for a few moments, reassuring Amanda that she was at work and that her stay at the home was only temporary, but the call depleted her already shot nerves.

Shaky hands applied lip gloss and she put drops in her swollen eyes. Charlotte was nervous and embarrassed to be facing Nico, but more than that dreaded that she might see Zander, and wondered how on earth she should react to him if she did. But surely he had checked out, Charlotte consoled herself. After all, he had said his piece to his brother, had made it clear that he would not be selling the land and wanted nothing to do with him whatsoever. What reason could he have to be here? She attempted to reassure herself, trying to ignore the fact that he practically owned the south of Xanos and had *every* reason to stay for a few days at the very least.

Somehow she had to tell Nico that she was not able to stay any longer on Xanos, that she had to get home. But how could she possibly assert herself after what had just taken place? Of all the stupid things to do with Zander, of all the blind, stupid things. Nico was hardly going to accept demands from her now when by her own actions she had suddenly become extremely dispensable.

Damn you, Zander!

It was a relief to be angry.

A welcome change from guilt and remorse and shame. In fact, so angry was Charlotte that as she stepped out of the lift and headed across the foyer to the restaurant, to the table where Nico waited, instead of burning in a blush when she saw Zander sitting on the other side of the restaurant, looking up from the paper he was reading and sipping on coffee as if he did not have a care, instead of looking hurriedly away, she positively glowered at him. Her anger forced her to hold her head high as she crossed the room and joined her boss.

Nico had ordered two coffees—a milky one for Charlotte and a short black for himself. He gave a very tight smile as she approached. 'Well,' Nico said as she took a seat at the table. 'This is awkward.' He was as direct as ever and so honest with the circumstances that it made her smile, even made her laugh just a little as Nico rolled his eyes, but her smile soon faded. 'You should have told me you had spoken with Zander—you should have informed me that you had met him.'

'I know,' Charlotte said. 'I tried.'

'I know that you tried to call, and that you found out my father was ill.' Nico stirred sugar into his coffee, but even as she entered into the most difficult of conversations, her shoulder was burning, for she could feel Zander watching them. 'But, still, you should have said when you spoke with Constantine.' She was shamed by the pity in Nico's eyes now when he looked at her. 'I could have warned you what he is like.'

'You knew?' She was determined not to cry, not in front of Nico and certainly not with Zander close by, but, damn it, it was hard to sit there and have it confirmed just how easily she had been used. 'You knew that his intentions were not good?'

'When you rang and said that the owner was coming, that Zander...' Nico grimaced for it had been a painful realisation for him too. 'I went and got the house deeds, saw his signature and, call it twin intuition, I knew there was trouble brewing. I knew that Zander knew who I was, that he was coming to confront me.'

'I believed him when he said it would be a surprise.'

'You listen only to me now,' Nico warned. 'Your loyalty is only to me.'

And she nodded, because it had to be now, because Zander had let her down so badly. All their time together had been a sham of his making.

'What did he tell you?' Nico asked. 'Did he speak about our parents?'

'No.' She raked her mind back over their conversations, realised just how much he had avoided talking about himself. 'He gave nothing away.'

'He must have revealed something?' Nico urged. 'You met him on Saturday. Surely you spoke, not just...' He held his tongue and she was grateful, for they had not just tumbled into bed.

'We spoke a lot.'

'Did he say anything about our mother?'

'Nothing, just that he had never met her.'

'Charlotte?'

'That was it. He said that his time here on Xanos was not all happy.' And even if Zander had betrayed her in the vilest of ways, still she could not do the same to him, could not tell Nico about the markets and the thieving, about the taverna and the memories he had shared. She was sure, quite sure, Nico didn't need to know that. Already Constantine had said they knew the father was a brute. 'Nico, he told me nothing. He was using me to get information, not the other way around, and I told him nothing. Despite the mistakes I have made over the weekend, I was not indiscreet about you.'

He accepted that, and for that she was grateful. 'I need you to stay on in Xanos—perhaps into next week. I want you to look into the licensing for the club he is talking about building, just get some research together, and I have a lead on my mother. I need you to ring around, perhaps fly out to the mainland and visit a few homes.' He looked up. 'I trust that is not a problem.'

So badly she wanted to say that it was the most terrible problem, that she needed to get back to her mother, that travel was impossible, but the reality was that right now she needed a job, needed to pay for the bill that would come in for the nursing home, needed the wages that Nico paid. Cold reality beckoned in a way that it never had before. She needed this job, needed to work even if that might mean her mother had to live permanently in the home. It would be far easier to sit and weep now, but instead she forced her voice to be casual, even managed to look Nico in the eye as she spoke. 'Of course it's not.'

'And I want that land,' Nico said. 'I am not moving my wife and child from Xanos at his bidding. If he accepts my offer, you are to get it immediately in writing.'

'I am to deal with him?' That she could not handle.

'Of course.' Nico frowned. 'Though you will deal

with him rather more professionally this time, I hope.'
And he asked her again. 'Is that a problem?'

She knew what Nico was doing, knew that even if
he was giving her a chance to redeem herself, he also
saw her as a link to his brother. If she had had any energy left, she would have argued her case, but instead
Charlotte sat there, knew when she was beaten.

'No, it won't be a problem.'

Nico stood. 'Charlotte, I'm trusting you to do the
right thing.' She nodded, and closed her eyes. In a rare
move, Nico put a hand on her shoulder and gave it a
small squeeze, for he was more disappointed than angry.
Perhaps even a little guilty, for his private life had now
impacted badly on her and, yes, he did want her to find
out some more. 'All will be fine.'

Zander sat, watching his brother's hand on her shoulder, watching her back to him, watching the man he
hated most give Charlotte comfort. He knew she needed
comfort because of him, and it caused something to stir
inside as he recalled his words, recalled the gasp that
had come from her lips and the shock on her face.

His richly blended coffee tasted like acid as it slid
down his throat. There was a burn in his stomach and
a clench in his scalp as his brother walked past, as Nico
had the gall to give him a brief nod.

He did not want a polite greeting, did not want to
foster anything with him. Yet the eyes that had looked
in his direction felt like his own, the face, the walk—it
was like looking in the mirror, except different. Looking
at a reflection that was a better version of himself.

He looked over to where Charlotte remained and usually Zander did not entertain guilt, considered it a wasted emotion, an expensive emotion—but he could see her rigid posture. She turned her head and smiled as Nico said goodbye to her, and then he watched her shoulders drop, just a fraction, but he could see the internal collapse, see her hand tremble as she picked up her coffee, see her try to right herself, to sit up straight again, and then, when it didn't work, he watched as she stood to leave. He could see her eyes avoiding him as she walked across the restaurant. 'Charlotte.' He called her name, and of course she ignored him. He caught her wrist as she brushed past. 'Join me.'

'Join you!' She could not believe his audacity. It was way too soon to attempt professional. Surely she would be given a day's grace at the very least before she had to deal with him. 'Nico is still here. If you have business to discuss I can arrange—'

'I do not want to speak with him.'

'Then I can get Paulo…' She was having great trouble talking, could feel his fingers scalding her wrist. She wanted to slap him, to pick up his coffee and toss it in his lap, to hand back even an ounce of the hurt that he had landed her with, but Nico had spelt out the rules. Nico, she realised in that hopeless moment as she stood there, was using her too for she was, for now, the link to Zander, the pawn, the plaything that might make him linger, the trinket Zander wanted, perhaps for a while. She stood and remembered, remembered his cruel words, how he had sneered that her legs had been wrapped around him. And she didn't just hear his words, she saw the vision too, was back there in the passionate moments, remembering how deeply he had kissed her, how much he had ravished her, how pliant her body had been in arms, how good the bastard was, and it took everything she possessed just to stand there as his words were delivered.

'I don't want to speak with Paulo. I discuss business with you.'

'But you don't want to discuss business.'

'Of course I do. There are some questions I have about his future use of the land—and about the maintenance of the jetty.' He smiled and it lacerated. He lied and it killed her that he did.

'I'm a PA,' Charlotte said. 'It's not my job—'

'I choose who I liaise with. If you choose not to, then go and tell your boss that you refuse to speak with me.' He let go of her wrist then, for he knew she could not run. He snapped his fingers at a passing waiter and told him to organise a meeting room now, and it was said with such authority that the waiter immediately put down the plate he was carrying and Charlotte stood trembling, waiting as a room was hastily arranged. All she knew was that she did not want to be alone with him, did not trust him. Neither did she trust herself, for as they were led through the foyer her legs were like liquid.

They passed the bar where they had so recently sat together, where he had pressed his leg into her. How he must have inwardly been laughing. She glanced at the restaurant and the balcony beyond, where he had so skilfully seduced her. They turned to the function rooms, and into one of them. The slam of the door behind her told her why she was so very afraid, for she was back in his space, back alone with him, and for all he had done, still there was want.

Want as he turned to face her, want as he walked over to where she stood, her shoulders back against the door, want as she tried to be free of him, want for the man she had thought she had met.

'What I said about us to Nico—'

'Cannot be erased by an apology,' Charlotte cut in, for she must keep her head, must remember that it had all been a ruse, a lie, that she knew nothing about the man who stood before her now. 'You were right with what you said this morning—we never met. You're not the man I thought I knew, so let's just deal with the paperwork. I don't need to hear your feigned apology.'

'Why would I apologise?' She could not believe his audacity. 'I was offering you a job—a far better one than you have, working for him.'

'You really think that I'd ever work for you?' She could not, *could not*, believe what she was hearing. 'After what you did, you really think that I'd consider—?'

'I would pay you more than Nico does.'

'It's not about money.'

'What, then?' Zander asked. 'You prefer to be his mistress? To share him with his wife?'

She did slap him then, professional or not. A morning's worth of hurt leapt down her arm and was delivered by her palm and slammed into his cheek. He did not even flinch, he just stood there, then gave her a black smile as, stunned by her own actions, by the venom of her thoughts, she shrank against the door. *This* was what he had made her.

'I work for Nico,' she said through pale lips, 'because he is a wonderful boss. Because he has integrity, because I trust him, because he has never, and would never, expect what you clearly would from me. I could never work for you and I will never, ever sleep with you again.'

'You did not object last night.'

'Last night you seduced me.' She could see it so clearly now. 'Last night you set out to—'

'Ah, *po po po*…' He spoke in Greek, and she knew enough of the language to get his meaning, and it burned that he could tut, tut, tut away the night they had shared, could be so condescending about something that had been so wondrous. She felt as if she were back on the hillside with him, but with clarity now, could hear the birds calling, for war had already been declared, he just hadn't thought to tell her.

Charlotte had to bite on her lip for a moment to catch her voice, for she would speak her truth without breaking down and her voice rose as she forced herself to continue. 'Last night you let me think it was about me, that it was about us, when, in fact, you had another agenda entirely.' Her hand stung from the contact with him, her palm burnt red and she raked it through her hair to cool it, to wipe herself clean from him. He watched a moment as the blonde curtain lifted and he saw the bruise that his mouth had made, a visible reminder, proof of what had taken place; but the curtain fell and still the image remained, not of purple on pale flesh but the feel of her skin beneath his lips, how she had melted to him, how right they had been, how close he had come to sharing with another person, how she had been his. 'You really tell me you have not slept with Nico…'

'You have no right to ask me that!' And she hadn't, but her past was her own and certainly not for sharing with him. Still, she could not stay quiet, remembered now his push to the bed, and that it had not been just lust for her that had driven him. 'Did it turn you on, thinking that I had, Zander?' There was a warrior inside, a woman who rose, who would not let him destroy her, and she found her and moved from the door towards him, challenged him when it would have been so much easier to recoil. 'Did you like the idea, Zander, that you were better, that you made me come harder?' She taunted him as she reminded him because, damn, he deserved reminding about what he had done, what he had so readily destroyed. 'Well, you were wasting your time thinking about your brother—your mind should have been on me.'

'It was,' Zander said. 'I was not thinking of that.' The admission and the passion with which it was delivered surprised even him, because her words had taken him back there and, no, triumph over his brother had not been on his mind then; instead, it had all been her.

'It was *all* you were thinking of?' Charlotte sneered.

And he closed his eyes because, yes, at first it had been.

'Those little chats…' How it stung. How innocent she had been to lie in bed on a grey morning in London and listen to him, to recall how he had brightened her day, yet it had all been a game to him. How easily he had played her—how readily she had let him.

'I should have heeded the warnings.' She was furious not just at Zander but at herself, and then she threw back at him what Paulo had told her in Greek about his tawdry reputation, that he would sell his mother to the highest bidder, and she told him too how the islanders hated him.

'I am not here for a lecture from you.'

'Are you going to sign?' She just wanted out of there, she wanted away, she wanted done, or she would start crying.

'I have not decided.' He looked at her. 'Perhaps we go out on my yacht to discuss things, spend some time away…'

'Never,' Charlotte said.

'Never?' Zander checked.

'I hate you.'

'Tut tut.' Zander smiled. 'What would your boss say if he knew you were speaking to me like that? I thought Nico still wanted that land.'

'I'll resign before I have to spend a day with you.' She was trapped, completely trapped, and the slap she had delivered had not put out the fire inside, for it was flaring again, as it had done the whole wretched morning, building and building till it could not be contained. 'You have no idea what you've done to me. Because of you, I might have to put my mother in a home.' Which was perhaps a bit harsh, for it had been heading towards that for months now. It was hardly all his fault, but Zander had made it impossible to approach her boss at this moment, impossible to negotiate for a better arrangement, when she had let him down so badly, and the words tumbled out untamed.

'What are you talking about?' He sneered at the hysterical female who blamed a night of passion for every last ill, but something niggled inside Zander, something unfamiliar, for he had seen her so vibrant, so happy, and now she seemed to be choking with fury and fear almost. 'How can I be responsible for your mother's—?'

'Oh, what would you care about family?' Charlotte snapped, already regretting the words that had spilled out, wishing she could somehow sink to her knees and retrieve them, gather them up and put them in her bag and pretend they had never been said. But it was far too late for that now and the best she could do was look him briefly in the eye before walking out. She looked into black eyes that had once caressed her but were unrecognisable now. 'You're trying to destroy yours; I'm just trying to hold onto mine. What would you know about it?'

'The offer is there.' Zander would not enter a discussion on family, did not want to know of her ills. 'I will consider signing the papers *when* you decide to join me.'

CHAPTER NINE

SHE was his captor.

It felt absolutely like that.

The vast hotel felt like a goldfish bowl. Every time she turned, even if he wasn't there, she anticipated him.

The only relief was the occasional visit to nursing homes and hostels for the homeless on the mainland in the search for Roula Kargas. Nico's thorough search had already ruled out their mother being on Xanos or Lathira, but no matter how promising the lead, every time the result was same—the patient was too old, or the history wrong. Every time it was not their mother.

'Anything?' Nico asked when she rang early the next morning to report on her previous day, but they both knew it was bad news for had it been good she would immediately have told him. 'Nothing. Her name was right…' Charlotte gave a tense sigh. 'I thought I had found your mother, but she was from Rhodes, and the child she had given up was a girl. It was actually really sad.'

'I would have gone myself,' Nico explained. 'The trouble is, my father…' He did not need to explain further. Both knew there was little time left. The doctors were talking in hours now. 'I know that I am asking a lot from you, Charlotte, that this is not part of your more usual work, and it is much appreciated. You need to unwind. Ring the spa, it is world class. Have a massage…'

She might just do that. She could feel the knots in her neck, in her shoulders, in her jaw, even in her fingers that gripped the phone.

'Has Zander been in contact?'

'No.' She had told Nico about the offer to take her out on his boat and, though desperate for information, even Nico had agreed that would be too much to ask.

'If you do speak with him, though…' There was a rare pause from her boss, for their conversations were always brief. He always said what was needed and then hung up, except this was so personal and there was so much pain, it had shifted how things worked. 'I want to find my mother, Charlotte. Any clue, any information, no matter how small.'

'If he tells me anything, I shall pass it on.' She hung up the phone, cross with Nico, yet she could not blame him for his desperation to find out about his past.

She paced the room till she was sick of the walls and she stepped out to the balcony to breathe, to drag in some air, except there Zander was on his balcony, reading the newspaper, coffee in hand, and she raced back inside, only to hear a knock on the door. It couldn't be him, of course, given he was on his balcony, but her heart was thumping as she opened the door. The bellboy was hidden by a huge bunch of orchids and, on reading the attached card, an *apology* from Zander for any *indiscretions* and a summons, rather than an invitation, to join him for morning tea so that he could apologise in person. To add insult to injury, the florist had signed his name incorrectly.

Both card and flowers went in the bin.

Unless he contacted her about work, she would have nothing to do with him, Charlotte decided.

Indiscretions indeed! He was a brave man to request her presence.

The smell of orchids filled the room, but she refused to open the sliding doors, deciding instead that she *would* have the massage that Nico had suggested.

It was but a brief escape, although a pleasant one. Her body was smoothed and pummelled, oiled fingers massaged her scalp and she could almost feel the tension seeping out of her body and through her fingertips. As she was left alone for the lotions to work, as she lay in the warm, darkened room, her mind did not automatically drift to Zander, as it did all too often these days, for he was not the only problem she had. Neither did her thoughts drift to the constant worry about her mother. No, given this pause, for the first time in a long time there was a moment to focus on self, and the voice she had been silencing for a while now started to make itself known. It was a voice that was familiar from her childhood. It blamed others for her problems, heaped on the guilt—the voice of her mother was becoming her own and Charlotte did not like the sound of it a bit. Yes,

Zander had hurt her. Yes, his behaviour had been beyond appalling, but her problems were her own and she knew they needed to be sorted out rather than shelved, knew that so much had to change.

The massage both regenerated and soothed her, but it was a fix that Charlotte knew was only temporary for all too soon she was back in the lift, heading to her room. She swiped the card in her door, relieved to be inside, but her relief was short-lived for there he was, sitting on the chair. She didn't jump, for she put nothing past him.

'I'll complain.'

'To whom?' Zander said. 'I own the hotel.' He glanced over to the bin. 'I see that you don't like orchids.'

'I love orchids,' Charlotte said, 'or rather I used to.' She gave him a very tight smile. 'Though the scent of them will now forever make my stomach curl.'

'I asked you to join me in the restaurant.'

'To discuss business?' Charlotte asked, and watched his jaw tighten. 'Because if that was the case then a phone call would have sufficed—flowers and a second-hand apology weren't necessary.'

'Second-hand?'

'They spelt Zander with an X. Anyway it's irrelevant. I have nothing to discuss with you unless it's about business.' Zander was not used to being stood up or turned down and certainly not when he'd deigned to send flowers.

'I wish to talk.'

'You really think that you can just walk in anywhere and get whatever you want?'

'Of course.'

'You're just a spoiled rich boy…'

And he looked to where she stood and knew he could correct her, could tell her there had been nothing spoiled about his childhood, that the privileged life he led now had been built by his hands, but he spoke of his past with no one, although he had, occasionally, with her.

'You don't know anything about my life.'

'I thought I was starting to,' Charlotte said. 'I thought when we walked on that beach, when we went out to dinner, when you took me to bed…'

He was not here to discuss his past; he was here to find out about her, to put to rest the rare guilt she had generated in him, a feeling that did not sit well with him. 'What you said about your mother, about her having to go into a home…'

'I shouldn't have.' Charlotte's response was instant, that precious time in the spa allowing her to speak with clarity, on that subject at least. 'My problems are my own and they have nothing to do with what happened between us, so you can leave now.' She went to open the door, but Zander was not going anywhere.

'I want to know what is happening.'

'I don't want to discuss my mother, and I have nothing to say to you.'

For the first time with a woman he could not leave it there, did not want to leave it there—for although their day had been engineered, although their night had started with cruel intent, it had concluded differently, and he wanted her back. He wanted the Charlotte that had spoken with him, but her stance was closed, her face a mask, and he fought with the one thing he had left.

'What if I *am* here about business?' Zander said.

'Then I'll schedule you an appointment. '

'I have already been more than patient…'

'Really!'

'Do you know how valuable my time is? Instead, you keep me waiting in a restaurant. You will come out with me. I have arranged to take out the yacht. I am considering releasing the land…'

'I just need your signature.' Charlotte did her level best to keep her voice even. 'It isn't necessary to go out on your yacht.'

'Necessary for whom?' came his snobbish response. 'It is how I conduct business.' He paused for a moment. 'Okay, ring Nico and tell him to join me.'

'That's not possible now. I could speak with Paulo.'

'I have no time for him. It is to be Nico or you. We would go out on the boat, then naturally we would share a long lunch, we would talk, and then I would, *perhaps*, sign. In fact…' She could feel her nails digging into her palms as cruelly he continued. 'It should be Nico taking me out, given how much he wants this deal. Perhaps he is not so keen after all. Perhaps given his PA can only spare me a few minutes of her time…'

'You know that is not the case.'

'So where is he?' Zander pushed and of course she could not answer, knew that he had her trapped, and she did not want to be on a boat with him. She just wanted it over and done with, wanted him out of her life.

'You know you don't need to take me out for a signature.'

'I want to, though.'

'You think I'll change my mind, that you'll seduce me again...' The trouble was that he would, he absolutely would, and that was what most terrified her.

'I came here to do business,' Zander said coolly. 'I expect either Nico or yourself on the jetty at midday.' He looked at where she clutched her dressing gown to herself. 'Hopefully you will dress suitably. Speak with Ethina in the boutique, I will tell her to expect you.'

Bastard.

'Nico...' She apologised for disturbing him, but she would not make a move without telling him, and Nico listened as she explained what his brother had in store for her.

'I've told you, you don't have to go out on his yacht with him. I would never ask you to do that.'

'I'm willing to, though. I just want these papers signed, Nico. And then, I'm sorry, I just want to go home.' She took a deep breath for there was so little to lose now. 'I'm having some health issues with my mother and I really need to fly home first thing tomorrow.'

'I'm sorry to hear that. Is there anything I can do to help?'

'I don't know...' she admitted. 'I need to see how she is before I make any decisions.'

'You can cope?' Nico checked. 'With Zander?'

'Of course.'

'Charlotte…'

'I'm working for you, Nico,' she said, because she was, and, yes, she could cope.

If Zander thought she would succumb again to his charms, that a few hours in close confinement on his yacht with him would somehow dissipate the hurt, would have her falling into his bed again, he was wrong.

So wrong, Charlotte thought, and a small smile spread across her lips.

A smile that became more devilish.

A smile that, as she looked in the mirror, reminded her of the old Charlotte. Apart from her work clothes she was so behind with fashion these days, what heaven it would be to update. How wonderful to keep her head with Zander and look brilliant while doing so.

She stood in the boutique, facing a full-length mirror. Ethina, the owner, was far from gushing, was critical. Clearly it was Zander that Ethina had to impress, and, from the purse to her lips as she ran her eyes over Charlotte, she had her work cut out. She had to transform the lily-white body that hadn't so much as set foot in a gym into the groomed beauty expected by the wallet the boutique was attached to.

How many clothes did a signature from a billionaire require?

'Too harsh.' Ethina held a blood-red bikini up to Charlotte's shoulder and then a jade one and then white. Had her mind not been made up as to her course of action, Charlotte would have run out of the exclusive boutique rather than take the shame.

No doubt that was what Zander was expecting.

For her to make do with what was in her case or to grab the first offering Ethina held up. Instead, she stood there and fought down the shame. She listened and watched and slowly, very slowly, marvelled at the skill of the snooty Ethina.

She learnt that the dull silvery-gold string bikini that looked so tacky on the rack looked sensational on her, that it did not clash with the paleness of her skin and that it blended in with the gold of her hair.

'With the right sunglasses…' Ethina continued, 'the right sandals…' There were beautifully cut shorts and cool linen shirts and then for the first time since her project had entered there was a smile on Ethina's face as she eyed Charlotte in the mirror. 'My work is done.'

Even a bag was purchased for her and Ethina said that she would pack it. Charlotte was led to the salon, the oils washed out and her hair brushed, straightened and then curled, all to create one, oh, so casual ponytail, and she felt casual and elegant and possibly a little bit beautiful as she picked up her new bag and headed to the jetty.

Yes, she felt ready to face him.

Zander watched her walk along the jetty.

Saw her ponytail swishing in the breeze. He had expected hesitation, for her to stop and fiddle, to find a mirror, but it was a confident Charlotte who walked towards the boat—and she looked stunning, even with those gorgeous eyes shielded.

She did her best not to sulk.

Instead, she played the game and accepted champagne and the delicacies on offer, laughed at his comments, spoke with him—but not for a second was she herself, and he missed her, he craved her, he wanted her back.

'That is Lathira...' he pointed to the island in the distance '...where Nico grew up.'

'Oh.'

'You know that,' Zander said. 'It was the wealthier of the islands then.' She examined a manicured nail instead of commenting. She was at work, Charlotte reminded herself, there to gather information for Nico. There to confuse Zander with her confidence, there to reclaim some pride.

'And you grew up on Xanos,' Charlotte said. 'What about...?' She swallowed, for she felt like a spy. 'What about your parents?'

'What did he ask you to find out?' Worse than a spy, she felt like a double agent.

'I was just making conversation.'

'You blush when you lie,' Zander said. 'Not a lot, but your neck goes pink.'

They dropped anchor and she didn't feel so brave any more, but tried not to show it.

He took off his shirt and she yearned to do the same, to feel the breeze on her shoulders, but her body thrummed in his presence and it was safer covered. He smiled as she sat on the bench, trying to look detached, trying to ignore the scent of him as he leant over to pick up the sun lotion.

'Could you do my back?' He asked as if he were innocent, as if that olive skin could possibly burn, as if a man like Zander Kargas could possibly feel pain if it did.

'Of course.'

She was stronger than she even knew she was capable of being. Charlotte picked up the tube and imagined it was the vitamin E cream with which she daily oiled her mum. She refused to remember the sheen of his back when it had slid beneath her fingers, refused to notice the ripple of muscles, or to even acknowledge the faint scratches that her nails had made the other night.

'Done!' She even managed a gentle, sisterly slap on his back before she replaced the lid on the tube and felt the teeniest surge of triumph as, without words, she told him he wasn't quite as irresistible as he'd thought. 'How long will we be out for?'

'That depends.'

'On what?' For the first time her anger bubbled to the surface and she fought to check it. Did he think all this would erase the hurt, that a day trip on his luxury yacht would blind her to all he had done?

'I want to talk.'

'We are talking.'

'I want to talk like before.'

'I trusted you then,' Charlotte said.

She did not trust him now.

Did not trust the man who stripped off his shorts and stood before her.

'Time for a swim.' Black eyes met hers. 'Join me?'

'I'd rather not.'

What a lie. Her body was on fire and she wanted to be in the water. Only as he dived off the side did she venture a look from behind her dark glasses, saw the arms that had once held her slice through the water as easily as he had sliced her heart, yet she wanted to be in there with him, wanted the cool of the water, wanted so badly to join him.

Instead, she sat and the linen of her shirt felt like a horse blanket around her shoulders, so she finally allowed herself to take it off. He came back to the boat, dripping and cool and irritated now, for she spoke about the water and the view. She chatted but did not engage in the way they once had.

'We could sunbake,' he offered, 'go further out to the islands.'

'Whatever you want.'

'What do you want?' Zander demanded. 'What amuses Charlotte?'

Clearly nothing did.

'What will it take for you to enjoy it? What do I have to do to—?'

'There's nothing you can do,' she cut in, for did he really think she was so shallow, that a trip on his yacht and champagne could soothe the hurt? 'How can I ever enjoy time with you when I know what you did to me, when I know what you are capable of?'

'I have apologized,' Zander said. He did so rarely, but it had always worked in the past.

'But it still happened,' Charlotte said, and such was the visible regret in his dark eyes, she almost believed it was real. She felt the spell that he cast so easily start to work its charm and she flailed for something else, an antidote to the magic he made, and she found it. 'I know how you treated me, and I know how you treat others, how you do business, the lengths you will go to...' It felt good to say it, easier to be angry on other's behalf, for around him, for herself, she was weak. 'Look what you've done to Xanos.'

'It needed it,' Zander said. 'The place was falling apart, people were leaving in droves. Now it is prosperous.'

'For you, perhaps,' Charlotte said.

'It was a dwindling fishing village, now there are jobs, now the island is thriving.'

'There are no jobs for the locals, though.' She challenged him. 'Except for the taverna that feeds *your* labourers, all the other workers are from the mainland.' He heard her words and he moved to defend himself, to correct her, but there it was again, this guilt that seemed to invade at times when she was around. She was such a wisp of a thing, Zander thought, but she was stronger than most; not in her slender arms that stretched out, exasperated, and not in her voice, which could so easily be drowned by his, but in her resolve, in her beliefs, in her convictions, and he was silenced. 'Will you take me back now?'

'If that is what you want. But I brought you here to find out why, because of me, your mother needs to go in a home.' This time there was no derision in his voice. 'Charlotte, I need to know. I need to put that right at least.'

'Please,' Charlotte said, 'just leave it.'

'I cannot. If Nico is going to fire you because of what happened… I have told you, there is a job for you.'

'A paid mistress?' Charlotte sneered. 'I'm not even going to respond to that offer.'

'I don't understand how your mother—'

'Zander, stop!' Her voice was shrill and she tamed it. 'I'm sorry that I said that.'

'Sorry?' He could not make out this woman, was used to women pouring out their hearts rather than holding back.

'My mother is sick, she has Alzheimer's, and I've been looking after her at home. I don't have the party life that I told you I did. That life was a long time ago.' And she waited, waited for horror to cloud his features, for him to recoil, but still he stood there. 'I lied to you.' She spelt it out and *still* he stood there.

An angel had not been required, but she was close to it now. This was the woman he had thought sleeping with his brother, the party girl he had assumed could handle all he heaped on her. And he knew then how badly he had hurt her, that the heart he had broken this time had been a fragile one.

'Why?'

'I lied to you because…' She screwed her face up in

frustration. 'Because you didn't need to hear it, because it could never impact on you.'

It just had, though.

'I thought I could handle a fling,' Charlotte said simply. 'In fact, I'm quite sure I could have. I just never anticipated that you'd cause me so much pain.' She was terribly honest. 'I'm sorry that I blamed you about my mother, it just felt easier.'

'Easier?'

'I'm starting to sound like her.' She did not need to explain herself to him, Charlotte realised, she just needed to explain it to herself. 'You actually did me a favour...' She gave a wry smile. 'You learn a lot about yourself when difficult times hit.'

'So what did you learn?'

He was the man she'd first met, the man who made her unbend, the man she could talk to, but she was far more wary now. Still, it was a relief to voice what had been whirring in her head.

'That I'm starting to sound like her.' Charlotte explained. 'Bitter, a victim, berating—it was never my intention. She begged me not to put her in a home when she was first diagnosed, told me over and over that I was all she had, that she had done so much for me. I love my mum. Whatever decision I make it's going to hurt. But when I heard myself blaming you, when I used my mum as an excuse...'

'What do you want, Charlotte?'

'I want my life back.' There, she'd said it out loud. 'To go back to flying...'

'No. I don't want to be away all the time while I've still got Mum. Hopefully I'll keep my job and be able to visit Mum a lot.' She was talking as if it were a done deal, but she felt sick inside and she looked beyond the boat to the ocean, wished for a glimpse of peace, but it did not come from the view; instead, it came from a most unexpected source. He put his hand on her shoulder and for the first time her body did not respond to his with a leap of awareness. As his fingers rested on her shoulder, it was a caress that soothed, a caress she wanted to sink into, his voice somehow the one that calmed her.

'I can only imagine what you think of me, and I know my opinion might not mean much to you, but for what it's worth, I think you have made the right choice.'

And his opinion should not matter, except it did, and to hear him approve of her wretched decision brought a sting of relieved tears to her eyes.

'It's a horrible choice, though.'

'There isn't a nice one,' Zander pointed out. 'From impossible situations you make impossible choices. Maybe if your mother had her time again, if she knew how bad it would get, maybe she would be saying the same thing.'

'I doubt it!' Her smile was small but genuine. 'I love her dearly, but she really was the most difficult woman.'

'She probably did her best,' Zander offered, and Charlotte could tell he immediately wished that he hadn't because as her eyes jerked to his, he looked away. She knew he was going to change the subject.

'Maybe yours did, too.'

He stood, did not even attempt a response. 'Do you want to swim? Or we could head back…'

'No.'

He was the one resisting now, he was the one who wanted the safety of shore, and she wanted him to stop, wanted him to talk. 'Maybe she did do her best, Zander.'

'By selling one child and deserting the other?' Zander asked. 'She destroyed my father by leaving. He was a good man, an honourable man, till she left him.' He stopped but only because she put up her hand.

'Please, don't…' Her hand was shaking. She so badly wanted to know what had happened, but she had forgotten the reason was here, did not want him to confide in her when she would have to betray him. She could not reveal that to him, but Zander was one step ahead of her.

'You have to tell Nico what I say to you?'

'How do you know?'

'Rare, the woman who doesn't want to talk about feelings.' She looked up and was surprised to see him smiling. 'That's usually all they want to talk about. Tell him what you must, Charlotte, it makes no difference to me.'

'Why won't you talk to him?'

'There's nothing I want to discuss.'

'He's your twin,' Charlotte said. 'How can you not want to get to know him? How can you not want to find your mum?'

'Because neither of them interest me,' Zander said.

'I'll sign the papers, though—if it helps you.' Which was the reason she was there, yet all she felt was sad.

'If I were Nico…' she started, and then stopped, for Zander's signature was the reason she was there and she had it in her grasp now.

'Go on.'

She dared to go on, dared to speak her truth, whatever the eventual cost. 'I wouldn't want the land. I'd move as far away as I could.' She looked at the most beautiful man she had ever seen, a man who was capable of so very much but was determined to stay locked in hate. 'I don't know why Nico wants to prolong the agony. Why he doesn't just cut his losses…' She stopped talking then, because she understood why. For surely Nico loved him, wanted, however painful, contact with him, wanted the hope that things might one day change.

'You need oil.' He picked up the bottle and changed the subject, gave her the benefit of that beautiful smile that was, she had found out, just a small part of him. 'Your shoulders are burning.'

'Don't try and seduce me, Zander.' She must not give into him, must not just bend to his will. 'I'm not sleeping with you.'

'I just want to oil you.'

'Please.' She shrank away, for she knew what his touch could do. 'What do you want from me, Zander?'

And always Zander surprised her for, as he unstoppered the bottle, as he poured oil on her shoulders, he told her he wanted more than her body as he put in his bid. 'I am leaving Xanos tonight—and I want you to come with me.'

CHAPTER TEN

HER arms were rigid beside her when she felt the sliver of oil touch her skin.

He traced it across her shoulders; she felt first his fingers then his palms and felt as if she was being gently kneaded, moulded. She attempted to retain her self-possession.

'You want me to come with you?'

'Now I know your circumstances, now that I know the truth, we could come to some arrangement that suits.'

'That suits?' Her heart seemed to plummet from the dizzy heights it had soared to, and she berated herself for daring to dream, for considering for a foolish moment that he might purely want her.

'Relax, all I am doing is oiling you.'

'I don't trust you,' she said, for it was true. Neither did her body trust what it might do, for her legs were shaking so much she had to push down her feet to stop them.

'Lie down,' Zander said, removing her sunglasses, and she wished he hadn't for she felt braver behind them.

'I'll do your back.' And as she tensed in resistance, he gave her his word. 'We will not sleep together again till you trust me,' Zander said. 'And you will.'

I won't, her mind insisted, but he lowered the bars of resistance with velvet-cloaked words and she lay on her stomach and felt the oil drizzle on her back and then the bliss of his fingers.

'Come with me.'

'Where?' His hands were on her rib cage now, stroking in the oil.

'Anywhere,' Zander said. 'Away from Nico. I will take care of you. Whatever he pays you—'

'You mean you'll employ me?' She could feel the tears in her eyes and she squeezed them closed.

'Turn over,' he said, and she wanted to see him, she wanted to see him properly so she could understand what he was saying, so she did as he asked.

'I'm not asking you to work for me.' He poured oil to her stomach, but not once did his fingers edge towards gold. 'Just that you do not work for him. I will look after you.'

'Financially?' She pushed his hands away, but they were quickly back and she wanted to sob because they changed her, they made the wrong so very right, made all things possible as now they moved to her waist. She wanted him to tear off her bikini and cool her with his mouth. 'You mean that you'll pay me to be there for you. There's another word for that, Zander.'

And he was so loathsome because all he did was smile. He looked at her tears, her anger, and still all he did was smile, because what abhorred her was completely fine with him.

'If you're looking for my heart, I warn you,' he said, 'I have no heart to give.'

'Then I don't want you.'

'Liar.'

'I don't,' she said, except his hands were at her neck, unfastening the top of her bikini and then moving behind and working the tiny clasp, and so small were her breasts that they barely moved, but she felt sick with excitement and shame. He stared down at them, and she saw the lust in his eyes, the decadent lick of his lips.

'I can't…'

'Can't or won't?' His hands crept to her breasts,

'Can't.' She shuddered, her eyes flashing to his, telling him her truth in the hope it would repel. 'I've told you that I lied. I'm not what you think, I'm not able to travel. It nearly killed me to get away this time.'

'Because of your mother.'

'Yes,' she wept, because the truth should halt his hands, that she was not all she had said she was should have him pause, but his hands moved lower.

'How about a job with no work hours?' She frowned up at him. 'I don't need another PA, Charlotte.'

'I don't want to be kept.'

'Why?' he asked. 'When you'd get the best bits.' He was more tempting than the devil. She could see the best bits, the thick outline of them in his wet bathers. The lull of the boat beneath her back, the sun on her arms, the cool shade of his body shielding her torso did nothing to cool her.

Was it wrong, to want only the best bits?

Wrong to lie there as he eased her bikini bottoms down, to envisage a future as the occasional lover of Zander?

To go back to her life and not worry about bills?

To look after her mother and know she had this as an occasional reward?

She lay naked beneath him and he was so unabashed by her nakedness, so delighted by her, and wicked too, for he picked up the oil and squeezed it where her thighs were clamped closed, like her mind, trying to keep delicious prospects out, trying not to be seduced again by all Zander Kargas offered.

Except his fingers slid in, welcome if uninvited, and she kept her thighs closed but that offered no deterrent. She bit on her lip as he watched her, and she opened her eyes to the beauty of him and could not say no, did not want to say no, so she said nothing, her silence her consent.

He bought her to orgasm so easily.

Too easily almost. It made her feel ashamed, the kettle he could flick on at whim, not that a man like Zander had any need for a kettle. She wanted it all, even if it was impossible. She could not be at his bidding, for her sanity's sake.

'No.' Her hand was reaching out for him, for the supposed best bit, but she pulled it back for she wanted more, wanted the man that came with it, wanted his heart.

'You don't know me.' She thought of her life back home.

'I don't need to.'

And it was cruel but it was his truth.

She could play dress-up once maybe twice a month, escape to a fabulous hotel.

Inhabit a small corner of his life.

And it would be beyond cruel, Charlotte realised.

He did not offer escape. Instead, Zander offered prison, for she would be locked for ever with feelings she could not release. That was what held her hand back.

That made her say no.

'I can't.' She was completely honest. 'I want more than that.'

'There can be no more.'

'There has to be.'

'I don't understand what you want.' He was brutally honest. 'We have known each other one weekend. Isn't it a bit soon to be demanding for ever?'

'That's not what I'm saying.'

'What, then? I am offering you a chance for us to get to know each other better and to remove from you the division of loyalty you have working for Nico. I don't give out rings, Charlotte. I'm offering you now all I will ever give.' He made it completely clear, and she could only admire him for that—he warned her upfront that he would break her heart, and for Charlotte it made the final choice painful but easy.

'Then I choose to live with my head in the clouds. To believe that one day—'

'Someone better than me will come along.' It was his trump card and he played it. He was possibly the only man who could ever play it, for he had driven her to the edge in bed, and to the deepest places in her mind; he was exquisite and beautiful and there could be no better, for her heart had met his on that first phone call and they would forever be joined. He was the best, and it almost killed her to stay strong as he looked down at her naked, flushed body, a body that had just come at his command, and even think there could be someone better.

'He might,' Charlotte said.

'I told you—you blush when you lie. You know there can be no better than what we have.'

'And do you retain exclusive rights?'

'Of course.'

'Do I get the same privilege?' She watched as his tongue rolled in his cheek. She would rather be alone than share him and would go no further with this ridiculous conversation. She was stronger than she'd known, stronger even than Nico, for she could do what his identical twin could not—she could end the painful contact with him, could give up now the hope that things might one day change.

'Can you take me back now, please?'

She stood. Putting on a bikini seemed too complicated with a head that was spinning and hands that were shaking, so she fled down below, pulled on her new clothes from her new bag, and went back to her old heart.

To the one that had the dream that life could one day be different,.

That *he* was somehow waiting.

And clearly it wasn't a dream that Zander shared, for as she sat on a bed she would never sleep in, she heard the engine, felt the movement of the boat as Zander took her back to shore.

Zander spent the hour sailing towards Xanos wrestling with his thoughts.

He sailed the yacht past Lathira, the place his brother had been raised, and then he aimed towards Xanos, to the hell he had hated. Yet it was with new eyes he saw it now.

He saw the beach where he had met her, where they had walked and talked.

He saw the balcony of Ravels where they had kissed and the blackened windows where he had held her.

He saw his island through different eyes, new images made by Charlotte.

He had hurt her, had assumed she could take it, had not recognised her innocence, for he had none himself. He had hurt others too—he had looked at the land he had transformed with no thought to its history, or the people.

The seagulls were loud as the boat neared land, swirling overhead and finally daring to swoop onto the deck, screeching as they squabbled over the remnants of the meal, eating with far more relish than Charlotte had the delicacies he had ordered for her. Still they squawked for more, still, when they should be full, there was hunger, greed that was never satisfied—like his endless quest for a revenge.

For the first time he saw a future that was different, one that did not stink of the past, one that was better, one where he could be with her.

Maybe he did have a heart to give.

Maybe there could be trust.

Someone there for him, someone who did not leave.

He needed to think, he needed the safety of dry land and the solitude of his room before he made the most difficult decision of his life. Then she came up to the deck in shorts and a T-shirt, her hair down and her eyes shielded by glasses again.

'It was a lovely offer, but completely impossible, even if you did give out rings. You don't know my life…'

He wanted to, though.

For the first time he wanted someone in a way he never had. He wanted to know her, about her, to be there for her, to accept the baggage that came with her, instead of hurling it back to defend a black heart.

The sun must have been too strong, he thought. The sky was orange and he wanted it black. He wanted a safe, dark world that was bitter, but he was tired of strangers on his pillow.

'Here.' He handed her the signed contract of sale for the land that Nico wanted. He could not read her expression behind her dark glasses, but from the shake of her hand when he spoke, he guessed that she understood, for with his signature she was no longer obliged to see him for Nico's sake.

'Meet me.' He wanted her now, but he made himself wait. Till he was sure, till he had talked himself out of it perhaps…

Till the time was right.

'Ring Nico when we get back. Tell him you have my signature.' Then he looked at her and he tried for haughty, for assuming, for the arrogance that usually dripped from each word, but instead his eyes implored. 'Meet me tonight, not on behalf of Nico. Hear what I have to say.' And he turned his back to her, for more than anything he hated weakness. 'Meet me for dinner.'

He was a skilled seducer, Charlotte reminded herself. He had said, and would again, anything to get her to his bed.

It was hard to remember the hurt, though, when there was something else in his eyes.

'I don't know.' She was truly scared, not of him but of how he made her feel, how easily she believed in him when she had sworn that she never would again.

'Please be there.'

'If I'm not?'

'Then I'll know,' Zander said, and he took off her glasses and looked deep into her eyes. 'Do we say good-bye here?'

He was choosing to kiss her, Charlotte realised.

He chose to pull her into him to serve as a constant reminder. He kissed her better than the first time and maybe for the last time; he kissed her with his mouth and she felt it with her heart. 'Please…' He dropped contact for he had to think, but once he had done that, everything would change.

Change can be good, Zander thought as he looked into the blue that could perhaps forever entrance him.

The same can be good too, Zander mused as he thought of her head on the pillow beside him from this night for ever. 'Meet me tonight.'

CHAPTER ELEVEN

HE WENT to his suite and waited for sense to return.

He downed a drink as if were medicine, felt the burn in his gut and waited for normal services to resume, for him to remember how much she annoyed him. Except he could recall not an instant, not a laugh that had irritated him, or questions that had irked. For the first time he had wanted to tell all to another. Still, he racked his brains to find fault somehow, to prove himself right, to tell himself that this could not work, that he was mad to consider a future with her.

But consider it he did.

So too did she.

Had there been love in those coal-black eyes—was there more that he might be prepared to give?

It wasn't the yacht or the trappings that lured her, it was the voice that had filled her grey bedroom those mornings that she wanted to hear for ever; it was the man who had made her smile and melt. She wanted so much more of him.

She blasted her body and face with the shower, told

herself not to get her hopes up, that this was a man who had hurt her deeply, a man who had shamed her badly. Logic told her that this was a man she should not trust.

The phone rang and it was Nico. She had to remember where, for now at least, her duties lay. She would enjoy giving him the good news about the land. But instead of Nico it was Constantine with sad news.

'He passed away,' Constantine said. 'Nico's father passed away a couple of hours ago. In the end it was peaceful and they made their peace, which is good.'

Charlotte offered her condolences and then told Constantine to pass on that she had Zander's signature, but they both knew it was not really the land that Nico wanted but the brother and the mother and the history that came with it.

'Charlotte, you know we have tried all the homes and hostels on Xanos and Lathira but the nurses here were talking and there is one we have missed. It's in the nunnery in the northern hills of Xanos, they take in a few fallen women and care for them. I have rung and spoken to them and I think I might have found her. Please, Charlotte, can you go and find out? I don't want to tell Nico until I am certain. Can you go now?'

'Of course.' Charlotte looked at the clock. She could surely do it. If she was a bit late for dinner, Zander would have to understand.

It wasn't just for Nico that she said yes, neither was it for duty. She wanted to face Zander tonight with the truth on the table. As she walked through the foyer, past the various boutiques, she glanced at the jeweller's, at an empty space where the necklace had been, and she actually held hope.

She was sure, completely sure, that she was doing the right thing by him, that it was the truth that was needed here.

And she was almost sure that Zander wasn't about to break her heart again.

The driver was delighted by the blonde passenger who spoke a little Greek, but Charlotte barely replied to his questions as the car threaded its way along the hillside and came to rest at the nunnery.

There was no reception on her mobile phone, so she asked the driver to wait and stalled his protests with cash. Then she rang the bell and, when it was answered, she was welcomed into the old building. She spoke for a while with two kindly nuns, one of whom spoke a little English, which helped when Charlotte's Greek was not up to the job.

'She speaks of the twins all the time,' the nun explained. 'She has two plastic dolls that she holds and will not let go of. It is sad…'

'Can I see her?' Even now she dared not get her hopes up, for she had thought she was close to finding her so many times before.

'Of course. If she can see her sons, or even know that they are okay, maybe she can go to God in peace.'

'She's only young, though,' Charlotte said, for the woman they were speaking about was only around fifty, she had been told.

'She has lived a hard life.'

It was impossible to remember she was supposed to be working as she walked into the sparsely furnished room for as she walked over to Roula, it was Zander who was in her heart.

It *was* Roula. She could now, without hearing a word from the woman, ring Nico and tell him his mother had been found, for the eyes that stared into the distance had been passed on to her sons, the pain in them too. Charlotte wanted to embrace her, but instead she approached slowly.

'This is Charlotte,' the nun explained to a vacant-looking face of Roula. 'She works for Nico...' The old lady's eyes jerked to hers.

'He has been looking for you,' Charlotte said in Greek.

'Alexandros?' Roula begged, and Charlotte could not lie to her. Neither could she stand to tell her the truth, that the son she longed for hated her.

'I know Zander too,' she settled for and then, with Charlotte's sparse Greek and the nun's sparse English, they sat, slowly piecing together her story. Though she was supposed to be meeting Zander, Charlotte knew this was more important. She listened to the woman as her agony was slowly revealed. There was no question of rushing her, no impulse to ring Nico, no thought to the fading light outside or the taxi driver waiting, no thought even of Zander sitting waiting for her at a dinner table. Time did not matter for the moment, for these were words that Zander needed to hear.

CHAPTER TWELVE

'TONIGHT they have their own rooms,' Alexandros said. 'Separate rooms.'

'What harm...?' Roula started and then stopped. She had learnt not to question Alexandros's decisions, but on this one she had to stand up to him. It would be cruel to separate the babies, so she tried another route. 'They will wake you with their tears.'

'Let them cry—that is the way they will learn that at night you are with me.' He ran a hand between her thighs, told her that tonight there would be no excuses—not that he listened when she made them.

Her only relief was the slam of the door when he left to spend the day sitting outside the taverna, playing cards and drinking, but Roula's relief lasted just a moment before the countdown started, dreading his return.

Seventeen and the mother of twins, they were her only shining light. More beautiful than any other babies, she could watch them sleep for hours, the little snubs of their noses pushed up by their fingers as they sucked on their thumbs, eyelashes so long that they met the curve *of their cheeks. Sometimes one would open his eyes to the other. Huge black eyes would gaze at his brother, soothed by what he saw, and then close again.*

Mirror-image twins, the midwife had told Roula when she had delivered them. Identical, but opposite, one right-handed the other left. Their soft baby hair swirled to the right on Nico, to the left on little Alexandros.

At almost a year, they still shared a cot, screaming if she tried to separate them. Even if their cribs were pushed together their protests would not abate. Now he would force them into separate rooms.

And she would hear their screams all night as her husband used her body, and Roula could not take it any more.

Would not.

Her father would surely help if he knew. Alexandros did not like her to go out so she had seen her father only a couple of times since her marriage—he had wanted her to marry as the little money he got for his paintings could not support them both. He had been a little eccentric since her mother's death; he preferred to be alone. But he would surely not want this life for his daughter and grandsons.

'Now,' she told herself. 'You must do it now.' She had maybe five or six hours before Alexandros returned. She ran down the hallway, pulled out a case and filled it with the few clothes she had for her babies, and then she ran into the kitchen to a jar she had hidden, filled with money she had been secretly hoarding for months now.

'This is how you repay me?' Roula froze when she heard his voice, and then simply detached herself as he beat her, as he told her she was a thief to take from the man who put a roof over her head. 'You want to leave, then get out!' How her heart soared for a brief moment, but then Alexandros dealt his most brutal blow. 'You get half...' He hauled her to the bedroom where her babies lay screaming, woken by the terrible sounds. 'Which one is the firstborn?' He did not recognise his own sons. 'Which one is Alexandros?'

When she answered he picked up the other babe and thrust Nico at her.

'Take him, and get out.'

She ran to her father's, clutching Nico. She was terrified for Alexandros left alone with him, sure that her father would help her sort it out. Along the streets she ran till finally home was in view, except it was boarded up. Her father was now dead, the disgusted neighbours told her, for she had neglected him in his final days and had not bothered to attend his funeral. The worst was finding out that her husband had been informed, had known, and not thought to tell her.

'We will get your brother back,' she said to a screaming Nico. The local policeman drank regularly with Alexandros so he would be no help, but she would go to the main town of Xanos, which was on the north of the island, to the lawyer that was there.

She took a ride on a truck and had to pay the driver in the vilest of ways, but she did it for her son, and she *did it many times again when she found that the rich young lawyer wanted money up front before helping her.*

A little cheap ouzo from the lid meant Nico slept at night and she could earn more money. The rest of the bottle got her through.

And she tried.

Till one day, sitting holding her baby in an alleyway, she heard a man's voice.

'How much?'

Roula looked up and she was about to name her paltry fee, but there was a woman standing next to him, and that was one thing Roula would not do.

'I'm not interested.'

Except he did not want her body. 'How much for him?'

He told her they were childless, that they were on holiday from the mainland to get over their grief. He told her about the money and education they could give her beautiful boy, that they would move to the neighboring island of Lathira and would raise him as their own. She thought of Alexandros, who was still with that monster, and somehow she had to save him. She thought of the ouzo and the clients she would service tonight and all the terrible things she had done. Surely Nico deserved better.

He wailed in protest as the stranger's wife lifted him. Just as he had those first awful nights when he had missed little Alexandros so badly. But he would settle, Roula told herself as finally she sat in the lawyer's wait-

ing room and signed over one son in the hope of saving the other.

Nico would settle, Roula told herself again as the couple left with her baby. Soon Nico would forget.

She, on the other hand, would spend the rest of her life trying to.

CHAPTER THIRTEEN

'Zander...'

As soon as she had phone reception, she called Zander, though she should have called Nico first.

'I'm sorry I couldn't get there in time... I'm on my way now.'

'Are you okay?' She heard his immediate concern. 'You sound as if you have been crying.' Only in the taxi had she broken down, but she tried to disguise it from Zander, for surely it was not her place to weep about this to him.

'I'm okay. I should be there in an hour.'

The reception was terrible and Zander commented on it. 'Where are you?'

'I'm in the hills.'

'The hills? I thought you were meeting me.'

'I'm in a taxi and I'm on my way. Nico asked me...' She faltered, for the mention of Nico's name seemed to light a flare. 'I had something to do for Nico.'

'Something so important that you leave me waiting. You have my signature already, which was what he wanted.'

She looked to her watch. It was long after eight and though she *must* tell Nico first, it was Zander she loved. 'Nico had a lead on your mother that he asked me to follow up. Zander, I've found her. I've just come from speaking with your mother.'

And all she heard was the click of the phone and for a moment thought he had lost the signal, but when she rang again and he didn't answer, when she tried once more and it just rang, she knew he was leaving, knew that in his eyes it had happened again—that she had chosen against him.

She must ring Nico, must remember where her duty lay. 'I've found her,' she said when Constantine answered the phone. Unlike Zander, Constantine immediately asked how Roula was. 'She's fragile,' Charlotte said, and told her a little of the story, arranging to meet with them tomorrow, to explain better face to face. 'There's one thing I don't understand, though…' Charlotte frowned as she spoke with Constantine, for there was one thing she wanted to sort out before she spoke with Zander. 'Roula had the money when she sold Nico so why didn't she go back to the lawyer? Why didn't she use the money to try and get to Zander?'

'Because the lawyer kept upping his fees. Because the lawyer did not want to work for Roula and have her exposing all that he had done.'

'How do you know that?' Charlotte asked.

'Because that lawyer was my father.'

There was pain all around, Charlotte realised. A pain that ran so deep, perhaps too deep for healing, but surely if Nico and Constantine could work through it, then she and Zander stood a chance. She spent the rest of the journey pleading with the driver to please go faster and flew out of the taxi before it had even come fully to a halt. Dashing into the foyer, she saw luxurious cases on the gold trolley and almost wept with relief that Zander was still there.

'Zander, please…' She ran up to him as he walked out to the waiting car. 'I'm sorry but Nico—'

'Nico?' He hated that word and this time it showed. This time he spat it out. 'Nico snaps his fingers and you run. You had plans with me and yet you drop them for him.'

'I met your mum!' Charlotte said. 'I spoke with your mum. Don't you even want to know how she is?'

'No.' It was that simple to Zander. 'I care nothing for her. She is a poor excuse for you to use. I asked you to be there tonight, I was going to…' And he could not say it, for he had been a fool to even think it, think for a moment that they could ever be.

'Going to what?' she pushed, because she wanted to know, wanted to believe that love might have been on offer tonight, wanted to remind him of all he was losing.

'Give you this.' He handed her a thick velvet box, but it came with no meaning, for even rubies and diamonds shone dull without love.

'Just this?' Charlotte said, which seemed strange when the necklace was worth a small mortgage, but she was sure, so sure there had been more to come.

'What else were you expecting?' He frowned. 'Oh, and by the way, I've reconsidered the job offer.'

'Job offer?'

'We discussed you working for me?' He twisted the knife. 'I prefer someone a little more reliable—someone who does not dash off when we have plans. Still…' he gave a tight shrug '…we have had some pleasant times.' He glanced at the box. 'Have it.'

'For services rendered?'

'Don't be crass.'

'That's how you just made me feel.' And there was nothing left to dream, for it had always been impossible. 'I'd say no anyway.' She looked at the stone of his face, at eyes that refused to warm, at the immutable man that was Zander. 'Even if it was more than a job, even if it was more than your mistress, no matter what you were going to offer, I'd still say no.'

Was that a smirk on his face, yes, it was, and it incensed her.

'I would say no.'

'Liar.' It was the closest he would come to admitting that the night could have been very different, that had she not chosen Nico, he would have offered it all.

'Of course I would. You've got a mother who loves you. You don't know what happened, you don't know what she went through…'

'She's had thirty years to come up with her excuses. Whatever she told you—'

'It's nothing to do with what your mother told me,' Charlotte interrupted. 'It's to do with you, Zander.

You've got a whole family waiting, a whole parade of people who want to get to know you, and all you choose is pain. I would say no to whatever you offer, for it would be like living with my mother—and I've done my time with bitter.' And then she looked straight at him. 'It would be worse, in fact. My mother has genuinely forgotten her past, whereas you choose not to know. Your brother is grieving tonight but your black heart cares nothing for that.'

'Nico has what he wants from me—he has the land. Tell him I am selling Xanos. Run to your boss with that bit of information and see if he pays you a bonus for giving him the heads up.'

'It isn't Xanos Nico wants!' Charlotte said pleadingly. 'Can't you see that when you hurt Nico, you hurt me?' Her words came out wrong, her thoughts too jumbled, but she didn't attempt to explain. 'I know what I want, so thank you for helping me see it. I know what I want now.' She held out the box but he did not take it. Neither did he ask her to explain what it was she wanted, but she told him. She looked at him, and he did not flinch as she said it, but she watched his face turn grey, watched his jaw clench just a fraction.

'I want what your brother's got.'

She moved her lips closer to his ear and could have sworn she heard the thud of his black heart as she spoke on. 'I want everything your brother has—a home, babies, love, acceptance and forgiveness, all the things that you can never give.' How cruelly she taunted him, but better that than not say it, better that than he never see. 'I want what Nico has.'

'Well, you've made the right choice,' Zander responded, 'because you'll never get it from me.'

He climbed into a car that would take him the short distance to the jetty, and she stood watching the seaplane lift into the sky and it hurt, for she wanted to be on it, wanted so badly to be with him, but not this way, never this way. She walked the streets of Xanos that night and wandered down to the beach. How she longed to ring him, but knew she must not.

She felt rain start to fall, winter rain that came from the north and was cold and driving, but as she sat on the beach and shivered, it did not feel like rain. Zander had left, signed over the land, walked out, not just on her but the truth, and it felt as if right now, this minute, he was washing his hands of Xanos.

Cleansing himself of her.

CHAPTER FOURTEEN

HE TRIED.

Every part of him tried to remove Xanos from his heart. For the first time he ordered his team to respond to the expressions of interest in the hotel, the land, the entire development. He wanted it sold, he simply wanted it gone.

Zander wasn't baiting Nico, but it came as no surprise that Nico was a serious bidder. There were few who could afford it, fewer still who had a heart in the place, and of course his brother wanted it.

Nico wanted something else too, something Zander could never give.

'No.' Zander's response to his legal team was instant, for it was all done through them, there had been no conversations between the brothers. 'I'm not interested in a partnership.' He moved to the window, stared out to what was surely the most beautiful harbour in the world, to glimpses of beaches that should, after all this time, feel like home, so why was his heart in Xanos? 'He can buy it all or nothing.'

Why did it hurt as his lawyers made calls, as he shed

a painful past and moved towards his future? Why did it hurt to listen to his lawyer inform Nico's team they would be looking at all offers and get back to them soon.

'She wants to know how soon is soon.' The lawyer put the phone on mute. 'Apparently, Nico Eliades does not want to be kept waiting for your decision as he has been in the past. He has another development he is keen on and will be retracting his offer at the end of the week.'

'Tell Paulo—'

'It's not his lawyer on the line, it's his PA, with a direct message from Eliades.'

It was Nico baiting him this time, Zander realised, for Charlotte was the only thing that had bound them. Were it not for her, he might not even have bothered going to Xanos to confront his brother. It had been the lure of her voice that had changed his plans, had made him go to the island he hated. It had been Charlotte who'd had him stay on those extra days and Nico knew it.

'Tell her…' Zander said, but his voice trailed off, because it was late afternoon in Australia and early morning in London, and he *wanted* her voice and the image of her in bed; he wanted to go back to what they'd had before. Which was impossible of course, and it was impossible too to move forward, for he did not have a heart to give—except it seemed to be beating just now, pounding in his chest and demanding the sound of her voice to soothe it. And there beneath his heart, his soul also demanded, but he shut it down with bile, would not give in to Nico, would not let him use Charlotte as his pawn. 'Give me the phone,' Zander said, but did not ask for privacy, for there were few words to be said. 'My staff will get back to you when I tell them to. Tell your boss that, tell him too that he is the one *using* you, but I don't care who calls, I don't care—'

'I'll pass it on.' The clipped words halted him, the sound of a woman's voice, but not *hers*.

'I thought I was speaking with Eliades's PA.'

'You are.'

He did ask for privacy then, flicked his staff out of his office with a brief wave of his hand, before resuming the conversation. 'I usually deal with Charlotte.'

'Ms Edwards is no longer working for Mr Eliades.'

'Since?'

'I'll pass on your message to Mr Eliades.' Nico's incredibly efficient new PA was not going to waste a moment of her boss's valuable time discussing her predecessor.

It was she who rang off and Zander stood there as he lost that last link to Charlotte. She was away from Nico. It should bring relief.

But relief was absent.

He had looked forward to their calls far more than he should.

He gazed out at the richest view in Australia, felt a chill in his skin beneath his luxurious suit, for he had everything, yet he had nothing.

When you hurt Nico, you hurt me.

It was as if she were in the room with him.

He picked up the phone and rang what had once been

Charlotte's number and, of course, Nico's new PA answered. He knew there was only one way to find out about her. 'Can you arrange a meeting for me?' He would do it only for Charlotte. 'With my brother.'

CHAPTER FIFTEEN

'WHY would you want a partnership?'

Zander had been surprised at the choice of venue,
sure they would sit in a meeting room at Ravels or perhaps in an office in Athens, but instead Nico had asked
him to come to his home. Zander could taste bile as he
walked through the stone arch and up the steps of what
had once been his grandfather's house. He had accepted
the cool greeting of Nico's wife and now sat, grateful
for the drink she offered him, as he asked his brother a
question that burned.

'Is that not what brothers do?' Nico answered. 'I do
not like the plans you have for the remaining part of
the island, but I cannot deny what you have achieved
so far—'

'At the expense of the people.'

'You have sorted that,' Nico said. 'You have repaid
them. There are locals now working at the hotel, in the
shops and bars. Xanos is a happier place now. Why
would you want to walk away from it, from all you have
achieved?'

'Because…' Zander said, but did not qualify it, did

not tell Nico that achieving prosperity for Xanos had never been his intention. He had wanted it gone, to change the landscape he so hated, as if somehow he could erase the past. But he did not share his thoughts with others, did not confide, well, not usually. He had with Charlotte, but he chose not to go there yet. He wanted to know if Nico had fired her, wanted to know if she was doing okay, and if sitting here meant he found out, he'd do it.

'I am not going to play games. Your offer is fair and I accept it. I will have my staff move things along.' He glanced up at the wall behind Nico, to a picture that looked like a jigsaw, and saw that it was the garden he had just walked through. He could see two babies sitting in the grass and he tore his eyes away, would not ask if it was Nicos himself, would not stand and walk over to examine it more closely, he just would not be drawn in. He wanted Xanos gone, wanted distance, he was here for one thing only. 'I will speak with your PA…' He tried to do it casually, tried to change the subject naturally. 'I note that Charlotte is no longer working for you.'

'That's right.' His brother was far too like him, Zander realized, for he gave nothing away uninvited.

'Did you fire her?'

'My staff are not your concern.'

'I am not asking after your staff.' He felt ridiculously uncomfortable, would have liked to loosen his tie, but refused to. 'I am asking after Charlotte.'

'Her personal situation is not for me to discuss.'

'Is she okay?'

'Perhaps you should ask her.'

'I would, had I her number. I assume it was a work phone?'

'I'll ring her,' Nico offered, 'ask if she is okay with me giving her number to you.'

'Please, don't.' Zander stood. 'I just want to know that everything is okay. I don't want to make contact...'

'Why?'

'Because,' Zander said, and again did not qualify, for how could he confide, how could he say what he was feeling, and who on God's earth would understand?

'Why would you not want to speak with her?'

'Because it was just...' He couldn't even say it, could not relegate it to a one-night stand, so instead he sat in silence and the discomfort became unbearable. There was no relief to be had when Nico changed the subject.

'I spoke with our mother...'

'Good for you,' Zander said, and now he wanted out, he wanted to be gone.

'She had her reasons...'

'She's had many years to get her story straight.' Zander's heart was black and he knew it, far, far too black for the light that was Charlotte. A lifetime of hate must have burnt a hole in his soul and he would not taint her. 'I wish you well.' He went to shake his brother's hand and changed his mind. He could hardly stand to look at him, could hardly stand the sight of him, for it felt as if he were looking at himself—a better self, Zander realised, for again it was his brother who had everything, everything he wanted.

He could hear Constantine in the kitchen, could feel the love that filled the home, everything that must be denied him.

'Do you not want to see your nephew?' Nico asked.

He did not want to see him, did not want to fuss and admire a baby, did not want to see more of what he could never have, but Nico would have none of it. Nico walked along a hallway, clearly expecting Zander to follow him.

He would glance in and then leave, Zander decided.

Perhaps admire the babe and then ask once more after Charlotte, for he so badly needed to know that she was okay.

It was for her that he walked the corridor, for her he walked to the crib but for himself he stood there.

And he must have a soul, for right there beneath his heart it wanted to howl. Right there beneath his heart it seemed to shatter and destabilize the knees beneath it. He stared at the babe, his little nose pushed up by fingers, his eyes opening to find out what the noise was. And the baby did not know the man he was gazing at was not his father. All he saw were familiar black eyes and he smiled as if it was a face that comforted, smiled as if it was he, Zander, who soothed him. Then he closed his eyes and went back to sleep.

Nico knew how his brother felt, for his first real look at his son had been by this very crib. The first time he had looked into his son's eyes he had felt as if he was looking into his own, and he now knew he had been looking into his brother's. He knew Zander was remembering a time that could not logically be remembered, when life had been simple, a time when the sight of the other, a look at yourself, had been all it had taken to feel safe.

When you hurt Nico, you hurt me.

Zander could hear her voice in the room with him again, and more than anything he wished it was true, that at this difficult, agonising moment she was here, for he wanted to turn around and see her.

'This is the age we were parted,' Nico said, and to Zander his voice came from a distance. 'This was the age he made her leave and kept only you—the firstborn.'

'She left and chose you,' Zander corrected. 'The good one, the nice one…'

'No.'

He could not face the truth, could not hear it from his brother, could not believe it, for it changed every piece of the past. He raced from the house with questions unanswered, walked the beach and the streets like a drunk in a rage, for he could not stand to hear it, could not face the music, could not be alone as his pompous, lucky, chosen brother sat in a house that was a home.

So he took the plane to Rhodes, blasted the casino and hated himself more for winning. He drank hundred-year-old brandy and it barely touched sides. He wanted it to be easy, wanted to want, as he had before, the women who flocked to him, but knew tonight, for their sakes, that he was safer to be alone. So he paced the floors of the Imperial Suite, and nothing, not money, not brandy, could sate him; nothing in these luxurious confines could tame or sedate him. He waited for sunrise, for the clarity of a morning that was still a couple of hours away—but the sun did not rise, he remembered, it was we who moved towards it. He thought of that first morning phone call, the difference in time that had brought her to him, thought of her in London deeper in the darkness now than he.

She messed with his head, Zander decided. Charlotte messed with his head and changed things and he paced harder. He wanted to get on the plane and chase endless darkness, not run to the morning and the painful light it would bring. But he was weary from running, exhausted from it, knew he had to face the fact that there was nothing now that he would not do to be with her.

And he paced, for he did not know how to find her, did not know how to move forward without going back, yet he could not stand to go back without her.

Nico paced with him not beside him, but in Xanos, for he had worn the same path recently, knew the pit of despair that his brother was now in. He paced his house and garden through the night. He felt his brother's rage, the hurt and anger, but Nico believed in the pendulum, knew that Zander would calm down. He believed in it so fiercely, was so connected with his brother that night, that he knew the moment Zander made his decision.

'Nico.' He looked up at his wife, saw the concern in her face as she came out to the dark garden—the sound of the fountains audible now, the world coming back into focus as he stepped back from his brother's pain and looked into her eyes. How lucky he had been to have her there when the truth had surfaced, how much cooler she had made the hell he'd plunged into.

'I want to help him,' Nico said, as if it was that simple, as if the man who hated him would want his help. But even if she did not approve of his brother, Constantine was always there for him, with a word, with a smile that soothed.

'Then do.'

CHAPTER SIXTEEN

SHE missed him far more than she should.

Far more than one should miss a man who had caused so much pain, Charlotte reminded herself as she woke to the morning and another day without Zander.

The heating came on, the pipes filling, spreading warmth through the house, and she wished it would do the same for her heart, for Zander's heart too. She lay for a moment with her head in the clouds, imagined that he was near, that things were different, and though she loved visiting dreams, she knew she couldn't linger. She put a toe out to the carpet and then pulled it back in, but she had to get up. There was a nurse coming at nine and she wanted the house a little more ordered before she arrived.

Charlotte hauled herself out of bed. The bedroom was freezing as she walked across it but as she caught sight of herself in the mirror, the reflection was not unfamiliar. She did not see a woman living a life she was not happy with. Instead, she saw herself staring back. She was dressed in faded lemon pyjamas, her hair was in need of a wash, but she was wearing a hundred-thousand-dollar necklace, and she could look into the mirror and smile. The hardest weeks of her life lay ahead, yet somehow she knew she could handle it and was at peace with the choices she had made.

She *was* bound to her mother, Roula had taught her that. Sitting talking to Roula, listening as she'd relived the mistake made long ago, hearing her pain, Charlotte had realised that she was bound to her mother for ever— only not out of duty, but love.

Still, the ringing of the doorbell made her grumble, sure that the nursing agency had messed up the times again. She pulled the door open and then promptly closed it, not in anger, just in shock, for there should surely be a warning alert on a cold winter morning when the man of your dreams comes knocking at your door.

'Charlotte!' He opened the letterbox, which was in line with her crotch, and she jumped to the side.

'Can we talk?'

'Now?'

'Right now.' She heard the need, the plea, felt the urgency, and she opened the door to a man only her heart recognised. She saw the unkempt suit, a jaw that needed a razor and eyes that were bloodshot, and she could smell brandy, but his soul shone bright and she could never not let him in.

'It was not a job I was going to offer you...'

'I know.'

'And I was not going to ask you to be my mistress that night.'

'I know that too.'

'And would you still have said no?'

'No,' Charlotte admitted, for had she made it to dinner, had he offered her his world and an exclusive part in his life, hell, she'd have said yes in a heartbeat, but she was stronger than that now. 'Though I'm sure I'd have lived to regret saying yes.' It was such a hard thing to say. 'I want the Zander I thought I knew, the one I first met. The one who could not wait to meet with his brother...'

'I spoke to Nico. I went to see him yesterday.' Charlotte opened her mouth to speak, knew just how big this was, but she forced herself to say nothing, to let him tell her in his own time. 'He gave me your address, early this morning he texted it to me. I understand if you have little to say to me but I have to know, did I cost you your job?'

'No.' Immediately she shook her head. 'No...I...' She did not want to say it here, did not want to discuss such things in the hall. 'Come through.'

She saw him blink in surprise as she led him not to the lounge but to her bedroom, for it was the only place in the house that was truly hers. She sat on the bed and he perched on the jumble of clothes that hid her chair and she said the hardest words.

'I was going to put Mum in a home. I just couldn't keep looking after her and I had to work and it would have been the right decision at the time. But when I got back I had some bad news about her health—Mum's only got a few months left to live.' She took a big breath because it was so hard to say it, but she forced herself, said it quickly, lightly, even though it masked so much hurt. 'So I've bunged a bit of money on the mortgage and I'm taking a year off from my job.'

'You could have sold the necklace.' He smiled to see it around her neck, smiled that it was not locked up in a box but that she wore it with pyjamas. 'I was trying to take care of you with that.'

'I'd never sell it,' Charlotte said. 'No matter what it's worth, it's worth more than money to me.'

He looked at her face, at the dull eyes and the unwashed hair, and all he could see was Charlotte.

'You could have rung,' she said. 'You should have given me some warning.'

'I wanted to see you.'

'Well, now you have,' Charlotte said. 'And I'm fine. I still have a job when I'm ready to go back. You can leave with your conscience clear.'

But he did not.

'You must be exhausted,' Zander said, as even with a racing heart she stifled a yawn.

'A bit,' she admitted. 'But I just want to finish what I started. I couldn't go on looking after Mum indefinitely, I can see that now, but…' He said nothing, he just looked. 'It isn't indefinite any more and I want to focus on the time we have. I've got a nurse that comes in and we're going on holiday next week.' Charlotte rolled her eyes. 'Don't ask me how we'll manage but I've booked a cottage by the beach and, freezing or not, we're going to walk on the beach and feed the seagulls. Nico's actually been wonderful…' And she watched because this time his face did not darken, neither did he flinch at the mention of his brother, he just looked at her with eyes that were open to her questions now. 'You went to see him?'

'I went to see him to find out about you. When I spoke with his new PA I could not stand it that you had left, that Nico might have fired you...'

'I can go back any time,' Charlotte said, though she doubted she actually could, for it would kill her to see Nico and not Zander; it would be agony to be close to someone just a step away from the man she truly wanted. 'You went to see him just for that?'

He paused and then shook his head. 'No, I also went to find out about me, about him, about our mother.'

'And did you?'

'No.' He had run from the truth, for very deep reasons, but he could not keep running any longer. The truth was waiting and he had somehow to move forward and greet it, and the only way he could do that was with her. 'I would rather hear the truth from you,' Zander said. 'With you.'

'She loved you,' Charlotte said simply. 'She still does.' She watched as he pressed his fingers into his eyes, didn't understand the shake of his head and his unwillingness to believe it, and she told him his story as had been relayed to her through his mother and the nun, but still he denied it, still he refused to believe. 'She didn't choose Nico. Zander, your father gave her no choice in anything. He completely controlled her. She did everything she could to go back for you.'

'No.' Still he was adamant; still he argued that black was white and Charlotte just did not understand. Why would he refuse the antidote to his pain.?

'Why won't you believe her, Zander? Why do you…?' She closed her eyes in frustration, for still he would not be swayed, still he would not take the love that was all around him if only he reached out to it. 'She's sitting in a nursing home, clutching two plastic dolls, desperate to see her sons. It's cruel that you…' She halted herself for she did not want it to be so, did not want Constantine's words to be true, did not want the father-son rule to apply. 'Why can't you just accept…?'

'Because that's not what I *know*.' He did not shout it, but he might as well have. She felt the hairs rise on her neck, felt her body jolt as if he had roared, and Charlotte heard it so loud and so clear that it hurt. 'He fell apart when she left. The drinking and the misery and the hell was all of her making. She did that to him.' She watched as he stopped, as everything he knew dispersed. 'That is what I need to believe, needed to believe to survive. The man I loved…' He halted, for it hurt to admit it, hurt to be five years old and hear the roar of his father's voice, hurt to recall the confusion.

'You loved him?'

'Of course—he was my father,' Zander said, because to a child it was that simple. 'And then later I felt sorry for him, thought I made things worse for him by being there, and then all I did was hate him, for not being strong enough to move on from what she had done.' He looked at Charlotte. 'He told me he was a good man, an honourable man, a hard-working man till she left him. And I believed him, till this very moment I believed him—I had to. All he told me was a lie, and I should have seen it. As if he was ever going to sit down and tell me the truth…'

'She loved you,' Charlotte said. 'She always has.'

'What does that make him, then?' Zander asked. She had thought him blind, thought he had simply chosen pain, but she saw him very differently now. She saw how hard he had tried to remain loyal to the memory of the father that had raised him—a father, that despite it all, he had loved.

'Maybe he was hurting too?' Charlotte offered, but some things were very hard to forgive. 'Perhaps you need to find out more about him.'

And one day he would, Zander decided. One day he would, and he would try to do it without hate in his heart.

'I understand now what you said…' He saw her frown. 'That when I hurt him I hurt you.' Still her frown deepened. 'That Nico is a part of me and when I hurt him, I hurt myself…which hurts you.'

'Actually…' Oh, God, should she tell him she'd just got her words mixed up, that it wasn't some wise saying, just her mouth moving too fast?

'What I meant…' But she stopped talking and smiled instead, saw his exhaustion and wanted to extinguish it. She did not say another word but climbed into bed and closed her eyes.

And he made dreams real, because he undressed and climbed into her single bed, and held her for a moment.

'I have spent my life hating.' He said it to her neck. 'I cannot imagine the outcome had you not come into my life. The day that mattered the most to me, the day I had focused on for so very long, suddenly became less important than the day that came before it, the day I spent with you.'

He kissed her neck and then he said it.

'I love you, Charlotte.'

But she closed her eyes, because it was still impossible. 'This is me,' Charlotte said. 'I can't leave Mum.'

'You don't have to.'

'You say that now…' She was scared to look to the future, scared of the shouts when any moment now her mother awoke, scared of him making a promise that reality would not let him keep. 'When you see how hard it is…'

'Why would I change you?' Zander asked. 'I have never had a proper family. I am told most come with good and bad?'

'They do.'

'I will never hurt the good,' Zander said, 'and I will do my best to ease the bad.'

She could hear the rain against the window and the bus pulling up at the stop outside. His voice was in her ear, as it had been so many times, but this time there was the breath on her ear that meant he was close by.

He had said she must never make love with him till

she trusted him again, and now she handed her heart over willingly, knew it would be safe with him.

He made love for the first time in the morning; that morning they actually made *love*, and it was, as Charlotte told him afterwards as she lay in her bed with him, perfect.

'It would be perfect had I brought a ring,' Zander said. 'However, I was not exactly thinking straight on my way to you.'

'You don't give out rings, remember.' She did not need a ring to know his love.

'Not easily,' Zander said. 'But it is what I want for you. Mrs Kargas.' His name did not hurt now when he said it. With Charlotte bearing it, he could say it proudly.

For their future was together.

EPILOGUE

HE MADE every day a memory.

And not just for Charlotte.

She sat on the beach beside her mother, as she did most late afternoons, stared out at the glorious Mediterranean, and when her mother was starting to get tired, Charlotte would open up the package she had brought, toss out some food and wait for the seagulls. It never failed to make her mother smile, to laugh as she once had, and though Charlotte could not be sure if her mother was going back to earlier times or just smiling at today, every day it was more than worth it.

'Is she ready to go back to the house?' Agira asked, walking over and smiling, a genuine smile that was warm and caring, and Charlotte knew she was blessed to have Agira to nurse her mother.

So very blessed.

Zander had made good his word—he had made the good better and eased the bad. All her mother's furniture had been moved to Xanos, but the night-time wanderings had stopped and the aggression too. Their daily times on the beach, the salty air and the wonderful food seemed to calm and relax Amanda, or was it the change in her daughter that eased Amanda's mind? For with help and support Charlotte could finally enjoy her mother and help her enjoy the time she had left.

And she wanted more.

As she kissed her mother goodbye and Agira walked her back to the house, Charlotte caught sight of the seaplane coming in to land, and felt the wind whip away selfish tears, for surely when she had so much, when everything she had wished for had come true, it was wrong now to ask for just a little more time.

She watched as the plane landed at the jetty that both brothers now owned. The partnership that had once seemed impossible was a reality now. Old met new in Xanos, the taverna was bustling again with locals, the hotel and restaurants were vibrant, and Ravels was the shining jewel in the island's crown. Charlotte watched as a suited, dark-haired man stepped out, and though he looked like her husband, walked like her husband, to anyone else might well have been her husband, her heart didn't leap, and she knew that it was Nico.

Constantine recognised him too. Charlotte turned as she saw the woman come down to the beach, baby Leo on her hip. She waved to her husband and walked over to join Charlotte, whose heart did tighten now as another suited dark man stepped out, and it was just, just... What was the difference? So many times she tried to pin it down, sure their hair fell differently, one left-handed, the other right-, but from this distance it was impossible to make that out. It was just that her heart told her it was him.

It had told Roula too. For as long as she lived, Charlotte would never forget the smile of disbelief on the older woman's face when she had first seen her grown sons. She had named them immediately—correctly—had taken Zander's tense face in her hands and kissed him, told him how much she had missed him, grief mingling with joy as she held again the son she had been forced to leave behind. Her heart had held more than a three-decade vigil, her love at the centre, and there was no mistaking her heart shone for them. Had Zander had any doubts, Charlotte had watched them fade as he moved towards his mother.

'How do you think it went?' Constantine asked, clearly trying to gauge it, because though both men lived on the island, were in business together, it was still early days. They were two strong personalities and the relationship was still new and, at times, overwhelming, for bruises took time to fade completely.

'Well, they're still talking.' Charlotte smiled, because they were. Nico and Zander walked along the jetty. Zander was nodding at something his brother must have said, and then he looked up and saw her and smiled a smile that crossed the beach like a sunbeam. It warmed her on a cool spring day.

The trips to visit Roula were becoming more regular. Take things slowly, the doctors had warned them for Roula was still very fragile, but the brothers' short visits to Roula were growing longer, and last week, for the first time, the sons had brought their mother for a visit home. It had been hugely emotional watching the fragile woman tremble as she stepped into Nico's home, the home that had once been her father's, watching her stare at the picture on the wall of the babies she had lost.

Only now and then did Charlotte and Constantine join the visits to their mother, but one day, Charlotte was sure, they would bring her home.

'How was she?' Charlotte asked.

'Good,' Zander said. 'Better again. She asked after you.'

'Would you like to come for supper?' Constantine offered, for she was Greek and wanted family at her table. Normally Charlotte left it to Zander to accept or decline, but this time it was Charlotte who answered.

'We'd have loved to, but actually we've got plans to-night.'

They said goodbye. Zander gave little Leo a kiss and then took his wife's hand and walked along the beach toward the development and towards their home.

'What plans do you have for me?' he nudged.

'Oh, I'll think of something.' Charlotte smiled, but her heart wasn't in it and he must have heard the forced lightness to her voice and put his arm around her. 'How was the doctor?' Zander asked. 'How is your mother doing?'

'Good,' Charlotte said. 'He says she is doing well, better than expected.' She stopped walking then. 'I want more time for her...'

'Who knows?' Zander said. 'They did say a couple of months but already she has surpassed that.'

'I want more…'

And Zander heard the plea in her voice that was so rarely there. She asked for nothing and was delighted with everything. For Charlotte to beg, and for something that he could not give, had him turn and pull her into his arms, fighting for words.

'Let's just make each day count,' he settled for. 'Which you already do.'

'I want more!' If she was precise with her wish, maybe it would be answered. 'I want seven months more.' She watched him frown, watched *it* dawn, watched him realise the truth. 'I spoke to the doctor about me as well. We went back to the clinic, he did a test,' Charlotte said. 'A scan.'

'We're having a baby?' He looked at his wife, and he looked into his soul, and he wanted this so badly. He wanted everything that his brother had, not for selfish reasons now, but he had never expected that he would get more.

'We're having twins.'

He put his hand to her stomach, could not believe that it was two hearts that beat in her womb. He knew that things would be different for their babies and he felt the need to share, to spread the good news, to bring things full circle.

'Can we tell him?'

And she nodded with delight, for she did want to be with his family. She had just wanted to tell Zander alone first and would not have been able to hold onto the news for a moment longer.

They walked back along the beach hand in hand, back to the house that had once been Roula's childhood home.

Back to share wonderful news with family.

* * * * *

Beholden to
the Throne
CAROL MARINELLI

CHAPTER ONE

'SHEIKH King Emir has agreed that he will speak with you.'

Amy looked up as Fatima, one of the servants, entered the nursery where Amy was feeding the young Princesses their dinner. 'Thank you for letting me know. What time—?'

'He is ready for you now,' Fatima interrupted, impatience evident in her voice at Amy's lack of haste, for Amy continued to feed the twins.

'They're just having their dinner…' Amy started, but didn't bother to continue—after all, what would the King know about his daughters' routines? Emir barely saw the twins and, quite simply, it was breaking Amy's heart.

What would he know about how clingy they had become lately and how fussy they were with their food? It was one of the reasons Amy had requested a meeting with him—tomorrow they were to be handed over to the Bedouins. First they would be immersed in the desert oasis and then they would be handed over to strangers for the night. It was a tradition that dated back centuries,

Fatima had told her, and it was a tradition that could not be challenged.

Well, Amy would see about that!

The little girls had lost their mother when they were just two weeks old, and since his wife's death Emir had hardly seen them. It was Amy they relied on. Amy who was with them day in and day out. Amy they trusted. She would not simply hand them over to strangers without a fight on their behalf.

'I will look after the twins and give them dinner,' Fatima said. 'You need to make yourself presentable for your audience with the King.' She ran disapproving eyes over Amy's pale blue robe, which was the uniform of the Royal Nanny. It had been fresh on that morning, but now it wore the telltale signs that she had been finger-painting with Clemira and Nakia this afternoon. Surely Emir should not care about the neatness of her robe? He should expect that if the nanny was doing her job properly she would be less than immaculate in appearance. But, again, what would Emir know about the goings-on in the nursery? He hadn't been in to visit his daughters for weeks.

Amy changed into a fresh robe and retied her shoulder-length blonde hair into a neat ponytail. Then she covered her hair with a length of darker blue silk, arranging the cloth around her neck and leaving the end to trail over her shoulder. She wore no make-up but, as routinely as most women might check their lipstick, Amy checked to see that the scar low on her neck was covered by the silk. She hated how, in any conversation, eyes were often drawn to it, and more than that she hated the inevitable questions that followed.

The accident and its aftermath were something she would far rather forget than discuss.

'They are too fussy with their food,' Fatima said as Amy walked back into the nursery.

Amy suppressed a smile as Clemira pulled a face and then grabbed at the spoon Fatima was offering and threw it to the floor.

'They just need to be cajoled,' Amy explained. 'They haven't eaten this before.'

'They need to know how to behave!' Fatima said. 'There will be eyes on them when they are out in public, and tomorrow they leave to go to the desert—there they must eat only fruit, and the desert people will not be impressed by two spoiled princesses spitting out their food.' She looked Amy up and down. 'Remember to bow your head when you enter, and to keep it bowed until the King speaks. And you are to thank him for any suggestions that he makes.'

Thank him!

Amy bit down on a smart retort. It would be wasted on Fatima and, after all, she might do better to save her responses for Emir. As she turned to go, Clemira, only now realising that she was being left with Fatima, called out to Amy.

'Ummi!' her little voice wailed. 'Ummi!'

She called again and Fatima stared in horror as Clemira used the Arabic word for mother.

'Is this what she calls you?'

'She doesn't mean it,' Amy said quickly, but Fatima was standing now, the twins' dinner forgotten, fury evident on her face.

'What have you been teaching her?' Fatima accused.

'I have *not* been teaching her to say it,' Amy said in panic. 'I've been trying to stop her.'

She had been. Over and over she had repeated her name these past few days, but the twins had discovered a new version. Clemira must have picked it up from the stories she had heard Amy tell, and from the small gatherings they attended with other children who naturally called out to their mothers. No matter how often she was corrected, Clemira persisted with her new word.

'It's a similar sound,' Amy explained. But just as she thought she had perhaps rectified the situation, Nakia, as always, copied her sister.

'Ummi,' Nakia joined in with the tearful protest.

'Amy!' Amy corrected, but she could feel the disgust emanating from Fatima.

'If the King ever hears of this there will be trouble!' Fatima warned. 'Serious trouble.'

'I know!' Amy bit back on tears as she left the nursery. She tried to block out the cries that followed her down the long corridor as she made her way deep into the palace.

This meeting with the King was necessary, Amy told herself, as nerves started to catch up with her. Something had to be said.

Still, even if she *had* requested this audience, she was not relishing the prospect. Sheikh King Emir of Alzan was not exactly open to conversation—at least not since the death of Hannah. The walls were lined with paintings of previous rulers, all dark and imposing men, but since the death of Emir's wife, none was more imposing than Emir—and in a moment she must face him.

Must face him, Amy told herself as she saw the guards standing outside his door. As difficult as this conversation might be, there were things that needed to be said and she wanted to say them before she headed into the desert with the King and his daughters—for this was a discussion that must take place well away from tender ears.

Amy halted at the heavy, intricately carved doors and waited until finally the guards nodded and the doors were opened. She saw an office that reminded her of a courtroom. Emir sat at a large desk, dressed in black robes and wearing a *kafeya*. He took centre stage and the aides and elders sat around him. Somehow she must find the courage to state her case.

'Head down!' she was brusquely reminded by a guard.

Amy did as she was told and stepped in. She was not allowed to look at the King yet, but could feel his dark eyes drift over her as a rapid introduction was made in Arabic by his senior aide, Patel. Amy stood with her head bowed, as instructed, until finally Emir spoke.

'You have been requesting to see me for some days now, yet I am told the twins are not unwell.'

His voice was deep and rich with accent. Amy had not heard him speak in English for so very long—his visits to the nursery were always brief, and when there he spoke just a few words in Arabic to his daughters before leaving. Standing there, hearing him speak again, Amy realised with a nervous jolt how much she had missed hearing his voice.

She remembered those precious days after the twins had been born and how approachable he'd been then. Emir had been a harried king, if there was such a thing, and like any new father to twins—especially with a sick wife. He had been grateful for any suggestion she'd made to help with the tiny babies—so much so that Amy had often forgotten that he was King and they had been on first-name terms. It was hard to imagine that he had ever been so approachable now, but she held on to that image as she lifted her head and faced him, determined to reach the father he was rather than the King.

'Clemira and Nakia are fine,' Amy started. 'Well, physically they are fine…' She watched as his haughty face moved to a frown. 'I wanted to speak to you about their progress, and also about the tradition that they—'

'Tomorrow we fly out to the desert,' Emir interrupted. 'We will be there for twenty-four hours. I am sure there will be ample time then to discuss their progress.'

'But I want to speak about this well away from the twins. It might upset them to hear what I have to say.'

'They are turning one,' Emir stated. 'It's hardly as if they can understand what we are discussing.'

'They might be able to…'

Amy felt as if she were choking—could feel the scar beneath the silk around her neck inflame. For she knew how it felt to lie silent, knew how it felt to hear and not be able to respond. She knew exactly what it was like to have your life discussed around you and not be able to partake in the conversation. She simply would not let this happen to the twins. Even if there was only a slight chance that they might understand what was being said, Amy would not take that risk. Anyway, she was here for more than simply to discuss their progress.

'Fatima told me that the twins are to spend the night with the Bedouins…'

He nodded.

'I don't think that is such a good idea,' Amy went on. 'They are very clingy at the moment. They get upset if I even leave the room.'

'Which is the whole point of the separation.' Emir was unmoved. 'All royals must spend time each year with the desert people.'

'But they are so young!'

'It is the way things have long been done. It is a rule in both Alzan and Alzirz and it is not open for discussion.'

It hurt, but she had no choice but to accept that, Amy realised, for this was a land where rules and traditions were strictly followed. All she could do was make the separation as easy as possible on the twins.

'There are other things I need to speak with you about.' Amy glanced around the room—although she was unsure how many of the guards and aides spoke English, she knew that Patel did. 'It might be better if we speak in private?' Amy suggested.

'Private?' Emir questioned. His irritation made it

clear that there was nothing Amy could possibly say that might merit clearing the room. 'There is no need for that. Just say what you came to.'

'But…'

'Just say it!'

He did not shout, but there was anger and impatience in his voice, and Emir's eyes held a challenge. Quite simply, Amy did not recognise him—or rather she did not recognise him as the man she had known a year ago. Oh, he had been a fierce king then, and a stern ruler, but he had also been a man sensitive to his sick wife's needs, a man who had put duty and protocol aside to look after his ailing wife and their new babies. But today there was no mistaking it. Amy was speaking not with the husband and father she had first met, but to the King of Alzan.

'The children so rarely see you,' Amy attempted, in front of this most critical audience. 'They *miss* seeing you.'

'They have told you this, have they?' His beautiful mouth was sullied as it moved to a smirk. 'I was not aware that they had such an advanced vocabulary.'

A small murmur of laughter came from Patel before he stepped forward. 'The King does not need to hear this,' Patel said. Aware that this was her only chance to speak with him before they set off tomorrow, Amy pushed on.

'Perhaps not, but the children do need their father. They need—'

'There is nothing to discuss.' It was Emir who terminated the conversation. Barely a minute into their meeting he ended it with a flick of his hand and Amy was dismissed. The guards opened the door and Patel indicated that she should leave. But instead of following the silent order to bow her head meekly and depart, Amy stood her ground.

'On the contrary—there's an awful lot that we need to discuss!'

She heard the shocked gasp from the aides, felt the rise in tension from everyone present in the room, for no one in this land would dare argue with the King— and certainly not a mere nanny.

'I apologise, Your Highness.' Patel came over to where Amy stood and addressed the King in a reverential voice. That voice was only for the King—when he spoke to Amy Patel was stern, suggesting in no uncertain terms that she leave the room this very moment.

'I need to be heard!'

'The King has finished speaking with you,' Patel warned her.

'Well, I haven't finished speaking with *him*!' Amy's voice rose, and as it did so, it wavered—but only slightly. Her blue eyes blinked, perhaps a little rapidly, but she met the King's black stare as she dared to confront him. Yes, she was nervous—terrified, in fact—but she had come this far and she simply could not stay quiet for a moment longer.

'Your Highness, I really do need to speak with you about your daughters before we go to the desert. As you know, I have been requesting an audience with you for days now. On my contract it states that I will meet regularly with the parents of the twins to discuss any concerns.'

It appalled her that she even had to request an appointment with him for such a thing, and that when he finally deigned to see her he could so rapidly dismiss her. He didn't even have the courtesy to hear her out, to find out what she had to say about his children. Amy was incensed.

'When I accepted the role of Royal Nanny it was on the understanding that I was to *assist* in the raising of the twins and that when they turned four...' Her voice trailed off as once again Emir ignored her. He had turned to Patel and was speaking in Arabic. Amy stood quietly fuming as a file—presumably *her* file—was placed in front of Emir and he took a moment to read through it.

'You signed a four-year contract,' Emir stated. 'You will be here till the twins leave for London to pursue their education and then we will readdress the terms, that is what was agreed.'

'So am I expected to wait another three years before we discuss the children?' Amy forgot then that he was a king—forgot her surrounds entirely. She was so angry with him that she was at her caustic best. 'I'm expected to wait another three years before we address any issues? If you want to talk about the contract, then fine—we will! The fact is the contract we both signed isn't being adhered to from your end!' Amy flared. 'You can't just pick and choose which clauses you keep to.'

'Enough!'

It was Patel who responded. He would not let his

King be bothered with such trivialities. He summoned the guard to drag her out if required, but as the guard unceremoniously took her arm to escort her out, Amy stood firm. The veil covering her hair slithered from its position as she tried to shake the guard off.

It was Emir who halted this rather undignified exit. He did not need a guard to deal with this woman and he put up his hand to stop him, said something that was presumably an instruction to release her, because suddenly the guard let go his grip on her arm.

'Go on,' Emir challenged, his eyes narrowing as he stared over to the woman who had just dared to confront him—the woman who had dared suggest that he, Sheikh King Emir of Alzan, had broken an agreement that bore his signature. 'Tell me where I have broken my word.'

She stood before him, a little more shaken, a touch more breathless, but grateful for another chance to be heard. 'The twins need a parent...' He did not even blink. 'As I said, my role is to assist in the raising of the twins both here in the palace and on regular trips to London.' Perhaps, Amy decided, it would be safer to start with less emotive practicalities. 'I haven't been home in over a year.'

'Go on,' he replied.

Amy took a deep breath, wondering how best to broach this sensitively, for he really was listening now. 'The girls need more than I can give them—they...' She struggled to continue for a moment. The twins needed love, and she had plenty of that for them, but it was a parent that those two precious girls needed most. Somehow she had to tell him that—had to remind him what Hannah had wanted for her daughters. 'Until they turn four I'm supposed to *assist* in their raising. It was agreed that I have two evenings and two nights off a week, but instead—'

He interrupted her again and spoke in rapid Arabic to Patel. There was a brief conversation between the aides before he turned back to her. 'Very well. Fatima will help you with the care of the children. You will have your days off from now on, and my staff will look into your annual leave arrangements.'

She couldn't believe it—could not believe how he had turned things around. He had made it seem as if all she was here for was to discuss her holiday entitlements.

'That will be all.'

'No!' This time she did shout, but her voice did not waver—on behalf of the twins, Amy was determined to be heard. 'That isn't the point I was trying to make. I am to *assist*—my job is to *assist* the parents in the raising of the children, not to bring them up alone. I would never have accepted the role otherwise.' She wouldn't have. Amy knew that. She had thought she was entering a loving family—not one where children, or rather female children, were ignored. 'When Queen Hannah interviewed me...'

Emir's face paled—his dark skin literally paled in the blink of an eye—and there was a flash of pain across his haughty features at the mention of his late wife. It was as if her words were ice that he was biting down on and he flinched. But almost instantaneously the pain dispersed, anger replacing it.

He stood. He did not need to, for already she was silent, already she had realised the error of her ways. From behind his desk Emir rose to his impressive height and the whole room was still and silent. No one more so than Amy, for Emir was an imposing man and not just in title. He stood well over six foot and was broad shouldered, toned. There was the essence of a warrior to him—a man of the desert who would never be tamed. But Emir was more than a warrior, he was a ruler too—a fierce ruler—and she had dared to talk back at him, had dared to touch on a subject that was most definitely, most painfully, closed.

'Leave!'

He roared the single word and this time Amy chose to obey his command, for his black eyes glittered with fury and the scar that ran through his left eyebrow was prominent, making his features more savage. Amy knew beyond doubt that she had crossed a line. There were so many lines that you did not cross here in Alzan, so many things that could not be said while working at the palace, but to speak of the late Queen Hannah, to talk of happier times, to bring up the past with King Emir wasn't simply speaking out of turn, or merely crossing a line—it was a leap that only the foolish would take. Knowing she was beaten, Amy turned to go.

'Not you!' His voice halted her exit. 'The rest of you are to leave.'

Amy turned around slowly, met the eyes of an angry

sheikh king. She had upset him, and now she must face him alone.

'The nanny is to stay.'

CHAPTER TWO

THE *nanny*.

As Amy stood there awaiting her fate those words re-played and burnt in her ears—she was quite sure that he had forgotten her name. She was raising his children and he knew nothing about her. Not that she would address it, for she would be lucky to keep her job now. Amy's heart fluttered in wild panic because she could not bear to leave the twins, could not stand to be sent home with-out the chance to even say goodbye.

It was that thought that propelled her apology.

'Please...' she started. 'I apologise.' But he ignored her as the room slowly cleared.

'Patel, that means you too,' Emir said when his senior aide still hovered, despite the others having left.

When Patel reluctantly followed the rest and closed the door, for the first time in almost a year Amy was alone with him—only this time she was terrified.

'You were saying?' he challenged.

'I should not have.'

'It's a bit late for reticence,' Emir said. 'You now have

the privacy that you asked for. You have your chance to speak. So why have you suddenly lost your voice?'

'I haven't.'

'Then speak.'

Amy could not look at him. Gone now was her boldness. She drew in a deep breath and, staring down, saw that her hands were pleated together. Very deliberately she separated them and placed her arms at her sides, forced her chin up to meet his stare. He was right—she had the audience she had requested. A very private, very intimidating audience, but at least now she had a chance to speak with the King. On behalf of Clemira and Nakia she would force herself to do so while she still had the chance. Amy was well aware that he would probably fire her, but she hoped that if he listened even to a little of what she had to say things might change.

They had to.

Which was why she forced herself to speak.

'When I was hired it was on the understanding that I was to assist in the raising of the children.' Her voice was calmer now, even if her heart was not. 'Queen Hannah was very specific in her wishes for the girls and we had similar values…' She faltered then, for she should not compare herself to the late Queen. 'Rather, I admired Queen Hannah's values—I understood what she wanted for her girls, and we spoke at length about their future. It was the reason why I signed such a long contract.'

'Go on,' Emir invited.

'When I took the job I understood that her pregnancy had made the Queen unwell—that it might take some considerable time for her to recover and that she might not be able to do all she wanted to for the babies. However—'

'I am sure Queen Hannah would have preferred that you were just *assisting* her in the raising of the twins,' Emir interrupted. 'I am sure that when she hired you, Queen Hannah had no intention of dying.' His lip curled in disdain as he looked down at Amy and his words dripped sarcasm. 'I apologise for the inconvenience.'

'No!' Amy refused to let him turn things around again—refused to let him miss her point. 'If Queen Hannah were still alive I would happily get up to the twins ten times in the night if I had to. She was a wonderful woman, an amazing mother, and I would have done anything for her...' Amy meant every word she said. She had admired the Queen so much, had adored her for her forward thinking and for the choices she had made to ensure the happiness of her girls. 'I would have done anything for Queen Hannah, but I—'

'You will have assistance,' Emir said. 'I will see that Fatima—'

She could not believe that he still didn't get it. Bold again now, she interrupted the King. 'It's not another nanny that the twins need. It's *you*! I am tired of getting up at night while their father sleeps.'

'Their father is the King.' His voice was both angry and incredulous. 'Their father is busy running the country. I am trying to push through a modern maternity hospital with a cardiac ward to ensure no other woman suffers as my wife did. Today I have twenty workers trapped in the emerald mines. But instead of reaching out to my people I have to hear about *your* woes. The people I rule are nervous as to the future of their country and yet you expect me, the King, to get up at night to a crying child?'

'You used to!' Amy was instant in her response. 'You used to get up to your babies.'

And there it was again—that flash of pain across his features. Only this time it did not dissipate. This time it remained. His eyes were screwed closed, he pressed his thumb and finger to the bridge of his nose and she could hear his hard breathing. Amy realised that somewhere inside was the Emir she had known and she was desperate to contact him again, to see the loving father he had once been returned to his daughters—it was for that reason she continued.

'I would bring Queen Hannah one of the twins for feeding while you would take care of the other.'

He removed his hand from his face, and stood there as she spoke, his fists clenched, his face so rigid and taut that she could see a muscle flickering beneath his eye. And she knew that it was pain not rage that she was witnessing, Amy was quite sure of it, for as sad as those times had been still they had been precious.

'And, no, I don't honestly expect you to get up at night to your babies, but is it too much for you to come in and see them each day? Is it too much to ask that you take a more active role in their lives? They are starting to talk…'

He shook his head—a warning, perhaps, that she

should not continue—but she had to let him know all that he was missing out on, even if it cost her her job.

'Clemira is standing now. She pulls herself up on the furniture and Nakia tries to copy—she claps and smiles and...'

'Stop.' His word was a raw husk.

'No!' She would not stop. Could not stop.

Amy was too upset to register properly the plea in his voice, for she was crying now. The scarf that had slipped from her head as she made her case unravelled and fell to the floor. She wanted to grab it, retrieve it, for she felt his eyes move to her neck, to the beastly scar that was there—her permanent reminder of hell—but her hands did not fly to her neck in an attempt to cover it. She had more important things on her mind—two little girls whose births she had witnessed, two little girls who had won her heart—and her voice broke as she choked out the truth.

'You need to know that things are happening with your children. It is their first birthday in two days' time and they'll be terrified in the desert—terrified to be parted from me. And then, when they return to the Palace, they'll be dressed up and trotted out for the people to admire. You will hold them, and they will be so happy that you do, but then you will go back to ignoring them...' She was going to be fired, Amy knew it, so she carried on speaking while she still could. 'I cannot stand to see how they are being treated.'

'They are treated like the princesses they are!' Emir flared. 'They have everything—'

'They have *nothing*!' Amy shouted. 'They have the best clothes and cots and furniture and jewels, and it means nothing because they don't have *you*. Just because they're gi—' Amy stopped herself from saying it, halted her words, but it was already too late.

'Go on.' His words invited her but his tone and stance did not.

'I think that I have already said enough.' There was no point saying any more, Amy realised. Emir was not going to change at her bidding. The country was not going to embrace the girls just because she did. So she picked up her scarf and replaced it. 'Thank you for your time, Your Highness.'

She turned to go and as she did his voice halted her. 'Amy…'

So he did remember her name.

She turned to look at him, met his black gaze full on. The pain was still there, witness to the agony this year must have been for him, but even as she recognised it, it vanished. His features were hardening in anger now, and the voice he had used to call her changed in that instant.

His words were stern when they came. 'It is not your place to question our ways.'

'What *is* my place?'

'An employee.'

Oh, he'd made things brutally clear, but at least it sounded as if she still had a job—at least she would not be sent away from the twins. 'I'll remember that in future.'

'You would be very wise to,' Emir said, watching as

she bowed and then walked out, leaving him standing for once alone in his sumptuous office. But not for long. Patel walked in almost the second that Amy had gone, ready to resume, for there was still much to be taken care of even at this late stage in the day.

'I apologise, Your Highness,' Patel said as he entered. 'I should never have allowed her to speak with you directly—you should not have been troubled with such trivial things.'

But Emir put up his hand to halt him. Patel's words only exacerbated his hell. 'Leave me.'

Unlike Amy, Patel knew better than to argue with the King and did as he was told. Once alone again Emir dragged in air and walked over to the window, looking out to the desert where tomorrow he would take the twins.

He was dreading it.

For reasons he could not even hint at to another, he dreaded tomorrow and the time he would spend with his children. He dreaded not just handing them over to the desert people for the night, but the time before that— seeing them standing, clapping, laughing, trying to talk, as Amy had described.

Their confrontation had more than unsettled him. Not because she had dared to speak in such a way, more because she had stated the truth.

The truth that Emir was well aware of.

Amy was right. He *had* got up at night to them when they were born. They *had* pulled together. Although it had never been voiced, both had seemed to know that

they were battling against time and had raced to give
Hannah as many precious moments with her babies as
they could squeeze in.

He looked to his desk, to the picture of his wife and
their daughters. He seemed to be smiling in the photo
but his eyes were not, for he had known just how sick
his wife was. Had known the toll the twins' pregnancy
had taken on her heart. Six months into the pregnancy
they had found out she had a weakness. Three months
later she was dead.

And while Hannah was smiling in the photo also,
there was a sadness in her eyes too. Had she known
then that she was dying? Emir wondered. Had it been
the knowledge that she would have but a few more days
with her daughters that had brought dark clouds to her
eyes? Or had it been the knowledge that the kingdom of
Alzan needed a male heir if it was to continue? Without
a son Alzan would return to Alzirz and be under Sheikh
King Rakhal's rule.

He hated the words Hannah had said on the birth of
their gorgeous daughters—loathed the fact that she had
apologised to him for delivering two beautiful girls. His
heart thumped in his chest as if he were charging into
battle as silently he stood, gave his mind rare permission to recall Hannah's last words. The blood seared as
it raced through his veins, and his eyes closed as her
voice spoke again to him. 'Promise you will do your
best for our girls.'

How? Emir demanded to a soul that refused to rest.

Any day now Rakhal's wife, Natasha, was due to

give birth. The rules were different in Alzirz, for there a princess could become Queen and rule.

How Rakhal would gloat when his child was born—especially if it was a son.

Emir's face darkened at the thought of his rival. He picked up the two stones that sat on his desk and held them. Though they should be cool to the touch the rare pink sapphires seemed to burn in his palm. Rakhal had been a prince when he had given him this gift to *celebrate* the arrival of the girls—a gift that had been delivered on the morning Hannah had died.

Hannah had thought them to be rubies—had really believed that the troubles between the two kingdoms might finally be fading.

Emir had let her hold that thought, had let her think the gift was a kind gesture from Rakhal, even while fully understanding the vile message behind it—sapphires were meant to be blue.

Without a male heir the kingdom of Alzan would end.

Emir hurled the precious stones across his office, heard the clatter as they hit the wall and wished they would shatter as his brain felt it might.

He hated Rakhal, but more than that Emir hated the decision that he was slowly coming to. For it was not only Hannah who had begged for reassurance on her deathbed—he had held his dying father out in the desert. He had not been able to see the King dying because blood had been pouring from a wound above Emir's eye, but he had heard his father's plea, had given his solemn word that he would do his best for his country.

Two promises he could not meet.

Emir knew he could keep but one.

His decision could not—*must* not—be based on emotion, so he picked up the photo and took one long, last look, tracing his finger over Hannah's face and the image of his girls. And then he placed it face down in a drawer and closed it.

He could not look them.

Must not.

Somehow he had to cast emotion aside as he weighed the future—not just for his children, but for the country he led.

CHAPTER THREE

IT WAS too hot to sleep.

The fan above the bed barely moved the still night air, and the fact that Amy had been crying since she put the twins down for the night did not help. Her face was hot and red, so Amy climbed out of bed, opened the French windows and stepped out onto the balcony, wishing for cool night air to hit her cheeks. But in Alzan the nights were warm and, despite a soft breeze, there was no respite.

The desert was lit by a near full moon and Amy looked out across the pale sands in the direction of Alzirz—there, the nights were cold, she had been told. Amy wished that she were there now—not just for the cool of the night, but for other reasons too. In Alzirz a princess could rule.

There girls were not simply dismissed.

But even that didn't ring true. In many ways Alzan was progressive too—there were universities for women, and on Queen Hannah's death the King had ordered that a state-of-the-art maternity hospital be built in her name—not only with the cardiac ward he had mentioned but free obstetric care for all. Sheikh King Emir had pushed his people slowly forward, yet the royals themselves stayed grounded in the ways of old, bound by rules from the past.

The two lands had long ago been one, she had been told—Alzanirz—but they had been separated many generations ago and were now fierce rivals.

She had met King Rakhal and his wife, Natasha, on a few occasions. Natasha was always disarmingly nice and interested in the girls; Rakhal, on the other hand, despite his cool politeness, was guarded. Amy had felt the hatred simmering between the two men, had almost been able to taste the deep rivalry that existed whenever they were both in a room.

Still, it was not the rival King who troubled her tonight, nor was it the King who employed her.

It was her own soul.

She had to leave. She was too involved. Of course she was. Realising the toll her job was taking on her daughter, Amy's mother was urging her to come home. But as Amy stared out to the sands she was conflicted—she simply could not imagine abandoning the twins.

Ummi.

It hurt to hear that word from Clemira and Nakia and to know she would never be one herself.

Amy gulped in air, determined not to start crying again, but though she was dealing with things better these days—though for the most part she had come to terms with her fate—on nights like tonight sometimes the pain surfaced. Sometimes all she could do was mourn a time when happiness had seemed more certain.

Or had it?

She closed her eyes and tried to remember, tried to peer into the dark black hole that was the months and weeks leading up to her accident. Slowly, painfully slowly, she was starting to remember things—choosing her wedding dress, the invitations—but all she could see were images. She simply couldn't recall how she had felt.

Amy had always worked with children, and had been about to marry and start a family of her own when a riding accident had ruined everything. Her hopes and dreams, her relationship and even her fertility had all been taken in one cruel swoop.

Maybe it was for best, Amy pondered—perhaps it was kinder *not* to remember happier times.

It had been a relief to get away from London, to escape the sympathy and the attention. But Amy's mother had warned her about taking this job—had said it was too much and too soon, that she was running away from her problems. She hadn't been.

The thought of being involved with two babies from birth, of having a very real role in their lives, had been so tempting. Queen Hannah had been well aware of the challenges her daughters would face, and she had told Amy about the disappointment that would sweep the country if her pregnancy produced girls—especially if it proved too dangerous for Hannah to get pregnant again.

Hannah had wanted the girls to be educated in London, to live as ordinary girls there. The plan had been that for four years Amy would take care of the girls in Alzan, but that they would then be schooled in the UK. Amy was to be a huge part of their lives—not a mother, of course, but more than an aunt.

How could she leave now?

How could she walk away because she didn't like the way they were being treated?

Yet how could she stay?

Amy headed down the corridor to do a final check on the twins, her bare feet making no sound. It was a path she trod many times during the day and night, especially now that they were teething. The link from her suite to the twins' sumptuous quarters was a familiar one, but as she entered the room Amy froze—for the sight that greeted her was far from familiar.

There was Emir, his back to her, holding Clemira, who slept on his chest, her head resting on his shoulder, as if it was where she belonged.

Emir stood, silent and strong, and there was a sadness in him that he would surely not want her to witness—a weariness that had only been visible in the first few days after Hannah's death. Then he had gone into *tahir*—had taken himself to the desert for a time of ritual and deep prayer and contemplation. The man who returned to the palace had been different—a remote, aloof man who only occasionally deigned to visit the nursery.

He was far from aloof now as he cradled Clemira. He was wearing black silk lounge pants and nothing else. His top half was bare. Amy had seen him like this before, but then it had not moved her.

In the first dizzy days after the twins had been born they had grappled through the night with two tiny babies. Amy had changed one nappy and handed one fresh, clean baby to Emir, so he could take her to Hannah to feed. Things had been so different then—despite their concern for Hannah there had been love and laughter filling the palace and she missed it so, missed the man she had glimpsed then.

Tonight, for a moment, perhaps that man had returned.

He'd lost weight since then, she noted. His muscles were now a touch more defined. But there was such tenderness as he held his daughter. It was an intimate glimpse of father and daughter and again she doubted he would want it witnessed. She could sense the aching grief in his wide shoulders—so much so that for a bizarre moment Amy wanted to walk up to him, rest her hand there and offer him silent support. Yet she knew he would not want that, and given she was wearing only her nightdress it was better that she quietly slip away.

'Are you considering leaving?

He turned around just as she was about to go. Amy could not look at him. Normally her head was covered, and her body too—she wondered if she would be chastised tomorrow for being unsuitably dressed—but for now Emir did not appear to notice.

She answered his question as best she could. 'I don't know what to do.'

Clemira stirred in his arms. Gently he placed her

back in her crib and stared down at his daughter for the longest time before turning back to Amy.

'You've been crying.'

'There's an awful lot to cry about.' His black eyes did not reproach her this time. 'I never thought I'd be considering leaving, When Hannah interviewed me—I mean Sheikha Queen—'

'Hannah,' he interrupted. 'That is the name she requested you call her.'

Amy was grateful for the acknowledgement, but she could not speak of this in front of the twins—could not have this conversation without breaking down. So she wished him goodnight and headed back to her room.

'Amy!' he called out to her.

She kept on walking, determined to make it to her room before breaking down, stunned when he followed her through the door.

'You cannot leave Alzan now. I think it would be better for the twins—'

'Of *course* it would be better for the twins to have me stay!' she interrupted, although she should not. Her voice rose again, although it should not. But she was furious. 'Of *course* the twins should have somebody looking after them who loves them—except it's not my job to love them. I'm an employee.'

She watched his eyes shutter for a moment as she hurled back his choice word, but he was right—she *was* an employee, and could be fired at any moment, could be removed from the twins' lives by the flick of his hand.

She was thankful for his brutal reminder earlier. She would do well to remember her place.

She brushed past him, trying to get to the safety of the balcony, for it was stifling with him in the room, but before she could get there he halted her.

'You do *not* walk off when I'm talking to you!'

'I do when you're in *my* bedroom!' Amy turned and faced him. 'This happens to be the one place in this prison of a palace where *I* get to make the rules, where I get to speak as I choose, and if you don't like it, if you don't want to hear it, *you* can leave.'

She wanted him out of the room, she wanted him gone, and yet he stepped closer, and it was Amy who stepped back, acutely aware of his maleness, shamefully aware of her own body's conflicted response.

Anger burnt and hissed, but something else did too, for he was an impressive male, supremely beautiful, and of course she had noticed—what woman would not? But down there in his office, or in the safety of the nursery, he was the King and the twins' father, down there he was her boss, but here in this room he was something else.

Somehow she must not show it, so instead she hurled words. 'I *do* love your children, and it's tearing me apart to even think of walking away, but it's been nearly a year since Hannah died and I can't make excuses any more. If they were my children and you ignored them, then I'd have left you by now. The only difference is I'd have taken them with me...' Her face was red with fury, her blue eyes awash with fresh tears, but there was something more—something she could not tell him. It meant

she had to—*had to*—consider leaving, because sometimes when she looked at Emir she wanted the man he
had once been to return, and shamefully, guiltily, despite herself, she wanted *him*.

She tore her eyes from his, terrified as to what he
might see, and yet he stepped towards her, deliberately
stepped towards her. She fought the urge to move towards him—to feel the wrap of his arms around her,
for him to shield her from this hell.

It was a hell of his own making, though, Amy remembered, moving away from him and stepping out onto the
balcony, once again ruing the sultry nights.

But it was not just the night that was oppressive. He
had joined her outside. She gulped in air, wished the
breeze would cool, for it was not just her face that was
burning. She felt as if her body was on fire.

'Soon I will marry…' He saw her shoulders tense,
watched her hands grip the balcony, and as the breeze
caught her nightdress it outlined her shape, detailing soft
curves. In that moment Emir could not speak—was this
the first time he'd noticed her as a woman?

No.

But this was the first time he allowed himself to properly acknowledge it.

He had seen her in the nursery when he had visited the children a few weeks ago. That day he had sat
through a difficult meeting with his elders and advisers,
hearing that Queen Natasha was due to give birth soon
and being told that soon he must marry.

Emir did not like to be told to do anything, and he rarely ever was.

But in this he was powerless and it did not sit well.

He had walked into the nursery, dark thoughts chasing him. But seeing Amy sitting reading to the twins, her blue eyes looking up, smiling as he entered, he had felt his black thoughts leave him. For the first time in months he had glimpsed peace. Had wanted to stay awhile with his children, with the woman he and Hannah had entrusted to care for them.

He had wanted to hide.

But a king could not hide.

Now what he saw was not so soothing. Now her soft femininity did not bring peace. For a year his passion might as well have been buried in the sands with his wife. For a year he had not fought temptation—there had been none. But something had changed since that moment in the nursery, since that day when he had noticed not just her smile but her mouth, not just her words but her voice. At first those thoughts had been stealthy, invading dreams over which he had no control, but now they were bolder and crept in by day. The scent of her perfume in an empty corridor might suddenly reach him, telling him the path she had recently walked, reminding him of a buried dream. And the mention of her name when she had requested a meeting had hauled him from loftier thoughts to ones more basic.

And basic were his thoughts now, yet he fought them.

He tried to look at the problem, not the temptation before him, the woman standing with her back to him. He wanted to turn her around, wanted to in a way he hadn't in a long time. But he was not locked in dreams now. He had control here and he forced himself to speak on.

'I did look through your contract and you are right. It has not been adhered to.'

Still she did not turn to look at him, though her body told her to. She wished he would leave—could not deal with him here even if it was to discuss the twins.

'After their birthday things are going to get busy here,' Emir said.

'When you select your bride and marry?'

He did not answer directly. 'These are complicated times for Alzan. Perhaps it would be better if the girls spent some time in London—a holiday.'

She closed her eyes, knew what was coming. Yes, a flight on his luxury jet, a few weeks at home with the twins, time with her family, luxurious hotels... What was there to say no to? Except... She took a deep breath and turned to him. 'Without you?'

'Yes,' Emir said.

She looked at the man who had so loved his children, who was now so closed off, so remote, so able to turn from them, and she had to know why.

'Is it because they remind you of Hannah?' Amy asked. 'Is that why it hurts so much to have them around?'

'Leave it,' he said. He wished the answer was that simple, wished there was someone in whom he could confide. 'I will have the trip scheduled.'

'So you can remove them a bit more from your life?'

'You do *not* talk to me like that.'

'Here I do.'

'Once I am married the twins will have a mother figure...'

'Oh, please!'

He frowned at her inappropriate response, but that did not deter her.

'Is it a mother for the twins you are selecting or a bride to give you sons?'

'I've told you already: it is not for you to question our ways. What would you know...?'

'Plenty.' Amy retorted. 'My parents divorced when I was two and I remember going to my father's; I remember when he married his new wife—a woman who had no interest in his children, who would really have preferred that we didn't inconvenience her one Saturday in two.' She stopped her tirade. There was no point. This was about the twins, not her past.

But instead of telling her off again, instead of telling her her words were inappropriate, he asked questions.

'How did you deal with it as a child?' Emir asked—because it mattered. He did want to make things better for his girls. 'Were you unhappy? Were you...?'

'Ignored?' She finished his sentence for him and Emir nodded, making her tell him some of her truth. 'Dad bought me a dolls' house.' She gave a pale smile at the memory. 'I spent hours playing with it. There the mum and dad slept and ate together. The kids played in the garden or in the living room, not up in their room...'

There she'd been able to fix things. Her smile faded and trembled. Here she couldn't fix things.

She felt his hand on her bare arm, felt his fingers brush her skin as if to comfort.

It did not.

She felt his flesh meet hers and it was all she could think of. His dark hand making contact was *all* she could think of when her mind should surely be only on the twins.

She hauled her thoughts back to them. 'Can I ask,' she said, 'that when you consider a bride you think of them?'

'Of course.'

His voice was soft and low, his hand still warm on her arm and there was a different tension surrounding them, the certainty that she was but a second away from a kiss.

A kiss that could only spell danger.

Perhaps that was his plan? Amy thought, shrugging off his hand, turning again to the desert. Perhaps he wanted her to fall in love with him. How convenient to keep her here, to bind her a little closer to the twins, to ensure that she did not resign. For he deemed her *better* for the twins.

'Leave!' She spat the word out over her shoulder, but still he stood. 'Leave…' she said again. But there was no relief when he complied, no respite when she heard the door close. Amy choked back angry tears as she stood on the balcony, she wanted to call him back, wanted to continue their discussion….wanted…

There was the other reason she had to consider leaving. Despite herself, despite the way he had been these past months, when he made any brief appearance in the nursery, on the rare occasions when he deigned to appear, her heart foolishly leapt at the sight of him—and lately her dreams had allowed more intimate glimpses of him. It confused her that she could have feelings for a man who paid so little attention to his own children.

Feelings that were forbidden.

Hidden.

And they must stay that way, Amy told herself, climbing into bed and willing sleep to come. But she was nervous all the same, for when she woke it would be morning.

And tomorrow she would be alone in the desert with him.

CHAPTER FOUR

'COME in.'

Amy's smile wasn't returned as the bedroom door opened and Fatima walked in.

'I'm nearly ready.'

'What are you doing?' Fatima frowned, her serious eyes moving over the mountain of coloured paper scattered over Amy's bed.

'I'm just wrapping some presents to take for the twins. I hadn't had a chance before.' She hadn't had a chance because after a night spent tossing and turning, wondering if she'd misread things, wondering what might have happened had she not told Emir to leave, Amy had, for the first time since she'd taken the role as nanny, overslept.

Normally she was up before the twins, but this morning it had been their chatter over the intercom that had awoken her and now, having given them breakfast and got them bathed and dressed, five minutes before their departure for the desert, she had popped them in their cots so she could quickly wrap the gifts.

'Their time in the desert is to be solemn,' Fatima said.

'It's their birthday.'

'The celebrations will be here at the palace.' She stood and waited as Amy removed the gifts from her open case. 'The King is ready to leave now. I will help you board the helicopter with the twins.' She called to another servant to collect Amy's case.

'You need to take the twins' cases also,' Amy told him.

'I have taken care of that.' Fatima clearly did not want the King to be kept waiting. 'Come now.'

Perhaps she had imagined last night, for Emir barely glanced at the twins and was his usual dismissive self with Amy as they boarded the helicopter. Amy was grateful for Fatima's help to strap the twins in. The twins were used to flying, and so too was Amy, but what was different this time was the lack of aides—usually at the very least Patel travelled with them, but this trip, as she had been told many times, would be different.

Amy could almost forgive his silence and his lack of interaction with the girls during the flight, for she was well aware that this was a journey he should have been making with his wife. Perhaps he was more pensive than dismissive?

Emir was more than pensive: he looked out to the desert with loathing, and the sun glinting on the canyons made him frown as he stared into the distance. He remembered the rebels who'd used to reside there—men who had refused to wait for the predictions to come true, who'd wanted Alzan to be gone and had taken matters into their own bloody hands.

'It's beautiful,' Amy commented as they swept deeper into the desert. She'd said it more to herself, but Emir responded.

'From a distance,' Emir said. 'But the closer you get…'

He did not finish. Instead he went back to staring broodily out of the window, replaying battles of the past in his mind, hearing the pounding hooves and the cries, feeling the grit of sand rubbed in wounds, history in every grain. Yet above all that he could hear *her*, reading a book to the twins, hear his daughters laughing as they impatiently turned the pages. He wanted to turn to the sound of them, to forget the pain and suffering, to set aside the past, but as King he had sworn to remember.

The heat hit Amy as soon as she stepped out of the helicopter. Emir held Nakia, while Amy carried Clemira and even though the helicopter had landed as close as possible to the compound of tents still the walk was hard work—the shifting soft sand made each step an effort. Once inside a tent, she took off her shoes and changed into slippers as Emir instructed. She thanked the pilot, who had brought in her suitcase, and then Emir led her through a passageway and after that another, as he briefly explained what would happen.

'The girls will rest before we take them to the Bedouins. There is a room for you next to them.'

They were in what appeared to be a lounge, its sandy floor hidden beneath layer after layer of the most exquisite rugs. The different areas were all separated by coloured drapes. It was like being in the heart of a vibrant labyrinth and already she felt lost.

'There are refreshments through there,' Emir explained, 'but the twins are not to have any. Today they must eat and drink only from the desert...'

Amy had stopped listening. She spun around as she heard the sound of the helicopter taking off. 'He's forgotten to bring in their luggage!' She went to run outside, but she took a wrong turn and ran back into the lounge again, appalled that Emir wasn't helping. 'You have to stop him—we need to get the twins' bags.'

'They do not need the things you packed for them. They are here to learn the ways of the desert and to be immersed in them. Everything they need is here.'

'I didn't just pack toys for them!' She could hear the noise of the chopper fading in the distance. Well, he'd just have to summon someone to get it turned around. 'Emir—I mean, Your Highness.' Immediately Amy corrected herself, for she had addressed him as she had so long ago. 'It's not toys or fancy clothes that I'm worried about. It's their bottles, their formula.'

'Here they will drink water from a cup,' Emir said.

'You can't do that to them!' Amy could not believe what she was hearing. 'That's far too harsh.'

'*Harsh?*' Emir interrupted. 'This land is harsh. This land is brutal and unforgiving. Yet its people have learnt to survive in it. When you are royal, when your life is one of privilege, it is expected that at least once a year you are true to the desert.'

Where, she wondered, had the caring father gone?

Where was the man who had rocked his tiny babies in strong arms? Who even last night had picked up his sleeping child just to hold her? Maybe she really had dreamt it—maybe she had imagined last night—for he stood now unmoved as Clemira and Nakia picked up on the tension and started to cry.

'We will leave soon,' Emir said.

'It's time for their nap now,' Amy said. She was expecting another argument, but instead he nodded.

'When they wake we will leave.'

'Is there anyone to help? To show me where they rest? Where the kitchen…?'

'It's just us.'

'Just us?' Amy blinked.

'There is a groundsman to tend to the animals, but here in the tent and out in the desert we will take care of ourselves.'

Oh, she had known they would be alone in the desert, but she had thought he had meant alone by royal standards—she had been quite sure that there would be servants and maidens to help them. Not once had she imagined that it would truly be just them, and for the first time the vastness and the isolation of the desert scared her.

'What if something happens?' Amy asked. 'What if one of the girls gets ill?'

'The Bedouins trust me to make the right decisions for their land and for their survival. It is right that in turn I trust them.'

'With your children?'

'Again,' Emir said, 'I have to warn you not to question our ways. Again,' he stated, 'I have to remind you that you are an employee.'

Her cheeks burned in anger but Amy scooped up the twins and found their resting area. Maybe he was right, she thought with a black smile. Maybe *she* needed time in the desert, for she was too used to things being done for her—a bit too used to having things unpacked and put away. And, yes, she was used to ringing down to the palace kitchen to have bottles warmed and food prepared. Now she had to settle two hungry, frazzled babies in the most unfamiliar surroundings.

The wind made the tent walls billow, and the low wooden cribs that lay on the floor were nothing like what the twins were used to—neither were the cloth nappies she changed them into. Emir came in with two cups of water for the girls, but that just upset them more, and when he'd left Amy took ages rocking the cribs to get the twins to settle. Her anger towards Emir rose as she did so, and it was a less than impressed Amy who finally walked out to the sight of Emir resting on the cushions.

He looked at her tightly pressed lips, saw the anger burning in her cheeks as she walked past him, and offered a rare explanation. 'There are traditions that must be upheld. Sit.' Emir watched her fingers clench at his command and perhaps wisely rephrased it. 'Please be seated. I will explain what is to take place.'

It was awkward to sit on the low cushions, but Amy remembered to tuck her feet away from him. It was difficult facing him again after last night—not that he appeared to remember it, for his eyes did not even search her face. Really he seemed rather bored at having to explain things.

'I understand that you think this is cruel, but really it is not…'

'I never said cruel,' Amy corrected. 'I said it was harsh on the girls. Had you told me earlier what was to happen I could have better prepared them. I could have had them drinking from cups.'

He conceded with a nod, and now he did look at her—could see not just the anger but that she was upset, and on behalf of his children. 'I know the year has been a difficult one. I am grateful the girls have had you.'

She was disarmed by his sudden niceness, forgot to thank him as she ought to, but Emir did not seem to notice. 'I have not been looking forward to this. Which is why, perhaps, I did not explain things. I have been trying not to think about it. Hannah was not looking forward to this time either.' Amy blinked at the revelation. 'Hannah wanted it left till the last moment—till they were a little older. I was trying to follow her wish, I did not think about cups…' He gave a shrug.

'Of course not,' Amy conceded. 'I don't expect you to. But if there was just more communication it might make things easier.'

'If she were alive still this would be difficult.'

Amy could see the battle in his face to keep his features bland, almost hear the effort to keep sentiment from his voice.

'If she were here Hannah would not have been able to

feed them, and that would have upset her.' Amy frowned as he continued. 'This is a time when babies are…' He did not know the word. 'Separated from their mother's milk.'

'Weaned off it?'

Emir nodded. 'Tradition states that they should travel for a week living on water and fruits. The desert people do not approve that I am only giving them the girls for one night, and King Rakhal also opposed it, but I explained that my children have already been…' he paused before he used the word that was new to his vocabulary '…weaned at two weeks of age.'

'And he agreed to reduce it?'

'Not for my daughters' sake.' Emir's voice deepened in hate. 'Only, I believe, because his wife is pregnant. Only because I reminded him that the rule would apply to his infant too.' He gave a rare smile. 'Perhaps Queen Natasha found out about it.'

Amy smiled back. She looked at him and was curious—more curious than she had ever been about a man. There was just so much about him she did not know, so much she had wrongly assumed. These past weeks it had not been bottles and cups on his mind, it had been their welfare. That this proud King had gone to his enemy to ask a favour spoke volumes, but it just confused her more.

'Natasha is English, like you.' Emir broke into her thoughts. 'And would be just as opposed, I presume.' His smile was wry now. 'Poor Rakhal!'

'Poor Natasha,' was Amy's response. 'If Rakhal is as stubborn as you.'

He told her some more about what would happen—that they would set off soon and would take lunch at the oasis. 'It must be soon,' Emir said, 'for the winds are gathering and we have to make it to the oasis today, so all this can take place before their first birthday.'

He did have their best interests at heart, Amy realised, even if he did not always show it. At every turn he confused her, for when the twins woke from that nap it was Emir who went to them, who helped her wrap them in shawls. When she saw him smile down at Clemira as they headed outside he was like the Emir she had once seen.

As they turned to the right of the tent Amy felt her heart sink at the familiar sound of horses whinnying—it was a sound that had once been pleasing to her, but now it only brought terror.

'Horses?' She looked at the beasts. 'We're riding to the oasis?'

'Of course.' He handed her Clemira, oblivious to the panic in her voice.

'Your Highness…'

'Emir,' he conceded.

'Emir—I can't. I thought we'd be driving.'

'Driving?' He shot out an incredulous laugh. 'You really have no idea what this is about.'

'I honestly don't think I can ride,' Amy said.

'Walk, then.' Emir shrugged. 'Though I suggest you

walk alongside a horse, for it will only be a short time before you surely decide you're not so precious.'

'It's not that!' He was so arrogant, so difficult to speak to at times. She certainly wasn't going to tell him about her accident. She didn't want a lecture on how it was better to get back on a horse, or some withering comment, or—worse—questions. 'I'm nervous around horses,' she offered.

Emir just shrugged. 'I will travel alone, then,' he said. 'You will help me to secure the twins.'

Amy bristled. He certainly wasn't going to baby her—after all, he didn't even pander to the twins. She wondered if they would fight and struggle as she secured them, but instead the girls were delighted with this new game—giggling as he balanced each one against his chest. It was Amy who was struggling as she wrapped a sash over his shoulder and tied a knot low on his waist, for she had never been closer to him.

'That's Clemira.' She did her best to keep her voice light, hoped he would not notice her shaking fingers as she wrapped the second twin and was glad to walk around to his back so he would not see her blush. She lifted his *kafeya* a little, ran the cloth behind it. Her fingers paused as she felt dark skin. She bit on her lip as she saw the nape of his neck, resisting the urge to linger.

'Done?' he asked.

'Nearly.' She finished the knot on his shoulder. 'Are you sure you can manage them both?'

'I have carried much more.' He indicated to Raul, the groundsman, to bring over his horse. As he mounted with ease the twins started to get upset—perhaps realising that they were leaving Amy behind.

'They will be fine,' Emir said.

But wasn't it *her* job to make this transition easier for them? As painful as it would be, she wanted to be there for the girls when they were handed over to strangers— wanted this last bit of time with them.

'I'll come.' The words tumbled out. 'It will be better for the girls if I ride along beside them and give them their lunch.'

'It is up to you.' Emir's voice did not betray the fact that he was relieved. He had privately been wondering how he would manage—not the ride, but the time at the oasis.

When he saw her tentativeness as she approached her animal, saw that her fear was real, he halted their departure for a moment and called to Raul, translating for Amy. 'I have asked him to bring Layyinah. She is, as her name attests, the most gentle mare.'

Layyinah was gorgeous—white and elegant, and more beautiful than any horse Amy had seen. She had huge eyes and nostrils, her forehead was broad, and Amy ran a hand over a magnificent mane.

'She's beautiful,' Amy said. 'I mean *seriously* beautiful.'

'Pure Arabian,' Emir explained. 'That bulge between her eyes is her *jibbah*. There is more...' he did not know the word '...more room that helps with her breathing in the hot air. They are built for this land. In our horses we put a lot of trust and they return it. She will look after you.'

Amy actually wanted to get on, although she was incredibly nervous. The once familiar action took her a couple of attempts, and though her robes had enough cloth in them to allow for decency it felt strange to be climbing onto a horse wearing them. But Emir had managed, Amy told herself. As she took to the saddle she was glad he had mounted his horse first, because he was there beside her, surprisingly patient and encouraging, as she took a moment to settle. The horse moved a few steps as it became accustomed to a new rider.

'*Kef*.' Emir leant over and pulled at the rein. 'It means stop,' he explained, and waited till Amy had her breath back. 'How does it feel?'

'Good,' Amy admitted. 'It feels scary, but good.'

'We will take it slowly,' Emir said. 'There is nothing to be nervous about.'

Oh, there was—but she chose not to tell him.

As they set off, even though it felt different riding on sand, the motion was soon familiar, and Amy realised how much she had missed riding. It had been a huge part of her life but she had never considered resuming it. Had never envisiaged the day she would be brave enough to try again—unexpectedly, that day was here.

She breathed in the warm air, felt the beauty of her surrounds, and for the first time she put anger and her questions aside, just drank in the moment. She heard Emir talk to his children, heard their chatter and laughter as they set off on an adventure. It was nicer just to enjoy rather than think about where this journey would take them.

'It's gorgeous.'

Emir merely shrugged.

'So peaceful.'

'When she chooses to be,' came Emir's strange answer, and he looked over to her. 'Don't let the desert seduce you. As my father told me, she is like a beautiful woman: she dazzles and lulls you, but she is always plotting.'

'What happened to your father?'

'He was killed.' Emir pointed to the distance. 'Over there.'

Despite the heat she shivered. 'And your mother?'

He did not answer.

'Emir?'

'It is not a tale to be told on your first night in the desert.' He changed the subject. 'Soon we will be there.' He pointed ahead to a shimmer on the horizon. 'Do you see the shadows?'

'Not really,' Amy admitted, but as they rode on she started to see the shadows that were in fact huge trees and shrubs.

'What will happen?'

'We will select our lunch,' Emir said, 'and then we will wait for the desert people.' He looked over, saw her tense profile, and then he looked down at the twins, lulled by the motion of the horse, safe with their father. They had both fallen asleep and he did not want to hand them over either—hating so many of his kingdom's ways.

'They've missed you.'

He heard Amy's voice but did not respond, for he had missed then so much too, and he could not share with her the reasons why.

Or perhaps he could.

He looked over as, bolder now, she rode ahead of him, her eyes on the oasis. Her scarf kept slipping, her hair was blowing behind her, and the attraction he felt was acknowledged. What just a couple of generations ago would have been forbidden was a possibility now. After all, Rakhal had an English wife—maybe there could be a way…

Poor Rakhal?

Perhaps not.

Poor Natasha. Even if they had been said as a light joke, he recalled Amy's words, knew from their conversation she was not one who would be told what to do. She would not meekly comply to his request or be flattered that he'd asked.

She was trotting now, and Emir frowned. For someone so nervous around horses, someone who hadn't wanted to ride, she was doing incredibly well. She looked as if she had been riding for years. He had a glimpse then of a different future—riding through the Alzan desert alongside her, with Clemira and Nakia and their own children too.

He must not rush this decision—and he certainly must not rush *her*.

She pulled up her horse and turned and smiled then, her face flushed from the exertion, her eyes for once unguarded, exhilarated. Emir wanted to see more of that and, patience forgotten, kicked his horse faster to join her, his urgency building with each gallop. He wanted her wild and free in his bed. Today—tonight—he would convince her. And as he slowed to a walk beside her, as he saw the spread of colour on her cheeks darken as he looked over to her, as he registered she wanted him too, he thanked the desert that had brought him a simple solution.

Maybe his kingdom and his family could somehow remain.

CHAPTER FIVE

'*LA,*' Emir scolded, frowning as Nakia spat out the fruit he'd tried to feed her. 'I mean *no*!' He was fast realising that the twins mainly understood English. 'She copies her sister.'

Amy couldn't help but laugh. They were deep in the desert, sitting by the oasis, feeding the children fresh fruit that they had collected from the lush trees—or they were *trying* to feed the children, because a moment ago Clemira had done the same thing, spitting out the fruit and screwing up her face.

'Clemira is the leader.' Amy watched his jaw tighten. It would seem she had said yet another thing of which he did not approve.

Their time at the oasis was not exactly turning out to be a stunning success. As soon as Emir had put her down Clemira had promptly tried to eat the sand, and Nakia had copied and got some in her eyes.

These were two thoroughly modern princesses, thanks to Amy. They were more used to bopping around to a DVD she'd had sent from home, or swimming in the impressive palace pool, than sitting by an oasis waiting for some elder from the Bedouins to come and offer wisdom for the life journey ahead of them.

'They know nothing of our ways,' Emir said, and though Amy was tempted to murmur that she wondered why that was, she bit her tongue. 'Hannah was worried about this. She didn't like the idea of them fasting.'

'It's not fasting.' Amy was practical; she understood now why he had put this off. 'If they're hungry, they'll eat. They have finally started to drink water.'

'They are spoilt,' Emir said as Clemira again spat out the fruit he offered.

'I know,' Amy admitted. 'And it's completely my fault—I can't help it.'

To her utter surprise, he laughed. She hadn't heard him laugh in a very long while. Even though the twins were being naughty, since they had arrived at the oasis Emir had been different. He seemed more relaxed— like a father to the twins, even—and then she looked up and saw he was watching her. She blushed a little as she looked back, for he was still looking at her.

She had no idea she was being seduced, no idea that the man lounging beside her, relaxed and calm, nurtured serious intentions.

'I was not criticising you,' Emir said. 'I am glad that you spoil them. You are right—I should have given you more notice. Perhaps you could have prepared them.'

'Now I've thought about it, I don't know how I could have,' Amy admitted. 'They're going to be terrified when the Bedouin take them.'

'They are kind people,' Emir said. 'They will do them no harm.'

But his heart wasn't in it. He tasted again the fear he had felt when he was a child—could remember his screams as the wizened old man took him. He hated the rules that bound him.

Hated Rakhal.

It was kinder to his soul to look at Amy, to visit another possible option.

'What happens tomorrow when we get back to the palace?' Amy asked, unnerved by his scrutiny and desperately trying to think of something to say. 'Will it be very grand?'

'There will be a party. My brother Hassan, the second in line, should attend.'

'Should?'

'He has a great interest in horses too…' Emir gave a wry smile. 'They take up a lot of his time.'

She had heard about Prince Hassan and his wild ways, though she had never met him, just heard the whispers. Of course some things were never discussed, so she stayed silent.

She was surprised when Emir said more. 'Though his interest in horses is something I do not condone.'

She gave a small shocked laugh at his admission.

'He needs to grow up,' Emir said.

'Maybe he's happier not.'

'Perhaps,' he admitted, and thought perhaps now he understood his brother a little.

He had confronted him many times, to no avail. Emir

did not get the thrill his brother found in winning—did not understand why Hassan would roam the globe from casino to casino. Hassan had everything and more a man needed right here in Alzan. Riches aplenty, and any woman of his choosing.

He looked over to Amy. One of her hands was idly patting the sand into a mound. For the first time with a woman Emir was not certain of the outcome, but he glimpsed the thrill of the chase, the anticipation before victory.

He understood Hassan a little better now.

'King Rakhal will also be attending.'

'With his wife?' Amy checked. She had briefly met Natasha, but she remembered who she was speaking about. 'I meant will Queen Natasha be attending?'

'No.' Emir shook his head. 'She is due to give birth soon, so it is safer that she does not travel. She seems very happy here,' he pushed gently. 'At first I am sure it was daunting, but she seems to have taken well to her new role.'

'Can I ask something?' Emir was still looking at her, still inviting conversation.

Her question was not the one he was hoping for: it did not appear as if she was envisaging herself for a moment as Queen.

'Why, if their baby is a girl, can she rule?'

'Their laws are different,' Emir said. 'Do you know that Alzan and Alzirz were once the same country?'

'Alzanirz?' Amy nodded.

'There have always been twins in our royal lineage,'

Emir explained. 'Many generations ago a ruler of the time had twin sons. They were unexpected, and were not branded, so the people were unsure who the rightful heir was. It was a troubled time for the country and the King sought a solution. It was decided that the land would be divided, that each son would rule his own kingdom. The predictors of the time said that one day they would reunite...but we were both given separate rules. As soon as one rule is broken the country must become one again, the ruler being of the lineage which survived.'

'It doesn't seem fair.' She looked to his dark eyes and blinked, for they were not stern, and instead of chastising her he nodded for her to go on. 'If a princess can rule there, why not here?'

'They have another rule that they must abide by,' Emir explained. 'In Alzirz the ruler can marry only once. Rakhal's mother died in childbirth and he was not expected to survive—the prophecy was almost fulfilled.'

'But he survived?'

Emir nodded. 'Here...' He was silent for a moment before continuing. 'Here the law states that if the ruler's partner dies he can marry again.' Still he looked into her eyes. 'As must I.'

'Must?'

'The people are unsettled—especially with an impending birth in Alzirz.'

'But if you are not ready...' Amy bit her tongue, knew that to discuss would be pointless.

'Ready?' He frowned, for who was she to question him? But then he remembered she came from a land that relied on the fickle formula of attraction. The glimmer of his idea glowed brighter still. The answer to his dilemma sat beside him now, and her voice, Emir noticed, was just a little breathy when she spoke to him.

'Perhaps a year is too soon to expect...' She licked dry lips, wished she could suddenly be busy with the twins, for this conversation was far too intimate, but the girls were sitting playing with each other. 'Marriage is a huge step.'

'And a step I must take seriously. Though...' He must not rush her, Emir was aware of that. 'I am not thinking of marriage today.'

'Oh...'

Sometimes he made her dizzy. Sometimes when he looked at her with those black eyes it was all she could do to return his gaze. Sometimes she was terrified he would see the lust that burnt inside her.

Not all the time.

But at times.

And this was one of them.

Sometimes, and this was also one of them, she held the impossible thought that he might kiss her—that the noble head might lower a fraction to hers. The sun must be making her crazy because she could almost taste his mouth... The conversation *was* too intimate.

His next words made her burn.

'You are worried about tonight?' Emir said. 'About what might happen?' He saw the dart of her eyes, saw her top teeth move to her lower lip. He could kiss her mouth *now*, could feel her want, was almost certain of it. He would confirm it now. 'They will be fine.'

'They?'

Her eyes narrowed as his words confused her and he knew then that in her mind she had been alone in the tent with him. Emir suppressed a triumphant smile.

'They will be looked after,' he assured her. And so too, Emir decided, would she.

Embarrassed, she turned away, looked to the oasis, to the clear cool water. She wished she could jump in, for her cheeks were on fire now and she was honest enough with herself to know why. Perhaps it was she who was not ready for the presence of a new sheikha queen?

How foolish had she been to think he might have been about to kiss her? That Emir might even see her in that way?

'I have thought about what you said—about the girls needing someone…' He should be patient and yet he could not. 'You love my daughters.'

He said it as a fact.

It *was* a fact.

She stared deeper into the water, wondered if she was crazy with the thoughts she was entertaining—that Emir might be considering her as his lover, a mistress, a proxy mother for his girls. Then she felt his hand on her cheek and she could not breathe. She felt his finger trace down to her throat and caress the piece of flesh she truly loathed.

'What is this from?' His strong fingers were surprisingly gentle, his skin cool against her warm throat, and his questions, his touch, were both gentle and probing.

'Please, Emir…'

The Bedouin caravan was travelling towards them, the moment they were both dreading nearing. A kiss would have to wait. He stood and watched them approach—a line of camels and their riders. He listened to his daughters laughing, knowing in a short while there would be the sound of tears, and he wanted to bury his head in Amy's hair. He wanted the escape of her mouth. And yet now there was duty.

He stood and picked up both daughters, looked into their eyes so dark and trusting. He could not stand to hand them over, for he remembered being ripped from his own parents' arms, his own screams and pleas, and then the campfire and the strange faces and he remembered his own fear. Right now he hated the land that he ruled—hated the ways of old and the laws that could not be changed without both Kings' agreement.

He had survived it, Emir told himself as the wizened old man approached. The twins shrieked in terror as he held out his arms to them.

Emir walked over and spoke with the man, though Amy could not understand what was said.

'They are upset—you need to be kind with them,' Emir explained.

'It is your fear that scares them.' The black eyes were young in his wizened old face. 'You do not wish to come and speak with me?'

'I have decisions I must make alone.'

'Then make them!' the old man said.

'They are difficult ones.'

'Difficult if made from the palace, perhaps,' the old man said. 'But here the only king is the desert—it always brings solutions if you ask for them.'

Emir walked back to Amy, who should be standing in silence as the old man prepared the sand. But of course she was not.

'Who is he?' Amy asked.

'He's an elder of the Bedouins,' Emir explained. 'He is supposed to be more than one hundred and twenty years old.'

'That's impossible.'

'Not out here,' Emir said, without looking over. 'He gives wisdom to those who choose to ask for it.'

'Do *you*?' Amy asked, and then stammered an apology, for it was not her place to ask such things.

But Emir deigned a response. 'I have consulted him a few times,' he admitted, 'but not lately.' He gave a shrug. 'His answers are never straightforward...'

The old man filled two small vials with the sand he had blessed and Emir knew what was to come.

Amy felt her heart squeezing as he took the sobbing babies, and her pain turned to horror as he walked with them towards the water.

'What's happening?'

'They are to be immersed in the water and then they will be taken to the camp.'

'Emir—*no*!'

'You have rituals for your babies, do you not?' Emir snapped. 'Do babies in England not cry?'

He was right, but in that moment Amy felt as if she were bleeding, hearing their shrieks and not having the chance to kiss them goodbye. Listening to them sob as they were taken, she was not just upset; she was furious too—with herself for the part she was playing in this and with Emir.

'Ummi!' both twins screamed in the distance, and worse than her fear of his anger was resisting her urge to run to them. 'Ummi!'

She heard the fading cry and then she heard her own ones—stood there and sobbed. She didn't care if he was angry about what they called her. Right now she just ached for the babies.

And as he stood watching her weep for his children, as he heard them cry out for her, Emir knew his decision was the right one.

'They will be okay,' he tried to comfort her. 'These are the rules.'

'I thought kings made the rules,' she retorted angrily.

'This is the way of our land.' He should be angry, should reprimand her, silence her, but instead he sought to comfort her. 'They will be taken care of. They will be sung to and taught their history.' His hand was on her cheek. 'And each year that passes they will understand more...'

'I can't do this again.' So upset was Amy she did not focus on his touch, just on the thought of next year and the next, of watching the babies she loved lost to strange laws. 'I can't do this, Emir,' she was frantic. 'I have to leave.'

'No,' Emir said, for he could not lose her now. 'You can be here for them—comfort them and explain to them.'

She could. He knew that. The answer to his prayers was here and he bent his mouth and tasted her, tasted the salty tears on her cheeks, and then his lips moved to her mouth and her fear for the girls was replaced, but only with terror.

She was kissing a king. And she *was* kissing him. Her mouth was seeking an escape from her agony and for a moment she found it. She let her mind hush to the skill of his lips and his arms wrapped around her, drew her closer to him. His tongue did not prise open her lips because they opened readily, and she knew where this was leading—knew the plans he had in mind.

He wanted her to be here for his daughters—wanted to ensure she would stay. She pulled back, as her head told her to, because for Amy this was a dangerous game. With this kiss came her heart.

'No.' She wanted to get away, wanted this moment never to have happened. She could not be his lover—especially when soon he would take a bride. 'We can't...'

'We *can*.' He was insistent. His lips found hers again and her second taste was her downfall, for it made her suddenly weak.

His hands were on her hips and he pulled her firmly in, his mouth making clear his intent, and she had never felt more wanted, more feminine. His passion was her pleasure, his desire was what she had been missing, but she could not be his plaything, could not confuse things further.

'Emir, no.'

'Yes.' He could see it so clearly now—wondered why it had taken so long. 'We go now to the tent and make love.'

Again he kissed her. His mind had been busy seeking a solution, but it stilled when he tasted her lips. The pleasure he had forgone was now remembered, except with a different slant—for he tasted not any woman, but Amy. And she was more than simply pleasing. He liked the stilling of her breath as his mouth shocked her, liked the fight for control beneath his hands. Her mouth was still but her body was succumbing; he felt her momentary pause and then her mouth gave in to him, and for Emir there was something unexpected—an emotion he had never tasted in a woman. All the anger she had held in check was delivered in her response. It was a savage kiss that met him now, a different kiss, and he was hard in response. The gentle lovemaking he had intended, the tender seduction he had pictured, changed as she kissed him back.

He was surprised by the intensity of her passion, by the bundle of emotion in his arms, for though she fought him still her mouth was kissing him.

It was Emir who withdrew. He looked down at her flushed, angry face.

'Why the temper, Amy?'

'Because I didn't want you to *know*!'

'Know?' And he looked down and saw the lust she had kept hidden, felt the burn of her arousal beneath him. It consumed him, endeared her to him, told him his decision was the right one. 'Why would you not want me to know?'

'Because...' His mouth was at her ear, his breath making her shiver. She turned her face away at the admission, but it did not stop his pursuit, more stealthy now, and more delicious. 'It can come to nothing.'

'It can...' Emir said. She loathed her own weakness, but now she had tasted him she wanted him so.

'Please...' The word spilled from her lips; it sounded as if she was begging. 'Take me back to the tent.'

Except he wanted her *now*. His hands were at the buttons of her robe, pulling it down over her shoulders. Their kisses were frantic, their want building. She grappled with his robe, felt the leather that held his sword and the power of the man who was about to make love to her. She was kissing a king and it terrified her, but still it was delicious, still it inflamed her as his words attempted to soothe her.

'The people will come to accept it...'

He was kissing her neck now, moving down to her exposed breast. She ached for his mouth there, ached to give in to his mastery, but her mind struggled to understand his words. 'The people...?'

'When I take you as my bride.'

'Bride!' He might as well have pushed her into the water. She felt the plunge into confusion and struggled to come up for air, felt the horror as history repeated itself. It was happening again.

'Emir—no!'

'Yes.' He thought she was overwhelmed by his offer—did not recognise she was dying in his arms, as his mouth moved back to take her again, to calm her. But when she spoke he froze.

'I can't have children.'

She watched the words paralyse him, saw his pupils constrict, and then watched him make an attempt to right his features. To his credit he did not drop her, but his arms stilled at her sides and then his forehead rested on hers as the enormity of her words set in.

'I had a riding accident and it left me unable to have children.' Somehow she managed to speak; somehow, before she broke down, she managed to find her voice.

'I'm sorry.'

'My fiancé was too.'

With a sob she turned from him, pulled her robe over her naked breasts and did up the buttons as she ran to where the horses were tethered. She didn't possess any fear as she untied her mare and mounted it, because fear was nothing compared to grief. She kicked her into a canter and when that did not help she galloped. She could hear the sound of Emir's beast rapidly gaining on her, could hear his shouts for her to halt, and finally she did, turning her pained eyes to him.

'I lay for five days on a machine that made me breathe and I heard my fiancé speaking with his mother. That was how I found out I couldn't have children. That was how I heard him say there really was no point marrying me...' She was breathless from riding, from anger, yet still she shouted. 'Of course that's not what he told me when I came round—he said the accident had made him realise that, though he cared, he didn't love me, that life was too short and he wasn't ready for commitment.' Emir said nothing. 'But I knew the reason he really left.'

'He's a fool, then.'

'So what does that make you?'

'I am King,' Emir answered, and it was the only answer he could give.

As soon as the tent was in sight, it was Emir who kicked his horse on, Emir who raced through the desert, and she was grateful to be left alone, to gallop, to sob, to think...

To remember.

The black hole of the accident was filling painfully—each stride from Layyinah was taking her back there again. She was a troubled bride-to-be, a young woman wondering if she wasn't making the most appalling mistake. The sand and the dunes changed to countryside; she could hear hooves pounding mud and feel the cool of spring as she came to an appalling conclusion.

She had to call the wedding off.

CHAPTER SIX

'I HAVE run you a bath.'

Emir looked up as Amy walked into the tent. He had told Raul to watch her from a distance and, after showering, had run the first bath of his life.

And it was for another.

As he had done so his gut had churned with loathing towards her fiancé—loathing that was immediately reflected in a mirror that shone back to him, for wasn't he now doing the same?

Yet he was a king.

Again that thought brought no solace.

'Thank you.'

Her pale smile as she walked into the tent confused him. He had expected anger, bitterness to enter the tent with her, but if anything she seemed calm.

Amy *was* calm.

Calmer than she had been since the accident.

She unzipped her robe and looked around the bathing area. It was lit by candles in hurricane jars—not, she realised, a romantic gesture from Emir, it was how the whole tent was lit. Yet she was touched all the same.

Amy slid into the fragrant water and closed her eyes, trying and failing not to think of the twins and how they would be coping. Doing her best not to think of Emir and what he had proposed.

Instead she looked at her past—at a time she could now clearly remember. It felt good to have it back.

She washed her hair and climbed out of the water, drying herself with the towel and then wrapping it around her. Aware she was dressed rather inappropriately, she hoped Emir would be in his sleeping area, but he was sitting on cushions as she walked quietly past him, heading to her sleeping area to put on something rather more suitable, before she faced a conversation with him.

He looked up. 'Better?'

'Much.' Amy nodded.

'You should eat.'

She stared at the food spread before him and shook her head. 'I'm not hungry,' she lied.

'You do not decline when a king invites you to dine at his table.'

'Oh, but you do when that king has just declined *you*,' Amy responded. 'My rule.' And the strangest thing was she even managed a small smile as she said it—another smile that caught Emir by surprise.

'I thought you would be...' He did not really know. Emir had expected more hurt, but instead there was an air of peace around her that he had never noticed before.

'I really am fine,' Amy said. She was aware there was a new fracture he had delivered to her heart, but it was too painful for examination just yet, so instead she explored past hurts. 'In fact I remembered something when I was riding,' Amy explained. 'Something I'd forgotten. I've been struggling with my memory—I couldn't remember the weeks before the accident.' She shook her head. 'It doesn't matter.'

She went again to head to her room, but again he called her back. 'You need to eat.' He held up a plate of *lokum* and Amy frowned at the pastry, at the selection of food in front of him.

'I thought it was just fruit that we could eat?'

'It is the twins who can eat only fruit and drink only water. I thought it better for them if we all did it.'

She saw the tension in his jaw as he spoke of the twins. Sometimes he sounded like a father—sometimes this dark, brooding King was the man she had once known.

'They will be okay.' He said it as if he was trying to convince himself.

'I'm sure they'll be fine,' Amy said. Tonight he was worried about his children. Tonight neither of them really wanted to be alone. 'I'll get changed and then I'll have something to eat.'

Was there relief in his eyes when he nodded?

There was not much to choose from—it was either her nightdress and dressing gown or yet another pale blue robe. Amy settled for the latter, brushed her damp hair and tied it back, and then headed out to him.

He was tired of seeing her in that robe. He wanted to see her in other colours—wanted to see her draped in red or emerald, wanted to see her hair loose around her shoulders and those full lips rouged. Or rather, Emir conceded as he caught the fresh, feminine scent of her as she sat down, he wanted to see the shoulders he had glimpsed moments earlier, wanted only the colour of her skin and her naked on the bed beneath him. But her revelation had denied them that chance.

'I apologise.' He came right out and said it. 'To have it happen to you twice…'

'Honestly…' Amy ate sweet pastry between words—she really was hungry. Perhaps for the first time in a year she knew what starving was. She'd been numb for so long and now it felt as if all her senses were returning. 'I'm okay.' She wondered how she might best explain what she was only just discovering herself. 'Since the accident I've felt like a victim.' It was terribly hard to express it! 'I didn't like feeling that way. It didn't feel like me. I didn't like my anger towards him.'

'You had every reason to be angry.'

'No,' Amy said. 'As it turns out, I didn't.'

'I don't understand.'

'There were a few days before I fully came round when I could hear conversations. I couldn't speak because I was on a machine.'

Emir watched her fingers go instinctively to her throat.

'That was when I heard the doctors discussing the surgery I'd had.' She was uncomfortable explaining things to him, so she kept it very brief. 'The horse had trampled me. They took me to surgery and they had to remove my ovaries. They left a small piece of one so that I didn't go into…'

'Menopause.' He said it for her, smiled because she was embarrassed, 'I do know about these things.'

'I know.' She squirmed. 'It just feels strange, speaking about it with you. Anyway, I lay there unable to speak and heard my fiancé talking to his mother—how he didn't know what to do, how he'd always wanted children. Later, after I was discharged from the hospital, he told me it was over, that he'd been having doubts for ages, that it wasn't about the accident. But I knew it was. Or rather I thought I knew it was.' She looked up at Emir's frown. 'When I was riding today I remembered the last time I rode a horse. I don't remember falling off, or being trampled, but I do remember what I was thinking. I was unhappy, Emir.' She admitted it out loud for the first time, for even back then she had kept it in. 'I felt trapped and I was wondering how I could call off the wedding. That was what I was thinking when the accident happened—he was right to end things. It wasn't working. I just didn't know it—till now.'

'You didn't love him?' Emir asked, and watched as she shook her head. As she did so a curl escaped the confines of the hair tie. He was jealous of her fingers as they caught it and twisted it as she pondered his question.

'I did love him,' she said slowly, for she was still working things out for herself, still piecing her life together. 'But it wasn't the kind of love I wanted. We'd been going out together since we were teenagers. Our engagement seemed a natural progression—we both wanted children, we both wanted the same things, or thought we did. I cared for him and, yes, I suppose I loved him. But it wasn't…' She couldn't articulate the word. 'It wasn't a passionate love,' Amy attempted. 'It was…' She still couldn't place the word.

Emir tried for her. 'Safe?'

But that wasn't the word she was looking for either.

'Logical,' Amy said. 'It was a sort of logical love. Does that make sense?'

'I think so,' Emir said. 'That is the kind of love we build on here—two people who are chosen, who are considered a suitable match, and then love grows.'

He was quiet for a moment. The conversation was so personal she felt she could ask. 'Was that the love you had with Hannah?'

'Very much so,' Emir said. 'She was a wonderful wife, and would have been an amazing mother as well as a dignified sheikha queen.'

Amy heard the love in his voice when he spoke of her and they were not jealous tears that she blinked back. 'Maybe my fiancé and I would have made it.' Amy gave a tight shrug. 'I'm quite sure we would have had a good marriage. I think I was chasing the dream—a home and children, doing things differently than my parents.'

'A grown-up dolls' house?' Emir suggested, and she smiled.

'I guess I just wanted…' She still didn't know the word for it.

'An illogical love?' Emir offered—and that was it.

'I did,' Amy said, and then she stood. 'I do.'

'Stay,' he said. 'I have not explained.'

'You don't need to explain, Emir,' Amy said. 'I know we can't go anywhere. I know it is imperative to your country's survival that you have a son.' But there was just a tiny flare of hope. 'Could you speak to King Rakhal and have the rule revoked?' Amy didn't care if she was speaking out of turn. 'It is a different time now.'

'Rakhal's mother died in childbirth,' Emir said. 'And, as I told you, for a while her baby was not expected to survive. The King of Alzirz came to my father and asked the same…' Emir shrugged his broad shoulders. 'Of course my father declined his request. He wanted the countries to be one.'

'You've thought about it, then?'

He looked at her and for the first time revealed to another person just a little of what was on his mind. 'I have more than thought about it. I approached Rakhal when my wife first became ill. His response was as you might expect.' He shook his head as he recalled that conversation. Could see again the smirk on Rakhal's face when he had broached the subject. How he had relished Emir's rare discomfort. How he had enjoyed watching a proud king reduced to plead.

Emir looked into Amy's blue eyes and somehow the chill in him thawed slightly. He revealed more of the burden that weighed heavily on his mind. 'I have thought about many things, and I am trying to make the best decision not just for my country but for my daughters.' He had said too much. Immediately Emir knew that. For no one must know everything.

She persisted. 'If you didn't have a son…'

'It would be unthinkable,' Emir said. And yet it was all he thought about. He looked to her pale blue eyes and maybe it was the wind and the sound of the desert, perhaps the dance of the shadows on the walls, but he wanted to tell her—wanted to take her to the dark place in his mind, to share it. But he halted, for he could not. 'I *will* have a son.' Which meant his bride could not be her. 'Marriage means different things for me. I am sorry if I hurt you—that was never my intention.'

'I didn't take it personally…' But at the last moment her voice broke—because her last words weren't true. She'd realised it as she said them. It was a very personal hurt, and one to be explored only in private, in the safety of her room. There she could cry at this very new loss. 'Goodnight, Emir.'

'Amy?'

She wished he would not call her back, but this time it was not to dissuade her. Instead he warned her what the night would bring.

'The wind is fierce tonight—she knows that you are new here and will play tricks with your mind.'

'You talk about the wind as if it's a person.'

'Some say she is a collection of souls.' He saw her instantly dismiss that. 'Just don't be alarmed.'

She wasn't—at first.

Amy lay in the bed and stared at the ceiling—a ceiling that rose and fell with the wind. She missed the girls more than she had ever thought possible and she missed too what might have been.

Not once had she glimpsed what Emir had been considering—not once had she thought herself a potential sheikha queen. She'd thought she might be his mistress—an occasional lover, perhaps, and a proxy mother to the twins.

Emir had been willing to marry her.

It helped that he had.

It killed that he never could.

Amy lay there and fought not to cry—not that he would be able to hear her, for the wind was whipping around the tent and had the walls and roof lifting. The flickering candles made the shadows dance as if the room were moving, so she closed her eyes and willed sleep to come. But the wind shrieked louder, and it sounded at times like the twins. She wept for them.

Later she could hear a woman screaming—the same sound she had heard the night they were born. The shouts had filled the palace a year ago this night, when the twins were being born. These screams sounded like a woman birthing—screams she would never know—and it was torture. She knew the wind played tricks, but the screams and the cries were more than she could bear.

Maybe they'd taunted Emir too, for when she opened her eyes he was standing there, still robed, his sword strapped to his hips. His *kafeya* was off. He stood watching, a dark shadow in the night, but one that did not terrify.

'When you kissed me back, when you said *please*, what did you think I meant?' he asked.

'I thought it was sex that was on offer.' If she sounded coarse she didn't care. Her hurt was too raw to smother it with lies.

'That is not our way.' Emir looked at her. 'In Alzirz they are looser with their morals. There are harems and...' He shook his head. 'I did not want that for you.'

Not for the first time, but for more shameful reasons now, she wished she were there—wished it was there that Emir was King.

'I never for a moment thought you would consider me for your bride. When we kissed—when we...' She swallowed, because it was brutal to her senses to recall it. 'When we kissed,' Amy started again, 'when we touched...' Her eyes were brave enough to meet his. 'I wasn't thinking about the future or the twins or solutions, I thought it was just me that you wanted...'

And he looked at her, and the winds were silenced. The screams and the tears seemed to halt. Surely for one night he could think like a man and not a king? Emir was honest in his response and his voice was low with passion. 'It was,' Emir said. Yes, at first he had been seducing, but later... 'When I kissed you I forgot.'

'Forgot?'

'I forgot everything but you.'

She looked over to him, saw the raw need in his eyes, saw the coffee colour of his skin and the arms that had held her, and she wanted his mouth back.

'I know we can't go anywhere. I know...' She just wanted to be a woman again—wanted one time with this astonishingly beautiful man. 'Just once…' she whispered, and Emir nodded.

'Just once,' came his reply, for that was all it must be, and with that he picked her up and carried her to his bed.

CHAPTER SEVEN

SHE lay on his bed and watched as he undid the leather belt and the sword fell to the floor with a gentle thud. She turned away from him then, for she was filled with terror. All too clearly she could see his braids and royal decorations and she knew what they were doing was wrong—she wanted the man, not the King, and his status was truly terrifying.

'Turn around,' Emir told her.

Slowly she did so, and saw him naked, and she feared that too—for he was more beautiful then she had even imagined and, yes, now it was safe to admit to herself that she had imagined. He hardened under her gaze. Her shy eyes took in more of him—the toned planes of his stomach, the long, solid thighs and the arms she now ached to have hold her again.

'This is wrong,' she said as he walked towards her.

'It doesn't feel wrong,' he said, and he climbed in beside her. The fact that the bodies that met were forbidden to each other only heightened their desire.

She cringed as he took off her nightgown, closed her eyes as he pushed down the bedclothes and fully exposed her. He wanted to know every piece of her skin. He kissed not her mouth but the breast that he had so nearly kissed in the desert, and she was as aroused in that instant as she had been then. She returned to that moment in the desert when he could have taken her. He kissed lower, kissed her stomach as deeply as if it were her mouth, and then he moved lower still, and she lay there writhing as he made her feel like a woman again.

Her body had craved passion for so long and he had returned it to her. She had denied herself touch, had felt untouchable, empty, and now he filled her with his tongue, touched her so intimately and not with haste.

With her moans he grew.

With her screams he lost himself more.

He had shared not an ounce of emotion since the death of his wife, but he shared it now.

There was a burden for this King that not the wisest of his council knew about. There was a decision in the making that he could only come to alone—a decision he had wrestled with for more than a year now. It was all forgotten.

He felt her fingers in his hair and the tightening of her thighs to his head. Her hips attempted to rise but he pushed her down with his mouth till she throbbed into him, and then he could wait no more.

He kneeled, looked down at all that beckoned, and she felt the roughness of his thighs part her legs further. Her body still quivered from his intimate exploration as he parted her with his thumbs. She looked with decadent, wanton fear at what would soon be deep inside her and, breathless, pleaded for it to be *now*.

He pulled back, for he must sheathe, and then he heard her whisper.

'We don't have to.'

For the first time, the fact that there could be no baby brought only relief, for neither wanted to halt things.

Now he lifted her hips, aimed himself towards her. A more deliberate lover he could not be, for he watched and manoeuvred every detail, and she let him—let him position her till he was poised at her entrance, and then he made her wait.

'Emir…'

His smile was as rare as it was wicked.

'Emir…'

He hovered closer and was cruel in his timing; that beat of space made her weep, and her mouth opened to beg him again, but her words faded as he filled her, as he drove into her with the ardour of a man ending his deprivation. He forgot his size and to be gentle, and never had she been so grateful to have a man forget.

He filled her completely, and then filled her again. He was over her, and the kiss he had first denied her was Amy's reward, for he hushed her moans with his mouth until it was Emir who could not be silent. The pleasure was now his, all pain obliterated, the shackles temporarily released. His mind soared in freedom as her body moved with his. Escape beckoned and he claimed it, groaning to hold on to it, yearning to sustain it. But the pulse of her around him was too much—the rapid tightening and flicker of intimate muscles, her hot wet cheek next to his, her breath, his name in his ear.

He lost himself to her, gave in to what was and spilled into her, called out her name as they dived into pleasure. The wind was their friend now, for it shrieked louder around them, carried their shouts and their moans and buried their secret in the sands.

CHAPTER EIGHT

OF COURSE it should never have happened.

And of course it must never be referred to again.

But it was a little before morning and they'd made love again after she'd turned and looked at him while she still could. She ran a finger across the scar above his eye about which she had often wondered and was brave enough now to ask.

'What is that from?'

'You don't ask that sort of thing.'

'Naked beside you I do.'

Maybe it was better she knew, Emir thought. Maybe then she could understand how impossible it was for them.

'Some rebels decided that they could not wait for the predictions, so they took matters into their own hands.' He did not look at her as he spoke. He felt her fingers over his scar and remembered again. 'They decided to take out one lineage.' He heard her shocked gasp. 'Of course our people had seen them approaching and they rallied. My father went out and battled, as did my brother and I…'

'And your mother?'

'She was killed in her bed.'

He removed her hand from his face, climbed out of bed, and dressed and headed to prayer. He had begged the desert for a solution and for a moment had thought one had been delivered; instead it had been a taunt. He must play by the rules, Emir realised as he remembered again that night and all he had inherited.

So he prayed for his country and his people.

He must forget about their lovemaking, the woman he had held in his arms. He had never felt closer to another, even Hannah, and he prayed for forgiveness.

He prayed for his daughters and the decision he was making and he got no comfort, for his heart still told him he was making the wrong one.

Then he remembered what his father had fought for and he knew he must honour it—so he prayed again for his country.

Amy lay silent, taking in this last time she would be in his bed, the masculine scent of him. Her hand moved to the warm area where he had slept and she yearned to wait for him to return to the bed and make love to her just one more time. But for both of them that would be unfair, so she headed to the bathing area and then to her own room.

She fixed her hair and put on the blue robe, became the nanny again.

For Emir there was both regret and relief when he returned from prayer and saw the empty bed. Regret and relief as they shared a quiet breakfast. She did not once refer to last night, but it killed him to see her in the familiar blue robe and to know what was beneath.

And when the silence deafened her, when she knew if she met his eyes just one more time, it would end in a kiss she wished him good morning and headed to her room. She lay on her bed and willed the twins to return, for sanity to come back to her life and to resume again her role.

But of course it felt different.

Her heart swelled with pride and relief when the birthday girls were returned.

Their squeals of delight as she kissed them made her eyes burn from the salt of unshed tears. She realised how close to being their mother she had come.

'What are these?' She attempted normal conversation, looked at the heart-shaped vials that now hung around their necks.

'They are filled with the sands of the desert—they must be worn till they go to bed tonight, then they are to be locked away until their wedding day.'

'They're gorgeous.' Amy held one between her finger and thumb. 'What are they for?'

'Fertility.' He almost spat the word out, his mood as dark as it had been the morning she had faced him in his office, and it didn't improve as they boarded the helicopter for their return to the palace.

The twins were crying as the helicopter took off.

'They are not to arrive with teary faces. There will be many people gathered to greet them. My people will line the streets.'

'Then comfort them!' Amy said, but his face was as hard as granite and he turned to the window. 'Emir, please.' Amy spoke when perhaps she should not, but he had been so much better with the girls yesterday, and it worried her that she had made things worse instead of better. 'Please don't let last night…'

He looked over to Amy, his eyes silencing her, warning her not to continue, and then he made things exceptionally clear. 'Do you really think what happened last night might have any bearing on the way I am with my daughters?' He mocked her with one small incredulous shake of his head. 'You are the nanny—you are in my country and you have to accept our laws and our ways. They are to be stoic. They are to be strong.'

But he did take Clemira and hold her on his knees, and when Clemira was quiet so too was Nakia.

Amy sat silent, craning her neck as the palace loomed into view, bouncing Nakia on her knee, ready to point out all the people, to tell the little girl that the waving flags were for her sister and herself.

Except the streets were empty.

She looked to Emir. His face was still set in stone and he said nothing.

He strode from the helicopter, which left Amy to struggle with the twins. He was greeted by Patel and whatever was said was clearly not good news, for Emir's already severe expression hardened even more.

Amy had no idea what was happening.

She took the twins to the nursery and waited for information, to find out what time the party would be, but with each passing hour any hope of celebration faded and again it was left to Amy to amuse the little girls on what should be the happiest of days.

Her heart was heavy in her chest and she fought back tears as she made them cupcakes in the small kitchen annexe. At supper time she sang 'Happy Birthday' to them, watched them smile in glee as they opened the presents she had wrapped for them. Amy smiled back— but her face froze when she saw Emir standing in the nursery doorway.

His eyes took in the presents, the teddies and the DVDs. He watched as Amy walked over to him, her face white with fury, and for a second he thought she might spit.

'They have everything, do they?' Her eyes challenged him. 'Some party!'

'My brother is too busy in Dubai with his horses.'

He walked over to the twins and kissed the two little dark heads. He spoke in his language to them for a few moments. 'I have their present.'

He called the servants to come in and Amy watched as the delighted twins pulled paper off a huge parcel. She bit on her lip when she saw it was a dolls' house— an exquisite one—built like the palace, with the stairs, the doors, the bedroom.

'I thought about what you said. How it helped you. I wanted the same for them.'

'How?' Even though it seemed like a lifetime ago, it had only been a couple of days. 'How on earth did you get this done so quickly?'

'There are some advantages to being King—though right now…' Emir almost smiled, almost met her eyes but did not '…I can't think of many.'

He stood from where he'd knelt with the twins and still could not look at her. He just cleared his throat and said what he had to—did what should have been done long ago.

'Fatima will be sharing in the care of the twins from now on,' Emir said, and Fatima stepped forward.

Not *assisting*, not *helping*, Amy noted.

'She speaks only a little English and she will speak none to the twins: they need to learn our ways now.'

She did not understand what had happened. For as blissful as last night had been she would give it back, would completely delete it, if it had changed things so badly for the girls.

'Emir…' She saw Fatima frown at the familiarity. 'I mean, Your Highness…'

But he didn't allow her to speak, to question, just walked from the nursery, not turning as the twins started to cry. Amy rushed to them.

'Leave them,' Fatima said.

'They're upset.' Amy stood her ground. 'It's been a long day for them.'

'It's been a long day for their country,' Fatima responded. 'It is not just the twins who will mark today— Queen Natasha gave birth to a son at sunrise.'

For a bizarre moment Amy thought of the screams she had heard last night, the cries she had thought might come from Hannah. Yet Natasha had been screaming too. She felt as if the winds were still tricking her, that the desert was always one step ahead, and watched as Fatima picked up the twins and took them to their cots. Fatima turned to go, happy to leave them to cry.

That was why there had been no celebrations, no crowds gathering in the streets. It had been a silent protest from the people—a reminder to their King that he must give them a son. Fatima confirmed it as she switched out the light.

'Unlike Alzan, the future of Alzirz is assured.'

CHAPTER NINE

'THEY won't stay quiet for that length of time unless you are holding them.'

It had been a long morning for Amy. They were practising the formalities for the new Prince's naming ceremony tomorrow, and as it was Fatima who would be travelling with the King and the Princesses, Amy had been tidying the nursery. The windows were open and she had heard their little protests, their cries to be held by their father and eventually, reluctantly, Emir had asked for Amy to be sent down.

'Fatima will be the one holding them.'

'They want you.'

'They cannot have me,' Emir said. She caught his eye then and he saw her lips tighten, because, yes, she knew how that felt. 'I will be in military uniform. I have to salute.' He stopped explaining then—not just because he'd remembered that he didn't have to, but because Nakia, who had been begging for his arms, now held her arms out to Amy. They both knew that there would be no problem if it was Amy who was travelling with him.

Not that Emir would admit it.

Not that she wanted to go.

She could not stand to be around him—could not bear to see the man she loved so cold and distant, not just with her but with the babies who craved his love.

'Can you hold *one*?' She tried to keep the exasperation from her voice as she hugged a tearful Clemira.

'I've tried that. Clemira was jealous,' he explained as Fatima sloped off with Nakia to get her a drink.

'If you can hold one then it needs to be Clemira. Keep Clemira happy and then usually Nakia is fine.' She saw him frown and she could not check her temper because he didn't know something so basic about his own daughters. 'Just hold Clemira,' she said, handing the little girl to him. 'God, it's like I'm speaking in a foreign language.'

'It is one to me!' Emir hissed, and she knew they were not talking about words.

Amy walked off, back to the palace, so she could listen to more tears from the window and do nothing, back to a role that was being eroded by the minute. She looked at the dolls' house and felt like kicking it, felt like ripping down the palace walls, but she stifled a laugh rather than turn into psycho-nanny. She polished the tables in the nursery and changed the sheets, tried to pretend she was working.

'It worked.'

She turned around at the sound of him, stood and stared. He held the twins, both asleep, their heads resting on his shoulders. She waited for Fatima to appear, except she didn't.

'Fatima is getting a headache tablet.' Emir gave a wry smile. 'I said I would bring them up.'

How sad that this was so rare, Amy reminded herself. How sad that something so normal merited an explanation—and, no, she told herself, she did *not* want him.

He went to put Clemira down and she moved to help him.

'I don't know how…' It was almost an apology.

'No.' She took one child from his arms. 'I can't put them down together now either,' she said. 'They're far too big for that.' She lowered Clemira to the mattress as Emir did the same with Nakia. 'It was easier when they were little.' She was jabbering now. 'But I've had to lower the mattress now they're standing.' She could feel him watching her mouth; she feared to look at him—just wanted Fatima to come.

'Amy…'

'They're enjoying the dolls' house.'

She kept her head down because she knew what would happen if she lifted it. She knew because it had almost happened the day before, and the day before that—moments when it had been impossible to deny, when it had almost killed not to touch, when it would have been easier to give in. But if she kissed him now this was what they would be reduced to—furtive snogs when Fatima wasn't around, a quick shag when no one was watching, perhaps? And she was better than that, Amy told herself.

But the tears were coming. She reminded herself that, even if she was crying she was strong.

It was Amy who walked out. Amy who left him watching his children as she headed to her room,

'You need to come home.'

Rather than cry she rang home, desperate for normality, for advice. Though Amy's mum didn't know all that had gone on, even if she did, Amy realised, her advice would be the same.

'Amy, you're not going to change things there. I told you that when you accepted the job.'

'But Queen Hannah…'

'Is dead.'

The harsh words hit home.

'Even Queen Hannah knew that the country would have little time for her daughters. That was why she wanted them to be educated in England.'

'I can't leave them.'

'You have no choice,' her mum said. 'Can you really stand another three years of this?'

No, Amy could not. She knew that as she hung up the phone. The last ten days had been hell. With the anniversary of Queen Hannah's death approaching the palace was subdued, but more than that, worse was to come, for there would be a wedding in a few weeks and how could she be here for that?

She couldn't.

Rather than being upset, Amy had actually been relieved that Fatima had been selected to travel with the King. She had decided that the time she would spend alone must be used wisely, but really her decision was made.

Her mother was right: she had no choice but to go home.

She had to, she told herself as she made it through another night.

By morning, she was already wavering.

She walked into the nursery where two beaming girls stood in their cots and blew kisses. They wriggled and blew bubbles as she bathed them, spat out their food and hated their new dresses, pulled out the little hair ribbons faster than Fatima could tie them.

Amy knew every new tooth in their heads, every smile was a gift for her, and she could not stand to walk away.

Except she had to.

Amy packed cases for the little girls, putting in their swimming costumes, because she knew there were several pools at the Alzirz palace.

'They won't be needing those,' Fatima said. 'I shall not be swimming with them.'

And their father certainly wouldn't, Amy thought, biting down on her lip as she struggled to maintain her composure.

She helped Fatima bring them down to wait for the King and board the helicopter.

'Be good!' Amy smiled at the girls when she wanted to kiss them and hold them. She was terribly aware that this might be the last time she would see them, that perhaps it would be kinder to all of them for her simply to leave while they were away.

As Emir strode across the palace he barely glanced at his daughters, and certainly he did not look in Amy's direction. He was dressed in military uniform as this was to be a formal event and she loathed the fact that this man still moved her. His long leather boots rang out as he walked briskly across the marble floor, only halting when Patel called out to him.

'La.' He shook his head, his reply instant, and carried on walking, but Patel called to him again and there was a brief, rather urgent discussion. Then Emir headed into his study, with Patel following closely behind.

'I'll say goodbye now!' Amy spoke to the girls, for they were getting increasingly fretful and so too was she. She must remember that they were not her babies, that they would be fine with Fatima, that they were not hers to love. But it killed her to turn around and walk up the grand staircase. It was almost impossible not to look around and respond to their tears, but she did her level best—freezing on the spot when she heard Patel's voice.

'The King wishes to speak with you.'

'Me?' Slowly Amy turned around.

'Now,' Patel informed her. 'He is busy—do not keep him waiting.'

It felt like the longest walk of her life. Amy could feel eyes on her as she walked back down the stairs, trying to quieten her mind, trying not to pre-empt what Emir wanted though her heart surely knew. She had never been summoned to speak to him before, and could only conclude that his thoughts were the same as hers—while he was gone, perhaps it was better that she leave.

It was terribly awkward to face him. Not since their night together had it been just them, for Fatima was always around, her silent criticism following Amy's every move. There was no discomfort in Emir, she noted. He looked as uninterested and as imposing as he had the last time that she had stood there, and his voice was flat.

'*You* are to accompany the children to the naming ceremony of the new Prince of Alzirz.'

'Me?' Amy swallowed. This was so not what she had been expecting. 'But I thought it was considered more suitable for Fatima to travel with them? She is more well-versed—'

'This is not a discussion,' Emir interrupted. 'You are to go now and to pack quickly. The helicopter is waiting and I have no intention of arriving late.'

'But—' She didn't understand the change of plan. She needed this time alone and was nervous about travelling with him.

'That will be all,' Emir broke in. 'As I said, I did not call you in here for a discussion.'

It was Patel who offered a brief explanation as she left the office. 'Queen Natasha wishes to discuss English nannies and has said she is looking forward to speaking with you.'

This made sense, because of course a request from Queen Natasha during the new Prince's naming ceremony must be accommodated.

It mattered not that it would break her heart.

Amy packed quickly. She selected three pale blue robes and her nightwear, and threw a few toiletries into her bag. Even if there was the helicopter, the King and his entourage waiting, still she took a moment to pack the twins' swimming costumes and her own bikini—because, unlike Fatima, she *would* swim with the girls.

Emir was at the helicopter, and she felt his air of impatience as she stepped in. He had already strapped in the girls and Fatima gave Amy a long, cool look as she left the aircraft, for it was an honour indeed to travel with the King.

It was not the easiest of journeys, though Emir did hold Nakia as they neared their destination. Again Amy watched his features harden and, looking out of the window, thought perhaps she understood why. Alzirz was celebrating as Alzan should have been on the day of the twins' birthday. The streets around the palace were lined with excited people waving flags. They all watched in excitement as dignitaries arrived for the naming of their new Prince.

How it must kill him to be so polite, Amy mused as they arrived at the palace and the two men kissed on both cheeks. She could feel the simmering hatred between them that went back generations.

Queen Natasha didn't seem to notice it. She was incredibly informal and greeted both Amy and the twins as if they were visiting relatives, rather than a nanny and two young princesses. 'They've grown!' she said.

She looked amazing, Amy noted, wearing a loose fitting white robe embroidered with flowers. She certainly didn't look like a woman who had given birth just a few days ago, and Amy felt drab beside her.

'Come through!' Natasha offered, seeing the twins were more than a little overawed by the large formal gathering. 'I'll take you to the nursery. I have to get the baby ready.' She chatted easily as they walked through the palace. 'I'll introduce you to my nanny, Kuma. She's just delightful, but I really want him to learn English.' She smiled over to Amy. 'You're not looking for a job, by any chance?' she asked shamelessly.

'I'm very happy where I am,' came Amy's appropriate response, though she was tempted to joke that Natasha might find her on the palace doorstep in a couple of days. But, no, Amy realised, even if Natasha *was* nice, even if she *was* easy to talk to, in Alzirz as in Alzan the Royal Nanny would have to be obedient to royal command. She could never put her heart through this again.

Kuma really was delightful. She was far more effusive and loving than Fatima. She smiled widely when she saw the twins, put a finger up to her lips to tell them to hush, and then beckoned them over to admire the new prince. Nakia wasn't particularly interested, but Clemira clapped her hands in delight and nearly jumped out of Amy's arms in an effort to get to the baby. She was clearly totally infatuated with the young Prince.

'He's beautiful,' Amy said. His skin was as dark as Rakhal's, but his hair was blonde like Natasha's, and Amy was suddenly filled with hopeless wonder as to what *her* babies might have been like if Emir was their father. She was consumed again with all she had lost, but then she held Clemira tighter and qualified that—all that she was losing by walking away.

'Would you like to hold him?' Natasha offered.

'He's asleep,' Amy said, because she was terrified if she did that she might break down.

'He has to get up, I'm afraid,' Natasha said. 'I want to feed him before the naming ceremony.' She scooped the sleeping infant out of his crib and, as Kuma took Clemira, handed him to Amy.

Sometimes it had hurt to hold Clemira and Nakia in those early days, to know that she would never hold her own newborn, and the pain was back now, as acute as it had been then, perhaps more so—especially when the two Kings came in. Rakhal was proud and smiling down at his son. Emir was polite as he admired the new Prince. But there was grief in his eyes and Amy could see it. She was angry on behalf of his girls, yet she understood it too—for the laws in this land, like in the desert, could be cruel.

'Come,' Emir told her, 'we should take our places.'

Her place was beside him—for the last time.

She stood where in the future she would not: holding his daughters. She held Clemira and sometimes swapped. Sometimes he held both, when he did not have to salute, so he could give Amy a rest and once, when they girls got restless, she set them on the ground, for it was a long and complicated ceremony.

'They did well,' Emir said as they walked back to the nursery with the weary twins.

'Of course they did!' Amy smiled. 'And if they'd cried

would it really have mattered? Tariq screamed the whole ceremony.'

'He did.' Emir had been thinking the same, knew he must not be so rigid. Except his country expected so little from his daughters and somehow he wanted to show them all they could be. 'Just so you know, the Alzirz nanny will be looking after the twins tonight. They are to make a brief appearance at the party, but she will dress them and take care of that.'

'Why?' Amy asked, and she watched his lips tighten as she questioned him.

'Because.' Emir answered, and he almost hissed in irritation as he felt her blue eyes still questioning him. He refused to admit that he did not know why.

'Because what?'

He wanted to turn around and tell her that he was new to this, that the intricacies of parenthood and royal protocol confused him at times too. Hannah would have been the one handling such things. It was on days like today that the duty of being a single parent was the hardest. Yet he could not say all this, so his voice was brusque when he conceded to respond. 'Sheikha Queen Natasha wants them to be close. It is how things are done. If Prince Tariq comes to stay in Alzan you will look after him for the night.'

'I thought you were rivals?'

'Of course,' Emir said. 'But Queen Natasha is new to this. She does not understand how deep the rivalry is, that though we speak and laugh and attend each other's celebrations there is no affection there.'

'None?'

'None.' His face was dark. 'The twins will be looked after by their nanny tonight. They will be brought back to you in the morning and you will all join me at the formal breakfast tomorrow.'

'But the girls will be unsettled in a new…'

He looked at her. He must have been mad to even have considered it—crazy even to think it. For she would not make a good sheikha queen. There was not one sentence he uttered that went unquestioned, not a thought in her head that she did not voice.

'You keep requesting a night off. Why then, do you complain when you get one?'

Amy reminded herself of her place.

'I'm not complaining.' She gave him a wide smile. 'I'm delighted to have a night off work. I just wasn't expecting it.'

'You can ring down for dinner to be sent to you.'

'Room service?' Amy kept that smile, remembered her place. 'And I've got my own pool… Enjoy the party.'

Of course he did not.

He was less than happy as he took his place at the gathering. He could see the changes Natasha had brought to the rather staid palace, heard laughter in the air and the hum of pleasant, relaxed conversation, and it only served to make him more tense. He held his daughters along with Kuma, and Natasha held her son. He saw Kuma being so good with them and thought perhaps Fatima was not so suitable.

Maybe a gentler nanny would suit the children best,

Emir thought. For he knew that Amy was leaving—had seen it in her eyes—and he held Clemira just a touch tighter before he handed her back to Kuma. His heart twisted again, for they should not be in this world without their mother, and a king should not be worrying about hiring a new nanny.

There was the one big decision that weighed heavily, but there were others that must be made too: their nanny, their schooling, their language, their tears, their grief, their future. He must fathom it all unshared with another who loved them. As a single father he did not know how to be.

Black was his mind as the babies were taken upstairs to the nursery, and he looked over to Rakhal, who stood with his wife by his side. Never had he felt more alone. Tonight he grieved the loss of both Hannah and Amy, and he was so distracted that he did not notice Natasha had made her way over.

'I'm sorry. This must be so difficult for you.'

He shot her a look of scorn. How dared she suggest to his face such a thing? How dared she so blatantly disrespect his girls?

But just as his mouth formed a scathing retort she continued. 'It's Hannah's anniversary soon?'

He closed his eyes for a second. Grief consumed him.

He nodded. 'She is missed.'

Natasha looked at this King with grief in his eyes, who stood apart and polite but alone. 'Where's Amy?'

'She is enjoying a night off,' he clipped, for he did

not like to think about her when he wanted her here at his side.

'I didn't mean for her to stay in her room.' Natasha laughed. 'When I said that my nanny would look after the girls I was hoping that she would join us.'

'She is the nanny,' Emir said curtly. 'She is here only to look after the children.'

'Ah, but she's English,' Natasha sighed and rolled her eyes. 'Have you any idea how nice it feels to have someone here who is from home? I was so looking forward to speaking with her—we never really got a chance earlier.'

'She will bring the twins to breakfast tomorrow,' Emir responded, uncomfortable with such overt friendliness.

When he visited Alzirz, or when duty dictated that Rakhal visit Alzan, there were firm boundaries in place, certain ways things were done, but Natasha seemed completely oblivious to them. The new Sheikha Queen did not seem to understand that it was all an act between himself and Rakhal, that there was still a deep rivalry between the two Kings, born from an innate need to protect the kingdoms, their land and their people. Natasha simply didn't understand that although they spoke politely, although they attended all necessary functions, it was only mutual hate that truly united them.

'I'll have somebody sent to get her,' Natasha persisted.

Emir could only imagine how well that would go down with Amy. She didn't like to be told what to do at the best of times, and this certainly wasn't the best of times.

'She is staff,' Emir said, and that should have ended the conversation—especially as Rakhal had now come over. At least Rakhal knew how things were done. He would terminate this conversation in an instant, would quickly realise that lines were being crossed—unlike this beaming Englishwoman.

What *was* it with them?

Natasha smiled up to her husband. 'I was just saying to Emir that I was hoping to have Amy join us tonight. I do miss having someone from home to chat to at times.'

And love must have softened Rakhal's brain, Emir thought darkly, for instead of looking to Emir, instead of gauging his response, instead of playing by the unspoken rules he looked to his wife.

'Then why don't you have someone go to the suite and see if she would care to join us?' he said. Only then did he address Emir. 'Normally Natasha's brother and his fiancée would be here tonight, to join in the celebrations, but they are in the UK for another family commitment and couldn't make it.'

Emir did not care. Emir had no desire to know why Natasha's brother and his fiancée could not be here. Had Rakhal forgotten for a moment that this was all a charade? That there was more hate in the air than the palatial ballroom could readily hold? For when he thought of his daughters, thought of his late wife and the rule Alzirz refused to revoke, Emir could happily pull his knife.

'It would be unfair to her.' Emir did his best to keep

his voice even. 'She will have only her working clothes with her.'

'I'm not that mean.' Natasha smiled. 'I wouldn't do that to her. I'll have some clothes and maidens sent to her room to help prepare her. I'll arrange it now.'

There was so much he would like to say—Emir was not used to having any decision questioned—and yet protocol dictated politeness even in this most uncomfortable of situations. He could just imagine Amy, in her present mood, if one of the servants were to knock at her door and insist that she come down and join in with the feasting and celebrations. A smile he was not expecting almost spread his lips at the very thought, but he rescued his features from expression and nodded to the waiting Queen.

'Very well, if you wish to have Amy here, I shall go now and speak to her. I will ask her to come down, though she may already have retired for the night.'

Natasha smiled back at him and Emir could not understand why she could not see the hate in his eyes as he spoke. He strode out of the grand ballroom.

As he did so Rakhal turned to his wife. 'You are meddling.'

'Of course I'm not,' Natasha lied.

But her husband knew her too well. He had had the teachings too and his wife seduced with her beauty, dazzled like the sun low in the desert. He knew his wife was plotting now.

'Natasha? You do *not* interfere in such things.'

'I'm not,' Natasha insisted. 'You have to work the

room and I would like someone to talk to in my own language. Amy seems nice.'

But of course she *was* meddling. Natasha had seen King Emir's eyes linger a little too long on Amy at times, when the nanny hadn't been aware he was watching her. She had seen the sadness behind his eyes too. And, yes, perhaps it was for selfish reasons also that she was interfering just a little, but the thought of someone from her own land to be beside her at these endless functions...

She knew that Emir must soon take a new sheikha queen, and if that queen happened to be Amy—well, who could blame her for giving Cupid a little nudge? She loved her new country—loved it so much—but the rivalry between the two nations, the bitterness between them and all the impossible rules she simply could not abide, and she was quite sure that Amy must feel the same.

Amy had not retired for the night as Emir was silently hoping as he walked through the palace to her room.

She had rung down for dinner and enjoyed a delicious feast—or tried to. She had been thinking about the girls, thinking about Emir and trying to picture her future without them. But it was too hard. So she had telephoned home, hoping for a long chat, but everybody must be at work because she had spoken to endless answering machines. And, yes, a night off was what she had asked for, and the Alzirz palace was as sumptuous as even the most luxurious hotel, but after an hour or two of reading and painting her toenails she had grown restless. Simply because it was there for the taking Amy put on her bikini and went for a long swim in her own private pool.

It was glorious—the temperature of the water perfect, the area shaded with date palms for complete privacy and protection from the fierce Alzirz sun during the day. Lying on her back, she could see the stars peeking through. But just as she started to relax, just as she had convinced herself to stop worrying about leaving Alzan, at least for tonight, she heard a bell ring from her suite.

Perhaps the maid had come to take her tray, Amy thought and, climbing out of the pool, went to answer the door. She had left her towel behind so she tied on a flimsy silk robe and called for the maid to come in. As the bell rang again Amy realised that perhaps she didn't understand English and opened the door—completely taken aback to find Emir standing there.

'It was not my intention to disturb you.' It was close to an apology, but not quite. He was a king summoning a servant, Emir reminded himself—it was a compliment in itself that he had come to her door. 'You are required downstairs.'

Amy frowned. 'Is there a problem with one of the twins?'

'Not at all.' He felt more than a little uncomfortable, especially as two damp triangles were becoming visible where her wet bikini seeped into the silk of her gown. 'Sheikha Queen Natasha has requested that you join in the celebrations.'

'No, thanks.' Amy gave a tight smile and went to

close the door, but his booted foot halted it. 'Excuse me!' was Amy's brittle response.

'You don't understand,' Emir said, but he did remove his boot. 'That is why I came personally—to explain things to you. The Queen is hosting the party. It is the Queen who has requested you to come down, not me. It would be rude...'

'Rude for who?' Amy responded—because she did not want to go down there, did not want to be Natasha's little project for the night. She particularly did not want to spend any more time with Emir than she had to— things were already difficult enough.

Now he was at her door, and she could feel the cool wetness of her gown, knew from the flick of his eyes downwards that he had seen it too—that she might just as well not be wearing it. She was frantic to have him gone.

'It's rude to give me a night off and then revoke it!' She went to close the door again, did not want to pro- long this discussion.

Emir would not let things be, and unless she slammed the door in his face she'd have to stand there and listen as he spoke on.

'If the twins were awake you would be expected to bring them down.'

'The twins are not in my care tonight.'

'That is not the point.' Emir's voice was stern. He was less than impressed with Amy's behaviour—especially as a maid came into the corridor and bowed her head to him. He stood there bristling with indignation as she went in and retrieved Amy's dinner tray. 'It is not right for me to be seen standing here and arguing with...'

'An employee?' she finished for him. But she accepted it was not fitting behaviour, and once the maid had gone she held the door further open for him. 'I have nothing to wear to a party. I haven't showered. I'm not ready...'

'That is being taken care of.' He blocked her excuses as Natasha had blocked his. 'Queen Natasha is having some clothes and some maidens sent here to your room.' He turned to go. 'I expect you to be down there within half an hour.'

'Emir...'

There was a plea in her voice, a plea he had heard once before—the sound of her begging. He remembered her writhing beneath him and he hardly dared turn around.

'Don't make me do this. Go and enjoy the party on your own—make an excuse for me that is fitting. I don't know anything about...'

'Enjoy it?' He did turn around then, and he wished she were dressed—wished she looked anything other than she did now. For the gown was completely see-through. Three triangles taunted him. He could see the hard peaks of her nipples, see the flush on her neck. He should not be in this room with her for a whole set of reasons other than protocol. 'You will get dressed.'

When still she shook her head, he lost his temper. He spoke harsh angry words. It was far safer than pushing her onto the bed.

'You really think that I want to be down there? You really think that I'm enjoying making small talk, pretending that I do not hate them? If it were not for them…'

His black eyes met hers, as angry and savage as they had been the day she had first challenged him, but it did not scare her as it had then. His anger was not aimed at her, nor his words, Amy was quite sure. This would not be of his choosing, for this remote, private man to pour some of the pain out.

'Amy, please…'

Not once had he pleaded, not once that she knew of, and this came with a roar from the heart.

'I am asking you to please make this night easier for me—I am in hell down there.'

And he was. He was in hell tonight and no one knew. He could not share his burden; he carried it alone for he was King. He remembered his status and was ashamed of his words, his loss of control. But there was no smart retort from Amy. This time she stood stunned, as he was at his revelation, and he could see tears pooling in her eyes. She had glimpsed a little of his pain.

It was not that her mouth found his, nor was it his mouth which sought hers. Neither initiated the kiss. They simply joined, and he felt the bliss of oblivion. The pain ended for a moment and relief was instant. There was release and escape as her wet body pressed to his. He had craved her since that night, had wanted her each minute, and her tongue as it twisted with his, the heat of her skin through the damp gown, told him she had craved him as much.

She had.

His uniform was rough beneath her fingers, his mouth desperate on hers, his erection as fierce as his passion. She could feel him hard in her centre. It was happening again and it must not.

'Emir,' she whimpered, pulling her mouth back from his, though she did not want him to stop kissing her. Her lips ached for more as they moved from his. Regretting their departure, they returned, speaking into his mouth. 'We said just once.'

'Then get dressed,' he said, and his hands peeled off the damp robe, and his fingers worked the knot at the back of her bikini.

She moaned in his mouth as he stroked the aching peaks; his hands moved to her bottom and he pulled her up till her legs twined around him. This was way more than a kiss getting out of hand. The bed seemed an impossible distance, clothes their only barrier.

She felt the cold of brass buttons on her skin as he kissed her onto the bed, pulling at the damp bikini while his other hand moved to unbuckle his belt. And Amy realised her hands were helping his, for she was through with thinking. She could make decisions later, could work things out then. Right now she simply had to have him.

And she would have.

He would have had her.

Had the bell not rung again.

He looked down at where she lay, a breath away from

coming. Regret was in both their eyes—not just at the interruption, but at what had taken place.

'That didn't just happen,' Amy said. Except it had. And now, even more so than before, it was impossible for her to stay.

No longer could their night in the desert be put down to a one-off. The attraction between them was undeniable and yet soon he would be taking a wife.

'It won't happen again,' Emir said.

They both knew he was lying.

He buckled up his belt, took her by the hand and led her to the bathroom. He checked his appearance in the mirror and then called to open the door. He watched as maidens bought in an array of clothing. He told them that Amy was in the shower and they must quickly prepare her to be brought down, and then he called out to her where she sat, crouched and shivering on the bathroom floor.

'You will get ready quickly.' He spoke as a king would when addressing a belligerent servant. He tried to remember his place and so too must she. 'Queen Natasha is waiting for you.'

CHAPTER TEN

'TOMORROW we leave for the desert.'

Natasha was irritating. She insisted on chatting as if they were old friends. And yet, Emir conceded, he would find *any* conversation annoying now, for his mind was only on Amy and what had just taken place.

Fool, he said to himself. Fool for not resisting. Fool for being weak.

And fool because tonight he would take her, only to lose her again in the morning.

Only to have her leave.

'I'm looking forward to it.' Natasha persisted with their one-way conversation. 'After all the celebrations and pomp surrounding the birth, it will be nice to get some peace.'

Now Emir did respond—and very deliberately he chose to get things wrong. 'I'm sure that the Bedouins will take good care of him.' He saw the flare of horror in Natasha's eyes.

'Oh, it's not for that. It's way too soon to even *think* of being parted from him. That doesn't have to happen until he turns one.'

'*Before* he turns one,' Emir said, enjoying one pleasure in this night.

Two pleasures, he corrected, his mind drifting to Amy again. But he must stay focussed. He must concentrate on the conversation rather than anticipating her arrival, rather then remembering what had just happened. And perhaps it was time to give Natasha a taste of the medicine he had so recently sampled.

'I handed over the girls last week. Your husband was kind enough to grant a concession that they only stay in the desert for one night, given what happened to their mother.' He watched Natasha's lips tighten as he reminded her, none too gently, that her son would be in the desert for several nights—unless, of course, he lost his mother too. Unless he was forced to be weaned early, as Emir's daughters had been.

'How did the girls get on?' Natasha attempted to make it sound like a polite enquiry, as if she were asking after the girls rather than about what she could expect for her own son.

Emir knew that—it was the reason he didn't mollify her with his response. 'They screamed, they wept and they begged,' Emir said, watching as her face grew paler with each passing word. 'But they are the rules.' Emir shrugged. 'My daughters have been forced to be strong by circumstance, and so they survived it.'

He stopped twisting the knife then—not to save her from further distress, but because at that moment it seemed to Emir that everything simply stopped.

He had wondered far too often what Amy might look

like out of that robe—he had pictured her not just in her nightdress, or naked beneath him, but dressed as his Queen.

She stepped into that vision now and claimed it, and deep in his gut a knife twisted.

She was dressed in a dark emerald velvet gown, her lips painted red and her eyes skilfully lined with kohl. Her hair was down. But nothing, not even the work of a skilled make-up artist, could temper the glitter in her eyes and the blush of her cheeks that their kiss had evoked. A riot of ringlets framed her face.

The world was cruel, Emir decided, for it taunted him with what he could not have. It showed him exactly how good it could have been, had the rules allowed her to join him, to be at his side.

Little more than a year ago she would have been veiled and hidden. A year ago he would not have had to suffer the tease of her beauty. But there was a new Sheikha Queen in Alizirz and times were changing.

Amy was changing.

Before his eyes, as she chatted with Natasha, he witnessed the effortless seduction of her body. For even as she turned slightly away from him her gestures seemed designed for him. She threw her head back and laughed, and then, as he knew it would, her hand instinctively moved to cover the scar on her throat. She twisted her hair around her fingers and he fought his desire to snake a hand around her waist. He wanted to join in the conversation as he would with a partner, to squeeze her waist just once to remind her that soon it would be over and soon they would be alone.

He put down the glass he was gripping rather than break it.

He turned away, but her laughter filled his ears.

Emir tried to remember the shy woman who had first entered the palace. He had not noticed her—or at least not in that way. His mind had been too consumed with worry for his wife, who had been fading by the day, for him to notice Amy. He wanted that back. He wanted the invisible woman she had been then.

But she wasn't invisible now.

She was there before his eyes.

And for her he might not be King.

'Thank you so much for coming down.' Natasha kissed Amy's cheek an agonising couple of hours later. 'It was lovely to talk.'

'It was my pleasure,' Amy said. 'Thank you for the invitation.'

She meant not a word.

And neither did Emir as he too politely thanked Rakhal and headed to the stairs.

She could not do this.

She stepped out into a fragrant garden, breathed in the blossom and begged it to quell the hammering of her mind. She listened to the fountain that should soothe. Except it did not, for she understood now a little of what Emir had meant about being in hell.

To stand apart while their minds were together, to ignore the other while their bodies silently screamed, was a potent taste of what might be to come when he married.

If she stayed.

Her fury was silent as she walked to her room, but she knew what she had to do. Her eyes took in the empty bed, but the scent of him confirmed that he was there. She saw that the doors were open and looked beyond them to where he stood by the pool. His jacket was undone and his eyes met hers. She shook her head, for forbidden lovers they must not be.

'No.'

Brave in her decision, she walked towards him, her anger building as she did so, reminding herself of all she did not admire about this man. She tried to dull the passion he triggered, determined that it be over.

'I'm through with this, Emir.' She made herself say it. 'I don't even like you.'

He simply looked.

His silence let her speak.

'I could never be with a man willing to ignore his children—despite my health problems, despite the fact I can't have children. Even without that I'd never have said yes.' She was lying, she could hear it, but her mind begged for it to be true. 'How can I love a man who doesn't care about his children?'

She watched his eyes narrow. Perhaps this was not the conversation he'd been expecting. It was a mistress he wanted, Amy reminded herself, not an argument about his children. But her racing heart surely stopped for a moment when his low voice delivered a response *she* was not expecting.

'Never say that.'

She thought he might throw the drink he was holding in her face. He might just as well have, because nothing could have shocked her more than the passion in his voice when his next words were delivered.

'I love my children.'

Except his actions did not show it, even if his words sounded true.

'You say that…'

'Trust that I have my daughters' best interests at heart.'

And she looked at his pain ravaged face and into eyes that glittered with the flames of hell. Somehow she did trust him. Despite all evidence to the contrary, she did believe him.

What did this man do to her? she begged of herself.

'Please, Emir, go.'

She could not think when he was around; she lost herself when he was near.

'Go,' she said, and walked to the bedroom.

'Go.' She sobbed as still by the pool he stood.

And she knew it was hopeless. For to leave he would have to walk past her, and not to touch would be an impossible ask.

'*Go.*' She begged, even as she undressed for him, crying with shame at her own need.

She pulled down the zipper, slipped off the gown as he walked now towards her, her actions opposing her words as she removed her bra. Emir unbuckled his belt while entering the bedroom. Even then she shook her head. Even then she denied it as she took down her panties.

'No…' She changed her plea. She was sobbing as he kissed her down onto the bed, but she was grateful for the mattress that met her back for she got the gift of his full weight pressed into her. 'We mustn't…' She pushed at his bare chest but her fingers attempted to grip his skin, her nails wanted to dig in and leave her mark. 'Emir, you know that we mustn't…'

He took her hands and captured her wrists, held them over her head and hungrily kissed her. Then with words he fought for what they both needed tonight. 'We must.'

His words were truthful, and he was fierce. Even naked he ruled her as he told her that he would make it work.

'We *will* be together…'

'There is no way…'

'I will find a way,' he told her. 'I will make this work. I will come to you in the night-time and in later years I will visit you and the girls in London.'

'Your mistress…?'

'More than a mistress,' he said between frantic kisses. 'You will care for the twins. You will raise them.'

Was it possible to love and hate at the same time?

To be filled with both want and loathing as he bound her to him, but with a life of lies?

He offered her everything, yet gave her nothing.

A life with no voice, Amy realised, and it was then that she found hers.

'No.'

His hands released their grip but she did not push him off. Instead she wrapped her arms around his back. 'This ends tonight.'

Their bodies knew that she lied.

All night he had been wanting her, and all night she had been waiting for him. They met now and their kisses tasted of fury for the future they could not have. She felt his anger as he stabbed inside her—anger at the rules that denied him the woman he wanted by his side. But for now there was an outlet, and he was animal. He bucked inside her and she lifted her hips to him. Their eyes locked in a strange loathing of what they might make the other do so easily. So easily she came to him.

And so deeply he delivered.

He knew she would shout. He felt her lungs fill and the tension in her throat as he shot into her; he felt her scream even as it rose, for his body and his soul knew her.

She came in a way she never had before, tightened in possession as he drove her further. She was grateful for his hand that smothered her mouth, furious that the only restraint he could muster was to stifle her screams with the hand she could never take.

She told herself she hated him.

Reminded herself she did not want to be his wife.

She was relieved it was over, surely?

They lay for a suitable while, waiting for normality

to return, for the madness to subside, for him to rise from her bed and head to his own. But as he went to do so Amy's hand reached out to him and it was then that she cried, for she had proved that she lied.

Her fierce vow that it would end tonight had already been downgraded to the morning.

CHAPTER ELEVEN

MORNING came whether she wanted it to or not.

The sun did not care that it ended them.

It did what it was born to—it rose and dictated that their time was over.

She knew Emir was awake next to her. She watched the fingers of light spread across the floor and before they reached the bed she felt his hand on her hip, then her waist. She closed her eyes as he tucked her body towards him, felt his erection and wanted to wake every morning to him. She did not want to be a woman who settled for a slice of his life—didn't want to fit into allocated times. Yet had the phone not rung Amy knew that she would have.

'The twins are on their way.' Her voice was urgent as she hung up, 'Kuma is bringing them now.'

There was no time for Emir to dress and leave, but he dealt with it instantly. Picking up the uniform he had so readily discarded last night, he headed to her en suite bathroom. This time it was he who hid there.

More than a little breathless, Amy searched for something to put on. Her panic was broken by a smile as a well-manicured hand appeared from the bathroom, holding her robe.

'You need to relax,' he warned her.

It was far easier said than done, because even as she tied the knot on her robe there was a knock on the door. When she opened it, there stood Kuma holding the smiling twins, who were clearly delighted to see Amy.

'They had a wonderful night,' Kuma explained, putting them down. The twins crawled happily in. 'Clemira is really taken with the new Prince, but I think they both want someone more familiar this morning. How was your night?' Kuma beamed. 'I hear you were asked to join in the celebrations.'

'I was.' Amy nodded, nervous and trying not to show it, attempting to carry on the conversation as if she *didn't* have the King of Alzan hiding in her room.

But thankfully Kuma did not prolong things. She wanted to get back to her young charge, so she wished Amy good morning and reminded her that the twins were expected to join the royals for breakfast in hour. 'I hope that your time in Alzirz has been pleasant,' Kuma said and then she was gone.

As was their time.

Like two homing devices, or observant kittens, the twins had made a beeline for the bathroom door, their dear little hands banging, calling out to the rather big secret behind it.

'She's gone.' Amy's face was burning as the door opened and out stepped Emir. She had expected him to be wearing his uniform, but instead he was dressed in a more standard thick white towelling robe.

'I will say that I'm looking for the twins if someone sees me in the corridor.' He had already worked out how to discard all evidence. 'If you can pack my uniform...?'

'Of course.' Amy nodded, telling herself that this was what it would be like were they to continue.

The twins let out a squeal of delight as they realised the two people they loved most in the world were together in the same room. And the man who had asked her to believe that he had his daughters' best interests at heart, even if he did not always show it, the man who so often did not reveal his feelings, confused her again as he picked up the girls and greeted them tenderly.

He went to hand them to Amy, but changed his mind.

'I hear you take them swimming at the palace?'

'Every day,' Amy said. 'They love it.'

Go, her eyes begged him.

'Show me,' he said.

And so she dressed them in their little costumes, put on yesterday's red bikini, and now he wasn't a distant sheikh king who watched from the poolside. Instead he made do with his surprisingly modern black hipsters and took to the water with his daughters.

Amy was suddenly shy.

It felt wrong at first to be in the water with him— wrong to join them, wrong when he splashed her, when he caught her unguarded, when he pulled her into the trio. But after a moment she joined in.

Amy knew what was wrong—it was because it felt

right. For a little while they were a family—a family on vacation, perhaps—and they left their troubles behind.

Emir was a father to his daughters this morning, and the twins delighted at the love and affection surrounding them. Emir splashed around with Nakia, hoisted Clemira on his shoulders as she giggled in delight. And in the water with them was Amy, and he did not leave her out. They stopped for a kiss.

The pool was shaded by the palms, but the sun did not let them be. It dotted through the criss-cross of leaves and glimmered on the water. It chased and it caught up and there was nothing they could do.

'Let me get a photo,' Amy said. 'For the nursery.' She wanted the girls to have a picture with their father—a picture of the three of them together and happy.

This was how it could be, Amy realised as she looked at the image on her phone, looked at the people she felt were her family.

An almost family.

It wasn't enough.

'Get the girls ready,' Emir said as they walked back inside. 'And then bring them down to breakfast.'

She blinked at the change in him, and then she understood—in a few moments they would face each other at the breakfast table, would be expected to carry on as if nothing was between them.

Emir was back to being King.

CHAPTER TWELVE

AND so the feast continued.

The birth of the new Prince demanded an extensive celebration, and Amy could see the tiredness in Natasha's eyes as she greeted the never ending stream of guests.

It was a semi-formal breakfast. There was a long, low table groaning with all the food Amy had come to love in her time there, but she was not here to socialise or to eat, but to make sure that the twins behaved. It was assumed she would have eaten before the Princesses rose.

Of course, she was starving.

Starving, her eyes told him. He watched them linger on the *sfiha* he reached for. He was at Rakhal's table, and it would be rude not to indulge, but it tasted of guilt on his tongue.

He was weak for her. Emir knew that.

And weak kings did not make good decisions.

'Have something!' Natasha insisted, sitting next to Amy as she fed the girls. 'For goodness' sake.'

'I already ate,' Amy responded. 'But thank you.'

'I insist,' Natasha said. She saw her husband's eyes

shoot her a warning but she smiled sweetly back, for there was something that Rakhal did not know—something she had not had time to tell him.

When he had gone riding that morning she had taken tea on the balcony—had heard the sound of a family together, had felt the love in the air. She knew only too well the strain of being considered an unsuitable bride, yet things were changing here in Alzirz and they could change too in Alzan.

Amy did her best to forget she was hungry as she fed the twins. Did her best not to give in to the lure of his voice, nor turn her head when he spoke. She tried to treat him with the distant, quiet reverence that any servant would.

The twins were a little too loud, but very funny, smiling at their audience as they entertained, basking in the attention. As the breakfast started to conclude she wiped their faces, ready to take them back to their room and to pack for the journey home.

Not home, she reminded herself. She was returning to the palace.

With the evidence of last night in her case.

Just for a brief moment she lost focus, daydreamed for a second too long, considering the impossible as she recalled last night. Of course Clemira noticed her distraction.

Clemira demanded attention. 'Ummi!'

Amy snapped her eyes open, prayed for a futile second that no one had heard. But just in case they hadn't Nakia followed the leader as she always did.

'Ummi!'

'Amy!' She forced out the correction, tried to sound bright and matter of fact, but her eyes were filling with tears, her heart squeezing as still the twins insisted on using the Arabic word for mummy.

'I'll go and get them ready for the journey home.' She picked up Clemira, her hands shaking, grateful when Natasha stood and picked up Nakia.

Natasha was the perfect hostess, instantly realising the *faux pas* the little girls had made. Doing her best to smooth things over, she followed Amy out of the room with Nakia. But as Amy fled past the table she caught a brief glimpse of Emir. His face was as grey as the incoming storm—and there *would* be a storm. Amy was certain of it.

The tension chased her from the room. The realisation that continuing on was becoming increasingly impossible surrounded her now. She wished Natasha would leave when they reached the nursery, wished she would not try to make conversation, because Amy was very close to tears.

'I will go back and explain to them.' Natasha was practical. 'I know how difficult things can be at times, but once I explain how similar the words are…' She tried to make things better and, perhaps selfishly, yearned for Amy to confide in her. The only thing missing in her life was a girlfriend—someone from home to chat to, to compare the country's ways with. 'Anyway, it's surely natural that they would think of you in that way.'

'I'm not their mother.'

'I know.' Natasha misinterpreted Amy's tears as she cuddled Clemira into her—or perhaps she didn't. Her words were the truth. After all, she had heard them as a family that morning. 'It must be so hard for you—to detach, I mean, you've known them since the day they were born.'

'Why would it be hard for me to detach?' Amy met the Queen's eyes and frowned, her guard suddenly up. Natasha sounded as if she really did know how hard it was for her, and she must never know—no one must ever know. But Amy was suddenly certain that Natasha did, and her attempt to refute it was desperate. 'I'm a royal nanny—as Kuma is.'

Natasha knew she had meddled too far, but she stepped back a little too late. 'Of course you have to keep a professional detachment.' Natasha nodded. Amy was not going to confide in her, she realised, so she tried to salvage the conversation as best she could. 'After all, you will have your own babies one day.'

Amy was tired—so tired of women who assumed, who thought it was so straightforward, that parenthood was a God-given right. Maybe, too, she was tired of covering up, tired of saying the right thing, tired of putting others at ease as they stomped right over her heart.

She looked up at Natasha. 'Actually, I can't have children.' She watched the blush flood Natasha's cheeks and then fade till her skin was pale. She knew then that somehow Natasha knew about herself and Emir—perhaps they had given themselves away last night at the celebration? Perhaps they'd ignored each other just a touch too much? Or was their love simply visible to all?

Yes, love, Amy thought with a sob of bitterness—a bitterness that carried through to her words. 'So, yes, while it might have been a touch awkward for everyone at breakfast to hear the twins call me Ummi, for me it hurts like hell. Now...' She wanted her tears to fall in private, for Natasha was not her friend. 'If you'll excuse me...?'

'Amy—'

'Please!' Amy didn't care if it was the Queen she was dismissing, didn't care if this was Natasha's home. She just wanted some privacy, some space. 'Can you please just leave it?'

Had she looked up she would have seen tears in Natasha's eyes too as she nodded and left her. And Natasha's eyes filled again when she took her place back at the table and saw Emir sit tall and proud, but removed.

Natasha had seen that expression before. It was the same as it had been when he had lost Hannah. Grey and strained, his features etched in grief.

As Emir looked up, as he saw the sympathy in Natasha's expression, he knew she had been told—that Amy must have somehow confided the truth.

That it was impossible for her to be Queen.

CHAPTER THIRTEEN

HE MET the day he dreaded and rose at dawn.

His prayers were deep.

Guilt lashed like a whip to his back. He had not allowed a year to pass before he touched another woman and deep was Emir's prayer for forgiveness; yet there was nothing to forgive, his soul told him. That wasn't the prayer that she needed to hear.

He could feel Hannah reaching from the grave, desperate for him to say it, for without those words how could she rest?

'I will make the best decision.'

Still it was not what she wanted; still he was forced to look deeper. Yet he dared not.

He visited the nursery. There was Amy, curled up on the sofa, reading a book with the twins. He could not look at her. Later they rode with him in the back of a car to the edge of the desert, to visit Hannah and pay their respects.

Amy sat in the vehicle and watched the trio. When he turned to walk back to the car she watched him unseen, for the windows were heavily tinted. She ached to comfort him, to say the right thing, but it was not and could never be her place.

It had been five days since they'd returned from Alzirz.

Five days of ignoring her, Emir thought as they drove back.

Five days of denial.

And a lifetime of it to look forward to.

She could see his pain, could feel his pain as they walked back into the palace, and she proved herself a liar again.

'I'm sorry today is so hard.'

He could not look at her.

'If…' She stopped herself, but with a single word it was out there: *If it gets too tough, if things get too hard, if the night is too long…*

He turned and did not wait for the guards to open his office door; instead he strode in, saw Patel and the elders quickly shuffle some papers. But Emir knew. He did not attempt politeness, nor even ask to see what was written. He just strode to the desk and picked them up. He looked through them for a moment, a muscle flickering in his cheek as he read them.

'Sheikha Princess Jannah of Idam?' He looked to Patel—a look that demanded a rapid answer.

'She has many brothers.' Patel's voice was a touch high from fear. It was his turn to be on the receiving end of the King's anger and he did not like it one bit. 'She has many brothers. Her father too has many brothers…'

'Sheikha Noor?' Emir's voice was low, but no less ferocious.

'A strong male lineage also…' Patel's words were rapid. 'And a family of longevity.'

'Today is the anniversary of the death of Queen Hannah, and instead of being on your knees in prayer you sit and discuss the next royal intake.'

'In my defence, Your Highness, we really need to address this. The people are impatient. Today they mourn, but tomorrow they will start asking…'

'Silence!' Emir roared. It was not today that he dreaded, he realised, but tomorrow, when he must move on, and the tomorrow after that one and the next. 'You will show respect to your departed Sheikha Queen. You will give thanks for the Royal Princesses's mother.'

'Of course.'

'You do not mention the Princesses here, I note,' Emir said. 'You do not seem concerned in the least as to the new Queen's suitability for *them*.' He cursed his aide and Patel did not wait to be told to leave. Neither did the elders. Within a moment the room was cleared and he stood alone. He did not want the day over—did not want it to be tonight. For it was killing him not to go to Amy, not to draw on the comfort she would give, not to have her again and again.

He was an honourable man.

And soon he must take a wife.

He looked again to the list that had been drawn up, tried to picture himself standing with his new bride at his side while his lover, the woman he really wanted, stood next to him, holding his children as he made solemn vows.

It had never been harder to be King.

He picked up his phone. It was answered in an instant and he was grateful, for given two seconds he might have paused and changed his mind.

'Send the children's nanny to speak with me,' Emir said, and then specified, 'the English one.' He could only stand and wait to do this to her, to himself, but once, Emir needed it done this very moment. He had to bring things to a conclusion tonight—needed a clear head with which to make his decision. And with Amy in the palace it was an impossible ask. He could not get through this night with her near and yet out of reach to him.

Not an army, only distance could hold him back from her tonight.

'Are you in trouble again?' Fatima asked the minute Amy returned from her swim with the twins.

Amy was starting to warm to Fatima, and the twins were too—she was very firm, but she was also fair and kind and, perhaps more importantly, she had grown fond of the twins. They were taking over her heart, which was something they could easily do.

'Trouble?' Amy smiled, assuming the kitchen had rung again to complain about her meal choices for the twins. Or perhaps they had made too much noise when they were swimming on such a revered day. 'Probably. Why?'

'I just took a phone call and the King wishes to speak with you immediately.'

At some level she had known this was coming. Deep down she had known it was only a matter of time before it happened. She just hadn't expected it today.

She had thought they might have this night, but she could not hope for anything as Fatima suggested that she tidy herself before she met with him, because Amy's hair was still wet from the pool.

'I don't think that will be necessary,' Amy said— there seemed no point having a mini makeover when you were about to be fired.

She looked around the nursery to the twins, who were now hungrily eating the grapes Fatima was passing to them, counting them out in Arabic as she did so.

They would be okay, Amy told herself as she took the long walk through the palace.

The guards opened the door as she approached, and reminded her to bow her head until the King spoke.

She discarded that advice.

Amy walked in with her head held high, determined she would leave with grace. Except the sight of him, standing tall but so remote, made her want to be his lover again, to salvage what little they had. She opened her mouth to plead her case, but his eyes forbade her to speak and it was Emir who spoke first.

'You will leave late this afternoon. I have arranged all transport. That gives you some time to spend with the girls. I have a new nanny starting. She will assist Fatima.'

Yes, she'd wanted to do this with grace, but at the final hurdle she faltered—could not stand the thought of yet another woman taking care of *her* girls. 'No! You know the girls are better off with me—you said it yourself.'

'I did not realise then that they were learning only to speak in English, that they knew nothing of our ways…'

'They would know a whole lot more if you spent more time with them. They don't need another nanny!'

'She will be more suitable. We must hold on to the ways of old.'

'What about London? What about their education and all Queen Hannah wanted for them?'

'*This* is their land.'

She really would never see them. Amy knew this was a goodbye for ever, and she forgot to be brave and strong. 'What you said before…about me being your lover…' She could not bear to leave—would give anything, even her pride, if it meant that she could stay. Because it was three times her heart was being broken here. She was losing three of the people she most loved. 'What you said about me raising the girls in London…'

'It is the type of thing men say when they want a woman in their bed. It is the type of thing a man says when his thoughts are not clear.' Completely devoid of emotion, he threw the most hurtful words at her, a round of bullets shot rapidly straight to her heart. He didn't stop firing. 'You really think I would choose *you* for that role?' He let out an incredulous laugh at the very thought. 'Here a mistress is a man's respite—a woman he can go to to relax and not be bombarded with everyday trivialities. You would be most unsuitable.'

He was right.

Amy felt the colour flood back to her cheeks, and she felt the fire in her soul return too—a fire that had been doused by the accident, that had flared only on occasion in recent times. But it was back now, and burning even more brightly, fuelling her to stand up to him.

'I *would* be a most unsuitable mistress.' She gathered her dignity and held on to it tightly, determined that she would never let it go again. She could hardly believe the offer she had made him just a few moments before and she told him why. 'I'd be a terrible mistress, in fact. I'd bombard you with news about your daughters. Every achievement, every tear I would share with you. I would busy your distinguished brain with my voice and my opinions, and…' She walked over to him—right over to where he stood. He lifted his jaw, did not look at her as she spoke, but it did not stop her. Her words told him all he would be missing. 'And there would be *no* relaxing.'

'Go!' Emir said, and still he could not look at her.

Amy knew why. He was resisting his need for her, refusing the comfort that was within his grasp.

'Go and spend time with the twins.'

'I'm going now to pack,' Amy said. 'I'll spend the afternoon at the airport.'

There was nothing left to say to him, no point pleading with him, nothing she could do for the twins. She was an employee, that was all.

But she had been his lover.

'We both know why you need me out of here today, Emir. We both know you'd be in my bed tonight, and heaven forbid you might show emotion—might tell me what's going on in the forbidden zone of your mind. You can stop worrying about that now—I'll be gone within the hour,' Amy said. 'All temptation will be removed.'

'You flatter yourself.'

'Actually, I haven't for a while. But I will from now on.'

Amy had once read that people who had been shot sometimes didn't even know, that they could carry on, fuelled by adrenaline, without realising they had been wounded. She hadn't believed it at the time, but she knew it to be true now.

She packed her belongings and rang down to arrange a car to take her to the airport. There wasn't an awful lot to pack. She'd arrived with hardly anything and left with little more—save a heart so broken she didn't dare feel it.

And because it was a royal nanny leaving, because in this land there were certain ways that had to be adhered to, Emir came out and held Clemira while Fatima held Nakia.

Amy did the hardest thing she had ever done, but it was necessary, she realised, the right thing to do. She kissed the little girls goodbye and managed to smile and not scare them. She should probably curtsy to *him*, but Amy chose not to. Instead she climbed into the car, and after a wave to the twins she deliberately didn't look back.

Never again would she let him see her cry.

CHAPTER FOURTEEN

HE HEARD the twins wail and sob late into the night. He need not have—his suite was far from the nursery—but he walked down there several times and knew Fatima could not quieten them.

'They will cry themselves out soon,' Fatima said, putting down her sewing and standing as he approached once again. She had put a chair in the hallway while she waited for the twins to give in to sleep.

Still they refused to.

He could not comfort them. They did not seem to want his comfort, and he did not know what to do.

He walked from the nursery not towards his suite but to Amy's quarters. It was a route he took in his head perhaps a thousand times each night. It was a door he fought not to open again and again. Now that he did, it was empty—the French doors had been left open to air it, so he didn't even get the brief hit of her scent. The bed had been stripped and the wardrobes, when he looked, were bare, so too the drawers. The bathroom had been thoroughly cleaned. Like a mad man, he went through the bathroom cupboards, and then back out to the bedroom, but there was nothing of her left.

He walked back to the nursery where the babies were still screaming as Fatima sewed. When she rose as he approached he told her to sit and walked into the nursery. He turned on the lights and picked up his screaming girls.

He scanned the pinboard of photos and children's paintings. There he was, and so too Hannah, and there were hundreds of pictures of the girls. But there was not a single one of Amy—not even a handprint bore her name. Emir realised fully then that she was gone from the palace and gone from these rooms—gone from his life and from his daughters' lives too.

The twins' screams grew louder, even though he held them in his arms, and Emir envied their lack of restraint and inhibition—they could sob and beat their fists on his chest, yell with indignant rage, that she was gone.

He looked out of the window to the sky that was carrying her home now. If he called for his jet possibly he could beat her, could meet her at the airport with the girls. But she was right, Emir thought with a rueful smile—she would make a terrible mistress.

She should be his wife.

'Ummi?' Clemira begged. Now she had two mothers to grieve for. He held his babies some more until finally they were spent. He put them down in one crib, but still they would not sleep, just stared at him with angry eyes, lay hiccoughing and gulping. He ran a finger down Clemira's cheek and across her eyebrows as

Amy had shown him a year ago, but Clemira did not close her eyes. She just stared coolly back, exhausted but still defiant. Yes, she was a born leader.

As was Emir.

Except the rules did not allow him to be.

'I'm leaving for the desert,' he told Fatima as he left the nursery. 'The new nanny starts in two days.'

Fatima lowered her head as he walked off. She did not ask when he would return, did not insist that he tell her so she could tell the girls. That was how it was supposed to be, yet not as it should be, Emir realised.

He joined Amy in the sky—but in his helicopter.

Once in the desert, he had Raul ready his horse and then rode into the night. He was at the oasis for sunrise. The first year was over and now he must move on.

He prayed as he waited for counsel from the wizened old man—for he knew that he would come.

'Hannah will not rest.'

The old man nodded.

'Before she died she asked that I promise to do my best for the girls.' He looked into the man's blackcurrant eyes. 'And to do the best for me.'

'And have you?'

'First I have to do the best by my country.'

'Because you are King?'

Emir nodded. 'I made that promise to my father when he died,' he said. He remembered the loss and the pain he had suffered then. His vow had been absolute when he had sworn it. 'The best for me is to marry Amy. It is the best for the girls too. But not the best for my country.' Emir told the old man why. 'She cannot have children.' He waited for the old man to shake his head, to tell him how impossible it was, to tell him there was no dilemma, that it could not be; instead he sat silent, so Emir spelt it out for him. 'She cannot give me a son.'

'And the new wife you will take can?' the old man checked.

Emir closed his eyes.

'Perhaps your new wife will give you girls too?' the old man said. 'As Queen Hannah did.'

'Without a son my lineage ends,' Emir hissed in frustration. 'Alzirz will swallow Alzan and the two lands will be become one.'

'That is the prediction,' the old man said. 'You cannot fight that.'

Emir was sick of predictions, of absolutes, of a fate that was sealed in the sand and the stars. 'It must not happen,' Emir said. He thought of his people—the people who had rejected his daughters, was his first savage thought. Yet they were not bad—they were scared. Emir knew that. He loved his people and his country so much, and they needed him as their leader. 'I cannot turn my back on them. There are rules for Alzan...'

'And for Alzirz too,' the old man said, and Emir grew silent. 'You are King for a reason.'

He reminded Emir of his teachings and Emir knew again that the year had passed and it was time for Hannah to rest, time for him to face things, to come to his decision. He stood. The old man stayed sitting.

'You will know what to do.'

He knew what to do now, and nothing could stop him.

Emir mounted his stallion and kicked him on, charged towards a land where he was not welcome uninvited. No one stopped him.

On his entering Alzirz, Rakhal's guards galloped behind and alongside him, but no one attempted to halt a king propelled by centuries of fury.

King Rakhal was alerted, and as Emir approached he saw Alzirz's King standing waiting for him outside his desert abode. His tearful wife was by his side, refusing to return to the tent; yet she would be wise to, for both men would draw swords if they had to—both men would fight to the death for what was theirs.

Emir climbed from his horse and it was he who made the first move, reaching not for his knife but deep into his robe. He took out the two precious stones that had been sent to taunt him and hurled them at Rakhal's feet. 'Never insult me again!'

Rakhal gave a black laugh. 'How did my gift insult you? They are the most precious sapphires I could find. I had my people look far and wide for them. How could they offend?'

'They arrived on the morning of Sheikh Queen Hannah's death. The insult was for her too.' He spat in the sand in the direction of the stones and then he spat again, looking to Rakhal as he told him how it would be. 'I am marrying soon.'

'I look forward to the celebrations,' Rakhal said 'Who, may I ask, is the fortunate bride?'

'You have met her,' Emir answered. 'Amy.'

'Congratulations!' Rakhal answered, and then, because of course his wife would have told him, he smiled at Emir. 'Shouldn't you also offer congratulations to me? After all, Alzan will be mine.'

'No.' Emir shook his head.

'What? Are you considering your brother as King when you step aside?' Rakhal laughed. 'That reprobate! Hassan would not stay out of the casino or be sober long enough to take the vow.' Again Rakhal laughed. 'Congratulations to me will soon be in order.'

'Not in my lifetime,' Emir said. 'And I plan to live for a very long time. I am the King and I will die the King. Alzan will cease existing when I do.' He watched the mocking smile fade from Rakhal's face. 'I pray for a long life for your son, who will inherit all that you pass on to him. I pray that the rules are kind to him and he marries a bride who gives him healthy children. I pray for a long life for her too—for your father was lonely when his wife died, was he not? But because of your rule he could not marry again. I will pray history does not repeat for your son.' He heard Natasha really weeping now, but Rakhal stood firm.

'Your people will not be happy. Your people will never accept—'

'I will deal with my people,' Emir interrupted. 'And I will continue to pray for your son. I hope that his time in the desert proves fruitful, and hardens and prepares him for all he faces. Yes, my people will be unhappy when their King has gone. They will rise and fight as their country is taken.' He watched as for the first time

Rakhal faltered when he realised the burden being placed on his newborn son, the weight both Kings carried being passed onto one. 'We are Kings, Rakhal, but without real power. For now I will rule as best I can, and do the best that I can for my children too.'

He meant it. Knew this was the right thing to do. He could no longer fight the predictions.

He rode back through the desert with rare peace in his soul. He could feel the peace in Hannah's too, for now she could rest.

Suddenly Emir halted his horse so abruptly it rose on its hind legs for a moment—or was it the shock that emanated from his master that startled the beast? Emir's realisation dawned: he had not yet discussed this with Amy. Yet surely his concern was unnecessary, he told himself. Surely no woman would refuse such a request.

But she was not from this land, and she was like no woman he knew. His last words to her had not been kind. He was back to being troubled as he realised she might not want to rule with him a people who with each passing year would grow more and more despondent. She might well prefer not to live in a land where her fertility or lack of it was a constant topic.

It dawned on him fully then—Amy might not say yes.

CHAPTER FIFTEEN

It was hell being back in England.

It was lovely to see everyone, and it was good to be home, Amy told herself. Good to be at her mother's.

For about one day, seven hours and thirty-six minutes.

But when she was told by her mother again that she'd warned her not to get too attached, as if the twins were like the hamsters she'd once brought home to care for during the school holidays, Amy knew that she had to move out.

It took her a week to find a small furnished rental while she looked around for something more permanent, something that might one day feel like home. Right now her heart still lived at the palace. At night she yearned to be next to Emir, and she still slept with one ear open for the twins. Her breasts ached as if she *were* weaning them, but she knew she had to somehow start healing—start over, start again. She'd done it once, she told herself. The next time would surely be easier. Right?

She tried to hold it together—she went out with friends, caught up with the news, bought a new London wardrobe and even went and had her hair done, in a nice layered cut with a few foils. Her friends told her she looked amazing. Those days swimming in the pool with the twins meant that she had arrived in the middle of a London winter with a deep golden tan.

She had never looked better—except her appearance didn't match the way she felt.

'You look great,' her ex fiancé told her.

If she heard it again she thought she might scream. But he'd heard she was back and wanted to catch up, and Amy was actually glad for the chance to apologise.

'For what?' he asked.

For the year of bitterness she had needlessly carried. He'd been right to end things, Amy told him.

'Are you sure about that?' he asked, before dropping her home. Fresh from a break-up with a single mum, he had revised his paternity plans and suggested that they might try again.

She *was* sure, she told him. Because it wasn't a logical love she wanted, Amy knew as she headed inside, it was an illogical one.

She knew what love was now.

Even if she did not understand it.

Even if it could never be returned.

She'd had her heart broken three times.

The accident, losing her fiancé, the aftermath—they didn't even enter the equation. They had been tiny tasters for the real grief to come.

She missed her babies, loved each little girl as fiercely as she would have loved her own. She had been there at their birth and held them every day since and she ached for them. She felt she had let Hannah down—not by sleeping with Emir, but by leaving the girls.

She was tired of being told she'd get over it—as if the love she felt didn't count, as if in a few days' times she'd wake up not missing them—but somehow she had to work out how to do just that.

She would not cry, Amy told herself. She had to keep it all together. She would look for a job next week and make some appointments—catch up on the life she'd left behind. Except as she went in her bag for her phone it was not to see if he'd called—because it had been two weeks now and still he had not—but to look at the photo of Emir and the girls that she had taken on that precious morning in Alzan.

She was horrified when she opened her bag to find that her phone was missing. Amy tipped out the contents, frantically trying to remember when she had last used her phone, positive she had taken it out with her. Perhaps she had left it at the restaurant? But, no—Amy remembered that she had sneaked a peek of the photo in the car.

It wasn't the phone that concerned her but that image of Emir, Clemira and Nakia that she could not stand to lose. It was all she had left of them.

Amy couldn't even telephone her ex to ask if he had it, because his number was in her phone. Just as she started to panic the doorbell rang. Amy ran to it, hoping he had found it, even smiling in relief as she opened the door. Her smile faded as soon as she saw who it was.

'Emir?'

There were so many questions behind that single
word, but his name was all she could manage. She wasn't
even sure that it was him. For a moment she even wondered if he had sent his brother, for the man standing
in her doorway was the Emir she had never seen—a
younger looking, more relaxed Emir—and he was smiling at her shocked expression. How dared he look so
happy? How dared he look so different? For though she
knew he wore suits in London, she had never seen him
wear one and he truly looked breathtaking.

'Not the man you were expecting?'

'Actually, no.' She didn't have to explain herself and
refused to, because even if he *had* seen her ex drop her
off it was none of his business any more.

'You're a very hard person to find.'

'Am I?'

'Your mother wouldn't give me your address.'

'I wouldn't have expected her to.' Amy gave a tight
shrug. 'So how *did* you find me?'

'Less than honourable ways,' he admitted.

He was powerful enough to get anything he set his
mind to, and she must remember to keep her guard up
around him. She could not take any more hurt, but she
had to know one thing. 'Are the girls okay?'

'They're fine,' Emir said. 'Well, they miss you a lot.'

She remembered standing in his office, telling him
practically the same thing, and she remembered how it
had changed nothing. Yet she did ask him in—she had
to know what he was here for, had to see this conversation through in the hope that she might one day move on.

'Are they here in London?'

'No.'

Emir quickly crushed that hope, but perhaps it was for the best, because she could not bear to say goodbye to them again.

'They have a new nanny. She is younger and not as rigid as Fatima. They are just starting to really settle in with her and I didn't think I should interrupt—'

'Emir, please…' She put a hand up to stop him. She really didn't need to hear how quickly and how well they were adapting to her replacement. 'I'm glad the girls are fine.'

She forced a smile and then for the first time since he'd arrived at her door remembered he was a sheikh king, she honestly forgot at times, and now that she remembered she didn't really know what to do with him.

Aware of her rather sparse furnished rental, and wondering if instant coffee would do, she remembered her manners and forced a smile for him. 'Would you like a drink?'

'I came here to talk to you.'

'You could have done that on the phone.' Except now she'd lost hers, Amy remembered. But what had seemed so devastating a few moments ago became a triviality. 'Have a seat. I'll make a drink.'

'I didn't come here for a drink.'

'Well, I'm having one.'

She headed to the fridge and opened it, grateful for the cool blast of air as she rummaged around and found some wine and then looked for glasses. She was glad for something to do—needed to have her back to him for a couple of moments as she composed herself. Amy did not want her broken heart on clear display to him, for she could be hurt so easily.

'What are you thinking?' Emir asked, the tiny kitchen area shrinking as he stepped in.

'Do you really want to know?'

'I really want to know.'

'That it's just as well this is a screwtop bottle because I don't have a corkscrew...'

'Amy!'

'And I'm wondering what happened to all the people who made the corks.' She was, and she was also wondering if the trees they came from were called cork trees, because it was safer than thinking about the man who was in her home, the man who was standing right behind her now. She knew that if she turned around it would be to a man she could not resist.

'What else are you thinking?'

'That it is cruel that you are here,' Amy said. 'That I don't want to be your mistress.' She stopped pouring the wine. She was making a mess of it anyway. Her eyes were filling with tears and she couldn't really see; she screwed her eyes closed as his hand touched her arm and swore to be strong as he turned her around. 'And I'm thinking how right I was to leave—that I don't want to be with you.'

'I don't believe that,' he said.

And his mouth was there, and already she was weakening. That in itself forced her to be strong, made her look into his eyes to speak. 'I wouldn't even want to be your wife.'

'I don't believe that either.'

'I mean it.' She reminded herself that she did. 'As I've said before, if you were my husband and they were my children I'd have left ages ago.'

'I told you that there were reasons I could not be the father I wanted to be for them, but those reasons are gone now.'

She shook her head. 'I don't want you, Emir.'

'You *do* want me.'

He was so bloody arrogant, so assured…so right.

'No.'

'That's not what your body is saying.'

He ran a hand down her arms, then removed it. She shivered, for only his touch could warm her.

'And it's not what I see in your eyes.'

So she hid them, lowered her head, and because the bench was behind her and she could not step back she lifted her hands to push him—yet she dared not touch. 'Just go, Emir,' she begged. 'I can't think straight when you're around.'

'I know,' Emir said.

She shook her head, because how could he know how it felt? After all, he was standing calm and controlled and she was a trembling mess.

'I know how impossible it is to make a wise decisions when love clouds the issue.'

She did look up then, shocked to hear him speak of love. A gasp came from her lips when he spoke next, when he said what no king should. 'I have been considering abdicating.'

'*No.*' He must not think it—let alone say it. She knew from her time in Alzan the implications, knew how serious this was, but Emir went on undaunted. This distant man invited her closer, and not just to his body, but to his mind; he pulled her in so her head was on his chest as he told her, shared with her his hell.

'Whenever I saw the twins laughing and happy, or crying and sad, I wanted them to come first—I did not want to rule a country that is disappointed by my daughters, that does not celebrate in their birthday, that will only be appeased by a son. When I am with my daughters all I want to do is step down...'

'You can't.'

'I am not sure that I want to rule a country where I cannot change the rules. I'm not sure I want to give the people the son they want just to pass the burden on to him.' He shook his head. 'No, I will not do that to my son.' He lifted her chin and looked into the eyes of the woman he loved and was completely sure. 'I love you, and I cannot lose the woman I love again.'

And it was right, Amy thought, that he acknowledged Hannah—even right that the love he felt should be compared to the love he had had for the Queen. And it was said so nicely that she could not help but cry.

'And neither can I put Clemira and Nakia through it again,' he went on. 'You have made my daughters so happy. They call you their mother—which is how it will be.' He watched her shake her head at the impossibility of it all. 'As soon as you left I wanted to get on a plane, but I knew I had to think this through. I will rule Alzan as best as I can in my lifetime, and if the people grow hostile, if things get too hard for you there, then the country will see less of their leader—for I will divide my time between there and here.'

'No…' Amy said, but he was close, and she was weak whenever Emir was around.

'Yes,' he said, and held her tight. 'Anyway, we will have time to work things out.' He could not help but tease, watching the colour spread up her cheeks as he spoke. 'No one needs to find out for a while yet that you cannot have children.'

'I told Natasha.' She thought his features would darken with surprise, but instead he smiled.

'I know you did.'

'I was just tired of everyone assuming…'

'I know.' And he was smiling no longer. 'I confronted Rakhal. I have told him my position.'

'What did he say?'

'That Alzan will be his.' Emir shrugged. 'I pointed out that if he does outlive me and inherit, one day it will be his son's too.' His voice was forboding, but the loathing was not aimed at her. She knew that. 'If Rakhal takes it upon himself to inform my people that you cannot have a child…' his features were dark, and now he was not smiling '…he will have *me* to deal with.'

'I can't marry you, Emir,' Amy said. 'I can't stand knowing that I'm going to disappoint your people.' That he loved her so much brought her both comfort and fear.

That he would leave his country's future in darkness for her was almost more than she could take.

'It is not your burden to carry,' Emir said. 'I was coming to this decision even before the twins were born. I was already considering this. For Hannah's heart was so weak I could never have asked her to be pregnant again. This is not of your making. We have time before the people know—time to work out how best to tell them.'

He was doing his best to reassure her, but even if his decision was right, she knew the pain behind it.

'I can't do it, Emir.'

'You can with me by your side. I will shield you as I will shield the twins. You will be a wonderful queen,' Emir said. 'The people could not have better.'

'They could.'

'No.'

He meant it.

Every word of it.

His heart was at peace with the decision he had made. He would do everything he could for his people, but his heart belonged to his girls and he was strong enough to end the impossible burden, to cease the madness. He would not place that burden on a child of his.

And here it was—the illogical love that she wanted. Love was a strange thing: it made you both strong and weak. Strong enough to stand by your convictions... Weak enough maybe to give in.

Except this was Emir, and even if she forgot at times he was King this was her life and it would be in the spotlight.

As she wrestled with indecision the doorbell rang. She opened it to the man she had once thought she loved, and blinked at the phone he held out in his hand.

'Thank you.'

She saw him look over her shoulder to where Emir was standing, saw the raising of his eyebrows, and then without a word he turned and Amy closed the door. She was nervous to turn around and face the man she knew she loved and would love for ever. But she had to be strong, had to say no, and that slight pause had given her a moment to regroup.

'I left my phone...' She felt his black eyes on hers and couldn't quite meet them. 'We went out before...'

'I saw you return,' Emir said. 'I was waiting in my car for you. Now, we were talking about—'

'Nothing happened,' Amy broke in. 'He just wanted...'

'I do not care.' She frowned, because surely he *should* care. 'We were discussing our marriage—'

'Emir!' she interrupted him. 'My ex-fiancé just came to the door, you know we've been out together tonight, and you don't *care*?' She couldn't believe what she was hearing. 'You don't have questions?'

'None,' Emir said.

She was less than flattered. A bit of jealousy wouldn't go amiss—after all, she *had* just been out with her ex.

'Am I supposed to take it as a compliment that you trust me so much? For all you know—'

'You could take a thousand lovers, Amy.' It was Emir who interrupted now. Emir who walked to where she stood. 'But each one would leave you empty. Each one would compare poorly to me.'

'You're so sure?'

'Completely,' Emir said. 'And you could sit through a hundred dinners and dates and your mind would wander even as the first course was served.' He stood right in front of her, looked down at her, and spoke the absolute truth. 'Your mind would wander straight back to me,' he said.

And, damn him, he was right. Because tonight all she had thought of was Emir, her efforts to concentrate and to listen had been half-hearted at best.

'And when you were kissed,' he said, and put his mouth right up to hers, 'you would crave what another man could not deliver. Because my mouth knows best what to do.'

She closed her eyes, opened her mouth to deny him. For there must be no future for them. She was going to say that she would find love again—except his tongue slid into her protesting mouth and he gave her a taste, and then he drew his head back, warned her again of the life she would lead if she did not say yes.

'You would miss me for ever.'

'No,' she begged, though she knew he spoke the truth.

'You would regret the decision for the rest of your days.'

'No,' Amy insisted, though she knew he was right.

'We will be married,' he concluded, through with talking. It had taken what felt like a lifetime to come to his decision, and now that he had he wanted it sealed.

He pulled her tighter to him, so close she could hear his heart—not galloping, but steady, for he knew he was right.

His hand lifted her chin and he looked down at her mouth. 'There are so many kisses we have not had.'

He lowered his mouth and tender were the lips that met hers in an unhurried kiss that reminded her of nothing—for this side of him she had not met.

'This is the kiss I wanted to give you one morning when I saw you walking in the gardens.' His mouth claimed her for another brief moment. He ran his hands down to her waist and his lips tasted of possession and promise for later. Then he he let her go. 'That was the kiss I wanted to greet you with when you joined the party.'

'What is this?' She would not cry in front of him. She had promised herself. Yet she was failing. 'Guess the kiss?'

'Yes,' he said, and she started to cry.

He held her again and his mouth drank her tears. He held her as he had wanted to, comforted her as he had wanted to after the breakfast, when Clemira had said *Ummi* and her heart had ached for a baby of her own. He held her as had wanted to that day.

'You will never face it alone again,' he promised, for he knew his kiss had taken her back to that day.

Then he kissed her again, both hands on her face, and it tasted of regret. She was leaving him again. They were back at the palace and he was letting her go. His arms were around hers and his tongue met hers. He was ferocious as he rewrote that moment—he kissed her back to his world. Then he kissed her hard and with intent, and *this* was a kiss she recognised. His tongue was lavish in its suggestion and he pulled her into him, to let her feel his want. His hands moved over her body. This was a kiss that could lead only to one thing.

Except he stopped.

He looked down to her mouth, which was wet and wanting. He did not believe in negotiation—not when he knew that he was right. He *would* get his way. 'You will return to Alzan and we will be married.'

'You don't just *tell* me!' Amy said. 'And that's hardly a proposal. You're supposed to get down on one knee.'

'Not where I come from,' Emir said.

He took her hand and held it over his erection. She kept her palm flat, but that did not deter him. He moved her hand up and down, till her fingers ached from not holding him, till all she wanted was to slide down his zipper and free him.

Free *them*.

'You can say yes,' Emir said, 'or you can kiss it goodbye if you care to.'

She could not help but smile as his usually excellent English wavered.

'You mean, kiss it *all* goodbye.'

'No,' Emir said. 'I mean exactly what I said.' And he pulled her into him. His mouth found her ear. 'Either way I bring you to your knees.'

And he would, because she could not be without him.

'Say yes, Amy.'

'I can't.'

'Then you can't have me.'

He confused her, because he kissed her again.

He kissed her mouth when still she questioned. He kissed her eyes closed when she tried to look at all that lay ahead. He kissed her until she was in the moment—kissed her all the way to her unmade bed. He did not bring her to her knees; instead he lay her down and removed every piece of her clothing.

First he took off her shoes, and when she sat with her arms by her sides he raised them.

'Emir...'

'Tell me to stop and I will.'

Her hands stayed in the air as he took off her top.

'Tell me we should not be together,' Emir said as he unhooked her bra, 'and I will go.'

And she felt his eyes on her breasts and she wanted his mouth to be there, but still she stayed silent, so he unzipped her skirt and pushed her back on the bed. When he pulled at the hem she did not lift her hips to help him. He stared down at her and it did not deter him. Instead he undressed himself.

He took off his jacket and placed it over a chair, took ages with each shoe, and as he pulled off his socks Amy found her toes curling.

'You do not get me till you say yes.' With a cruel lack of haste he removed his tie and unbuttoned his shirt. He gave her plenty of time to halt things but still she did not and he slid off his trousers and hipsters and stood over her, naked. 'I can't hear you, Amy.'

'Because I haven't said anything,' came her response, but this time when he tugged at her skirt she did lift her hips. How could she not say yes to him? How could she not be his wife? She tried to look to the future, when she would surely regret this decision, but *yes* waited to spill from her mouth.

He took off her panties so she was naked, and still she would not give in.

Emir kneeled between her legs, kissed up one thigh and then back down, and then he turned his attention to the other one till she writhed beneath him, wanting him there at her centre. He didn't play fair. He played mean. He lifted his head and focussed instead on himself, and she watched, fascinated, desperate. He stroked himself right there at her entrance and she watched, wanted. He would make her comply.

'I can't wait for ever,' he warned.

And he was right. There would never be a better lover. Always her mind would return to him. She heard his breath quicken. She wanted him more than she wanted her sanity and she hated this game he was playing.

'You can't seduce me into saying yes.'

'I can.'

He could.

He actually could.

'Yes,' she begged, for she wanted it to be ended.

'Manners?' How cruel was his teasing.

'I've forgotten them!' she screamed, and then screamed again as he drove into her.

Fierce was the passion that filled her. He did not stop

for a second to let her think, did not let her draw breath to reconsider. He had her and he would keep her. Each buck inside Amy told her that. Each pounding thrust confirmed she was his and Amy knew that was what she wanted.

'Please…' she sobbed, her legs coiling around him, possessing him, locking him in while ensuring his release.

She gave in as he did—gave in to the ultimate pleasure, lost in the throes of an orgasm that sealed their union as they pulsed together in time, lost with the other and returned together, lying with each other as they would now every night.

And Emir slept as he never had, in an untroubled sleep, for he knew that this was right.

Except Amy could not rest beside him. She heard every car that passed and listened to the rain battering the window in the early hours of the morning. She was petrified about what she'd agreed to.

She was going to be Queen.

CHAPTER SIXTEEN

'You need to come home,' was his answer when she told him her fears, and she knew that he was right—knew that Alzan was where she wanted to be.

They did not stay long in London. Just long enough to sort out her things and for Amy to try and convince her mum, who would fly to Alzan for the wedding, that she knew what she was doing, that it would all be okay.

And how could they not be okay? she asked herself. For it felt so right to have Emir by her side.

The journey home was a blur—the luxurious plane a mere mode of transport that allowed her to follow her heart. Even the people cheering the arrival of their King and soon to be new Sheikha Queen did not really register. But for all it was a blur, for all her mind was too busy to take in every detail, Amy would never forget her return to the palace.

He held her hand as they walked through the foyer where he had *not* kissed her goodbye, as they walked up the stairs—together this time—and then to the nursery. Emir let go of her hand, stepped in first, and she walked in quietly behind and smiled at the delighted reaction when the twins saw him. They were playing with their dolls' house, making everything right in a world where they could, but their beloved toy was instantly forgotten. Their father was back and that was all the girls needed to know—and then they saw her.

'Ummi!' It was Nakia who squealed it first and Clemira frowned, glanced at her sister and chastised her, for she had learnt that word was bad.

And then Clemira looked over to where her little sister was pointing and when she saw who was there she forgot to be the leader; she just burst into tears and took first steps towards Amy.

'It's okay.' Amy realised how much she had been hurting because her pain was gone the second she picked up Clemira. Poor Nakia stood too, but her legs didn't know how to walk yet, so she burst out crying too, and cried some more when Amy picked her up. Overwhelmed, the twins cried till they were smiling, kissing her face because Amy was crying too. She looked to Emir and it was the closest to tears she had ever seen him.

He had lost so much—his parents, his wife and almost Amy. That he could trust in love again was a feat in itself, and his decision was the right one, Amy told herself as she held his new family.

How could this be wrong?

Yet Amy awoke on the morning of her wedding with dread in her heart. She understood why Emir had been unable to make his decision when love was around, for when he was close, when he was near, it felt so *right* that they marry, that love was the solution. But Emir had spent the eve of his wedding in the desert, and without him it was far more than pre-wedding jitters Amy was struggling with. This morning she didn't even have the twins to keep her busy, for they were being readied for the wedding by the new nanny.

She felt as if she were cheating the people.

The maid came in and opened the window and the room was filled with humid desert air. Amy felt as if it was smothering her as she tried to swallow the ripe fruit that had been picked at dawn in the desert and prepared and served to her.

As was the tradition for the future Queen of Alzan.

The maids watched as she drank fertility potions from huge goblets and with every mouthful Amy felt sicker. Each taste of bridal tradition choked her and reminded her of the cheat and liar she was.

She bathed and had her make-up and hair done. Her eyes were lined with kohl and her cheeks and lips rouged. But she could see the pallor in her face and the guilt in her eyes as blossom was pinned into her hair—'For innocence,' the maiden explained. Amy closed her eyes on another lie as she remembered the love they had already made.

A dress of pale gold slithered over her head and she thought of her mother who, though there for the wedding, was stressed. She had done all she could to dissuade Amy. As late as last night she had warned her daughter of the mistake she was making, had offered to take her home; she had told Amy that she was taking on too much, that though the country was cheering at the union now it would soon turn against her, and maybe in time her husband would too.

'No.' Amy was adamant. 'He loves me.'

Yet she felt guilty accepting that love. What should be the happiest day of her life was blighted by the knowledge that she could never be the Queen the people really wanted.

And now the final touches. She could hear the excitement and anticipation building in the streets outside, for the wedding was to take place in the gardens and the people had gathered around the palace.

'The people are happy,' the maiden said as a loud cheer went up.

'It is King Rakhal and Queen Natasha, arriving,' a younger maiden informed the busy room, watching the proceedings from the window. 'They have the young Prince with them.' She looked to Amy and smiled. 'They won't be able to gloat over us for much longer.'

And now the maiden tied a necklace around her throat which had a small vial at the end of it. Amy knew even before the maiden told her that it was for fertility, for Clemira and Nakia had received a similar necklace in the desert. Emir's response then had been brusque, but the maiden was more effusive as she arranged it around Amy's throat.

'It is to ensure that the sands remain as Alzan.' She placed it over the scar on Amy's throat and Amy could feel her rapid pulse beating there against the vial, could hear the cheers from the people of Alzan building outside, she could feel the sweat removing her carefully applied make-up as the humid desert air made it impossible to breathe.

'Amy?'

She heard the concern in the young maiden's voice, and the shocked gasps from the others as they saw how much she was struggling.

'I can't do this,' was all Amy remembered saying as she slid to the ground.

CHAPTER SEVENTEEN

'SHE is late.'

Emir heard the whispers in the crowd and stared fixedly ahead. Though outwardly calm and in control, he was kicking himself, for he should not have left her alone last night. He knew the reason Amy was late was because she was reconsidering the union. He realised that perhaps, for her, it was too much too soon—after all, his decision had been more than a year in the making. But Emir knew he could not lose his love to a prediction, knew he was right, and he would go now and tell her the same.

'That is not necessary,' Patel informed him. 'She is better now, apparently. They have given her salts to smell and some fluids to drink and she will soon be on her way.'

As Amy approached she reminded Emir of the first time he had met her—pale and quiet but somehow strong. She had helped him so much at that heartbreaking time and he wanted to help *her* now, wanted to take her away from the gathered crowd, to talk to her, soothe and reassure her, but of course it was impossible.

'You are okay?' Emir checked as she joined him at his side, and his hand found hers.

She was touched at the gesture, for he had told her that today was duty, that feelings would not be on display—for in Alzan love usually came later.

Not today.

'Nervous,' Amy admitted, which was perhaps the understatement of the century.

The magnitude of what was about to take place had hit her again as she'd walked through the fragrant gardens and seen the crowd, and she had thought she might pass out again. There was Hassan, the reprobate brother, standing tall and silent by his brother's side. King Rakhal and Natasha were there too, regal and splendid, but she'd barely glanced at them. First she had looked to the twins, dressed in pale lemon and sitting on the grass holding flowers, but though she'd melted at the sight of them today it was Emir who won her heart a thousand times over.

His robe was pale gold too, as was the *kafeya* on his head, and she was overwhelmed by such male beauty, by the curve of his lips that barely smiled as they greeted her but that would caress her mouth tonight. She ached for tonight, to be in the desert with him, but of course there were formalities first.

For a country so steeped in tradition, the wedding was surprisingly simple.

'He asks,' Emir translated, 'if you agree to this union.'

'Yes,' Amy said, and then remembered and answered for the judge. *'Na'am.'*

'He asks that you will obey me.'

He saw the slight pursing of her lips, for they had discussed this a few times.

She pressed her thumb into his palm, to remind him of the million subclauses to her agreement, and then she answered, *'Na'am.'*

'He asks will you nurture the fruits of our union?' Emir saw the tears fill her eyes and he wanted to hold her, but all he could do was press his own thumb to her palm to remind her that this was right.

She could not look beyond his shoulder to where King Rakhal stood, and beside him Natasha, so she looked to her soon to be husband and answered him. The press of his thumb was a reminder of just how much this man loved her. *'Na'am.'*

The judge spoke for a few moments and she waited, then Emir's hand was in the small of her back, telling her to turn around.

'What happens now?' Amy asked.

'We go back to the palace.'

'Back?' Amy asked. 'But the wedding…?'

'We are married,' Emir said, and then he broke with tradition.

Even if it was brief she felt his arms around her, and the soft warmth of his mouth as Emir kissed his bride. It was not the cough of the elders that halted them but the two little girls who protested at the lack of attention.

Back to the palace they walked, holding one twin each, and she watched as Emir glanced up to the sky.

She knew he was telling Hannah she could rest now, that the girls would be looked after as she had wanted.

And they would be.

Amy wanted to be alone with him, wanted their night in the desert, but first came more formalities— a sumptuous meal and endless speeches. Finally it was Rakhal's turn to speak, and Amy felt her hand tighten on the glass she was holding. She wondered what barb was about to be delivered—not that she would know it when it came, for the speeches were in Arabic. Emir would translate for her.

She took a deep breath as Rakhal addressed the room, realised her fingers were suddenly tight around Emir's for he squeezed her hand back.

'My wife predicted this.' Rakhal spoke in English and Amy's head jerked up. 'She said she knew on the day she met you,' he said. 'It was the day of my father's passing.'

Amy blinked, because that was a long time ago—long before she had had feelings for Emir. Or had she? She remembered that time. Emir had gone to offer his fare-well and she had spoken briefly with Natasha. She had been so confused and bitter then, so angry with Emir for the distance he put between himself and his daughters.

'I said she was wrong.' Rakhal looked at the new Queen of Alzan. 'And I said she was wrong again at my son's naming ceremony. But this is one prediction that has been proved right.' Rakhal looked to Emir. 'Your Highness, I congratulate you on your wedding.' He spoke in Arabic, some words she recognised—long life, good health—and then again he spoke in English. 'The Kingdom of Alzirz celebrates with you today.'

How hard it was to smile as he raised a glass to them.

Hard too, to make small talk with Natasha a while later, for she was so determined to be friendly.

'You look wonderful.' Natasha smiled, but Amy could not help but be cool in her responses—could not so easily manage the feigned politeness between the rivals. 'Rakhal tells me you are honeymooning in London?'

'That's right.'

'With the girls?'

'Of course,' Amy said through gritted teeth.

'When you return we must get the children together, Clemira is so taken with Tariq, and…'

'We'll see.' Amy gave a tight smile. 'Now, if you'll excuse me…'

She turned straight into the chest of Emir and he rescued her with a dance. 'You will be polite,' Emir warned her. 'You will be pleasant.'

'I *am* being.'

'No.' He had seen the ice behind her smile as she spoke with Queen Natasha. 'When a queen speaks to you…'

'I'm a queen now too.'

He smiled down at her angry eyes. 'I will speak with you later. For now I will tell you to be polite.'

'I don't get it, Emir,' she bristled.

It annoyed her how well Emir and Rakhal were getting on tonight—oh, she knew it was all for show, but still it riled her. She put it aside, for it seemed impossible to hold a grudge on this night. The whole palace was alive with celebration, there were parties in the streets outside, and though she ached to be alone in the desert with Emir, to be with her new husband, it was the best night of her life.

Amy allowed herself simply to enjoy it right up to the end, when she accepted a kiss to her hand from Rakhal and, as instructed, smiled and chatted briefly to Natasha as they prepared to leave for the desert. Then it was time to say goodbye to the twins.

God, but she loved them. Nakia was now literally following in her big sister's footsteps, toddling too, and both loved calling out 'Ummi'. They would always know about their real mother, but it was bliss not to correct them, just to scoop them into her arms. She did it now, kissed their little faces and told them she would see them tomorrow.

She feared the wedding night in the desert more than a little—always felt as if the desert knew something she didn't, as if somehow it was a step ahead of them.

'It's dark.'

The last time she had been there the sands had been lit by a huge moon, and there had been stars, but tonight the desert was clouded—not that Emir seemed concerned.

'There will be rain, which is good,' he said. 'After rain comes new growth.'

The rain met them as they landed—a driving rain that had the helicopter flounder for a moment, a pelting rain that soaked through her gown. As she stepped into the tent maidens were waiting, wrapping her in shawls, and a feast was laid out for them. There were a thousand things to get through when all she wanted was to be alone with him, to speak with him. Emir must have sensed that, for he dismissed the maidens and took her into his arms.

'Should I be offended,' Emir asked, 'that my wife did not enjoy her wedding day?'

'I loved it, Emir.' She looked up to him. 'Every moment of it.'

'Every moment?'

'I struggle to be polite to Natasha and Rakhal. I understand that I have to be, that without communication…' She did not want to talk about them on her wedding night but, yes, she might have been a little rude. 'I struggle sometimes to stay quiet when I believe there is injustice.'

'I *had* worked that out,' Emir said. 'I know there is much on your mind. All day I have wanted to speak with you. There is something you need to know, but there has not been a suitable moment.'

'Oh!' Amy had been about to say the same thing. 'Emir, there is something—'

'Amy,' he interrupted, for his news was too important not to share. 'You know I spent last night in the desert? Usually the night before the King marries is a time for feasting and celebrating; instead I spent that time speaking with Rakhal.'

'And you didn't pull your swords?'

He heard the teasing in her voice. 'Rakhal listened

to all I said to him that day—he thought long and hard about it and though things have worked out for him, though he is happy, he does not want the burden he carried to be passed on to his son. He agrees that we are Kings without power unless we make our own rules for our own lands.' Emir picked up the vial that hung around her throat, knew the terrible pressure that had been placed on her. 'Our decision will be refuted by the elders, of course, but with both Kings in full agreement there will be no going back.'

'I don't understand?'

'The predictors are wrong,' Emir said. 'Alzan and Alzirz are two strong and proud countries. It is time for them to break free from the rules of old. Of course the people and the elders will challenge this. They believe...'

'Emir!' That whooshing sound was back in her ears, 'Emir, wait!' Anguished eyes looked up to him. 'I did enjoy today, every moment of it, and if I seemed distracted at times...' Amy took a deep breath. 'I didn't faint from nerves.' She still couldn't take the news in, had been reeling from it all day. 'Well, maybe a bit. But when the palace doctor examined me...' She'd never thought she'd hear herself say these words. 'I'm pregnant, Emir.' Amy was crying now, and not just a little bit. 'I had him retake the test and he is certain—it would seem that first night...'

'But you said it was impossible.' It was Emir who didn't understand.

'There was always a slim chance, apparently,' Amy explained. 'I just didn't hear that and neither did my fiancé. And I never went back to the doctor to properly discuss things.'

Emir held her as she cried. The news was as shocking as it was happy, and it took a moment for it to sink in.

'The rules might not need to change. I might have a son,' Amy said.

And he held the bride whom he loved, come what may, and he loved her all over again.

'Soon we will be able to find out what I'm having.'

'There is no need to find out,' Emir said. 'For whatever we are given we will love. The rules *will* change.' Emir's voice was firm. 'Clemira is a born leader, that much I know, and Nakia will be a wonderful support for her. It is right she be second in line.'

'But the predictions!'

'Are just that,' Emir said, and he looked to the woman who had healed his black and tortured heart, the woman who had swept into his office and challenged his way of thinking, and he could not believe what he had. His instinct was to kiss her, to hold her and soothe her fears, and then he paused for just a moment as the news truly started to hit him. And he told her why the predictions were surely wrong. 'They did not factor in that a king might fall in love.'

EPILOGUE

'HE is beautiful,' Emir said.

Amy could not stop looking at her newborn son—could scarcely believe that she was holding her own baby in her arms. Just feeling him there, she knew all the hurts of the past were forgotten, the pain of the last twenty-four hours simply deleted as she looked down into his dark eyes.

'Are you sure he's mine?' Amy teased, because he was completely his father's son. She looked up to Emir and he kissed her gently, and she was bathed in a happiness made richer because he loved her and his daughters, with or without the gift of a son.

He took the baby in his arms and held him for a long moment, and Amy could see the pride and also the pain on his strong, proud features, for he was surely remembering the bittersweet time when he'd last held a tiny infant.

'I don't want to miss a moment of his life,' Emir said. 'I missed way too much of the twins' first year.' He closed his eyes in regret.

'Emir, there was a reason.' She understood that now.

'Every time I saw them, every time I held them, all I wanted was to do what was best for them, and yet I had the responsibility to put the future of my country first.'

'It must have been agony.'

'I was made better knowing they were looked after by you. When you left, when it was Fatima, when the ways of old were being adhered to, I knew I could not rule a country that rendered my daughters worthless. It worked in the past, but not now,' Emir explained. 'Yet it was a decision that required distance.'

'It did,' Amy agreed. 'I wish you could have spoken with me…' Her voice trailed off, because Emir was right. It was a decision that could only have been reached alone. 'It's all worked out.' She looked at her sleeping baby. 'The rules don't even have to change.'

'They do,' Emir said. 'For I never want my son to have to make a choice like the one I was forced to make. The predictors were wrong: the two countries are better separated. I am glad I have a son for many reasons, but it will prove once and for all that we are doing this because it is right rather than necessary. The people will love him as they now love the girls—as they love you.'

The changes of the past few months had been less tumultuous than Amy had feared. The old Bedouin man had laughed when Rakhal and Emir consulted him, had shrugged and shaken his head when they'd said that the predictions were wrong. But the people in the main had accepted it, reassured that their two Kings were united and strong in their decision. And even before they'd found out that Amy was expecting a baby they had cheered for the twins, and a newspaper had celebrated with a headline about the future Queen Clemira.

'Your mother should be here any time,' Emir said, because as soon as Amy had gone into labour Emir had organised a plane for her.

Amy could not wait to see her mother's face when, after all the anguish, she got to hold her grandson.

'Shall I bring the girls in to meet their new brother?' Emir asked, handing his son back to her outstretched arms.

'Okay,' Amy said, excited about their reaction.

She smiled as he brought the girls in. She loved them so much—every bit as much as the baby in her arms. She had loved them from the moment they were born. She watched Nakia's face light up when she saw her new brother. She was completely entranced, smothering him with kisses, but Clemira seemed less than impressed. She looked at him for a moment or two and then wriggled down off the bed and toddled off. Following her sister's lead, soon so too did Nakia. Emir called for the nanny to take them back to the playroom.

'Do you think she is jealous?' Emir asked, taking the now sleeping baby and placing him in his crib, then climbing onto the bed beside her. 'She barely looked at him.'

'It's early days,' Amy said. There was no nicer place in the world than to be in bed next to Emir with their baby sleeping by their side. 'I'm surprised, though. She was so taken with Tariq. I guess it will take a bit of getting used…' She did not finish her sentence because it was taken over by a yawn.

Emir pulled her in. 'You need to rest.'

'Stay.'

'Of course,' Emir said. 'But you must sleep while you have the chance. The next weeks will be busy— your family arriving and the naming ceremony… And Natasha has rung and wants to come over before then. She is so looking forward to seeing the baby.'

Amy smiled, half dozing. All was well in her world as she rested safe in his arms. She would look forward to Natasha's visit—they were firm friends now and met often. Their children delighted in playing together.

'I'd love to see her, and Clemira will be thrilled to see Tariq…' Her voice trailed off again, but for a different reason. An impossible thought formed between waking and sleep. 'Emir?'

'Rest,' he told her, his eyes closed, but Amy couldn't.

'If Clemira is still as taken with Tariq in…oh, say in twenty years or so…'

She looked up and his eyes opened. The frown that had formed faded as a smile broke onto his face. 'That would make things incredibly complicated.'

'Really?'

'Or incredibly simple.' He kissed the top of her head. 'Sleep now,' he said. 'It is not something we are going to consider or force. That is not a decision we will ever make for them.'

'But if it *did* happen?' Amy pushed. 'Then the countries would become one again?'

'Perhaps,' Emir said.

She closed her eyes and stopped thinking about the future, relished the present.

Emir was the one who broke the silence, the possibility perhaps still on his mind.

'Maybe I was wrong?' Emir said, pulling her in closer, feeling absolute peace in his once troubled heart. 'Who am I to say that when the predictions were made, they did not factor in love?'

* * * * *

Hers for One Night Only?

CAROL MARINELLI

CHAPTER ONE

'YOU'RE far too available.' Bridgette didn't really know how to respond when her friend Jasmine's sympathy finally ran out. After all, she knew that Jasmine was right. 'It's me and Vince's leaving do and you won't come out *in case* your sister needs a babysitter.'

'You know it's not as simple as that,' Bridgette said.

'But it *is* as simple as that.' Jasmine was determined to stand firm this time. Her boyfriend, Vince, was a paediatric intern at the large Melbourne hospital where Bridgette had, until recently, worked, and he was heading off for a year to do relief work overseas. At what felt like the last minute the rather dizzy Jasmine had decided to join him for three months, and after a lot of paperwork and frantic applications, finally tonight there was a gathering to see them both off. 'You've put everything on hold for Courtney, you've given up a job you love so you can do agency and be more flexible— you've done everything you can to support her and look at where it's got you.'

Jasmine knew that she was being harsh, but she wanted Bridgette to cry, damn it, wanted her friend to admit the truth—that living like this was agony, that something had to give. But Bridgette refused to cry, insisting instead that she was coping—that she didn't mind doing agency work, that she loved looking after Courtney's son, Harry. 'Come out, then,' Jasmine challenged. 'If everything's as fine as you say, you deserve a night out—you haven't had one in ages. I want you there—we all want to see you. Everyone will be there...'

'What if...?' Bridgette stopped herself from saying it. She was exhausted from going over the what-ifs.

'Stop hiding behind Harry,' Jasmine said.

'I'm not.'

'Yes, you are. I know you've been hurt, but you need to put it behind you.'

And it stung, but, then, the truth often did and, yes, Bridgette conceded, maybe she was using Harry as a bit of an excuse so as not to get out there. 'Okay!' Bridgette took a deep breath and nodded. 'You're on.'

'You're coming?' Jasmine grinned.

'Looks like it.'

So instead of sitting at home, Bridgette sat in the hairdresser's and had some dark foils added to her mousey-brown hair. They made her skin look paler and her sludgy-grey eyes just a bit darker, it seemed, and with Jasmine's endless encouragement she had a wax and her nails done too and, for good measure, crammed in a little shopping.

Bridgette's bedroom was in chaos, not that Jasmine cared a bit, as they fought over mirror space and added another layer of mascara. It was a hot, humid night and already Bridgette was sweating. Her face would be shining by the time she got there at this rate, so she climbed over two laundry baskets to open her bedroom window and then attempted to find her shoes. 'I must tidy up in here.' Bridgette searched for her high-heeled sandals.

Her bedroom had once been tidy—but when Harry had been born Courtney had moved in and Bridgette's two-bedroom flat had never quite recovered from housing three—actually, four at times if you counted Paul. Her love life hadn't recovered either!

Bridgette found her sandals and leant against the wall as she put them on. She surveyed the large boxes of shelves she had bought online that would hopefully help her organise things. 'I want to get these shelves put up. Dad said he'd come around and find the studs in the wall, whatever they are…'

Jasmine bit her tongue—Maurice had been saying that for months. The last thing Bridgette needed tonight was to have her parents criticised but, honestly, two more unhelpful, inflexible people you could not meet. Maurice and Betty Joyce just closed their eyes to the chaos their youngest daughter created and left it all for Bridgette to sort out.

'How do you feel?' Jasmine asked as, dressed in a guilty purchase, make-up done and high heels on, Bridgette surveyed herself in the mirror.

'Twenty-six.' Bridgette grinned at her own reflection, liking, for once, what she saw. Gone was the exhausted woman from earlier—instead she literally glowed and not with sweat either. No, it was the sheer silver dress she had bought that did the most amazing things to her rather curvy figure, and the heavenly new blusher that had wiped away the last remnants of fatigue in just a few glittery, peachy strokes.

'And single,' Jasmine nudged.

'Staying single,' Bridgette said. 'The last thing I want is a relationship.'

'Doesn't have to be a relationship,' Jasmine replied, but gave in with a small laugh. 'It does with you, though.' She looked at her friend. 'Paul was a complete bastard, you know.'

'I know.' She did not want to talk about it.

'Better to find out now than later.'

'I know that,' Bridgette snapped. She *so* did not want to talk about it—she didn't even want to think about it tonight—but thankfully Jasmine had other things on her mind.

'Ooh, I wonder if Dominic will be there. He's sex on legs, that guy…' Even though she was blissfully happy with Vince, Jasmine still raved about the paediatric locum registrar, Dominic Mansfield.

'You're just about to fly off to Africa with your boyfriend.' Bridgette grinned. 'Should you be noticing such things?'

'I can still look.' Jasmine sighed. 'Honestly, you can't help looking when Dominic's around—he's gorgeous. He just doesn't belong in our hospital. He should be on some glamorous soap or something… Anyway, I was thinking of him more for you.'

'Liar. From what you've told me about Dominic, he's not the *relationship* kind.'

'Well, he must have been at some point—he was engaged before he came to Melbourne. Mind you, he wouldn't do for you at all. He hardly speaks. He's quite arrogant really,' Jasmine mused. 'Anyway, enough about all that. Look at you.' She smiled at her friend in the mirror. 'Gorgeous, single, no commitments… You're allowed to have fun, you know.'

Except Bridgette did have commitments, even if no one could really understand them. It was those commitments that had her double-check that she had her phone in her bag. She didn't feel completely single—more she felt like a single mum with her child away on an access visit. Courtney and Harry had lived with her for a year and it had ended badly, and though she spoke little to Courtney now, she was an extremely regular babysitter.

She missed him tonight.

But, she reminded herself, he wasn't hers to miss.

Still, it was nice to be out and to catch up with everyone. They all put in some money for drinks, but unfortunately it was Jasmine who chose the wine and it was certainly a case of quantity over quality. Bridgette took a sip—she was far from a wine snob, but it really was awful and she sat on one drink all night.

'When are you coming back to us?' was the cry from her ex-colleagues.

'I'm not sure,' Bridgette responded. 'Soon, I hope.'

Yes, it was a good night; it just wasn't the same as it once had been.

She wasn't one of them any more.

She had no idea who they were talking about when they moaned about someone called Rita—how she took over in a birth, how much her voice grated. There had been a big drama last week apparently, which they were now discussing, of which Bridgette knew nothing. Slipping her phone out of her bag, she checked it, relieved to see that there were no calls, but even though she wasn't needed, even though she had nowhere else to be right now, the night was over for her.

She wasn't a midwife any more, or at best she was an occasional one—she went wherever the agency sent her. Bridgette was about to say goodbye to Jasmine, to make a discreet exit, when she was thwarted by some late arrivals, whom Jasmine marched her over to, insisting that she say hello.

'This is Rita, the new unit manager.' Jasmine introduced the two women. 'And, Rita, this is Bridgette Joyce. She used to work with us. We're trying to persuade her to come back. And this is...' He really needed no introduction, because Bridgette looked over and fell into very black eyes. The man stood apart from the rest and looked a bit out of place in the rather tacky bar, and, yes, he was as completely stunning as Jasmine had described. His black hair was worn just a little bit long and swept backwards to reveal a face that was exquisite. He was tall, slim and wearing black trousers and a fitted white shirt. He was, quite simply, divine. 'This is Dominic,' Jasmine introduced, 'our locum paediatrician.'

He didn't look like a paediatrician—oh, she knew she shouldn't label people so, but as he nodded and said hello he didn't look in the least like a man who was used to dealing with children. Jasmine was right—he should be on a soap, playing the part of a pretend doctor, or... She imagined him more a surgeon, a cosmetic surgeon perhaps, at some exclusive private practice.

'Can I get anyone a drink?' He was very smooth and polite, and there was no hint of an accent, but with such dark looks she wondered if his forebears were Italian perhaps, maybe Greek. He must have caught her staring, and when he saw that she didn't have a glass, he spoke directly to her. 'Bridgette, can I get you anything?'

'Not for me, thanks, I'm—' She was just about to say that she was leaving when Jasmine interrupted her.

'You don't need to buy a drink, Dominic. We've got loads.' Jasmine toddled over to their loud table and poured him a glass of vinegary wine and one for

Bridgette too, and then handed them over. 'Come on.' Jasmine pushed, determined her friend would unwind. 'Drink up, Bridgette.'

He was terribly polite because he accepted it graciously and took a sip of the drink and managed not to wince. But as Bridgette took a tiny sip, she did catch his eye, and there was a hint of a shared smile, if it could even be called that.

'It's good that you could make it, Dominic.' Vince came over. He had just today finished his paediatric rotation, and Bridgette had worked with him on Maternity for a while before she'd left. 'I know that it hasn't been a great day.'

She watched as Dominic gave a brief nod, gave practically nothing back to that line of conversation—instead, he changed the subject. 'So,' he asked, 'when do you fly?'

'Monday night,' Vince said, and spoke a little about the project he was joining.

'Well,' said Dominic, 'all the best with it.'

He really didn't waste words, did he? Bridgette thought as Jasmine polished her cupid's bow and happily took Vince's hand and wandered off, leaving Bridgette alone with him and trying not to show just how awkward she felt.

'Careful,' she said as his glass moved to his lips. 'Remember how bad it tastes.'

She was rewarded with the glimpse of a smile.

'Do you want me to get you something else?'

Yikes, she hadn't been fishing for drinks. 'No, no…' Bridgette shook her head. 'Jasmine would be offended. I'm fine. I was just…' Joking, she didn't add, trying to make conversation. Gorgeous he might be to look at but he really didn't say very much. 'You're at the hospital, then?' Bridgette asked.

'Just as a fill-in,' Dominic said. 'I've got a consultant's position starting in a couple of weeks in Sydney.' He named a rather impressive hospital and that just about summed him up, Bridgette decided—rather impressive and very, very temporary.

'Your family is there?'

'That's right,' he said, but didn't elaborate. 'You work on Maternity?' Dominic frowned, because he couldn't place her.

'I used to,' Bridgette explained. 'I left six months ago. I've been doing agency…'

'Why?'

It was a very direct question, one she wasn't quite expecting, one she wasn't really sure how to answer.

'The hours are more flexible,' she said, 'the money's better…' And it was the truth, but only a shred of it, because she missed her old job very badly. She'd just been accepted as a clinical nurse specialist when she'd left. She adored everything about midwifery, and now she went wherever the agency sent her. As she was qualified as a general nurse, she could find herself in nursing homes, on spinal units, sometimes in psych. She just worked and got on with it, but she missed doing what she loved the most.

He really didn't need to hear it, so back on went the smile she'd been wearing all night. 'And it means that I get to go out on a Saturday night.' The moment she said them, she wanted those words back, wished she could retrieve them. She knew that she sounded like some sort of party girl, especially with what came next.

'I can see it has benefits,' Dominic said, and she

swore he glanced down at the hand that was holding the glass, and for a dizzy moment she realised she was being appraised. 'If you have a young family.'

'Er, no.' Oh, help, she *was* being appraised. He was looking at her, the same way she might look at shoes in a window and tick off her mental list of preferences—too flat, too high, nice colour, shame about the bow. Wrong girl, she wanted to say to him, I'm lace-up-shoe boring.

'You don't have children?'

'No,' she said, and something twisted inside, because if she told him about Harry she would surely burst into tears. She could just imagine Dominic's gorgeous face sort of sliding into horrified boredom if the newly foiled, for once groomed woman beside him told him she felt as if her guts were being torn, that right now, right this very minute, she was having great difficulty not pulling out her phone to check if there had been a text or a call from Courtney. Right now she wanted to drive past where her sister was living with her friend Louise and make sure that there wasn't a wild party raging. She scrambled for something to say, anything to say, and of course she again said the wrong thing.

'Sorry that you had a bad day.' She watched his jaw tighten a fraction, knew, given his job, that it was a stupid thing to say, especially when her words tumbled out in a bright and breezy voice. But the false smile she had plastered on all night seemed to be infusing her brain somehow, she was so incredibly out of practice with anything remotely social.

He gave her the same brief nod that he had given Vince, then a very brief smile and very smoothly excused himself.

'Told you!' Jasmine was over in a flash the minute he was gone. 'Oh, my God, you were talking for ages.'

'For two minutes.'

'That's ages for him!' Jasmine breathed. 'He hardly says a word to anyone.'

'Jasmine!' She rolled her eyes at her friend. 'You can stop this very moment.' Bridgette let out a small gurgle of laughter. 'I think I've just been assessed as to my suitability for a one-nighter. Honestly, he's shameless… He asked if I had children and everything. Maybe he's worried I've got stretch marks and a baggy vagina.'

It was midwife-speak, and as she made Jasmine laugh, she laughed herself. The two women really laughed for the first time in a long, long time, and it was so good for Bridgette to be with her friend before she jetted off, because Jasmine had helped her through this difficult time. She didn't want to be a misery at her friends' leaving do, so she kept up the conversation a little. They giggled about lithe, toned bodies and the temptresses who would surely writhe on his white rug in his undoubtedly immaculate city apartment. It *was* a white rug, they decided, laughing, for a man like Dominic was surely far too tasteful for animal prints. And he'd make you a cocktail on arrival, for this was the first-class lounge of one-night stands, and on and on they went… Yes, it was so good to laugh.

Dominic could hear her laughter as he spoke with a colleague, as again he was offered yet more supposed consolation for a 'bad day'. He wished that people would just say nothing, wished he could simply forget.

It had been a… He searched for the expletive to best describe his day, chose it, but knew if he voiced it he might just be asked to leave, which wouldn't be so bad, but, no, he took a mouthful of vinegar and grimaced as it met the acid in his stomach.

He hated his job.

Was great at it.

Hated it.

Loved it.

Did it.

He played ping-pong in his mind with a ball that broke with every hit.

He wanted that hard ball tonight, one that bounced back on every smash, one that didn't crumple if you hammered it.

He wanted to be the doctor who offered better answers.

Today he had seen the dominos falling, had scrambled to stop them, had done everything to reset them, but still they'd fallen—click, click, click—racing faster than he could halt them till he'd known absolutely what was coming and had loathed that he'd been the only one who could see it.

'Where there's life there's hope' had been offered several times.

Actually, no, he wanted to say as he'd stared at another batch of blood results and read off the poisons that had filled this tiny body.

'There is hope, though…' the parents had begged, and he had refused to flinch at the frantic eyes that had scanned his face as he'd delivered news.

He loved hope, he craved hope and had searched so hard for it today, but he also knew when hope was gone, said it before others would. Unlike others, he faced the inevitable—because it was either cardiac massage and all lights blazing, or a cuddle without the tubes at the end.

Yes, it came down to that.

Yes, it had been a XXXX of a day.

He had sat with the parents till ten p.m. and then entered a bar that was too bright, stood with company that was too loud and tasted wine that could dissolve an olive, and hated that he missed her. How could you miss a woman you didn't even like? He hated that she'd ring tonight and that he might be tempted to go back. That in two weeks' time he'd see her. Shouldn't he be over Arabella by now? Maybe it was just because he had had a 'bad day'. Not that he and Arabella had ever really spoken about work—oh, they'd discussed their career paths of course, but never the day-to-day details. They'd never talked about days such as this, Dominic mused.

Then he had seen her—Bridgette. In a silver dress and with a very wide smile, with gorgeous nails and polished hair, she had drawn his eye. Yet on inspection there was more behind that polished façade than he cared to explore, more than he needed tonight.

He *had* been checking for a wedding ring.

What no one understood was that he preferred to find one.

Married women were less complicated, knew the rules from the start, for they had so much more to lose than he did.

Bridgette was complicated.

He'd read her, because he read women well. He could see the hurt behind those grey eyes, could see the effort that went into her bright smile. She was complicated and he didn't need it. But, on the way down to her ring finger, he'd noticed very pale skin and a tapestry of freckles, and he'd wondered where the freckles stopped, had wondered far too many things.

He didn't need an ounce of emotion tonight, not one more piece, which was why he had excused himself and walked away. But perhaps he'd left gut instinct in his car tonight, the radar warning that had told him to keep his distance dimmed a fraction as he looked over to where she stood, laughing with her friend.

'Hey, Dominic…' He heard a low, seductive voice and turned to the pretty blonde who stood before him, a nurse who worked in Theatre and one whose husband seemed to be perpetually away. 'So brilliant to see you tonight.' He looked into eyes that were blue and glittered with open invitation, saw the ring on her finger and the spray tan on her arm on the way down. 'I just finished a late shift. Wasn't sure I'd make it.'

'Are you on tomorrow?' someone asked.

'No,' she answered. 'And I've got the weekend to myself. Geoff's away.' Her eyes flicked to his and Dominic met her gaze, went to take another sip of his drink and then, remembering how it tasted, changed his mind, and he changed his mind about something else too—he couldn't stomach the taste of fake tan tonight.

Then he heard Bridgette laughing, looked over and ignored his inner radar, managed to convince himself that he had read her wrong.

He knew now what Bridgette's middle name was. Escape.

'People are talking about going for something to eat…' Vince came over and snaked his arm around Jasmine, and they shared a kiss as Bridgette stood, pretending not to feel awkward—actually, not so awkward now

that she and Jasmine had had such a laugh. She wasn't
going out to dinner, or to a club, but at least she and
Jasmine had had some fun—but then the waitress came
over and handed her a glass.

'For me?' Bridgette frowned.

'He said to be discreet.' The waitress nodded her
head in Dominic's direction. 'I'll get rid of your other
glass.'

Double yikes!

She glanced over to black eyes that were waiting to
meet hers.

Wrong girl, she wanted to semaphore back—so very,
very wrong for you, Dominic, she wanted to signal. It
took me weeks to have sex with Paul, I mean weeks,
and you're only here for two. And I don't think I'm very
good at it anyway. At least he hinted at that when we
broke up. But Bridgette didn't have any flags handy
and wouldn't know what to do if she had them anyway, so she couldn't spell it out; she only had her eyes
and they held his.

She lifted the glass of temptation he offered and the
wine slipped onto her tongue and down her throat. It
tasted delicious—cold and expensive and not at all what
she was used to.

She felt her cheeks burn as she dragged her eyes from
him and back to her friend and tried to focus on what
Jasmine was saying—something about Mexican, and a
night that would never end. She sipped her champagne
that was far too nice, far too moreish, and Bridgette
knew she had to get out of there. 'Not for me,' she said
to Jasmine, feeling the scald of his eyes on her shoulder
as she spoke. 'Honestly, Jasmine…' She didn't need to
make excuses with her friend.

0800 054 2211

'I know.' Jasmine smiled. 'It really is great that you came out.'

It had been. Bridgette was relieved that she'd made it this far for her friend and also rather relieved to escape from the very suave Dominic—he was so out of her league and she also knew they were flirting. Dominic had the completely wrong impression of her—he thought she worked agency for the money and flexibility, so that she could choose her shifts at whim and party hard on a Saturday night.

If only he knew the truth.

Still, he was terribly nice.

Not nice, she corrected. Not *nice* nice, more toe-curlingly sexy and a dangerous nice. Still, no one was leaving. Instead he had made his way over, the music seemed to thud low in her stomach and for a bizarre moment as he joined them she thought he was about to lean over and kiss her.

Just like that, in front of everyone.

And just like that, in front of everyone, she had the ridiculous feeling that she'd comply.

It was safer to leave, to thank him for the drink, to say she wasn't hungry, to hitch up her bag and get the hell out of there, to ignore the dangerous dance in her mind.

'I'll see you on Monday,' she said to Jasmine.

'You can help me pack!'

The group sort of moved out of the bar as she did and walked towards the Mexican restaurant. There had been a burst of summer rain but it hadn't cleared the air. Instead it was muggy, the damp night air clinging to her cheeks, to her legs and arms as her eyes scanned the street for a taxi.

'Are you sure you don't want something to eat?' Dominic asked.

And she should say no—she really should walk away now, Bridgette told herself. She didn't even like Mexican food, but he was gorgeous and it had been ages since there had been even a hint of a flirt. And she was twenty-six and maybe just a bit flattered that someone as sophisticated as he was was paying her attention. Her wounded ego could certainly use the massage and she'd just checked her phone and things seemed fine, so Bridgette took a deep breath and forced back that smile.

'Sounds great.'

'Good,' he replied, except she was confused, because he then said goodbye to Vince and Jasmine as Bridgette stood on the pavement, blinking as the group all bundled into a restaurant and just the two of them remained. Then he turned and smiled. 'Let's get something to eat, then.'

'I thought…' She didn't finish her sentence, because he aimed his keys at a car, a very nice car, which lit up in response, and she glanced at her phone again and there wasn't a single message.

Her chariot awaited.

She climbed in the car and sank into the leather and held her breath as Dominic walked around to the driver's side.

She didn't do things like this.

Ever.

But there was a part of her that didn't want to say goodnight.

A part of her that didn't want to go back to an empty flat and worry about Harry.

They drove though the city; he blasted on the air-conditioner and it was bliss to feel the cool air on her cheeks. They drove in silence until his phone rang and she glanced to the dashboard where it sat in its little charger and the name 'Arabella' flashed up on his screen. Instead of making an excuse, he turned for a brief second and rolled his eyes. 'Here we go.'

'Sorry?'

'The maudlin Saturday night phone call,' Dominic said, grinding the gears. 'How much she misses me, how she didn't mean it like that...'

The phone went black.

'Your ex?'

'Yep.' He glanced over to her. 'You can answer it if she rings again.' He flashed her a smile, a devilish smile that had her stomach flip. 'Tell her we're in bed—that might just silence her.'

'Er, no!' She grinned. 'I don't do things like that.'

On both counts.

'Were you serious?' she asked, because she couldn't really imagine him serious about anyone. Mind you, Jasmine had said they'd been engaged.

'Engaged,' he said. 'For a whole four weeks.'

And he pulled his foot back from the accelerator because he realised he was driving too fast, but he hated the phone calls, hated that sometimes he was tempted to answer, to slip back into life as he once had known it.

And end up like his parents, Dominic reminded himself.

He'd lived through their hellish divorce as a teenager, had seen their perfect life crumble, and had no intention of emulating it. With Arabella he had taken his time. They had been together for two years and he thought he had chosen well—gorgeous, career-minded and she didn't want children. In fact, it had turned out, she didn't want anything that was less than perfect.

'You're driving too fast.' Her voice broke into his thoughts. 'I don't make a very good passenger.' She smiled. 'I think I'm a bit of a control freak.'

He slowed down, the car swishing through the damp city streets, and then they turned into the Arts Centre car park. Walking through it, she could hear her heels ringing on the cement, and even though it was her town, it was Dominic who knew where he was going—it had been ages since she had been in the heart of the city. She didn't feel out of place in her silver dress. The theatres were spilling out and there were people everywhere dressed to the nines and heading for a late dinner.

She found herself by a river—looking out on it from behind glass. She was at a table, with candles and silver and huge purple menus and a man she was quite sure she couldn't handle. He'd been joking in the car about telling his ex they were in bed, she knew it, but not really—she knew that too.

'What do you want to eat?'

Bridgette wasn't that hungry—she felt a little bit sick, in fact—but she looked through the menu and tried to make up her mind.

'I…' She didn't have the energy to sit through a meal. Really, she ought to tell him now, that the night would not be ending as he was undoubtedly expecting. 'I'm not very hungry…'

'We can get dessert and coffee if you want.'

'I wouldn't mind the cheese platter.'

'Start at the end.' He gave her a smile and placed the order—water for him and cognac for her, he suggested, and, heaven help her, the waiter asked if she wanted it warmed.

'Dominic…' She took a deep breath as their platter arrived, a gorgeous platter of rich cheeses and fruits. 'I think—'

'I think we just ought to enjoy,' he interrupted.

'No.' Bridgette gulped. 'I mean…' She watched as he smeared cheese on a cracker and offered it to her.

'I don't like blue cheese.'

'Then you haven't had a good one.'

He wasn't wrong there!

He took a bite instead and her hand shook as she reached for the knife, tasted something she was quite sure she didn't like and found out it was, in fact, amazing.

'Told you.'

'You did.' She looked at the platter, at the grapes and dates, like some lush oil painting, and she knew the dance that was being played and the flirting and the seduction that was to come, and it terrified her. 'I don't think I should be here…' She scrabbled in her bag, would pay the bill, knew that she must end this.

'Bridgette.' He wasn't a bastard—he really wasn't. Yes, he'd been playing the field since his engagement had ended, and, yes, he had every intention of continuing to do so, but he only played with those who were happy with the rules, and he knew now for sure that she wasn't. 'It's cheese.'

She lifted troubled eyes to his.

'No, it isn't—it's the ride home after.'

He liked her. He hadn't wanted emotion tonight, and yet she made him smile as a tear washed away the last of her foundation and he could see freckles on her nose.

'Bridgette, it's cheese and conversation.' He took her hand, and she started to tell him he didn't want just cheese and conversation, oh, no, she knew it very well. She told him she wasn't the girl in the silver dress who partied and he held her hand as she babbled about zebra-print rugs, no white ones, and cocktails. 'Bridgette.' He was incredibly close to adoring her, to leaning over and kissing her right now. 'It's cheese and conversation and then I'll take you home.' He looked at her mouth and he was honest. 'Maybe just one kiss goodnight.'

Oh, but she wanted her kiss.

Just one.

'That leads nowhere,' she said.

'That leads nowhere,' he assured her.

'We're not suited,' she said, and was incredibly grateful that he nodded.

'We're completely incompatible,' Dominic agreed.

'And I'm sorry if I've misled you…'

'You didn't.' He was very magnanimous, smearing more cheese and this time handing it to her, no, wait, feeding her, and it wasn't so much seductive as nice. 'I *let* myself be misled,' he said, and he handed her her cognac. 'I knew from the start you were nice.' He gave her a smile. 'And you are, Bridgette.'

'So are you.'

'Oh, no,' he assured her. 'I'm not.'

CHAPTER TWO

IT FELT so good to feel so good and it was as if they both knew that they didn't have long. It was terribly hard to explain it, but now that there wasn't sex on the menu, now they'd cleared that out of the way, they could relax and just be.

For a little while.

She took a sip of cognac and it burnt all the way down, a delicious burn.

'Nice?' Dominic asked.

'Too nice,' she admitted.

And he hadn't wanted conversation, or emotion, but he was laughing, talking, sharing, and that XXXX of a day melted away with her smile.

So they worked the menu backwards and ordered dessert, chocolate soufflé for Bridgette and water-melon and mint sorbet for him. As he sampled his dish, Bridgette wanted a taste—not a spoonful, more a taste of his cool, watermelon-and-mint-flavoured tongue—and she flushed a little as he offered her the spoon. 'Want some?' Dominic said.

She shook her head, asked instead about his work, and he told her a bit about his plans for his career, and she told him about the lack of plans for hers.

'You love midwifery, though?' Dominic checked.

'I am hoping to go back to it.' Bridgette nodded. 'It's just been a bit of a complicated year…' She didn't elaborate and she was glad that he didn't push. Yes, she loved midwifery, she answered, loved babies.

'You want your own?' He asked the same question that everyone did when they heard her job.

'One day maybe…' Bridgette gave a vague shrug. Had he asked a couple of years ago she'd have told him that she wanted millions, couldn't wait to have babies of her own. Only now she simply couldn't see it. She couldn't imagine a place or a time where it might happen, couldn't imagine really trusting a man again. She didn't tell him that of course—that wasn't what tonight was about. Instead she gave a vague nod. 'I think so. You?' she asked, and he admitted that he shuddered at the very thought.

'You're a paediatrician.' Bridgette laughed.

'Doesn't mean I have to want my own. Anyway,' he added, 'I know what can go wrong.' He shook his head and was very definite. 'Nope, not for me.' He told her that he had a brother, Chris, when Bridgette said she had a sister, Courtney. Neither mentioned Arabella or Paul, and Bridgette certainly didn't mention Harry.

Tonight it was just about them.

And then they ordered coffee and talked some more.

And then another coffee.

And the waiters yawned, and Dominic and Bridgette looked around the restaurant and realised it was just the two of them left.

And it was over too soon, Bridgette thought as he paid the bill and they left. It was as if they were trying to cram so much into one night; almost as if it was understood that this really should deserve longer. It was like a plane trip alongside a wonderful companion: you knew you would be friends, more than friends perhaps, if you had more time, but you were both heading off to different lives. He to further his career and then back to his life in Sydney,

She to, no doubt, more of the same.

Except they had these few hours together and neither wanted them to end.

They walked along the river and to the bridge, leant over it and looked into the water, and still they spoke, about silly things, about music and videos and movies they had watched or that they thought the other really should see. He was nothing like the man she had assumed he was when they had been introduced in the bar—he was insightful and funny and amazing company. In fact, nothing at all like the remote, aloof man that Jasmine had described.

And she was nothing like he'd expected either when they had been introduced. Dominic was very careful about the women he dated in Melbourne; he had no interest in settling down, not even for a few weeks. Occasionally he got it wrong, and it would end in tears a few days later. Not his of course—it was always the women who wanted more than he was prepared to give, and Dominic had decided he was never giving that part of himself again. But there was a strange regret in the air as he drove her home—a rare regret for Dominic—because here was a woman he actually wouldn't mind getting to know a little more, one who might get him over those last stubborn, lingering remnants of Arabella.

He'd been joking about Bridgette answering the phone.

Sort of.

Actually, it wasn't such a bad idea. He couldn't face going back to Sydney while there was still weakness, didn't want to slip back into the picture-perfect life that had been prescribed to him since birth.

And it was strange because had they met at the start of his stay here, he was sure, quite sure, time would have moved more slowly. Now, though, it seemed that the beach road that led to her home, a road he was quite positive usually took a good fifteen minutes, seemed to be almost over in eight minutes and still they were talking, still they were laughing, as the car gobbled up their time.

'You should watch it.' She was talking about something on the internet, something she had found incredibly funny. 'Tonight when you get in.' She glanced at the clock on the dashboard and saw that it was almost two. 'I mean, this morning.'

'You watch it too.' He grinned. 'We can watch simultaneously...' His fingers tightened on the wheel and he ordered his mind not to voice the sudden direction it had taken—thankfully those thoughts went unsaid and unheard.

'I can't get on the internet,' Bridgette grumbled, trying desperately not to think similar thoughts. 'I've got a virus.' She swung her face to him. 'My computer, I mean, not...' What was wrong with her mouth? Bridgette thought as she turned her burning face to look out of the window. Why did everything lead to sex with him? 'Anyway,' she said, 'you should watch it.'

There was a roundabout coming up, the last roundabout, Bridgette knew, before her home, and it felt like her last chance at crazy, their last chance. And, yes, it was two a.m., but it could have been two p.m.; it was just a day that was running out and they wanted to chase it. She stole a look over at his delectable profile and to the olive hands that gripped the steering-wheel—it would be like leaving the cinema in the middle of the best movie ever without a hope of finding out the end. And she wanted more detail, wanted to know how it felt to be made love to by a man like him. She'd been truthful when she'd spoken to Jasmine—a relationship was the very last thing that she wanted now. Maybe this way had merit... '*We* should watch it.'

'Your computer's not working,' he pointed out.

'Yours is.' The flick of the indicator signalling right was about half the speed of her heart.

'Bridgette...' He wasn't a bastard—he was incredibly, incredibly nice, because they went three times round the roundabout as he made very sure.

'I don't want you to regret...' He was completely honest. 'I leave in two weeks.'

'I won't regret it.' She'd firmly decided that she wouldn't. 'After much consideration I have decided I would very much regret it if I didn't.' She gave him a smile. 'I want my night.'

She did. And he was lovely, because he did not gun the car home. It was so much nicer than she would ever be able to properly remember, but she knew for many nights she would try.

She wanted to be able to hold on to the moment when he turned and told her that he couldn't wait till they got all the way back to the city for the one kiss they had previously agreed to. She wanted to remember how they stopped at a lookout, gazed out at the bay, leant against his bonnet and watched the glittering view, and it felt as if time was suspended. She wanted to bottle it somehow, because she wasn't angry with Courtney at that moment, or worried for Harry. For the first time in ages she had a tiny glimpse of calm, of peace, a moment where she felt all was well.

Well, not calm, but it was a different sort of stress from the one she was used to as he moved his face to hers. Very nicely he kissed her, even if she was terribly nervous. He let her be nervous as he kissed her—till the pleats in her mind unfurled. It was a kiss that had been building all night, a kiss she had wanted since their introduction, and his mouth told her he had wanted the same.

'I was going to stay for one drink...' His mouth was at her ear, his body pressed into hers.

'I was just leaving,' she admitted as his face came back to view.

'And now look at us.'

So nice was that kiss that he did it again.

'You smell fantastic.' She was glad, to be honest, to have only him on her mind. He smelt as expensive as he looked and he tasted divine. She would never take this dress to the dry cleaner's, she thought as his scent wrapped around them, and his mouth was at her neck and under her hair. He was dragging in the last breaths of the perfume she had squirted on before going out and soaking in the scent of the salon's rich shampoo and the warm fragrance of woman.

'So do you,' he said.

'You taste fantastic,' Bridgette said. She was the one going back for more now.

'You too.'

And he liked the weight of responsibility that cloaked

him as he pressed her against the bonnet and his hands inched down to a silver hem. He could feel her soft thighs and wanted to lift her dress, but he wanted to know if her legs too were freckled, so he ended the kiss. He wanted more for her than that, more for himself than that.

Just tonight, Dominic assured himself as she did the same.

'What?' He caught her looking at him as they headed for his home, and grinned.

'Nothing.' She smiled back.

'Go on, say what you're thinking.'

'Okay.' So she did. 'You don't look like a paediatrician.'

'What is a paediatrician supposed to look like?'

'I don't know,' Bridgette admitted. 'Okay, you don't *seem* like a paediatrician.' She couldn't really explain it, but he laughed.

They laughed.

And when she told him that she imagined him more a cosmetic surgeon, with some exclusive private practice, his laugh turned wry. 'You're mistaking me for my father.'

'I don't think so,' Bridgette said.

And he pulled her towards him, because it was easier than thinking, easier than admitting he wasn't so sure of her verdict, that lately he seemed to be turning more and more into his father, the man he respected least.

It was three o'clock and she felt as if they were both trying to escape morning.

There wasn't a frantic kiss through the front door—instead the energy that swirled was more patient.

It was a gorgeous energy that waited as he made

her coffee and she went to the bathroom and he had the computer on when she returned. They did actually watch it together.

'I showed this to Jasmine—' there were tears rolling down her face, but from laughter '—and she didn't think it was funny.'

And he was laughing too, more than he ever had. He hadn't had a night like this in ages—in fact, he couldn't recall one ever.

Okay, she would try to remember the details, how he didn't cringe when she pretended his desk was a piano; instead he sang.

It was the most complicated thing to explain—that she could sing to him, that, worse, he could take the mug that was the microphone and do the same to her!

'We should be ashamed of ourselves.' She admired their reflection in the computer as they took a photo.

'Very ashamed,' he agreed.

She thought he was like this, Dominic realised, that this was how his usual one-night stands went. Didn't she understand that this was as rare for him as it was for her? He hadn't been like this even with Arabella.

He didn't just want anyone tonight; he wanted her.

It was an acute want that tired now of being patient and so too did hers. As their mouths met on time and together, he kissed her to the back of the sofa. It felt so seamless, so right, because not for a second did Bridgette think, Now he's going to kiss me. One moment they were laughing and the next they were kissing. It was a transition that was as simple as that.

It was his mouth and his taste and the slide of his tongue.

It was her mouth and a kiss that didn't taste of plastic, that tasted of her tongue, and he kissed her and she curled into it. She loved the feel of his mouth and the roam of his hands and the way her body was craving his—it was a kiss that was potent, everything a kiss could be, distilled into one delicious dose.

He took off her dress, because he wanted to see *her*, not the woman in silver, and his eyes roamed. They roamed as he took off her bra and he answered his earlier question because her freckles stopped only where her bikini would be. There were two unfreckled triangles that wanted his mouth, but he talked to her as well and what she didn't know was how rare that was.

He left control behind and was out of his mind.

He wanted her in France, he told her as he licked her nipple.

Topless and naked on the beach beside him, and new freckles on her breasts. She closed her eyes and she could smell the sun oil, could feel the heat from the sun that shone in France and the coolness of his tongue on sunburnt nipples. He pressed her into the couch and she pressed back to him.

She was lying down and could feel him hard against her and she didn't think twice, just slid his zipper down.

She could hear her own moan as she held him and he lifted his head.

'We're not going to make it to the bedroom, are we?'

'Not a hope,' she admitted.

Was this what it was like?

To be free.

To be irresponsible.

More, please, she wanted to sob, because she wanted to live on the edge for ever, never wanted this night to end.

She wanted this man who took off his trousers and kept condoms in his wallet, and it didn't offend her—she already knew what he was like, after all.

'Bastard.' She grinned.

And he knew her too.

'Sorry,' he said. In their own language he apologised for the cad that he was and told her that he wasn't being one tonight.

This was different.

So different that he sat her up.

Sank to his knees on the edge of the sofa.

And pulled her bottom towards him.

'Let's get rid of these.' He was shameless. He dispensed with anything awkward, just slid her panties down, and she did remember staring up at the ceiling as his tongue slid up a pale, freckled thigh that didn't taste of fake tan and then he dived right in. As he licked and teased and tasted she would remember for ever thinking, Is this me?

And she was grateful for his experience, for his skill, for the mastery of his tongue, because it was a whole new world and tonight she got to step into it.

'Relax,' he said, when she forgot to for a moment.

So she did, just closed her eyes and gave in to it.

'Where's the rug?' she asked as he slid her to the floor.

'No rug,' he said.

He maybe should get one, was her last semi-coherent thought, because the carpet burnt in her back as he moved inside her, a lovely burn, and then it was his turn to sample the carpet for he toppled her over, still deep inside her, and she was on top.

Don't look down.

It wasn't even a semi-coherent thought; it was more a familiar warning that echoed in her head.

Don't look down—but she did, she looked down from the tightrope that recently she'd been walking.

She glimpsed black eyes that were open as she closed hers and came, and he watched her expression, felt her abandon, and then his eyes closed as he came too. Yes, feeling those last bucks deep inside her she looked down and it didn't daunt her, didn't terrify. It exhilarated her as greedily he pulled her head down and kissed her.

'It's morning,' he said as they moved to the bedroom, the first sunlight starting.

Better still as she closed her eyes to the new day, there was no regret.

CHAPTER THREE

IT WAS like waking up to an adult Christmas.

The perfect morning, Bridgette thought as she stretched out in the wrinkled bed.

She must have slept through the alarm on her phone and he must have got up, for there was the smell of coffee in the air. If she thought there might be a little bit of embarrassment, that they both might be feeling a touch awkward this morning, she was wrong.

'Morning.' Dominic was delighted by her company, which was rare for him. He had the best job in the world to deal with situations such as this—in fact, since in Melbourne, he had a permanent alarm call set for eight a.m. at weekends. He would answer the phone to the recorded message, talk for a brief moment, and then hang up and apologise to the woman in his bed. He would explain that something had come up at work and that he had no choice but to go in.

It was a back-up plan that he often used, but he didn't want to use it today. Today he'd woken up before his alarm call and had headed out to the kitchen, made two coffees and remembered from last night that she took sugar. He thought about breakfast in bed and perhaps another walk to the river, to share it in daylight this time. Sunday stretched out before him like a long, luxurious yawn, a gorgeous pause in his busy schedule.

'What time is it?' Bridgette yawned too.

'Almost eight.' He climbed back into bed and he was delicious. 'I was thinking…' He looked down at where she lay. 'Do you want to go out somewhere nice for breakfast?'

'In a silver dress?' Bridgette grinned. 'And high heels?'

'Okay,' he said. 'Then I guess we've no option but to spend the day in bed.' She reached for her coffee and, as she always did when Harry wasn't with her, she reached for her phone to check for messages. Then she saw that it wasn't turned on and a knot of dread tightened in her stomach as she pressed the button.

'Is everything okay?'

'Sure.' Only it wasn't. She hadn't charged her phone yesterday; with Jasmine arriving and going out she hadn't thought to plug it in. Her phone could have been off for hours—anything could have happened and she wouldn't even know. She took a sip of her coffee and tried to calm herself down. Told herself she was being ridiculous, that she had to stop worrying herself sick, but it wasn't quite so easy and after a moment she turned and forced a smile. 'As much as I'd love to spend the day in bed, I really am going to have to get home.'

'Everything okay?' He checked again, because he could sense the change in her. One moment ago she'd been yawning and stretching; now she was as jumpy as a cat.

'Of course,' Bridgette said. 'I've just got a lot on…'

She saw the flash of confusion in his eyes and it could have irritated her—in fact, she wanted it to irritate her. After all, why shouldn't she have a busy day planned? Why should he just assume that she'd want a day with him? But that didn't work, because somehow last night had not been as casual as she was now making it out to be. It needed to be, Bridgette reminded herself as she turned away from his black eyes—she felt far safer with their one-night rule, far safer not trusting him. 'I'll get a taxi,' she said as she climbed out of bed and found her crumpled dress and then realised she'd have to go through the apartment to locate her underwear.

'Don't be ridiculous—I'll drive you home,' Dominic said, and he lay there as she padded out. He could hear her as she pulled on her panties and bra, and he tried not to think about last night and the wonderful time they'd had. Not just the sex, but before that, lying on the sofa watching clips on the computer, or the car ride home.

It wasn't usually him getting sentimental. Normally it was entirely the other way round.

'You really don't have to give me a lift.' She stood at the door, dressed now and holding her shoes in her hand, last night's mascara smudged beneath her eyes, her hair wild and curly, and he wanted her back in his bed. 'It's no problem to get a taxi.'

'I'll get my keys.'

And she averted her eyes as he climbed out of the bed, as he did the same walk as her and located his clothes all crumpled on the floor. She wished the balloon would pop and he'd look awful all messed and unshaven. She could smell them in the room and the computer was still on and their photo was there on the screen and *how* they'd been smiling.

'Bridgette…' He so wasn't used to this. 'You haven't even had your coffee.'

'I really do need to get back.'

'Sure.'

And talking was incredibly awkward, especially at the roundabout.

She wanted the indicator on, wanted him to turn the car around and take them back to bed, and, yes, she could maybe tell him about Harry.

About Courtney.

About the whole sorry mess.

End the dream badly.

After all, he was only here for two weeks, and even if he hadn't been, she could hardly expect someone as glamorous and gorgeous as him to understand.

She didn't want him to understand, she didn't want him to know, so instead she blew out a breath and let the sat nav lead him to her door.

'Good luck in Sydney.' She really was terrible at this one-night thing.

'Bridgette.' He had broken so many rules for her and he did it again. 'I know that you're busy today, but maybe…'

'Hey!' She forced a smile, dragged it up from her guts and slathered it on her face and turned to him. 'We're not suited, remember?'

'Completely incompatible.' He forced a smile too.

He gave her a kiss but could sense her distraction.

She climbed out of the car and she didn't say good-bye because she couldn't bear to, didn't turn around because she knew she'd head back to his arms, to his car, to escape.

But she couldn't escape the niggle in her stomach

that told her things were less than fine and it niggled louder as she made a half-hearted attempt at cleaning her room. By midday her answer came.

'Can you have Harry tonight?'

'I can't,' Bridgette said. 'I'm on an early shift in the morning…' Then she closed her eyes. She had reported her sister a couple of months ago to social services and finally voiced her concerns. Oh, there was nothing specific, but she could not simply stand by and do nothing. Since she'd asked Courtney to leave her flat, things had become increasingly chaotic and in the end she'd felt she had no choice but to speak out. Not to Jasmine or her friends—she didn't want to burden them. Instead she had spoken to people who might help. Her concerns had been taken seriously, and anger had ripped through her family that she could do such a thing. Sour grapes, Courtney had called it, because of what had happened between her and Paul. And then Courtney had admitted that, yes, she did like to party, she was only eighteen, after all, but never when Harry was around. She always made sure that Harry was taken care of.

By Bridgette.

And as she stood holding the phone, Bridgette didn't want to find out what might happen if she didn't say yes.

'I'll ring the agency,' Bridgette said. 'See if I can change to a late shift.'

Even if it was awkward talking to her sister when she dropped him off, Bridgette really was delighted to see Harry. At eighteen months he grew more gorgeous each day. His long blond curls fell in ringlets now and he had huge grey eyes like his aunt's.

Courtney had been a late baby for Maurice and Betty. Bridgette delivered babies to many so-called older women, but it was as if her parents had been old for ever—and they had struggled with the wilful Courtney from day one. It had been Bridgette who had practically brought her up, dealing with the angst and the crises that always seemed to surround Courtney, as her parents happily tuned out and carried on with their routines.

It had been Bridgette who had told them that their sixteen-year-old daughter was pregnant, Bridgette who had held Courtney's hand in the delivery room, Bridgette who had breathed with hope when Courtney, besotted with her new baby, had told Harry that she'd always be there for him.

'And I'll always be there for you,' Bridgette had said to her sister.

And Courtney was taking full advantage of that.

By seven, when Harry had had supper and been bathed, dressed in mint-green pyjamas, one of the many pairs Bridgette kept for him, and she had patted him off to sleep, she heard a car pulling up outside. She heard an expensive engine turning off, and then the sound of shoes on the steps outside her ground-floor flat, and she knew that it was him, even before she peeked through the blinds.

There was a loud ring of the bell and the noise made Harry cry.

And as Dominic stood on the step, there was his answer as to why she'd had to dash off that morning.

He waited a suitable moment, and Bridgette waited a moment too, rubbing Harry's back, telling him to go back to sleep, ignoring the bell. They were both quietly relieved when she didn't answer the door.

Still, last night had meant many things to Bridgette— and it wasn't all about the suave locum. Seeing her old colleagues, hearing about the midwifery unit, she'd re-alised just how much she was missing her old life. She knew somehow she had to get it back.

It was a curious thing that helped.

When Harry woke up at eleven and refused to go back to sleep, she held him as she checked her work sheet for the week. She was hoping that Courtney would be back tomorrow in time for her to get to her late shift when an e-mail pinged into her inbox.

No subject. No message. Just an attachment.

She had no idea how Dominic had got her e-mail address, no idea at all, but she didn't dwell on it, just opened the attachment.

It didn't upset her to see it. In fact, it made her smile. She had no regrets for that night and the photo of them together proved it. The photo, not just of him but of her-self smiling and happy, did more than sustain her—it inspired her.

'Harry Joyce,' she said to the serious face of her nephew. 'Your aunty Bridgette needs to get a life.'

And she *would* get one, Bridgette decided, carefully deleting Dominic's e-mail address so she didn't suc-cumb, like Arabella, in the middle of the night. The photo, though, became her new screensaver.

CHAPTER FOUR

'HE'LL be fine.'

It was six-thirty a.m. on Monday morning and Bridgette's guilt didn't lift as she handed a very sleepy Harry over to Mary, whom she had been introduced to last week. 'It seems mean, waking him so early,' Bridgette said.

'Well, you start work early.' Mary had the same lovely Irish brogue as Bridgette's granny had had and was very motherly and practical. 'Is his mum picking him up?'

'No, it's just me for the next few days,' Bridgette explained. 'She's got laryngitis, so I'm looking after Harry for a while.'

'Now, I know you'll want to see him during your breaks and things, but I really would suggest that for the first week or two, you don't pop down. He will think you're there to take him home and will just get upset.' She gave Bridgette a nice smile. 'Which will upset you and you'll not get your work done for worrying. Maybe ring down if you want to know how he is, and of course if there are any problems and we need you, I'll be the first to let you know.' Holding Harry, Mary walked

Bridgette to the door and gave her a little squeeze on the shoulder. 'You're doing grand.'

Oh, she wanted Mary to take her back to some mystical kitchen to sit at the table and drink tea for hours, for Mary to feed her advice about toddlers and tell her that everything was okay, was going to be okay, that Harry was fine.

Would be fine.

It felt strange to be back in her regular uniform, walking towards Maternity. Strange, but nice. It had been a busy month. She was so glad for that photo— their one night together had caused something of an awakening for Bridgette, had shown her just how much she was missing and had been the motivation to really sort her life out as best she could. She had been to the social-work department at the hospital she had once worked in and taken some much-needed advice. They suggested daycare and allocated Harry a place. At first Courtney had resisted. After all, she had said, she didn't work, but Bridgette stood firm—relieved that there would be more people looking out for Harry. She was especially glad that she had held her ground when the day before she started her new job, Courtney had come down with a severe throat infection and asked if Bridgette could step in for a few days.

Bridgette's interview with Rita had been long and rather difficult. Rita wasn't at all keen to make exceptions. She would do her best to give Bridgette early shifts but, no, she couldn't guarantee that was all she would get, and certainly, Rita said, she wanted all her staff to do regular stints on nights.

It all seemed a little impossible, but somehow Bridgette knew she had to make it work and get through things one day at a time—and today would be a good day, Bridgette decided as she entered the familiar unit, the smell and sound of babies in the air. This was where she belonged. She made herself a coffee to take into the long handover. Bridgette was hoping to be put into Labour and Delivery—she really wanted to immerse herself in a birth on her first day back.

'You're nice and early.' Rita was sitting at the computer, all busy and efficient and preparing for the day. 'Actually, that helps. It's been a very busy night, a busy weekend apparently. I've got a nurse who has to leave at seven. She's looking after a rather difficult case— would you mind taking handover from her and getting started?'

'Of course.' Bridgette was delighted. It often happened this way, and it would be lovely to get stuck into a labour on her first day back. She took a gulp of her coffee and tipped the rest down the sink, rinsed her cup and then headed off towards Labour and Delivery.

'No, it's room three where I want you to take over— twenty-four weeks with pre-eclampsia. They're having trouble getting her blood pressure back down.'

Okay, so she wasn't going to witness a birth this morning, but still, it was nice to be back using her midwifery brain. 'Hi, there, Heather.' She smiled at the familiar face. The room was quite crowded. Dr Hudson, the obstetrician, was there with the anaesthetist, and the anxious father was holding his wife's hand. The woman's face was flushed and she looked very drowsy. Thankfully, she was probably oblivious to all the activity going on.

'It's so good to see you.' Heather motioned to head

to the door and they stepped just a little outside. 'I've got to get away at seven.'

'Is that why it's good to see me?' Bridgette smiled.

'No, it's just good to see you back, good to have someone on the ball taking over as well. I'm worried about this one. Her name is Carla. She came up from Emergency yesterday evening.' Heather gave Bridgette a detailed rundown, showing her all the drugs that had been used overnight in an attempt to bring Carla's blood pressure down. 'We thought we had it under control at four a.m., but at six it spiked again.' Bridgette grimaced when she saw the figures. 'Obviously, they were hoping for a few more days at the very least. She's supposed to be having a more detailed scan this morning. They were estimating twenty-four weeks and three days.' That was very early. Every day spent in the womb at this stage was precious and vital and would increase the baby's chance of survival.

The parents wanted active treatment and the mother had been given steroids yesterday to mature the baby's lungs in case of premature delivery, but even so, to deliver at this stage would be dire indeed. 'She's just been given an epidural,' Heather explained, 'and they're fiddling with her medications through that as well. They're doing everything they can to get her blood pressure down.' It just didn't seem to be working, though. The only true cure for pre-eclampsia was delivery. Carla's vital signs meant that her life was in danger. She was at risk of a stroke or seizures and a whole host of complications if she didn't stabilise soon—even death. 'They were just talking about transferring her over to Intensive Care, but I think Dr Hudson now wants to go ahead and deliver. The paediatrician was just in…he's warned them what to expect, but at that stage we were still hoping for a couple more days, even to get her to twenty-five weeks.'

It wasn't going to happen.

'I hate leaving her...'

'I know,' Bridgette said.

'Dillan starts at a new school today.' Bridgette knew Heather's son had had trouble with bullying and it sounded as if today was a whole new start for him too. 'Or I wouldn't dash off.'

'You need to get home.'

The monitors were beeping and Heather and Bridgette walked back in.

'Carla...' Heather roused the dozing woman. 'This is Bridgette. She's going to be taking care of you today, and I'll be back to take care of you tonight.'

The alarms were really going off now. The appalling numbers that the monitors were showing meant the difficult decision would have to be made. Bridgette knew that Heather was torn. She'd been with Carla all night and at any moment now Carla was going to be rushed over to Theatre for an emergency Caesarean. 'Go,' Bridgette mouthed, because if Heather didn't leave soon, she would surely end up staying, and Dillan needed his mum today.

'Let Theatre know we're coming over,' Dr Hudson said to Bridgette, 'and we need the crash team from NICU. I'll tell the parents.'

Bridgette dashed out and informed Rita, the smooth wheels of the emergency routine snapping into place. Five minutes to seven on a Monday was not the best time. Staff were leaving, staff were starting, the weekend team was exhausted, the corridors busy as they moved the bed over to the maternity theatres.

'Okay.' Bridgette smiled at the terrified father, whom Dr Hudson had agreed could be present for the birth. 'Here's where you get changed.' She gave him some scrubs, a hat and some covers for his shoes. 'I'm going to go and get changed too and then I'll come back for you and take you in.'

Really, her presence at this birth was somewhat supernumerary. For a normal Caesarean section she would be receiving the baby; however, the NICU team was arriving and setting up, preparing their equipment for this very tiny baby, so Bridgette concentrated on the parents. Frank, the husband, wanted to film the birth, and Bridgette helped him to work out where to stand so that he wouldn't get in the way. She understood his need to document every minute of this little baby's life.

'It's all happening so fast…' Carla, though groggy, was clearly terrified, because now that the decision had been made, things were moving along with haste.

'We're just making sure we've got everything ready for your baby,' Bridgette explained as Dr Hudson came in. The anaesthetist had topped up the epidural and the operation would soon be starting.

'We're just waiting on…' Kelly, one of NICU team called out, when asked if they were ready, and then her voice trailed off. 'No problem. Dr Mansfield is here.'

Bridgette looked up and straight into those familiar black eyes, eyes that she stared at each day on her computer, except they didn't smile back at her now. She tore her gaze away from him and back to her patient. She completely halted her thoughts, gave all her attention to her patient, because the operation had started, the inci-

sion made at seven-eighteen, and just a few moments
later a tiny baby was delivered.

'She's beautiful,' Bridgette told Carla. 'She's moving.' She was, her red, spindly limbs flailing with indignation at her premature entry to the world.

'She's not crying,' Jenny said.

'She is.' There was a very feeble cry and her face
was grimacing. Frank was standing back, filming their
tiny daughter. Bridgette watched the activity and for the
first time she took a proper look at Dominic.

He needed to shave, his face was grim with concentration and he looked exhausted. Bridgette remembered
Rita saying that it had been a very busy weekend, and
this emergency had come right at the tail end of his
on-call shift.

'Can I see her?' Carla asked, but already the team
was moving the baby and she was whisked past. Carla
got only a very brief glimpse.

'They're taking her into another area,' Bridgette explained, as the team moved away, 'and then she'll be
taken up to the NICU.'

'Can I go with her?' Frank asked. 'Can I watch? I
won't get in the way. I just want to see what they're
doing.'

'I'll go and find out.'

Bridgette walked into the resuscitation area, where
the baby would be stabilised as much as possible before being moved to NICU. Even though she had seen
premature babies, now and for evermore the sight of
something so small and so fragile and so completely
tiny took her breath away. Bridgette loved big, fat
babies, little scrawny ones too, but a scrap like this
made her heart flutter in silent panic.

'She's a little fighter.' Kelly came over. 'We're going to move her up in a couple of minutes.'

'Dad wants to know if he can come and watch. He's promised not to get in the way. He just wants to see what's happening.'

'Not yet,' Dominic called over. 'I'll talk to him as soon as I can.'

'Tell him to stay with his wife for now,' Kelly suggested. 'I'll come and fetch him when Dominic is ready to talk to him.'

Kelly was as good as her word, and by the time Carla had been moved to Recovery, Kelly appeared, holding some new photos of their tiny daughter, which she handed to Mum and explained a little of what was going on. 'The doctors are still with her, but Dominic said if I bring Frank up he'll try to come out to speak with him. He'll come down and talk to you a bit later.'

It was a busy morning. Carla spent a long time in Recovery before being transferred back to the maternity unit, but even there she still required very close observation as her vital signs would take a while to stabilise after the birth. Carla was still very sick and of course wanted more information about her baby, whom they'd named Francesca. Frank had seen her very briefly and was now back with his wife and clearly a little impatient about the lack of news.

'Mary from daycare is on the phone for you.' Nandita, the ward clerk, popped a head around the door and handed Bridgette the phone.

'Nothing to worry about at all' came Mary's reassuring voice as Bridgette stepped out into the corridor. 'I'm just about to head off for lunch and I thought I'd let you know how well he's gone today. He's found a stack of bricks, which amused him for most of the morning.'

'Thanks so much for letting me know.'

'He's heading for an afternoon nap now. Anyway, you can get on with your day without fretting about him.' Bridgette felt a wave of guilt when she realised she hadn't even had time to worry about Harry and how he was doing on his first day at crèche and a wave of sadness too when she found out that, no, neither had Courtney rung to find out.

'Hi, Carla.' She gave the phone to Nandita, and as she walked back into her patient's room she heard Dominic's voice. If he had looked tired that morning then he looked exhausted now. 'Hi, Frank.' He shook the other man's hand. 'Sorry that it's taken so long to come and speak with you. I've been very busy with your daughter and another child who was delivered yesterday. I wanted to take the time to have a proper talk with you both.' He sat down next to the bed. 'Carla, you'll remember I spoke with you yesterday.' He didn't bog them down with too much detail. Apparently yesterday he had explained the risks of such a premature delivery and he didn't terrify them all over again. He told them their daughter's condition was extremely serious, but there was some good news. 'She seems a little further on than first estimated. I'd put her well into twenty-five weeks, which, though it's just a few days' difference, actually increases the survival rates quite dramatically. She's got size on her side too,' Dominic explained. 'Even though she's tiny, she is a little bit bigger than we would expect at twenty-five weeks, and she's had the benefit of the steroids we gave yesterday. She's a vigorous little thing, and she's doing absolutely as well as can be expected.'

'When can I see her?' Carla asked.

'I spoke to Dr Hudson before I came down, and as much as we know you want to see your daughter, you're not well enough at the moment.'

'What if…?' Poor Carla didn't even want to voice it, so Dominic did.

'If her condition deteriorates, we'll sort something out and do our best to get you up there.' He glanced over at Bridgette and so too did Carla.

'Of course we will,' she said.

'But right now the best you can do for your baby is to rest and get well yourself.' He answered a few more questions and then turned to Frank. 'You should be able to see her for a little while now. I've told them to expect you.'

'I'll get Nandita to walk you up,' Bridgette offered.

'Lunch?' Rita suggested as Bridgette walked over to speak with Nandita. 'Emma will take over from you.'

It was a late lunch, and as Bridgette hadn't had a coffee break, it was a sheer relief to slip off her shoes and just relax for a few moments. Well, at least it was until Dominic came in and sat on the couch opposite and unwrapped a roll. He gave her a brief nod but did not make any attempt at conversation, instead choosing to read a newspaper. It was Bridgette who tried to tackle the uncomfortable silence.

'I thought you were in Sydney.'

'It didn't work out.' He carried on reading the paper for a moment and then finally elaborated a touch. 'The professor I would be working under was taken ill and has gone on long-term sick leave—I didn't really care for his replacement, so I'm just waiting till something

I want comes up, or the professor returns. I'm here for a few more weeks.'

He sounded very austere, such a contrast to the easy conversations they had once shared. He didn't say anything else, didn't even read his paper, just sat and ate his roll.

Couldn't he have done that on NICU or on the paed ward? Bridgette thought, stirring her yoghurt. If he was going to sit there all silent and brooding, couldn't he do it somewhere else? Surely it was already awkward enough?

For Dominic, in that moment, it wasn't awkward, not in the least. He was too busy concentrating on not closing his eyes. Fatigue seeped through him. He'd had maybe six hours' sleep the entire weekend and he just wanted to go home and crash. Thank goodness for Rita, who had noticed his pallor and given him a spare cold patient lunch and suggested that he take five minutes before he saw the baby he had come down to examine, as well as speaking with Frank and Carla. Rebecca, his intern, came in. Bridgette recognised her from that morning, and then a couple of other colleagues too, which should have broken the tension, but instead Dominic ignored everyone and made no attempt to join in with the chitchat.

And later, he didn't look up when she had no choice but to sit and join him at the nurses' station to write up her notes before going home.

He told, rather than asked, Rebecca to take some further bloods on a baby born over the weekend, and then when one of the midwives asked if he'd mind taking a look at some drug orders, holding out the prescription chart to him, he didn't take it. Rather rudely, Bridgette thought, he didn't even look up.

'Is it a patient of mine?'

'No, it's a new delivery.'

He just carried on writing his own notes. 'Then you need to ring the doctor on call.'

The midwife rolled her eyes and left them to it, and the silence simmered uncomfortably between them, or at least it was uncomfortable for Bridgette.

'I'm sorry this is awkward.' She tried to broach it, to go ahead and say what was surely on both their minds, to somehow ease the tension, because the Dominic she had seen today was nothing like the man she had met, and she certainly didn't want to cause any problems at work. 'Had I known you were still working here, I wouldn't have…' Her voice trailed off—it seemed rather stupid to say that she'd never have taken the job, that she wouldn't have come back to the unit she loved. But had she known he would be here for a little while more, there might have been a delay in her return—with Jasmine being away she was completely out of the loop as to what was going on at work.

'Awkward?' Dominic frowned as he carried on writing. 'Why would it be awkward?' And then he shook his head. 'Are you referring to…?' He looked over and waited till her skin was burning, till there was no question that, yes, she was referring to that night. 'Bridgette, it was months ago.' She swallowed, because it was actually just a few weeks; she'd counted them. 'We shared one night together.' How easily he dismissed it, relegated it, reduced it to a long-ago event that had meant nothing—something so trivial that it didn't even merit a moment's reflection. Except she was quite sure that wasn't true.

'Thanks for the e-mail,' she said, to prove it had been more than that, that he had come back to her door, had later that night sent her a photo, yet he frowned as if trying to place it and then he had the nerve to give a wry laugh.

'Oh, that!'

'You got my e-mail address?'

'On some stupid group one from Vince and…' He gave a shrug, clearly couldn't remember Jasmine's name. 'Just clearing out my inbox, Bridgette.' She felt like a stalker, some mad, obsessed woman, and he clearly must be thinking the same. 'It was one night— hardly something to base your career path on. Don't give it another thought. There really is no problem.'

'Good.'

'And as for awkward, it's not in the least. This is how I am at work.' And then he corrected himself. 'This is how I am—ask anyone.' He gave a very thin smile. 'I'm not exactly known for small talk. It has nothing to do with what took place. It really is forgotten.'

And over the next few days he proved his point. She saw that Dr Dominic Mansfield *was* cool and distant with everyone. He was mainly polite, sometimes dismissive, and just never particularly friendly. There was an autonomous air to him that wasn't, Bridgette realised, solely reserved for her. Not that she should mind—nothing had shifted her heart. She was still way too raw to contemplate a relationship. And the patients, or rather their parents, didn't seem to mind the directness of his words in the least. In fact, as Bridgette wheeled Carla up later in the week for a visit with her newborn, Carla admitted it was Dr Mansfield's opinion she sought the most about her daughter.

'I don't want a doctor who tries to spare my feelings,' Carla said as they waited for the lift. 'He tells it like it is, which Frank and I appreciate.

'Mind you…' she smiled as Bridgette wheeled her in '…he's not exactly chatty. Gorgeous to look at he may be, but you wouldn't want to be stuck in a lift with him.' Whether she agreed or not, Bridgette smiled back, pleased to see her patient's humour returning, along with colour to her cheeks. It really had been a hellish ride for Carla. It had been four days until she had been well enough to see her baby, and there was still, for Francesca, a long road ahead.

'Carla.' Dominic gave a nod to the patient as Bridgette wheeled her over.

'Is everything okay?' Carla asked, anxious to see him standing by Francesca's incubator.

'She's had a good morning, by all reports,' Dominic said. 'I'm just checking in.'

He gave Bridgette the briefest nod of acknowledgement then moved on to the next incubator. He wasn't, she now realised, being rude or dismissive towards her. It was the way Dominic was to everyone.

It hurt more than she had time to allocate to it. Her days were so busy, and more and more Courtney was asking her to have Harry. It was hard trying to achieve some sort of routine and work full-time with a toddler— a toddler who worryingly didn't toddle very much, one who seemed far happier to sit with his building blocks, happier in his own world than hers. But sometimes at night, when all she should do was close her eyes and get some much-needed sleep, it was then that Bridgette's mind wandered. It was on those occasions that she realised not so much what she'd lost but more what she'd been privy to that night.

A side to Dominic that was rare indeed.

CHAPTER FIVE

'Harry!' Bridgette gave him a wide smile but Harry didn't look up. He was engrossed with the pile of bricks in front of him. 'How has he been today?' Bridgette asked.

'Busy building!' Mary answered. 'He loves his bricks.'

Bridgette saw her own fingers clench around the pen as she signed Harry out for the day, saw the white of her knuckles as her brain tightened just a fraction, wondering if Mary's comment was friendly chatter or a more professional observation. She was being paranoid, Bridgette told herself, seeing problems where there were surely none, but as she picked up Harry she wished, and not for the first time, that Harry was just a little bit more pleased to see her, a little more receptive.

There couldn't be something wrong with him. It wasn't just for selfish reasons that she panicked at the thought—it was Courtney's reaction that troubled Bridgette, or rather Courtney's lack of reaction towards her son. Her sister wasn't exactly coping now, let alone if her son had special needs.

Special needs.

It was the first time that she had actually said it, even

if only in her mind, and instantly she shoved it aside because there was just so much to deal with at the moment. She had so many things to contend with, without adding the unthinkable to the pile. But she had to approach it.

'How do you think he's doing?' she asked Mary.

'Grand.' She beamed. 'Mind, he does have a bit of a temper—' she tickled him under the chin '—if one of the other littlies knocks over his bricks.'

'What about his talking?' Bridgette looked at Mary, who just smiled at Harry.

'He's not much of a talker,' Mary said, 'but, then, he's just been here a couple of weeks and is still settling in so maybe he's a bit shy. If you're concerned, though…' Mary was lovely, but she told Bridgette what she already knew, that maybe his mum should take him to his GP if she was worried that he wasn't reaching his milestones.

'How is Mum?' Mary asked, because, despite Courtney collecting him a couple of times, it mainly fell to Bridgette.

'She's okay,' Bridgette answered. 'Though I'll be bringing Harry in for the next couple of days. She's got some job interviews lined up in Bendigo and is staying there with friends for a few nights.'

'Bendigo!' Mary's eyebrows rose. 'That's a good few hours away.'

'Well, it's early days,' Bridgette said, 'but it's good that she's looking for work.'

Bridgette had mixed feelings. Yes, she wanted her sister to get a job and to make a fresh start, but the thought of her, or rather Harry, so far away had Bridgette in a spin. She was doing her best not to dwell on it as she left the crèche.

'Excuse me!' She heard the irritation in the man's

voice as she, a woman who wasn't looking where she was going, collided with him as she walked out of the daycare centre. And then Dominic looked down, saw who he was talking to, saw who she was holding, and she was quite sure that he frowned as he gazed into Harry's eyes. Eyes that were exactly the same sludgy grey as hers, and though he quickly moved his features to impassive and gave her a very brief nod, she could feel the tension. They walked down a long corridor, Bridgette several steps behind him. As he headed out through the ambulance bay and turned left, it was clear they were both heading for the car park.

She should have managed to avoid him, given that she now walked incredibly slowly, but one of the security guards halted him and they spoke for a moment. No matter how Bridgette dawdled, no matter how hard she tried not to catch up, the security guard gave him a cheery farewell at the very second Bridgette walked past and, like it or not, for a moment or two there was no choice but to fall in step alongside him.

'Is that why you had to dash off?'

It was the first time he acknowledged he even *recalled* the details of that night, that morning, the slice of time when things had felt more than right.

'I should have explained…' She really didn't know what to say, what could she say. 'I didn't know how…' She still didn't. Should she plead, 'I'm his aunt. He's not my responsibility'? Harry was, he was solid in her arms—and whether Harry understood her words or not, he certainly did not need to be present as she defended her reasons for not telling this man of his existence. Instead she walked to her car that, unlike his, which lit up like a Christmas tree the second he approached, needed keys. Bridgette had to scrabble in her bag for them, with Harry, who was becoming increasingly heavy, but she was too nervous to put him down in the middle of a car park. He was, she realised, just too precious to let go.

As Dominic's sleek silver car slid past her, she deliberately did not look up, did not want to remember the night he'd driven her to heaven then returned her home again.

She was very close to crying, and that Harry did not need, but finally she found her keys and unlocked the car, opening the windows to let it cool down before she put Harry in.

'Here we go.' The car still felt like a sauna but she strapped Harry in, climbed into the seat and looked in the rear-vision mirror at his wispy curls and serious grey eyes. She gave him a very nice smile. 'You're ruining my love life, Harry!'

CHAPTER SIX

'Wow!' Bridgette walked into the delivery room, where Maria was pacing. 'I turn my back for five minutes...' She smiled at Maria, who had progressed rapidly in the past half hour.

'I was worried you wouldn't make it back,' Maria said.

'I'm sorry I had to dash off.' Harry had been a touch grizzly this morning when she'd dropped him off and had, half an hour ago, thrown the most spectacular temper tantrum, bad enough for Mary to call her on the ward and for Bridgette to take an early coffee break.

'I know what it's like,' Maria said. 'I've got three of my own.'

'Four soon,' Bridgette said, and Maria smiled.

'I can't wait to meet her.'

'Neither can I,' Bridgette admitted. It was, so far, turning out to be a gorgeous labour—especially as it was one that could have been labelled 'difficult' because the testing and scans had revealed that Maria and Tony's baby had Trisomy 21. The diagnosis, Maria had told Bridgette, had caused intense upset between both families—Spanish passion combined with pointless accusations and blame had caused a lot of tension and heartache indeed. Maria and Tony, however, once they had got over the initial shock, had researched as much as they could, and had even met with a local support group who ran a regular playgroup.

'It took away a lot of the fear,' Maria had explained, when Bridgette admitted her. 'Seeing other Down's syndrome babies and toddlers and their parents coping so well. We're so looking forward to having our baby. I just wish our families would stop with the grief.'

So upset was Maria with the response of her family that she hadn't even wanted them to know that she had gone into labour, but with three other small children to care for she'd had no choice but to tell them. And now two anxious families were sitting in the maternity waiting room. Still, Maria was doing beautifully and was helped so much by her husband's unwavering support. He rubbed her back where she indicated, stopped talking when she simply raised a hand. They had their own private language and were working to deliver their daughter as a team.

'How are things?' Rita popped her head around the door. 'The family just asked for an update.'

'It's all going well,' Bridgette said.

'Tell them it will be born when it's good and ready,' Maria snapped, and then breathed through another contraction. She was suddenly savage. 'You'd think they were preparing for a funeral more than a birth!' She let out an expletive or three in Spanish and Tony grimaced, then she told him *exactly* what she thought of Abuela.

'Grandmother,' Tony translated with a smile when Bridgette winked at him. 'My mother.' He rolled his eyes. 'She does a lot for us, but she can be a bit too much at times, though she means well.' He rubbed his wife's back as Maria said a little more of what she thought about her mother-in-law. 'Maria always does this when…' And Bridgette smiled, knew as Tony did, what was coming. Maria leant against the bed, her face changing to a familiar grimace.

'I want to push.'

'That's good,' Bridgette cheered.

'Come on, Tony,' she said and they both helped Maria up onto the bed. 'I'm just going to let Dr Hudson know—'

'No need.' Dr Hudson came in.

'How's she doing?' Rita popped her head around the door again and Bridgette gritted her teeth, while trying not to let Maria see.

'Can we get the paediatrician down?' The obstetrician's tone was a little brusque and Bridgette saw the flare of panic in Maria's eyes.

'It's fine, Maria,' Bridgette reassured her as Rita went to make the call. 'The fact Dr Hudson wants the paediatrician to come down means that you're getting close now and it won't be long till your baby's born.'

'The paediatrician is on his way,' Rita called over the intercom. 'I'll come in and give you a hand in a moment.'

Bridgette watched as Maria's eyes closed; as she dipped into her own private world and just tried to block the gathering crowd out. She had wanted the birth to be as low-key and as relaxed as possible, and had three other births with which to compare, but because of the possible health complications, more staff would be present with this one. Though potentially necessary, it just compounded things for Maria.

'Have you got everything ready?' Rita bustled into the room. 'Dominic is just a couple of minutes away.'

Bridgette felt incredibly confident with Dominic. He was an amazing doctor and very astute. However, for Maria, perhaps it was not the best combination of staff. Dr Hudson believed in planning for every eventuality—*every* eventuality—and Rita was one of those high-energy people who somehow didn't soothe. Now Dominic, a rather aloof paediatrician, was being added to the mix, except... 'Dominic Mansfield?' Tony looked over at Bridgette. 'Is that the paediatrician who's coming?' When Bridgette nodded, Tony hugged his wife. 'That's good news, Maria.'

'Bridgette?' Rita was checking and double-checking everything Bridgette had already done. 'Have you got the—?'

'Shut up!' roared Maria, just as Dominic came into the room.

For once Bridgette was grateful for his silence. He gave Tony a nod as Maria quietly laboured. Dominic took off his jacket and headed to the sink to wash his hands and then tied on a plastic apron.

'Big breath, Maria,' Bridgette said gently. 'Come on, another one...' The birth was imminent. 'And then push until Dr Hudson tells you to stop.' Maria was very good at this. There was grim concentration on her face as she bore down and Bridgette held her leg, relaying Dr Hudson's gruff instructions but in more encouraging tones. 'Don't push now. Just breathe. The head's out.'

The baby didn't even require another push. She slithered out into Dr Hudson's hands, where Rita was waiting to cut the cord and whisk the baby off for examination.

'Up onto Mum's stomach,' Dominic said. 'Tony can cut the cord.' Bridgette silently cheered as his calm, authoritative voice slowed the haste.

'Do you want the baby moved over for examination?' Rita checked when, again, she didn't need to. It had been a very beautiful birth, and Bridgette was especially thrilled that Dominic seemed in no rush to whisk the baby off and examine her—instead, he just quietly observed.

The little girl was small and Bridgette placed a towel over her, rubbing her to stimulate her, but she felt very calm with Dominic's stoic presence so close.

As the baby took her first breaths, Dominic called Tony over and the cord was cut—and Bridgette felt a blink of tears because the birth Maria had wanted so badly for her baby was happening.

'I can examine her here,' Dominic said, when Rita checked again if he wanted the baby moved over. And he did. He checked the little baby's muscle tone and her palate and listened to her heart for a long time. He told Maria he would perform a more comprehensive examination in a little while. 'But for now I'll let you enjoy her.'

There really was a lot to enjoy. She peered up at her mum, her almond-shaped eyes huge and gorgeous; she was very alert, and even though she let out a few little cries, she was easily comforted by Maria.

'Do you want me to let your family know?' Rita asked, and Bridgette's jaw tightened. She could understand the conversation that had been held at Jasmine's leaving do now. Rita really did try and take over.

'They'll want to come in,' Maria said. 'I just don't

want...' She held her baby closely. 'I want it to be a celebration, the same as it was with my others.'

'It will be,' Dominic said. 'They just haven't met
her yet.'

'She wants to feed,' Maria said, as her daughter frantically searched for her breast.

'Let her.'

'You said they'd scan her first,' Maria said, because,
though detailed prenatal scans had not shown anything,
the nature of the syndrome meant the little girl was at
risk of a heart defect and would need to be checked by
a paediatric cardiologist soon after birth, but Dominic
was clearly happy with his findings.

'She's looking great,' he said, quietly observing, and
the baby did latch on, but Bridgette helped with the po-
sitioning.

It was one of those births that confirmed her voca-
tion—there was no greater gift than watching a new
life come into the world, and today's so-called difficult birth had been made especially wonderful by the
calm presence of Dominic. Again he had surprised her.
He wasn't particularly effusive or gushing, he was so
much *more* than that, and he was everything this little
family needed today.

Dominic stayed and wrote up his notes while the
little girl fed and Bridgette watched for any signs that
the baby was having trouble sucking and swallowing
but she was doing very well. 'Dominic said that breast
feeding might be more difficult than with the others...'
Maria looked down at her daughter, who was tiring, so
Bridgette suggested she take her off now.

'She's doing an awful lot right,' Bridgette said,

checking the babe and then filling in her own notes. 'She's cried, pooed, wee'd and fed.'

Dominic came over. 'You remember I said that I'd take her up to NICU for a little while after she was born,' he said. 'I want that scan done. Everything looks good,' he reassured the parents, 'but I just want her thoroughly checked. Hopefully she'll be back down with you soon.'

Maria nodded and then took a deep breath. 'Can you bring in my family first?' Her eyes went to her husband's. 'If they start, I want you to…'

'We'll be here,' Bridgette said. 'You won't have to say a thing. I'm very good at bringing up excuses as to why people have to leave. If you start getting upset, or you've just had enough, you just have to let me know.' They worked out a little code, and she gave Tony a smile as he walked out. Dominic, she noted, instead of heading out to the desk, was sitting on a couch in the corner of the room, finishing his notes—a quiet, unobtrusive presence that was welcome.

Maria and Tony set the tone, but Bridgette's heart did go out to the family. They were trying to be brave, to not be upset, but there was so much tension, so many questions as they all peered at the newest member of the clan. Then Maria's three-year-old, Roman, climbed up on the bed and gazed at his sister, kissing her on the forehead, and the old *abuela* laughed.

Dominic came over and checked the baby briefly again, more for the family's benefit, or rather Maria's, Bridgette rightly guessed, because the questions they had been asking Maria were aimed at him now.

'She's doing very, very well,' he said, and answered more of their questions and told them that, yes, the prenatal diagnosis was correct. Yes, shortly there would be further testing, but for now she was doing perfectly. And then Bridgette blinked as he chatted with the *abuela* in what appeared to be fluid Spanish for a moment. *'Sí, ella es perfecta...'*

'We're going to move her up now.' Kelly from NICU had come down just as all the cameras came out.

'Photo with *el medico*,' the *abuela* said.

'We really ought to get moving.' Dominic was reluctant, but then obliged, and it struck Bridgette that though of course he held babies in the course of examining them, he wasn't the type to steal a cuddle.

He held the new infant and gave a smile for the camera and then he looked down at her.

'She's gorgeous, isn't she?' Maria said.

'Oh, I don't do the cute-baby thing,' Dominic answered, 'but, yes, I think I have to agree in this case. You have a very cute baby. Has she got a name?'

'Esperanza,' Maria said.

'Hope!' Dominic smiled.

He popped her back in her cot and at the last minute Tony asked if he might be able to stay with the baby during her tests. When Dominic agreed, the family all followed Dominic, Kelly and the porters in a little procession down the hall.

'He's lovely, isn't he?' Maria said. 'Dominic, I mean. He sort of tells you like it is.'

'He's very good,' Bridgette said, and gave Maria a wink. 'Speaks Spanish too.'

'Abuela was very impressed.' Maria grinned. 'Dominic's mother is Spanish apparently.' She had to find out about him from a patient! 'He's been great. We went to him when we got the amnio back and he told us what to expect. Well, I guess he'd know as his brother has Down's.' She must have seen Bridgette's eyes widen. 'Sorry, maybe I shouldn't have said—it was just that Tony was crying and so was I and it seemed like a disaster when we first found out, but Dominic was terribly patient. He told us what we were feeling was completely normal. We saw him again a couple of weeks ago and we were embarrassed about the scene we'd made, but he said not to give it another thought. It was all very normal, that his mother had been the same.'

They knew nothing about each other, Bridgette realised.

Which had been the point, she remembered.

She really was lousy at one-night stands.

Still, she didn't have time to dwell on it. L and D was busy and she was soon looking after another birth, a first-time mum called Jessica, who was very nervous, as well as keeping an eye on Maria.

Esperanza was gone for about an hour, and her heart test was clear, which was brilliant news, and by the time she was back, Bridgette had just transferred Maria to the ward. Having checked on her next patient, Bridgette was more than ready for lunch.

'What's all this?' Bridgette tried not to care that Dominic was sitting in the staffroom. After all, if he didn't care, why should she? Anyway, Rita was there too and there were other distractions this lunchtime. Instead of plain biscuits the table was heaving with fruit platters, small filled rolls and a spread of cheese.

'Leftovers from the obstetricians' meeting.' Rita gave a wry smile. 'I rescued some for the workers. Enjoy.'

Bridgette selected a roll and a few slivers of fruit. She glanced at the cheese—even though that would usually be her first option, even if it seemed stupid, with Dominic there she chose to give it a miss.

'How's Harry?' Rita asked.

'Better,' Bridgette answered. 'He was just having a bit of a tantrum. He's not in the best of moods today. I'm sorry I had to dash off.'

As annoying and inflexible as she could be, Rita could, Bridgette conceded, also be very nice. 'No problem. It's to be expected in the first weeks at daycare. He'll soon get used to it. The real question is, how is his aunt doing?'

'Trying to get used to it too,' Bridgette admitted. 'But we're getting there.'

Unfortunately Rita's break was soon over and word couldn't yet have got around about the spread on in the staffroom because only Dominic and Bridgette remained. Well, she wasn't going to give up a single minute of the precious break by going back early. Her feet were killing her and she was hungry too, and Jessica, her new patient, was progressing steadily. If Dominic wasn't feeling awkward then why on earth should she be? And if she wanted cheese, why not?

Bridgette stood and refilled her plate with some Cheddar and Brie and a few crackers and went to sit back down, selecting a magazine to read as she did so.

'I thought you liked blue cheese.'

'Maybe.' Bridgette refused to look up, just carried on reading the magazine. She was not going to jump to make conversation just because he suddenly deigned to do so.

'How's Maria?'

'Marvellous.' She refused to be chatty, just because he suddenly was.

'The baby I saw you with yesterday...' Still she did not fill in the spaces. 'He's your nephew?' When still he was met with silence, Dominic pushed a little further. 'Why didn't you just say so?'

'I don't really see that it's relevant,' Bridgette answered, still reading her magazine. 'Had our one-night stand been two years ago and you'd seen me walking out of daycare carrying a mini-Dominic, then, yes, perhaps I'd have had some explaining to do. But I don't.' She smirked with mild pleasure at her choice of words and looked up. She was rather surprised to see that he was smiling—not the Dr Mansfield smile that she had seen occasionally since her return to work but the Dominic smile she had once been privy to.

'I'm sorry about yesterday. I just jumped to conclusions. I saw you with—' he paused for a brief second '—Harry, and I thought that was the reason...' He really felt awkward, Bridgette realised. Despite insisting how easy this was, Dominic seemed to be struggling.

'The reason?' She frowned, because he'd done this to her too, made her blush as she'd revealed that she thought about that night—but Dominic didn't blush in the same way Bridgette had.

'The reason that you went home that morning.'

'Oh, I needed a reason, did I?' She went back to her magazine.

What was it with this woman? She had made it very clear that morning that she didn't want more than their one night. Normally it would have come as a relief to Dominic, an unusual relief because he was not the one working out how to end things.

'Excuse me.' Her phone buzzed in her pocket and

Bridgette pulled it out, taking a deep breath before answering.

'Hi, Mum.'

Why did he have to be here when she took this call? Hopefully he'd choose now to leave, but instead he just sat there.

'I might need a hand a little bit later,' she said to her mother. She'd left a message for her parents earlier in the day, when she'd realised that Harry might not last out the day in crèche and also she wanted to stay longer for Jessica. 'There's a chance that I won't be able to get away for work on time and it would really help if you could pick up Harry at four for me.' She closed her eyes as her mother gave the inevitable reply. 'Yes, I know the crèche doesn't close till six, but he's a bit grizzly today and I don't want to push things—it's been a long day for him.'

Bridgette looked down and realised she was clicking her pen on and off as her mother reeled out her excuses. She could hear the irritation creeping into her own voice as she responded. 'I know Dad's got the dentist but can't he go on his own?' She listened to the train of excuses, to how they would love to help, but how nervous Dad got at the dentist, and if he did need anything done when they got there... 'You mean he's just having a check-up?' Now Bridgette couldn't keep the exasperation from her voice. She really wanted to be there for Jessica and didn't want to be nervously keeping one eye on the clock in case the crèche rang. With a pang that she didn't want to examine, her heart ached for the long day Harry was having. She wanted some back-up, and despite her parents' constant reassurances that they would help, she never seemed to ask at the right time.

'Don't worry about it' Bridgette settled for, and managed a goodbye and then clicked off the phone. Then she couldn't help it—she shot out a little of the frustration that her parents so easily provoked. 'Why can't he go to the dentist by himself?' Bridgette asked as Dominic simply grinned at her exasperation. 'They go shopping together, they do the housework together… I mean, are they joined at the hip? Honestly, they don't do anything by themselves.'

'Breathe.' Dominic grinned and she did as the doctor recommended, but it didn't help and she stamped her feet for a moment and let out a brief 'Aagggh!'

'Better?' Dominic asked.

'A bit.'

Actually, she did feel a bit better. It was nice to have a little moan, to complain, to let some of her exasperation out. Her parents had always been the same—everything revolved around dinner, everything in the house was geared towards six p.m. They were so inflexible, right down to the brand of toothpaste they used, and that was fine, that was how it was, that was how they were, but right now Bridgette needed more hands and their four seemed to make a poor two.

'Have you got no one else who can help?' Dominic asked.

'I miss Jasmine for things like this,' Bridgette admitted. It was nice that they were finally talking but of course now that they were, Rita buzzed and told her Jessica was in transition and it was time for her to go back.

'You might be out by four,' he said, and she shook her head, because Jessica was a first-time mum.

'I doubt it.'

Dominic's phone was ringing as she left, and when he saw that it was his father, he chose not to answer it. Stupid, really, because his father would just ring again in an hour, Dominic thought, and every hour after that, till he could tick it off his to-do list.

He finally took the call at three.

'Hi.'

Dominic rolled his eyes as his father wished him a happy birthday. 'Thanks.' Dominic was being honest when he said that he couldn't talk for long, because he was summoned urgently and headed down to Theatre when paged for a child who was having an allergic reaction in Recovery. There was that theatre nurse, her blue eyes waiting, when he and the anaesthetist had finished discussing the child's care.

'Long shift?' Dominic asked when she yawned, because on certain occasions he did make conversation.

And today was a certain occasion.

It was, after all, his birthday.

'It's been busy.' She nodded.

'Back again in the morning?'

'Yes…though I shouldn't moan. My husband's away so I can just go home and sleep.'

He was always away, Dominic thought.

'What does he do?' He broke one of their rules and he watched her cheeks go pink. There were colleagues around, and they were seemingly just chatting, so of course she had to answer.

'He drives a coach,' Blue Eyes said. 'Overnight, Melbourne to Sydney.'

He gave a nod and walked off, felt a bit sick in the guts really, which wasn't like him, but he thought of the poor bloke driving up and down the freeway as Dominic bonked his wife. No questions asked, no real conversation.

Maybe he was growing up, Dominic thought. He hadn't been with anyone in weeks, not since Bridgette, in fact, though he rapidly shoved that thought out of his mind.

Well, why wouldn't he be growing up? It was his birthday, after all.

And birthdays were supposed to be enjoyed.

Never doubt the power of a woman in labour—Bridgette should really have known better. Jessica was amazing, focused and gritty, and the birth was wonderful, so wonderful that she was still high on adrenaline as she sped down the corridor to daycare.

'Bridgette.' He was walking towards her and this time he nodded *and* said her name—progress indeed!

'Dominic.' She grinned and nodded back at him, ready to keep walking, except he stopped in front of her.

'I was wondering,' Dominic said. 'Would you like to come out tonight? You're right, this is awkward, and I'd really like to clear the air.'

This she hadn't been expecting. 'The air is already clear, Dominic.' Except it wasn't, so Bridgette was a little more honest. 'You were right. Harry is the reason that I didn't want you to come in that first night. My computer didn't have a virus.' She gave a guilty grin. 'Well, it wasn't Harry exactly, more the cot and the stroller and the rather blatant clues that were littered around my flat at the time.' And with Bridgette, he did ask questions, and got some answers. 'I look after my nephew a lot. My sister's really young.' He didn't

look away, his eyes never left her face, and she rather
wished that they would. 'So!' She gave him a smile as
his pager went off and Dominic glanced down at it and
then switched it off. 'That's a little bit what my life is
like when Harry's with my sister—I'm permanently
on call.' Yes, the air had been cleared, and now they
could both move on; she truly wasn't expecting what
came next.

'Bridgette, would you like to come out tonight?'

She turned around slowly and he looked the same
as he had before—completely unreadable. She didn't
want a charity dinner, didn't want him taking her out
because he'd already asked her. To make things easier
for them both she gave him a small smile, shook her
head and politely declined. 'That's really nice of you,
thanks, but I have to say no—it's hard to get a babysitter.' There, she'd given him the out. It was over and
done with, and she awaited his polite smile back—it
didn't come. Instead he looked at his watch.

'How long does a dental check-up take?' He even
smiled. 'Can you try?' He pulled out a card and wrote
his mobile-phone number on it and handed it to her.
Maybe he read her too well because instead of saying
that he would wait to hear if she could make arrangements, he lobbed the ball firmly back into her court.
'I'll pick you up at seven, unless I hear otherwise. Ring
me if you can't get a babysitter.'

It was utterly and completely unexpected. She had
thought he would run a mile—she'd given him an out,
after all.

She wanted him to take it.

Bridgette really did. She just wasn't ready to get back
out there and certainly not with Dominic. Still, maybe

tonight he would just tell her how impossible it all was; maybe she would receive a long lecture on how they found each other attractive and all that, but how unsuitable they were—yet, remembering just how good they had been, it was very hard to say no.

'Hi, Mum.' It was the second time that day she'd asked her mum for help. 'Is there any chance you and Dad could babysit tonight?'

'You mean have our grandson over?' Betty laughed. 'We'd love to.' As Bridgette blinked in surprise, as she paused just a fraction, her mother filled the gap. 'Though we do have a couple of friends coming over tonight. Old friends of your dad's—remember Eric and Lorna?' Bridgette felt her jaw tense. Her parents insisted they were accommodating, but it was always on their terms—when it suited them. 'Could we maybe do it tomorrow?'

'I've got an invitation to go out tonight, Mum. I'd really like to go.'

'But we've got people over tonight. Tomorrow we can come over to you and stay. It might be easier on Harry.' Yes, it might be easier on Harry, but it certainly wouldn't be easier on her—or Dominic. He was already taking a leap of faith in asking her out. Though he wasn't asking her out, she reminded herself—he simply wanted to clear the air. Still, no doubt he was used to having the door opened by a groomed, glossy beauty who invited him in for a drink as she applied a final layer of lip gloss—somehow she couldn't imagine inflicting her mother and father and Harry on the guy.

'Mum, I haven't had a night out in weeks.' She hadn't, not since that night with Dominic. 'I'm sorry for the short notice. If you can have Harry, that would be great. If not...' If not, then it simply wasn't meant to be, Bridgette decided. If she couldn't get away for one single night without planning it days in advance, she might just as well text Dominic now with the whole truth.

It would be quite a relief to, actually, but after a moment's silence came her mother's rather martyred response. 'Well, make sure you bring a decent change of clothes for him. I want Harry looking smart. I've got Eric and Lorna coming over,' she repeated. 'Have you had his hair cut yet?' Bridgette looked at the mop of blond curls that danced in the afternoon sun as Harry built his bricks and wondered why her mother assumed that Harry's hair was Bridgette's responsibility. His mop of unruly hair was a slight bone of contention between them—Courtney would never think to get a haircut for her son and though at first it had irritated Bridgette, more and more his wild curls suited him. Bridgette was now reluctant to get them cut—she certainly wasn't going to rush out and get a haircut just to appease her parents' guests and, anyway, there wasn't time. 'No, Courtney hasn't had his hair cut, but he's looking beautiful and I've got a gorgeous outfit for him.'

And with Harry dropped off and the quickest bath in history taken, the flat had to be hastily tidied, not that she had any intention of Dominic coming in. She'd be ready and dressed at the door, Bridgette decided, so she had about sixteen minutes to work out a not-so-gorgeous outfit for herself.

There was a grey shift dress at the back of her wardrobe and she had to find her ballet pumps but first she had a quick whiz with hair tongs and her magical blusher.

'Please be late,' she begged as she remembered her

screensaver was of them. Her computer was in the spare bedroom, but in case of earthquake and it was the room they ended up in, she had to change it.

'Please be late,' she said again as she stashed dishes in the cupboard beneath the sink and shovelled piles of building bricks into the corner.

'Please be late,' she said as she opened her bedroom door to get her pumps and was distracted by the shelves she'd been meaning to build and the million-thread-count sheets she'd bought in a sale and had been saving for when the room was painted.

But the bedroom was too untidy to even contemplate bringing him in and, no, her prayers weren't answered.

Bang on seven, she heard the doorbell.

CHAPTER SEVEN

'READY!' Bridgette beamed as she opened the front door and stepped out, because there was no way he was coming in.

'Shoes?' Dominic helpfully suggested just after she closed the door.

'Oh. Yes.' Which meant she had to rummage in her bag for her keys as he stood there. 'They must be in here.'

'Can't the babysitter let you in?'

'He's at my parents',' she said as she rummaged.

'Have you locked yourself out?'

'No, no,' Bridgette said cheerfully. 'I do this all the time—here they are.' She produced them with a 'ta ra!' and she let herself in, which of course meant that she had to let him in too—well, she couldn't really leave him on the doorstep.

'Go through,' she said, because she didn't even want him to get a glimpse of the chaos in the bedroom. 'I'll just be a moment.' Except he didn't go through. He stood in the hallway as she slipped through the smallest crack in the door and then scrambled to find her shoes. She must get more organised. Bridgette knew that, dreamt of the day when she finally had some sort of routine. She'd had a loose one once, before Harry was born, but now the whole flat seemed to have gone to pot.

There they were, under the bed. She grabbed her pumps and sort of limbo-danced around the door so that he wouldn't see inside. 'Sorry about that,' she said. 'Just been a bit of a mad rush.'

'Look, if you're too tired to go out for dinner…'

She gave him a strange look. 'I'm starving,' Bridgette said. 'How could anyone be too tired to eat dinner?'

'I meant…'

'So we're not going out dancing, then,' she teased. 'You're not going to teach me the flamenco.' She was leaning against the wall and putting on her ballet pumps, hardly a provocative move, except it was to him.

'Impressed with my Spanish, were you?'

'No Flamenco Medico?' She pouted and raised her arm and gave a stamp of her foot. Dominic stood there, his black eyes watching and sudden tension in his throat.

'Any chance of a drink?'

'Sure!' She beamed and headed to the kitchen and opened the fridge. 'I've got…' She stared at a jug of cordial, kicked herself for not grabbing some beer or wine, or olives and vermouth to make cocktails, she frantically thought.

'I meant water.'

'Oh, I think I've got some somewhere.' She grinned and turned on the tap. 'Oh, yes, here it is.' Was that a reluctant smile on the edge of his lips? 'Here you go.' She handed him the glass as his phone rang, and because of his job he had no choice but to check it. Bridgette's smile was a wry one as 'Arabella' flashed up on the screen.

'She's hitting the bottle early tonight.'

He laughed. 'It's my birthday.'

'Oh!' It was all she could think of to say and then her brain sort of slid back into functioning. 'Happy birthday,' she said. 'I've got candles but no cake.'

Then the phone rang again and they stood there.

And she was annoyed at his ex, annoyed that he was standing there in her kitchen, and her eyes told him so. 'You really did break her heart, didn't you?'

'Long story,' he said. He didn't want to talk about it, hadn't ever spoken about it, and really he'd rather not now.

'Short version?'

'Come on,' he said, 'the table's booked.'

'You know what?' Bridgette said. 'I'm not very hungry.'

'You just said you were starving.'

'Not enough to sit through five hundred phone calls from your ex.'

'Okay, okay.' He offered a major concession. 'I'll turn it off.'

'No,' she said. 'I'm not doing it any more, putting up with crap.' She was talking about Paul, but she was talking about him too, or rather she was talking about herself—she would not put herself through it again. 'Even if you turn it off, I'll know she's ringing. What's that saying? If a tree falls in a forest, does it make a noise?'

'What?' He was irritated, annoyed, but certainly not with her. 'I've said I'll turn it off, Bridgette. She doesn't usually ring—I never thought when I asked you to come out that it was my birthday. I don't get sentimental, I don't sit remembering last year, blah blah blah.'

'Blah blah blah…' Bridgette said, her voice rising,

irritated and annoyed, and certainly it was with him. 'That's all she was, blah blah blah.' The night was over before it had even started. She really should have left it at one night with him. 'What is it with men?' She stormed past him, completely ready to show him the door, and it was almost a shout that halted her.

'She didn't want my brother and his friends at our engagement party.'

They both stood, in a sort of stunned silence, he for saying it, she that he had.

'He's got Down's,' Dominic said, and she was glad that she knew already. 'He lives in sheltered housing. When I'm there I go over every week and sometimes she came with me. She was great…or I thought she was, then when we were planning the engagement, my dad suggested it might be better if Chris didn't come, Chris and his friends, that we have a separate party for them, and she agreed. "It might be a bit awkward."' He put on a very plummy voice. '"You know, for the other guests. You know how he loves to dance."'

And Bridgette stood there and didn't know what to say.

'I couldn't get past it,' Dominic said, and he'd never discussed this with another person, but now that he'd started, it was as if he couldn't stop. Months of seething anger and hurt for his brother all tumbling out. 'My dad wanted nothing to do with him when he was born, he has nothing to do with him now, and it turned out Arabella didn't want him around either—well, not in the way I thought she would.'

'I'm sorry.' It was all she could say and she could hear the bitterness in his response.

'She keeps saying sorry too—that she didn't mean it

and if we can just go back of course he can come to our party. She claims that she said what she did because she was just trying to get on with my dad, except I heard it and I know that it was meant.' He shook his head. 'You think you know someone...'

And when the phone rang again she decided that she did know what to say, after all.

'Give it to me,' she said, and she answered it and gave him a wink and a smile as she spoke. 'Sorry, Dominic's in bed...' She looked at him, saw him groan out a laugh as she answered Arabella's question. 'So what if it's early? I never said that he was asleep.' And she put down the phone but didn't turn it off. Instead she put her hand to her mouth and started kissing it, making breathy noises. Then she jumped up onto the bench, her bottom knocking over a glass.

'Dominic!' she shrieked.

'Bridgette!' He was folded over laughing as he turned off the phone. 'You're wicked.'

'I can be,' she said.

And he looked at her sitting on the bench all dishevelled and sexy, and thought of the noises she had made and what she had done, and just how far they had come since that night. Her words were like a red rag to a bull—he sort of charged her, right there in the kitchen.

Ferocious was his kiss as he pushed her further up the bench, and frantic was her response as she dragged herself back.

His hands were everywhere, but she was just as bad—tearing at his shirt till the buttons tore, pulling out his belt, and she was delighted that they weren't going to make it to the bedroom again, delighted by her own condom-carrying medico. Except Dominic had other ideas.

'Bed.' He pulled her from the bench. 'This time bed.'

'No.' She pulled at his zipper. 'No, no, no.'

'Yes.' He didn't want the floor again. He was leading her to her room, dragging her more like as she dug her heels in.

'You can't go in there!'

'Why?' He grinned, except he'd already pushed the door open. 'Have you got more babies stashed away that you haven't told…?' He just stopped. She doubted anyone as glamorous as he had seen a really messy bedroom, like a *really* messy one. He looked at the chaos and then at the beauty that had somehow emerged out of it.

'I told you not to go in there!' She thought she'd killed the moment. Honestly, she really thought she had, but something else shifted, something even more breathtaking than before.

'In here now, young lady.' His voice was stern as he pointed, and she licked her lips, she could hardly breathe for the excitement, as she headed to her bedroom. 'You can hardly see the bed,' he scolded as he led her to it. 'I've a good mind…'

Yes, they *were* bad. He did put her over his knee, but she nearly fell off laughing and they wanted each other too much to play games. It was the quickest sex ever, the best sex ever.

Again.

Again, she thought as he speared into her. They were still half-dressed, just mutual in want. She'd wanted him so badly again and now he was inside her.

It was bliss to have him back, to be back, to scream out as he shuddered into her.

Bliss for it already to have been the perfect night and it was only seven-thirty p.m.

To be honest, as she looked over he seemed a bit taken back by what had happened.

'Bridgette...' Please don't say sorry, she thought. 'I had no intention...' He looked at her stricken face. 'I mean...I had a table booked and everything.'

'You're not sorry, then?'

'Sorry?' He looked over to her. 'I couldn't be less sorry, just...' He might even be blushing. 'I did want to talk, to take you out. We could still go...'

'If you can sew on your own buttons!' Bridgette looked at his shirt. 'But first you'd have to find a needle. And thread,' she added after a moment's thought.

They settled for pizza. Bridgette undressed and slid into bed, and there would be time for talking later, for now they filled the gap and her roaring hunger with kissing until the pizza was delivered, and then he undressed and got into bed too.

And they did have that grown-up conversation. It sort of meandered around other conversations, but the new rules were spoken by both of them. It was difficult and awkward at times too, but so much easier naked in bed and eating than at some gorgeous restaurant with others around. They spoke about nothing at first and then about work.

'I don't get close.' Dominic shook his head. 'I'm good at my job. I don't need to be like some politician and hold and cuddle babies to be a good doctor.'

'Never?' she checked.

'Never,' Dominic said. 'Oh, I held little Esperanza,

but that was more for the parents, for the *abuela*, but...'
He *did* try to explain it. 'I said she was cute and, yes,
she is, but they're not going to get a touchy-feely doctor if they are on my list.' He said it and he meant it. 'I
can't do that. I know all that might happen—I can't get
involved and then in a few weeks have to tell them that
the news isn't good.' He was possibly the most honest
person she had met. 'I'll give each patient and their parent or parents one hundred per cent of my medical mind.
You don't have to be involved to have compassion.' It
was too easy to be honest with her, but sometimes the
truth hurt. 'I couldn't do it, Bridgette. I couldn't do this
job if I got too close—so I stay back. It's why I don't
want kids of my own.' He gave her a nudge. 'That's why
I don't get involved with anyone who has kids.'

'I don't have kids.' Bridgette said. 'And I think it
wasn't just the long-term viability of our future you
were thinking about that night...' She nudged him and
he grinned, though she didn't repeat midwife-speak to
him; instead she spoke the truth. 'Here for a good time,
not a long time...and not have the night interrupted with
crying babies.'

'Something like that.'

'Didn't Arabella want kids?'

'God, no,' Dominic said.

The conversation sort of meandered around, but it
led to the same thing.

They both knew it.

'I will be moving back to Sydney.' He was honest.
'It's not just work. It's family and friends.' And she
nodded and took a lovely bite of cheesy dough and then
without chewing took another. She couldn't blame him
for wanting to be with them. She took another bite and

he told her about his brother, that he'd been thirteen when Chris was born. 'To be honest, I was embarrassed—I was a right idiot then. So was my dad,' he said. 'They broke up when he was three. I was doing my final year school exams and all stressed and self-absorbed and Chris would just come in and want to talk and play—drove me crazy.

'He didn't care that I had my chemistry, couldn't give a stuff about everything that was so important to me—except clothes. Even now he likes to look good, does his hair.' Dominic grinned. 'Loves to dance!' He rolled his eyes. 'Loves women…'

'Must be your brother!' Bridgette smiled—a real one.

'When I was doing my exams I'd be totally self-centred, angry, stressed. "What's wrong, Dom?" he'd ask. And I'd tell him and he'd just look at me and then go and get me a drink or bring me something to eat, or try to make me laugh because he didn't get it. You know, I stopped being embarrassed and used to feel sorry for him. My dad didn't have anything to do with him, but then I realised Chris was the one who was happy and feeling sorry for me!'

'We've got it all back to front, you know,' Bridgette admitted.

'He's great. And you're right…' He saw her frown. 'I'm not like a paediatrician. I was like my dad growing up—just me, me, me. Without Chris I would have been a sports doctor on the tennis circuit or something—I would,' he said, and she was quite sure he was right, because he had that edge, that drive, that could take him anywhere. 'I'd certainly have had a smaller nose.'

'What?' She frowned and he grinned. 'My father thought I needed a small procedure. I was to have it in the summer break between school and university. He had it all planned out.' He gave a dark laugh. 'The night before the operation I rang him and told him to go jump.'

'Do you talk now?'

'Of course.' He looked over. 'About nothing, though. He never asks about Chris, never goes in and sees him on his birthday or Christmas, or goes out with him.' He gave her a grin. 'I can still feel him looking at my nose when he speaks to me.'

'He'd be wanting to liposuction litres out of me!' Bridgette laughed and he did too.

Dominic lay and stared up at the ceiling, thought about today—because even if he did his best not to get close to his patients, today he hadn't felt nothing as he'd stood and had that photo taken. He'd been angry—yes, he might have smiled for the camera, but inside a black anger had churned, an anger towards his father.

He'd walked up to NICU and Tony had walked alongside him, had stood with his baby for every test, had beamed so brightly when the good news was confirmed that her heart was fine.

'I'll come back to Maternity with you in case Maria has any questions,' Dominic had said, even though he hadn't had to. He had stood and watched when Tony told his wife the good news and wondered what he'd have been like had he had Tony as a father. He didn't want to think about his father now.

'How long have you been looking after Harry?' he asked instead.

Bridgette gave a tense shrug. 'It's very on and off,' she said.

'You said she was a lot younger…'

'Eighteen,' Bridgette said. He'd been so open and honest, yet she just couldn't bring herself to be so with him. 'I really would rather not talk about it tonight.'

'Fair enough,' Dominic said.

So they ate pizza instead and made love and hoped that things might look a little less complicated in the morning.

They didn't.

'Do you want to go out tonight?' he asked, taking a gulp of the tea she'd made because Bridgette had run out of coffee. 'Or come over?'

'I'd love to, but I truly can't,' she said, because she *couldn't*. 'I've got to pick Harry up.'

'When does his mum get back?'

'Tomorrow,' Bridgette said. 'I think.'

'You think.' Some things he could not ignore. 'Bridgette, you seem to be taking on an awful lot.'

'Well, she's my sister,' Bridgette said, 'and she's looking for flats and daycare. It's better that she has a few days to sort it out herself rather than dragging Harry around with her.'

'Fair enough.'

And he didn't run for the hills.

Instead he gave her a very nice kiss, and then reached in for another, a kiss that was so nice it made her want to cry.

'Have breakfast,' she said to his kiss, trying to think what was in the fridge.

And he was about to say no, that he had to go to work in an hour and all that.

Except he said yes.

He thought of the frothy latte he'd normally be sipping right now.

Instead he watched Bridgette's bottom wiggle as she made pancakes because she didn't have bread.

Watched as she shook some icing sugar over them.

How could you not have bread? she screamed inside.

Or bacon, or fresh tomatoes. She had thrown on her nursing apron—it had two straps with buttons and big pockets in the front. She had ten of them and they were brilliant for cooking—so the fat didn't splat—but she was naked beneath.

'We should be sitting at a table outside a café—' she smiled as he watched her '—or at the window, watching the barista froth our lovely coffees.'

She must have read his mind.

As she brought over two plates of pancakes, where Bridgette was concerned, he crossed the line. 'How long ago did you break up with Paul?'

'Excuse me?' She gave him a very odd look as she came over with breakfast. 'I don't remember discussing him with you.'

'You didn't.' He gave a half-shrug. 'You really don't discuss yourself with me at all, so I've had to resort to other means.' He saw the purse of her lips. 'I didn't just happen across it—I asked Vince for your e-mail address. Guys do talk.' He saw her raise her eyebrows. 'He said there had been a messy break-up, that was all he knew.'

'Well, it wasn't very messy for me.' Bridgette shrugged. 'It might have been a bit messy for him because he suddenly had to find somewhere to live.' She shook her head. She wasn't going there with him. 'It's a long story…'

'Short version,' Dominic said.

'We were together two years,' Bridgette said. 'Great for one of them, great till my sister got depressed and moved in and suddenly there was a baby with colic and…' She gave a tight shrug. 'You get the picture. Anyway, by the time Harry turned one we were over.' She had given the short version, but she did ponder just a little. 'He felt the place had been invaded, that I was never able to go out.' She looked over at him. 'Funny, I'd have understood if it had been his flat.' She gave Dominic a smile but it didn't reach her eyes. He could see the hurt deep in them and knew better than to push.

'I'll see you at work on Monday,' she said as she saw him to the door.

'I'm still here for a while,' Dominic said.

'And then you won't be…'

'It doesn't mean we can't have a nice time.' If it sounded selfish, it wasn't entirely. He wanted to take her out, wanted to know her some more, wanted to spoil her perhaps.

'Like a holiday romance?' Bridgette asked.

'Hardly. I'm working sixty-plus hours a week,' he said to soften his offering, because, yes, a brief romance was the most he could ever commit to. But she hadn't said it with sarcasm. Instead she smiled, because a holiday romance sounded more doable. She certainly wasn't about to let go of her heart and definitely not to a man like him. A holiday romance maybe she could handle.

'I won't always be able to come out… I mean…' Bridgette warned.

'Let's just see.' He kissed the tip of her nose. 'Who knows, maybe your sister will get that job, after all, and move up to Bendigo.'

And you should be very careful what you wish for, Dominic soon realised, because a few days later Courtney did.

CHAPTER EIGHT

AT FIRST it was great. Out had come the silver dress, and he *had* taught her the flamenco—not that he knew how, but they'd had fun working it out.

In fact, with Courtney and Harry away, it had been Dominic who had found himself the one with scheduling problems.

'I'll get back to you within the hour.' There was a small curse of frustration as Dominic put down the phone and pulled out his laptop.

'Problem?' Bridgette asked.

'Mark Evans wants me to cover him till eleven a.m. I'm supposed to be picking up Chris from the airport then.' He pulled the airline page up. Chris had been missing his brother, and with Dominic unable to get away for a while, a compromise had been reached and Chris was coming down to Melbourne for the night. 'I'd say no to Mark except he's done me a lot of favours. I'll see if I can change his flight.'

'You could just ask me,' Bridgette said, unable to see the problem. 'Surely if Chris can fly on his own, he won't mind being met by a friend of his brother's.'

'You sure?'

'It's no big deal.'

To Dominic it was a big deal. Arabella would, he realised, have simply had Chris change his flight, which was maybe a bit unfair on her, because Arabella would have been at work too. Bridgette was, after all, not starting till later. 'What if the flight's delayed? It doesn't leave you much time to get to your shift as it is…'

'Then I'll ring work and explain that I'm delayed. What?' She misread his curious expression. 'You don't think I'd just leave him stranded?'

Chris's flight wasn't delayed. In fact, it landed a full ten minutes early and he had hand luggage only, which left plenty of time for a drink and something to eat at an airport café before she started her late shift. He told her all about his first time flying alone and then they drove back to Dominic's, getting there just as he arrived. There was no denying that the two brothers were pleased to see each other. 'Come over tonight if you want,' Dominic said, 'after your shift. We're just seeing an early movie so we could go out for something to eat if you like?'

'I'll give it a miss, thanks,' Bridgette said. 'I don't want to spoil your party and anyway I'm on an early shift tomorrow.' And he was always defensive around his brother yet not once did he think it was a snub. He knew Bridgette better than that—well, the part of Bridgette that she let him know. And he knew that she wouldn't even try to win points by hanging around to prove she was nothing like Arabella.

She *was* nothing like Arabella.

'See you, Chris.' She gave him a wave. 'Have a great night.'

'See you, Bridgette,' he said. 'Thanks for the cake.

'We went to a café,' Chris explained, when she had gone. 'Is that your girlfriend?'

'She's a friend,' Dominic said.

'Your girlfriend.' Chris grinned.

'Yeah, maybe,' Dominic admitted, 'but it's not as simple as that.' It wasn't and it was too hard to explain to himself let alone Chris.

There was a reason why holidays rarely lasted more than a few weeks—because any longer than that, you can't pretend there are no problems. You can't keep the real world on hold. Perhaps selfishly Dominic had wanted Courtney to leave, wanted to get to know a bit better the woman he had enjoyed dating, but once Chris had gone home, he realised that it wasn't the same Bridgette when Harry wasn't around. Over the next few days she couldn't get hold of Courtney and they were back to the morning after he'd met her—Bridgette constantly checking her phone. There was an anxiety to her that wasn't right.

He wanted the woman he'd found.

But Bridgette had that bright smile on, the one he had seen when they'd first met. She gave it to him the next Friday afternoon at work as she dropped off a new mum for a cuddle with her baby and he gave her his brief work nod back. Then she stopped by the incubator, as she often did, to speak with Carla.

'How are you?' she asked.

'Good today!' Carla smiled. 'Though it all depends on how Francesca is as to how I'm feeling at any moment, but today's been a good day. Do you want a peek?' There were drapes over the incubator and when she peeled them back Bridgette was thrilled by the change in the baby. She was still tiny, but her face was visible now, with far fewer tubes. It had been a precarious journey, it still was, but Francesca was still there, fighting.

'She gave us a fright last week,' Carla said. 'They thought she might need surgery on the Friday, but she settled over the weekend. Every day's a blessing still. I'm getting to hold her now—it's fantastic. Frank and I are fighting to take turns for a cuddle.'

It was lovely to see Francesca doing so well, but Bridgette's mind was on other things as she walked back to the ward, and she didn't hear Dominic till he was at her side.

'Hi.' He fell into step beside her. Not exactly chatty, he never was at work, but today neither was she. 'How's your shift?'

'Long,' she admitted. 'Everything's really quiet— I'm waiting for a baby boom.' She smiled when she saw Mary walking towards them.

'We're missing that little man of yours,' Mary said. 'How is he doing?'

'He's fine,' Bridgette said, expecting Dominic to walk on when she stopped to talk to Mary, but instead he stood there with them. 'I am sorry to have given you such short notice.'

'Hardly your fault.' Mary gave her a smile. 'You'd be missing him too?'

Bridgette gave a nod. 'A bit,' she admitted, 'but they should be home soon for a visit.'

'That's good.' Mary bustled off and Bridgette stood, suddenly awkward.

'Have you heard from her?'

Bridgette shook her head. 'I tried to ring but couldn't get through—I think she's out of credit for her phone.

Right.' She gave a tight smile. 'I'm going to head for home.'

'I should be finished soon,' Dominic said. 'And then I'm back here tomorrow for the weekend.' He gave her a wry grin. 'Some holiday romance.'

'We can go out tonight,' Bridgette offered. 'Or sleep.'

'Nope,' Dominic said, 'we can go out and then…' He gave her that nice private smile. 'Why don't you head over to mine?' he asked, because there were cafés a stone's throw away, unlike Bridgette's flat.

'Sure,' Bridgette said, because she couldn't face pizza again and the flat still hadn't been tidied. The cot was down, but stood taking up half the wall in her spare bedroom, which made it an obstacle course to get to the computer.

Next weekend she was off for four days and she *was* going to sort it.

Bridgette let herself into his flat, and wondered how someone who worked his ridiculous hours managed to keep the place so tidy. Yes, he'd told her he had someone who came in once a week, and she knew he did, but it wasn't just the cleaner, Bridgette knew. He was a tidy person, an ordered person.

Knew what he wanted, where his life was going.

She had a little snoop, to verify her findings. Yes, the dishes were done and stacked in the dishwasher; the lid was on the toothpaste and it was back in its little glass. She peered into the bedroom—okay, it wasn't exactly hospital corners, but the cover had been pulled back up. She wandered back to his lounge and over to his desk.

There was a pile of mail waiting for him, one a very thick envelope, from that exclusive hospital where he wanted to work, but it was too much to think about and she had a shower instead. Then she pulled on a black skirt with a pale grey top, because an awful lot of her clothes seemed to live here now. The outfit would look okay with ballet pumps or high heels—wherever the night might lead.

It was a holiday romance, Bridgette kept telling herself to make sense of it, and summer was coming to an end. The clock would change soon and in a couple of weeks it would be dark by now. She felt as if she were chasing the last fingers of the sun, just knew things were changing. Oh, she'd been blasé with Mary, didn't want to tell anyone what was in the bottom of her heart, that things were building, that at any moment now the phone would ring and it would all have gone to pot.

'Sorry about that…' He came in through the door much later than expected and gave her a very haphazard kiss as he looked at his watch and picked up his mail. He didn't want her to ask what the hold-up had been, didn't want her to know the scare little Francesca had given him just a short while before. He had twelve hours off before a weekend on call and he needed every moment of it, but first… 'I've got to take a phone call.'

'No problem.'

'Hey,' Dominic said when his phone rang promptly at seven-thirty. 'How are you?'

'Good,' Chris said, and got straight to the point. 'When are you coming back to Sydney?' Chris was growing impatient. 'It's been ages since you were here.'

And Dominic took a deep breath and told him the news he hadn't really had time to think about, let alone share with Bridgette. 'I got a phone call today, an—' he didn't want to say too much at this early stage '—I'm coming home for a few days next weekend. We'll go out then.'

'It's been ages.'

'I know,' Dominic said, and he knew how much his brother missed him, but he tried to talk him around, to move the conversation to other things. 'What are you doing tonight?'

'A party,' Chris said, and normally he'd have given him details as to who was going, the music that would be played, what they were eating, but instead he had a question. 'Bridgette *is* your girlfriend, isn't she?'

And normally Dominic would have laughed, would have made Chris laugh with an answer like 'One of them', but instead he hesitated. 'Yes.'

And usually they would have chatted for a bit—until Chris's Friday night kicked off and he was called out to come and join the party, but instead Chris was far from happy and told Dominic that he had to go and then asked another question.

'When are you properly coming back?'

'I've told you—I'm coming back soon for a few days,' Dominic said.

It wasn't, from Chris's gruff farewell, a very good answer.

'Right.' He came out of his room and saw that Bridgette was writing a note. 'Finally... Let's go and get something to eat. I've still got the sound of babies crying ringing in my ears.'

'Actually—' she turned '—my sister just called.' Back on went that smile. 'Things didn't work out in Bendigo and she's back. She's a bit upset and she's asked if I can have Harry tonight. I called and asked my parents, but they're out.'

'Oh.' He tried to be logical. After all, apart from one time in the corridor he'd never even seen Harry, and if her sister was upset, well, she needed to go. And even if more children was the last thing he needed tonight, she really had helped out with Chris and, yes, he did want to see her. 'We can take him out with us.'

'It's nearly eight o'clock,' Bridgette said, though when Harry was with her sister his bedtime was erratic at best.

'It's the Spaniard in me,' Dominic said.

Courtney, Dominic thought as he sat in the passenger seat while Bridgette collected Harry, didn't look that upset. But he said nothing as Bridgette drove. They'd gone out in her car because of baby seats and things, but they drove along to the area near his house and parked. It was cool but still light as they walked. She felt more than a little awkward. Walking along, pushing a stroller on a Friday night with Dominic felt terribly strange.

They sat out in a nice pavement café. They were spoiled for choice, but settled for Spanish and ate tapas. It was a lovely evening, but it was cool, even for summer. For Bridgette it was made extra bearable by one of Dominic's black turtlenecks and a big gas heater blazing above them. It was nice to sit outside and Harry seemed content, especially as Bridgette fed him *crema catalana*. Dominic had suggested it, a sort of cold custard with a caramel top, and Harry was loving his first Spanish dessert, but the mood wasn't as relaxed as it usually was. Dominic was lovely to Harry, there was no question about that, but Bridgette knew this wasn't quite the night he'd had planned.

'So, what's Courtney upset about?' He finally broached the subject

'I didn't really ask.'

'Does she do this a lot?'

Bridgette shot him a glance. 'It's one night, Dominic. I'm sorry for the invasion.' She was brittle in her defence and he assumed she was comparing him with Paul. She changed the subject. 'Have you been to Spain?'

'We used to go there in the summer holidays,' Dominic said. 'Well, their winter,' he clarified, because in Australia summer meant Christmas time. 'My father had a lot of social things on at that time, you know, what with work, so Chris and I would stay with Abuela.'

'And your mum?' Bridgette asked.

Dominic gave her an old-fashioned look, then a wry grin. 'Nope, she stayed here, looking stunning next to Dad. And I spent a year there when I finished school. I still want to go back, maybe work there for a couple of years at some point. It's an amazing place.'

And there were two conversations going on, as she ate thick black olives and fried baby squid, and he dipped bread in the most delicious lime hummus, and Harry, full up on the custard, fell asleep.

'I'd better get him back.'

They walked back along the beach road, a crowded beach full of Friday night fun, except Dominic was pensive. He was trying to remember the world before Chris had come along and Bridgette was for once quiet too.

She drove him back to his place. Harry was still asleep, and she didn't want to wake him up by coming in. Dominic had to be at work tomorrow, so there was no way really he could stay at hers.

And they kissed in the car, but it was different this time.

'Not your usual Friday night,' she said. 'Home by ten, alone!'

He didn't argue—she was, after all, speaking the truth.

CHAPTER NINE

Rather than change things, the situation brought what was already coming to a head.

Dominic didn't know how best to broach what was on his mind.

He was used to straight talking, but on this Tuesday morning, lying in bed with Bridgette warm and asleep beside him, he didn't know where to start. He'd been putting this discussion off for a couple of days now, which wasn't at all like him.

'Hey, Bridgette.' He turned and rolled into her, felt her sleepy body start to wake, and he was incredibly tempted to forget what had been on his mind a few seconds ago and to concentrate instead on what was on his mind now. 'When do you finish?'

'Mmm...?' She didn't want questions, didn't want to think about anything other than the delicious feel of Dominic behind her. She could feel his mouth nuzzling the back of her neck and she wanted to just sink into the sensations he so readily provided, to let him make love to her, but automatically she reached for the phone that was on her bedside drawer, checked there were no messages she had missed and frowned at how early it was—it wasn't even six a.m.

'It's not even six,' she grumbled, because they hadn't got to bed till one—an evening spent watching movies and eating chocolate, laughing and making love, because neither wanted to talk properly.

'I know that you're off next weekend, but when do you actually finish?'

'I've got a long weekend starting Thursday at three p.m. precisely.' She wriggled at the pleasurable thought. 'I'm not back till Wednesday when I start nights. Why?'

'Just thinking.'

Though he didn't want to think at the moment, it could surely wait for now, Dominic decided, because his hands were at her breasts, and how he loved them, and her stomach and her round bottom. She was the first woman he loved waking up with.

It was a strange admission for him, but he usually loathed chatter in the morning. Arabella had driven him mad then too.

'Do you want coffee?' Arabella would ask every morning.

It was just the most pointless question.

Okay, maybe not for a one-nighter, but two years on, had she really needed to start each day with the same?

He looked at Bridgette's back, at the millions of freckles, and she was the one woman who could make him smile even in her sleep. 'Do you want coffee?' he said to a dozing Bridgette.

'What do you think?' she mumbled, and then... 'What's so funny?' she asked as he laughed and his mouth met her neck.

'Nothing.'

'So what are you lying there thinking about?'

'Nothing.'

'Dominic?'

He hesitated for an interminable second, his lips hovering over her neck and his hand still on her breast. 'I've been invited for an informal interview.' He was back at her neck and kissing it deeply. 'Very informal. It's just a look around…'

'In Sydney?'

Her eyes that had been closed opened then. She'd sort of known this was coming. He'd always said he wanted to work there; they'd been seeing each other just a few short weeks and there had been that envelope she'd peeked at.

'Yep—there's a position coming up, but not till next year. It's all very tentative at this stage—they just want me to come and have a look around, a few introductions…'

'That's good.'

And that wasn't the hard bit.

They both knew it and they lay there in silence.

Like an injury that didn't hurt unless you applied pressure, they'd danced around this issue from day one, avoided it, but they couldn't keep doing that for ever.

'Come with me,' he said. 'We could have a nice weekend. You could use the break before you start nights.'

She didn't want to think about it.

Didn't want to think about him going to Sydney, and there was still something else to discuss. Bridgette knew that, and Dominic knew it too.

There was a conversation to be had but it was easier to turn around, to press her lips into his. 'Bridgette…' Dominic pulled back. 'It would be great.' He gave her a smile. 'I won't inflict my family on you.'

'What?' She tried to smile back. 'You'll put me in some fancy hotel?'

'We'll be staying at my flat,' Dominic said—and there it was, the fact that he owned a flat in Sydney but he was only renting here. He had a cleaner there, coming in weekly to take care of things while he was temporarily away. 'Bridgette, you've known from the start that was where I was going.'

'I know that.'

'It's only an hour's flight away.'

She nodded, because his words made sense, perfect sense—it was just a teeny flight, after all—but her life wasn't geared to hopping on planes.

'Look,' Dominic said, 'let's just have a weekend away. Let's not think about things for a while. I'll book flights. The interview will be a morning at most. I'll see Chris…'

And so badly she wanted to say yes, to say what the hell, and hop onto a plane, to swim in the ocean, shop and see the sights, to stay in the home of the man she adored, but… 'I can't.'

'You've got days off,' Dominic pointed out.

'I really need to sort out my flat.' She did. 'I've been putting it off for ages.'

'I know,' Dominic said. 'Look, why don't I come round a couple of nights in the week and help with those shelves?'

'You!' She actually laughed. 'Will you bring your drill?' She saw his tongue roll in his cheek. 'Bring your stud finder…' she said, and dug him in the ribs. He would be as hopeless as her, Dominic realised. After all, his dad had never been one for DIY—he wouldn't know how to change a washer. But it wasn't the shelves that were the real problem. Yes, it would be so much easier to talk about stud finders, to laugh and to roll into each other as they wanted to, but instead he asked her again.

'If I can't do it—' he had visions of her being knocked unconscious in the night by his handiwork '—then I will get someone in and those shelves will be put up on your return,' he said. 'But it really would be nice to go away.'

'I can't,' she said, because she simply could not bear to be so far away from Harry. Courtney's silence was worrying her and it couldn't be ignored; also, she couldn't bear to get any closer to Dominic. To open up her heart again—especially to a man who would soon be moving away.

'Look, I have to go back this weekend.'

'Go, then!' Bridgette said. 'I'm not stopping you. I'm just saying that I can't come.'

'You could!' he said. He could see the dominos all lined up, so many times he'd halted them from falling, and he was halting them now, because when talking didn't work he tried to kiss sense into her. She could feel her breasts flatten against his chest and the heady male scent of him surrounding her, and she kissed him back ferociously. It was as close as they had come to a row: they were going to have a row in a moment and she truly didn't want one, knew that neither did he. This way was easier, this way was better, this simply had to happen, because somehow they both knew it was the last time.

He kissed her face and her ears, he pushed her knees apart and they were well past condoms now. He slid into her tight warmth, went to the only place she would come with him and she did. They both did.

It was a regretful orgasm, if there was such a thing,

because it meant it was over. It meant they had to climb back out of the place where things were so simple.

'I think a weekend away would be great.' He tried again. He'd heard the first click of the dominos falling and still he was trying to halt them. 'I think we need to get away. Look, if you don't want to go to Sydney…' He didn't want to let down Chris, didn't want to reschedule the interview, but he didn't want things to end here. He wanted to give them a chance. 'We could drive. There's a few places I want to see along the coast…'

'I can't this weekend,' she said. 'I told you, I've got the flat to sort out. Courtney's still upset…'

'Well, when can you?' And he let them fall. 'I want to get away on my days off.' He really did—it had been a helluva weekend at work. He wanted to be as far away from the hospital as possible this next weekend, didn't want to be remotely available, because he knew that if they called, he'd go in. What was he thinking, driving to the coast when he had an interview, letting down Chris? For what? So that they could stay in and wait for her sister to ring?

'Look, I know you help out your sister…' He simply did not understand her. In so many things they were open, there were so many things they discussed, but really he knew so little about her. There was still a streak of hurt in her eyes, still a wall of silence around her. 'But surely you can have a weekend off.'

'Maybe I don't want one,' Bridgette said. 'Maybe I don't want to go up to Sydney and to see the life you'll soon be heading back to.'

'Bridgette…' He was trying to prolong things, not end them. 'I don't get you.'

'You're not supposed to, that's not what we're about.'

It wasn't, she told herself. It was supposed to be just a few short weeks—a break, a romance, that was all. It was better over with now. 'Just go to Sydney,' Bridgette said. 'That's what you want, that's where you've always been heading. Don't try and blame us ending on Harry.'

'I'm not blaming Harry,' Dominic said, and he wasn't. 'I'll admit I was a bit fed up with his aunt on Friday.'

'Sorry to mess up your night.' She so wasn't going to do this again. 'God, you're just like—'

'Don't say it, Bridgette,' Dominic warned, 'because I am nothing like him.' He'd heard a bit about her ex and wasn't about to be compared to Paul. 'I'll tell you one of the differences between him and me. I'd have had this sorted from the start. Your sister's using you, Bridgette.' He looked at her, all tousled and angry, and truly didn't know what this was about.

'Do you think I don't know that?'

'So why do you let her?' He gave an impatient shake of his head. 'Do you know, I think you hide behind Harry. He's your excuse not to go out, not to get away.' Bridgette was right, Sydney *was* where he'd always intended to be—that was his hospital of choice and he wasn't about to have his career dictated to by Courtney.

'I'm going for the interview. I'm flying out on Thursday night. I'll text you the flight times. We'll be back Sunday night.'

'Don't book a ticket for me,' Bridgette said. 'Because I can't go.'

'Yes, you can. And, yes, I am booking for you,' Dominic said. 'So you've plenty time to change your mind.'

He did book the tickets.

But he knew she wouldn't come.

CHAPTER TEN

'SORRY to call you down from NICU.' Rebecca, the accident and emergency registrar, looked up from the notes she was writing. It was four a.m. on Tuesday morning. It had been a long day for Dominic and a very long night on call. After the interviews in Sydney and long walks on the beach with Chris, his head felt as if it was exploding, not that Rebecca could have guessed it. He was his usual practical self. 'I'm trying to stall Mum by saying we're waiting for an X-ray.'

'No problem. What do we know so far?'

'Well, the story is actually quite consistent—Mum heard a bang and found him on the floor. He'd climbed out if his cot, which fits the injury. She said that he was crying by the time she went in to him. It was her reaction that was strange—complete panic, called an ambulance. She was hysterical when she arrived but she's calmed down.'

'Are there any other injuries you can see?'

'A couple of small bruises, an ear infection, he's a bit grubby and there's a bit of nappy rash,' Rebecca said, 'but he is a toddler, after all. Anyway, I'm just not happy and I thought you should take a look.' She handed him the patient card and as Dominic noted the name, as his stomach seemed to twist in on itself, a young woman called from the cubicle.

'How much longer are we going to be waiting here?' She peered out and all Dominic could think was that if he had not recognised the name, it would never have entered his head that this woman was Bridgette's sister. She had straggly dyed blond hair and was much skinnier. Her features were sharper than Bridgette's and even if she wasn't shouting, she was such an angry young thing, so hostile in her actions, so on the edge, that she was, Dominic recognised in an instant, about to explode any moment. 'How much longer till he gets his X-ray or CT or whatever?'

'There's another doctor here to take a look at Harry,' Helga, the charge nurse, calmly answered. 'He'll be in with you shortly—it won't be long.'

'Well, can someone watch him while I get a coffee at least?' Courtney snapped. 'Why can't I take it in the cubicle?'

'You can't take a hot drink—' Helga started, but Dominic interrupted.

'Courtney, why don't you go and get a coffee? Someone will sit with your son while you take a little break.

'Is that okay?' He checked with Helga and she sent in a student nurse, but Rebecca was too sharp not to notice that he had known the name of the patient's mother. 'You know her?' She grimaced as Courtney flounced out, because this sort of thing was always supremely awkward.

'I know his aunt.' Dominic was sparse with his reply but Helga filled in for him.

'Bridgette. She's a midwife on Maternity. She's on

her way. I called her a little while ago—Courtney was in a right panic when she arrived and she asked us to.'

'Okay.' Dominic tried not to think about Bridgette taking that phone call—he had to deal with this without emotion, had to step out and look at the bigger picture. 'I'm going to step aside.' He came to the only decision he could in such a situation. 'I'm going to ring Greg Andrews and ask him to take over the patient, but first I need to take a look at Harry and make sure that there's nothing medically urgent that needs to be dealt with.' His colleague might take a while. He did not engage in further small talk; he did not need to explain his involvement in the case. After all, he was stepping aside. Dominic walked into the cubicle where Harry lay resting in a cot with a student nurse by his side. Rebecca came in with him.

'Good morning, Harry.' He took off his jacket and hung it on the peg and proceeded to wash his hands and then made his way over to the young patient. He looked down into dark grey eyes that stared back at him and they reminded him of Bridgette's. He could see the hurt behind them and Dominic did not try to win a smile. 'I expect you're feeling pretty miserable? Well, I'm just going to take a look at you.' Gently he examined the toddler, looking in his ears for any signs of bleeding, and Harry let him, hardly even blinking as he shone the ophthalmoscope into the back of each eye, not even crying or flinching as Dominic gently examined the tender bruise. Through it all Harry didn't say a word. 'Has he spoken since he came here?' Dominic asked

'Not much—he's asked for a drink.' The curtains opened then and Helga walked in. Behind her was

Bridgette, her face as white as chalk, but she smiled to Harry.

'Hey.' She stroked his little cheek. 'I hear you've been in the wars.' She spoke ever so gently to him, but her eyes were everywhere, lifting the blanket and checking him carefully, even undoing his nappy, and he saw her jaw tighten at the rash.

'How is he?'

'He just gave everyone a fright!' Helga said, but Bridgette's eyes went to Dominic's.

'Could I have a quick word, Bridgette?'

He stepped outside the cubicle and she joined him.

'He's filthy,' Bridgette said. She could feel tears rising up, felt as if she was choking, so angry was she with her sister. 'And he didn't have any rash when I saw him on Friday. I bought loads of cream that she took—'

'Bridgette,' he interrupted, 'I'm handing Harry's care over to a colleague. You will need to tell him all this. It's not appropriate that I'm involved. You understand that?' She gave a brief nod but her attention was diverted by the arrival of her sister, and he watched as Bridgette strode off and practically marched Courtney out towards the waiting room.

'I'll go.' Helga was more than used to confrontations such as this and called to the nurses' station over her shoulder as she followed the two sisters out. 'Just let Security know we might need them.'

And this was what Courtney had reduced her to, Bridgette thought, standing outside the hospital early in the morning, with security guards hovering. But Bridgette was too angry to keep quiet.

'He climbed out of his cot!' Courtney was immediately on the defensive the moment they were outside.

'I didn't know that he climbed. You should have told me.' Maybe it was a good idea that security guards were present because hearing Courtney try to blame her for this had Bridgette's blood boiling.

'He's never once climbed out of the cot when I've had him,' Bridgette answered hotly. 'Mind you, he was probably trying to get out and change his own nappy or make himself a drink, or give himself a wash. You lazy, selfish…' She stopped herself then because if she said any more, it would be way too much. She paused and Helga stepped in, took Courtney inside, and Bridgette stood there hugging her arms around herself tightly, mortified when Dominic came out.

'This has nothing to do with you,' Bridgette said, still angry. 'You've stepped aside.'

'You know I had to.'

She did know that.

'Is this why you couldn't get away?' Dominic asked, and she didn't answer, because a simple yes would have been a lie. 'Bridgette?'

'I don't want to talk about it.'

'You never do,' he pointed out, but now really wasn't the time. 'I know that it doesn't seem like it now,' Dominic said, 'but Harry being admitted might be the best thing that could have happened. Things might get sorted now.'

As an ambulance pulled up she gave a nod, even if she didn't believe it.

'Bridgette, I was actually going to come over and see you today,' Dominic said, and she knew what was coming. 'I didn't want you to hear it from anyone else—I've just given notice. I'm leaving on Saturday.' He chose not to tell her just how impossible the decision had been, but in the end it had surely been the right one—he wanted simple, straightforward, and Bridgette was anything but. He'd opened up to her more than he had with anyone, and yet he realised that, still, despite his question, he knew very little about her and even now she said nothing. 'Anyway, I thought I should tell you myself.'

'Sure.'

'I'd better get up to...' His voice stopped, his stomach tightened, as the ambulance door opened and he met Tony's frantic eyes.

CHAPTER ELEVEN

DOMINIC checked himself, because it should make no difference that it wasn't Esperanza on the stretcher. Instead it was Roman, their three-year-old, and he needed Dominic's help and concentration just as much as his little sister would have. 'Dr Mansfield's here…' Tony was talking reassuringly to his son, who was struggling hard to breathe as they moved him straight into the critical area. 'The doctor who looked after Esperanza. That's good news.'

'He did this last year…' Tony said as Dominic examined him, and Tony explained about his severe asthma. 'He does it a lot, but last year he ended up in Intensive Care.'

'Okay.' Dominic listened to his chest and knew that Roman would probably have to head to Intensive Care again this morning.

Roman took up all of Dominic's morning, but by lunchtime, when he'd spoken to the family and the frantic *abuela*, things were a little calmer.

'While he's still needing hourly nebulisers it's safer that he is here,' Dominic explained, but then it was easier to speak in Spanish, so that Abuela understood. He told them things were steadily improving and would continue to do so.

Tony rang Maria, who was of course frantic, and Dominic spoke to her too.

'You get a taxi home,' Tony said to Abuela, 'and Maria can come in between feeds.'

Writing up his drug sheets, Dominic listened for a moment as they worked out a vague plan of action, heard that Tony would ring his boss and take today off.

'You think he might go to the ward tomorrow?'

'Or this evening.' Dominic nodded.

'I'll stay with him tonight and if you can come in in the morning to be with Roman I can go to work tomorrow,' Tony said to his mother. She rattled the start of twenty questions at him, but Tony broke in.

'We'll deal with that if it happens.'

Dominic headed down to the children's ward. Bridgette wasn't around and neither was Courtney. An extra layer had been added to Harry's cot, in case he was, in fact, a climber, and it stood like a tall cage in the middle of the nursery. He walked in and took off his jacket, washed his hands and then turned round and looked straight into the waiting grey eyes of Harry, who wasn't his patient, he reminded himself.

Harry's head injury wasn't at all serious, but he had been moved up to the children's ward mid-morning. Bridgette knew it was more of a social admission. Maybe she had done rather too good a job of reassuring her parents that it wasn't serious when she rang them, because they didn't dash in. After all, her father had to have a filling that afternoon, so they said they would come in the evening and, with a weary sigh, her mother agreed, yes, they would stop by Bridgette's flat and bring a change of clothes, pyjamas and toiletries.

Bridgette took the opportunity to voice a few of her concerns about his speech delay with the doctor and he gave her a sort of blink when she spoke about Harry's fixation with bricks and that he didn't talk much.

'Has he had his hearing checked?'

'Er, no.'

'He's had a few ear infections, though,' Dr Andrews said, peering through his examination notes. 'We'll get his hearing tested and then he might need an ENT out-patient appointment.'

Later they were interviewed by a social worker, but by dinnertime Courtney had had enough. 'I'm exhausted,' she said. 'I was up all night with him. I think I'll go home and get some sleep.'

'We can put a bed up beside his cot,' a nurse offered.

'I'd never sleep with all the noise,' Courtney said, gave Harry a brief kiss and then she was gone, safe in the knowledge that Bridgette would stay the night. Dominic was on the ward when Bridgette's parents arrived, talking with the charge nurse. She saw him glance up when her mother asked to be shown where Harry was.

'Here, Mum,' Bridgette said as they made their way over, all nervous smiles, slightly incredulous that their grandson was actually here.

'Here's the bits you wanted,' her mum said, handing over a bag.

Bridgette peered into the bag and flinched. 'Did you deliberately choose the ugliest pyjamas I own?' She grinned. 'I'd forgotten that I even had these!' They were orange flannelette, emblazoned with yellow flowers, and had been sent by her granny about five years ago.

'You're lucky I could find anything in *that* room!' Betty said. 'I could barely see the bed.'

Yes, she really must get organised, Bridgette remembered. Somehow she had not got around to it last weekend. She had either been worrying about Harry or mooching over Dominic. Well, Dominic was gone or going and Harry would be sorted, so she would get organised soon.

'So what is he in for?' Maurice asked. 'He looks fine.'

He certainly looked a whole lot better. He'd had a bath and hair wash and had a ton of cream on his bottom. There was just a very small bruise on his head.

'He didn't even need a stitch,' Betty said.

'You know why he's in, Mum.'

'For nappy rash!' Betty wasn't having it.

'Mum... He's getting his hearing tested tomorrow.' They were less than impressed. 'Aren't you going to ask where Courtney is?'

'Getting some well-deserved rest,' Betty hissed. 'She must have had the fright of her life last night.' They didn't stay very long. They fussed over Harry for half an hour or so and it was a very weary Bridgette who tried to get Harry off to sleep.

'How's he doing?' Dominic asked as she stood and rubbed Harry's back.

'Fine,' Bridgette said, and then conceded, as she really wasn't angry with him, 'he's doing great. We're going for a hearing test tomorrow. Dr Andrews said we should check out the basics.' Of course he said nothing. He was his 'at work' Dominic and so he didn't fill in the gaps. 'I thought he was autistic or something.' She gave a small shrug. 'Well, he might be. I mean, if he is, he is…'

'You nurses.'

'You'd be the same,' Bridgette said, 'if he was…' Except Harry wasn't his and he wasn't hers either and it was too hard to voice so she gave him the smile that said keep away.

She washed in the one shower available for parents, an ancient old thing at the edge of the parents' room, and pulled on the awful pyjamas her parents had brought and climbed into the roller bed at seven-thirty p.m., grateful that the lights were already down. But she found out that Courtney was right—it was far too noisy to sleep. When she was woken again by a nurse doing obs around ten and by a baby coughing in the next cot, she wandered down to the parents' room to get a drink and nearly jumped out of her skin to see Dominic sprawled out on a sofa.

He'd changed out of his suit, which was rare for him, and was wearing scrubs, and looked, for once, almost scruffy—unshaven and the hair that fell so neatly wasn't falling at all neatly now.

'Good God.' He peeled open his eyes when she walked in.

'Don't you judge me by my pyjamas,' Bridgette said, heading over to the kitchenette. 'I was just thinking you weren't looking so hot yourself—what happened to that smooth-looking man I met?'

'You did.' Dominic rolled his eyes and sort of heaved himself up. He sat there and she handed him a coffee without asking if he wanted one. 'Thanks.' He looked over at her. 'Bridgette, why didn't you say you were worried about Harry?'

'And worry you too? I haven't been ignoring things. I reported my concerns a few months ago, but I think I might have made things worse. I thought she was on drugs, that that was why she was always disappearing, but they did a screen and she's not. He's always been well looked after. Even now, he's just missed a couple of baths.' It was so terribly hard to explain it. 'They lived with me for nearly nine months, right up till Harry's first birthday.' She missed the frown on Dominic's face. 'And it was me who got up at night, did most of the laundry and bathing and changing. I just somehow know that she isn't coping on her own. Which is why I drop everything when she needs help. I don't really want to test my theories as to what might happen to Harry...'

'You could have told me this.'

'Not really holiday-romance stuff.'

'You've not exactly given us a chance to be anything more.'

'It's not always men who don't want a relationship,' Bridgette said. 'I always knew you were going back to Sydney and that I would stay here. It suited me better to keep it as it was.

'How was your weekend?' she asked, frantically changing the subject. 'How was Chris?'

'Great,' Dominic said. 'It's his twenty-first birthday this weekend, so he's getting all ready for that. Gangster party!' He gave a wry smile. 'I'm flying back up for that.'

'Have fun!' She grinned and didn't add that she'd love to be his moll, and he didn't say that he'd love it if she could be, and then his phone rang.

He checked it but didn't answer and Bridgette stood there, her cheeks darkening as Arabella's image flashed up on the screen.

'Well…' She turned away, tipped her coffee down the sink.

'Bridgette…'

'It doesn't matter anyway.'

Except it did.

He had seen Arabella—she'd found out he was back for the weekend and had come around. He'd opened the door to her and had surprised himself with how little he'd felt.

It would be easier to have felt something, to have gone back to his perfect life and pretend he believed she hadn't meant what she'd said about Chris. Easier than what he was contemplating.

'Bridgette, she came over. We had a coffee.'

'I don't want to hear it.' She really didn't, but she was angry too. It had been the day from hell and was turning into the night from hell too. 'It's been less than a week…' She didn't understand how it was so easy for some people to get over things. She was still desperately trying to get over Paul: not him exactly, more what he had done. And in some arguments you said things that perhaps weren't true, but you said them anyway.

'You're all the bloody same!'

'Hey!' He would not take that. 'I told you, we had coffee.'

'Sure.'

'And I told you, don't ever compare me to him.' He was sick of being compared to a man he hadn't met, a man who had caused her nothing but pain. 'I told you I'd have had this sorted.'

'Sure you would have.'

And in some arguments you said things that perhaps were true, but should never be said. 'And,' Dominic added, regretting it the second he said it, 'I'd never have slept with your sister.'

Her face looked as if it had been dunked in a bucket of bleach, the colour just stripped out of it. 'And you look after her kid—' Dominic could hardly contain the fury he felt on her behalf '—after the way she treated you?'

'How?' She had never been so angry, ashamed that he knew. 'Did Vince tell you? Did Jasmine tell him?' She was mortified. 'Does the whole hospital know?'

'I know,' Dominic said, 'because most people talk about their break-ups, most people share that bit at the start, but instead you keep yourself closed. I worked it out,' he explained. 'Courtney and Paul both happened to move out around Harry's first birthday…'

'Just leave it.'

'Why?'

'Because…' she said. 'I kicked my sister out, which meant I effectively kicked my nephew out, and look what it's been like since then.'

'Bridgette—'

'No.' She did not want his comfort, neither did she want his rationale, nor did she want to stand here and explain to him the hurt. 'Are you going to stay here? Tell me we should fight for Harry?' She just looked at him and gave a mocking laugh. 'You don't want kids of your own, let alone your girlfriend's nephew.' She shook her head. 'Your holiday fling's nephew.'

And he didn't want it, Dominic realised, and did that make him shallow? He did not want the drama that was

Courtney and he did not want a woman who simply refused to talk about what was clearly so important.

'I'm going back,' Bridgette said. 'You can take your
phone call now.'

And two minutes later he did.

She knew because she heard the buzz of his phone
as she stood in the corridor outside, trying to compose
herself enough to head out to the ward.

She heard his low voice through the wall and there
was curious relief as she walked away.

She was as lousy at one-night stands as she was at
holiday romances.

There was only one guy on her mind right now, and
he stood in the cot, waiting patiently for her return.

'Hey, Harry.' She picked him up and gave him a cuddle, and as Dominic walked past she deliberately didn't
look up; instead she concentrated on her nephew, pulling back the sheets and laying him down.

It felt far safer hiding behind him.

CHAPTER TWELVE

COURTNEY rang in the morning to see how Harry's night had been and said that she'd be in soon. Bridgette went with Harry for his hearing test and then surprisingly Raymond, the ENT consultant, came and saw him on the ward. 'Glue ear,' Raymond informed her. 'His hearing is significantly down in both ears, which would explain the speech delay. It can make them very miserable. We'll put him on the waiting list for grommets.' It might explain the temper tantrums too, Bridgette thought, kicking herself for overreaction.

By late afternoon, when Courtney still hadn't arrived and Harry was dozing, Bridgette slipped away and up to Maternity, even though she'd rung to explain things. Rita *was* nice and surprisingly understanding.

'We're having a family meeting tomorrow,' Bridgette explained. 'I really am sorry to let you down. I'll do nights just as soon as I can.'

'Don't be sorry—of course you can't work,' Rita said. 'You need to get this sorted.'

Though her family seemed convinced there was nothing to sort, and as Bridgette walked onto the ward, she could see Courtney sitting on the chair beside Harry, all smiles. She was playing the doting mother or 'mother of the year', as Jasmine would have said. Dominic was examining Harry's new neighbor, young Roman, and Bridgette stood and spoke to Tony for a moment. Harry, annoyed that Bridgette wasn't coming straight over, stood up, put up his leg and with two fat fists grabbed the cot, annoyed that with the barrier he couldn't get over it—he was indeed a climber, it was duly noted, not just by the nurses but by Courtney. And Bridgette wondered if she was going mad. Maybe there was nothing wrong with her sister's parenting and she, Bridgette, had been talking nonsense all along.

'Thanks so much for staying last night,' Courtney said. 'I was just completely exhausted. I'd been up all night with him teething. Mum said that that can give them the most terrible rash…and then when he climbed out, when I heard him fall…'

'No problem,' Bridgette said. 'ENT came down and saw him.'

'Yes, the nurse told me,' Courtney said, and rather pointedly unzipped her bag and took out her pyjamas. Brand-new ones, Bridgette noticed. Courtney was very good at cleaning up her act when required. 'You should get some rest, Bridgette.' Courtney looked up and her eyes held a challenge that Bridgette knew she simply couldn't win. 'You look exhausted. I'm sure I'll see you at the family meeting and you will have plenty to say about his nappy rash and that I put him to bed without washing him to Aunty Bridgette's satisfaction.'

Dominic saw Courtney's smirk after Bridgette had kissed Harry and left.

He spoke for a moment with Tony, told him he would see him tomorrow. And Dominic, a man who always stayed late, left early for once and met Bridgette at her

car. It wouldn't start, because in her rush to get to see
Harry last night, she'd left her lights on.

'Just leave me.' She was crying, furious, enraged,
and did not want him to see.

'I'll give you a lift.'

'So I can sort out a flat battery tomorrow! So I can
take a bus to the meeting.' She even laughed. 'They'll
think I'm the one with the problem. She's in there all
kisses and smiles and new pyjamas. She'll be taking
him home this time tomorrow.'

'She'll blow herself out soon,' Dominic said.

'And it will start all over again.' She turned the key
one last hopeless time and of course nothing happened.

'Come on,' Dominic said. 'I'll take you home.'

They drove for a while in silence. Dominic never carried tissues, but very graciously he gave her the little
bit of silk he used to clean his sunglasses. With little
other option, she took it.

'I do get it.'

'Sure!'

'No, I really do,' Dominic said. 'For three years after
Chris was born it was row after row. My father wanted
him gone—he never came out and said it, didn't have
the guts, and I can tell you the day it changed, I can
tell you the minute it changed.' He snapped his fingers
as he drove. 'My mother told him to get out because
Chris wasn't going anywhere. She told him if he stayed
in *her* home then he followed her rules.' They were at
the roundabout and she wanted him to indicate, wanted
to go back to his place, but instead he drove straight
on. 'She got her fire back.' He even grinned as he remembered his trophy-wife mother suddenly swearing
and cursing in Spanish. He remembered the drama as

she'd filled his father's suitcases and hurled them out, followed by his golf clubs, as she picked up Chris and walked back in. 'I really want you to listen, Bridgette. You need to think about what you want before you go into that meeting. You will need to sort out what you're prepared to offer or what you're prepared to accept, not for the next week or for the next month but maybe the next seventeen years—you need to do the best for yourself.'

'I'm trying my best.'

'Bridgette, you're not listening to me. My mum could have gone along with Dad—she could have had a far easier life if she hadn't been a single mum bringing up a special-needs child. Chris could have been slotted into a home. Instead he went to one when he was eighteen, to a sheltered home with friends, and my mother did it so that he'd have a life, a real one. She did not want him to have to start over in thirty years or so when she was gone. She thought out everything and that included looking out for herself. What I said was you have to do the best for you—you have to look out for yourself in this...'

Dominic gritted his teeth in frustration as he could see that she didn't understand what he meant and knew that he would have to make things clear. 'The best thing that could happen is that Courtney suddenly becomes responsible and gets well suddenly, becomes responsible and looks after Harry properly—and we both know that's not going to happen. Now, you can run yourself ragged chasing after Courtney, living your life ready to step in, or you can work out the life you want and what you're prepared to do.'

She still didn't get it.

'Bridgette, she could have another baby. She could be pregnant right now!' She closed her eyes. It was something she thought about late at night sometimes, that this could be ongoing, that there could be another Harry, or a little Harriet, or twins. 'Come away with me on Saturday,' he said. 'Come for the weekend, just to see...'

'What about Arabella?'

'What about her?' Dominic said. 'I told her last night the same thing I told her when we had coffee on Saturday. We're through. And I've told her that I'm blocking her from my phone.' He knew he was pushing it, but this time he said it. 'You could be my moll!'

'I've got other things to think about right now.'

'Yes,' he said as he pulled up at her door. 'You do.'

And she didn't ask him in, and neither did he expect her to, but he did pull her into his arms and kiss her.

'Don't...' She pulled her head back.

'It's a kiss.'

'A kiss that's going nowhere,' she said. 'I'm not very good at one-night stands, in case you didn't work it out. And I really think the holiday is over...'

'Why won't you let anyone in?'

'Because I can't stand being hurt again,' Bridgette admitted. 'And you and I...' She was honest. 'Well, it's going to hurt, whatever way you look at it.' And she did open up a bit, said what she'd thought all those days ago. 'My life's not exactly geared to hopping on planes.'

'You only need to hop on one,' Dominic said, and he was offering her the biggest out, an escape far more permanent than her flat.

'Think about it,' he said.

'I can't.'

'Just think about it,' Dominic said. 'Please.'

He wished her all the very best for the next day, then drove down the road and pulled out his phone.

'It's Wednesday,' Chris said. 'Why are you ringing me on a Wednesday?'

'I'm just ringing you,' Dominic said. 'It doesn't only have to be on a Friday.'

'It's about Bridgette?' Chris said, and Dominic couldn't help a wry grin that he was ringing his brother for advice. 'The one with the baby.'

'It's not her baby,' Dominic said, because he'd explained about Harry as they'd walked along the beach.

'But she loves him.'

'Yep.'

'Well, why can't they come and live here?'

'Because it's not going to happen,' Dominic said. 'His mum loves him too.'

'And you can't stay there because you're coming over on Saturday,' Chris reminded him. 'For my birthday.' He heard the silence. 'You said you would.'

'I did.'

'See you on Saturday,' Chris said.

And Dominic did know how Bridgette felt—he was quite sure of that, because he felt it then too, thought of his brother all dressed up with his friends and his disappointment if *he* wasn't there. He thought of Bridgette facing it alone.

'You are coming?' Chris pushed.

'You know I am,' Dominic said. 'I'll see you then.'

'Are you still going to ring me on Friday?' Chris said, because he loathed a change in routine.

'Of course.'

CHAPTER THIRTEEN

'HI, TONY!' Dominic said the next morning. 'Hi, Roman.' He tried not to look at Harry, who was watching him from the next cot. He'd seen all the Joyce family head off to the conference room, Courtney marching in front, the parents, as Bridgette would say, joined at the hip, and an exhausted-looking Bridgette bringing up the rear.

'Is this your last morning?' Tony said, because it was common knowledge now that he was leaving.

'No,' Dominic said. 'I'm on call tonight.'

'Well, if I don't see you I just want to be sure to thank you for everything with Roman and Esperanza and Maria,' Tony said.

'You're very welcome,' Dominic said. 'How are they both doing?'

'They're amazing,' Tony replied. 'Maria's a bit torn of course. She wants to be here more, but she doesn't want to bring Esperanza here…'

'Better not to,' Dominic said. He finished examining Roman and told his father he was pleased with his progress and that hopefully by Monday Roman would be home.

'It will be nice to have a full house again,' Tony

said. 'Thought we couldn't have children—three goes at IVF for the twins, then Roman surprises us and now Esperanza!'

Dominic carried on with his round and tried not to think what was going on in the conference room, tried not to think about the offer he had made last night.

Bridgette couldn't *not* think about it.

She had pondered it all night, had been thinking about it in the car park for the hour she had waited to sort out her battery, and she was feeling neither hopeful nor particularly patient with her family. She sat there and the meeting went backwards and forwards, like some endless round of table tennis, getting nowhere. She listened to Courtney making excuses and promises again, watched her parents, who so badly wanted to believe their youngest daughter's words. She listened to the social worker, who, Bridgette realised, was very willing for Harry's aunt to support her sister—and of course she didn't blame them; but she realised that no one was ever going to tell her that she was doing too much. She had to say it herself.

'This is what I'm prepared to do.' She looked around the room and then at her sister; she took over the bat and slammed out her serve and said it again, but a bit louder this time.

'This is what I'm prepared to do,' she repeated. And when she had the room's attention, she spoke. 'Harry is to attend daycare here at the hospital, whether he's staying with you or being babysat by me—there has to be some consistency in his life. I will pay for his place if that is a concern you have, but he has to be there Monday to Friday from now on.' She looked at the social worker. 'If I can get a place again.'

'I can sort that out.' She nodded. 'We have a couple of places reserved for special allocations.' Bridgette turned to her parents. 'Mum, if I'm on a late shift or working nights and Harry is in my care, for whatever reason, you have to collect him or stay overnight. I can't always work early shifts.'

'You know we do our best!' Betty said. 'Of course we'll pick him up.'

Bridgette looked over at the caseworker, who gave a bit of a nod that told her to go on. 'He's due to have surgery…' She was finding a voice and she knew what to do with it, was grateful for Dominic's advice because she'd heeded it. 'He's on the waiting list for grommets and if that comes up while he's in my care I want to be able to go ahead. I want written permission obtained so that when Harry is in my care, or at any time I'm concerned, I can speak to doctors and I can take him to appointments. And I want—'

'I don't want him in daycare,' Courtney chimed in. 'I've told you—I'm not going anywhere. I decide what treatment he has and who he sees.'

'That's fine.' Bridgette looked at her sister. 'You have every right to refuse what I'm offering. But I can't stand aside any more. If you don't accept my conditions…' It was the hardest thing she would ever say and could only be said if it was meant. Whether he was serious or not, she was incredibly grateful for Dominic's offer last night. 'Then you can deal with it. I'll move to Sydney.'

'Bridgette!' Her mum almost stood up. 'You know you don't mean that.'

'But I do—because I can't live like this. I can't watch Harry being passed around like a parcel. So it's either you accept my terms or I'm moving to Sydney.'

'You said you'd always be there for me.' Courtney started to cry, only this time it didn't move Bridgette. 'You promised…'

'Well, that makes us both liars, then,' Bridgette said. 'Because I can remember you saying exactly the same to Harry the day he was born.'

'Bridgette.' Her mum was trying to be firm, to talk sense into her sensible daughter. 'You know you're not going anywhere. Why Sydney?'

'I've met someone,' Bridgette said. 'And he's from there.' Betty had seen the happy couple, that were back as Bridgette's screensaver, when she'd had a nose in her daughter's spare room, had tutted at the two faces smiling back, and she had a terrible feeling her daughter might actually mean what she was saying.

'You love Courtney…' Maurice broke in.

'I'm not sure if I do,' Bridgette said, and she truly wasn't sure that she did. 'I honestly don't know that I do.'

'You love Harry.' Betty triumphed.

'Yes, I do. So if she wants my help then she can have it, but those are my conditions and she needs to know that any time I think Harry is at risk I will speak up.' She walked out of the meeting because she had nothing left to say. It had to be up to Courtney. She walked over to the ward and saw Harry sitting in his cot, building his bricks. She let down the cot side and held out her arms. She had meant every word she had said in that room, had convinced herself of it last night, but there was a piece of her that was hidden apart, a piece of her that no one must ever see, because as she picked up her nephew and buried her face in his curls, she knew she could never leave him. They just had to believe that she might.

Dominic watched her cuddling Harry and he wanted to go over, to find out what was happening, but instead he picked up the phone.

It was the longest morning, even though he had plenty to do, but he could not get involved, or be seen to be getting involved, which surely she knew, but still he felt like a bastard.

'Do you want me to give Harry his lunch?' Jennifer, one of the nurses, offered. 'You can go to the canteen, maybe have a little break?'

'I'm fine,' Bridgette said. 'They're still in the meeting. I'll give him his lunch and then—' she took a deep breath '—I'm going home.'

'Jennifer!' Dominic's voice barked across the ward. 'Can you hold on to Harry's lunch for now, please, and keep him nil by mouth until I've spoken to his mum?'

'What's going on?' Bridgette frowned.

'I've no idea,' Jennifer admitted. 'Wait there and I'll find out.' And she went over and spoke to Dominic, but instead of coming back and informing Bridgette, Jennifer headed off to the conference room. The group was just coming out and it was clear that Courtney had been crying but, along with Jennifer, they all headed back inside.

'What's going on?' She went up to him.

'Someone's coming down to speak to his mother.'

'Dominic!' She couldn't believe he'd do this to her.

'I'd go home now if I were you.'

'You know I can't.'

'Yes,' he said. 'You can.' She looked at him, met those lovely black eyes and somehow she trusted him.

'Go home,' he said. 'I'm sure you've got an awful lot to do.' She just stood there. 'Maybe tidy that bedroom, young lady.'

And she trusted him, she really did, but she knew he was leaving tomorrow, knew that right now he was saying goodbye.

'Go,' he said, 'and when she calls, don't come back.' He gave her a small wink. 'You only answer if it's me.'

'I can't do that. I can't just leave him.'

'You can,' he said. 'I'm here.'

CHAPTER FOURTEEN

WHEN her phone rang fifteen minutes later, she was driving, just approaching the roundabout, and she didn't pull over so she could take the call, as she usually would have. She didn't indicate when she saw that it was Courtney and instead she drove straight on.

Dominic was there.

She felt as if Dominic was there in the car beside her.

It rang again and this time it was her mum. Still, she ignored it.

Then it rang again as she arrived home and she sat at her computer before answering.

'Oh. Hi, Mum!'

'You didn't pick up.'

'I was driving.'

'Where are you?' she asked. 'I thought you'd gone down to the canteen.'

'I'm at home,' she said, as if she was breathing normally, as if home was the natural place she should be.

'Well, you need to get here!' Bridgette stared at her screensaver and tried to shut out the sound of her mother's panic. 'The doctors are here and they say Harry needs an operation. There's a space that's opened up on the list and they want him to have an operation!' she said again really loudly.

'What operation?'

'He has to have surgery on his ears, and if she doesn't sign the consent, he'll go back on the list…' She could hear the panic in her mother's voice. 'Bridgette, you need to get here. You know what your sister's like— Courtney can't make a decision. She's gone off!'

'It's a tiny operation, Mum. It could do him an awful lot of good.'

'Bridgette, please, they've added him to the list this evening. Courtney's going crazy!'

'Mum…' Bridgette looked into Dominic's eyes as she spoke, and then into her own and wanted to be her again, wanted to be the woman who smiled and laughed and lived. 'It's up to Courtney to give consent. If not, he can go on the waiting list and wait, but it would be a shame, because his hearing is really bad.' She stood up. 'I've got to go, Mum. I've got things to do. Give Harry a big kiss from his aunty Bridgette. Tell him that I'll bring him in a nice present for being brave.' And she rang off.

She took the phone into the bathroom with her and because she didn't have any bubble bath, she used shampoo, put on a load of washing while she was waiting for the bath to fill and every time the phone rang, she did not pick up.

And then she did her hair, straightened it and put on blusher and lipstick too, even though she knew Dominic was on call and wouldn't be coming round. Then when her phone finally fell silent, she tackled her bedroom, worked out how to use a stud finder and put up the shelves that had been sitting in cardboard for way too long. Then the phone bleeped a text and it was from Dominic.

She took a breath and read it.

Op went well—he's back on ward and having a drink. Home tomoz.

She felt the tension seep out of her.

Should I come in now?

She was quite sure what the response would be, that he'd tell her to stay put, that Courtney was there and to let her deal with it, but as she waited for his reply, there was a knock at the door and when her phone bleeped he didn't say what she'd thought he might.

No, stay put—your mum's with him.

She wanted to know what was happening so badly. She had this stupid vision it was him as, phone in hand, she opened the door.

Instead it was her father and Courtney.

CHAPTER FIFTEEN

IT WAS a long night and he was glad when it hit six a.m. and there were just a couple of hours to go.

'Cot Four.' Karan, the night nurse, looked up from the baby she was feeding. 'I'll be there in a minute.'

'I'll be fine,' Dominic said, and headed in.

He took off his jacket, glanced again at Harry, who sitting there staring, and then proceeded to wash his hands. When he turned around, Harry was smiling. Dominic couldn't help himself from looking at the pull-out bed beside him, relieved to see that Betty was there.

He didn't know what had happened.

He'd heard the explosions from the fuse he'd lit when he'd asked for a favour from Raymond and a certain blue-eyed theatre nurse, but he'd been up and down between here and NICU and had never caught up as to what had really gone on.

He smiled back at Harry and then headed over to the cot opposite him, carefully examining the baby who was causing concern, pleased with her progress.

'How's Harry Joyce?' he asked Karan. He had every right to enquire as he was the paediatrician on call that night and Karan wouldn't know that he had stepped aside from the case.

'He's doing well.' Karan smiled. 'You could see the difference in him almost as soon as he came back from Theatre. He must have been struggling with his ears for a while. He's much more smiley and he's making a few more noises, even had a little dance in his cot. He's off home in the morning to the care of Mum.' She pulled out a notebook. 'Hold on a moment. Sorry, he's home with his aunt tomorrow. There was a big case meeting today apparently. Lots of drama.' She rolled her eyes. 'I haven't had a chance to read the notes yet.' She stood up and collected the folder and put it in front of him. 'Should make interesting reading.'

Karan walked back to the nursery to put down the baby she had been feeding and Dominic sat there, tempted to read the notes, to find out all that had gone on. It would be so easy to. 'So this is your last morning.' Tony stopped by the desk, just as Dominic went to open the folder. Tony had been up and used the parent showers before all the others did, was dressed and ready for when Abuela came in.

'It is,' Dominic said. 'I'm flying to Sydney this afternoon.'

'Well, thanks again.' Tony stifled a yawn.

'You must be exhausted.' It was Dominic who extended the conversation.

'Ah, but it's Saturday,' Tony said. 'I'm going home to sleep. That's if the twins and Esperanza let me.'

'You've got a lot on your plate,' Dominic said, but Tony just grinned.

'Better than an empty plate.'

Dominic stood up and shook Tony's hand and

when Tony had gone he stepped away from the notes. Bridgette didn't deserve her ex reading up on her private life. If he wanted to know, he should ask her.

CHAPTER SIXTEEN

'HARRY!' She took him into her arms and wrapped him in a hug, truly delighted to have him home. 'I've got a surprise for you.' And she carried him in to what had been her study as well as Courtney's room and spare room. The cot had been folded and put away (well, it had been neatly put away under Bridgette's bed till she hauled it to the charity shop on Monday) and the bed that had been under a pile of ironing now had a little safety rail, new bedding and a child's bedside light. There were new curtains, a new stash of bricks in a toy box and an intercom was all set up.

'You've been busy,' her mum said when she saw Harry's new bedroom. 'Isn't he a bit young for a bed?'

'Well, at least he can't climb out of it. I'll just have to make sure I close the bedroom door or he'll be roaming the place at night.'

'It looks lovely.' Betty smiled at her daughter. 'I'm sorry that we haven't been much help.'

'You have been,' Bridgette said, because she couldn't stand her parents' guilt and they had probably been doing their best.

'No,' her mum corrected. 'We've been very busy burying our heads in the sand, trying to pretend that everything was okay, when clearly it wasn't. We're going to be around for you much more, and Harry too.'

'And Courtney?' Bridgette watched her mother's lips purse. 'She needs your support more than anyone.'

'We're paying for rehab,' Betty said.

'It's not going to be an instant fix,' Bridgette said, but she didn't go on. She could see how tired her parents looked, not from recent days but from recent years. 'We can get through this, Mum,' Bridgette said, 'if we all help each other.'

'What about you, though?' It was the first time her father had really spoken since they'd arrived. 'What about that young man of yours, the one in Sydney?'

'Let's not talk about that, Dad.' It hurt too much to explore at the moment. It was something she wanted to examine and think about in private—when she had calmed down fully, when she was safely alone, then she would deal with all she had lost for her sister, again. But her father was finally stepping up, as she had asked him to, and not burying his head in the sand as he usually did—which was a good thing, though perhaps not right now.

'We need to discuss it, Bridgette.' He sat down and looked her square in the eye. 'We didn't know you were serious about someone.'

'It never really got a chance to be serious,' Bridgette said.

'We should have had Harry more.'

Yes, you bloody should have, she wanted to say, but that wasn't fair on them, because really it wasn't so much Harry who had got in the way; it had been her too—she hadn't wanted a relationship, hadn't wanted to let another close. 'Things will be different now,' Bridgette said instead.

'You could go away for the odd weekend now and then…' her dad said. And teeny little wisps of hope seemed to rise in her stomach, but she doused them—it was simply too late.

After her parents had gone, Bridgette made Harry some lunch and then cuddled him on the sofa. She did exactly what she'd tried not to—she let herself love him. Of course she always had, but now she didn't hold back. She kissed his lovely curls and then smiled into his sleepy eyes and told him that everything was going to be okay, that Mum was getting well, that she would always be here for him.

And she would be.

It was a relief to acknowledge it, to step back from the conflict and ignore the push and pull as to who was wrong and who was right—she wasn't young, free and single, she had a very young heart to take care of.

'You wait there,' she said to Harry as the doorbell rang. They were curled up, watching a DVD. Harry was nearly ready to be put down for his afternoon nap and Bridgette was rather thinking that she might just have one too.

'Dominic!' He was the last person she was expecting to see, though maybe not. She knew that he did care about her, knew he would want to know how she was.

He wasn't a bastard unfortunately. It would be so much easier to paint him as one—they just had different lives, that was all.

'I thought you had a gangster party to be at!'

'I've got a couple of hours till the plane.' He was dressed in a black suit. 'I've just got to put on a tie and glasses—Mum's sent me a fake gun, though I'd better not risk it on the plane.' His smile faded a touch. 'I wanted to see how the meeting had gone...'

'Didn't you hear?' Bridgette said, quite sure the whole hospital must have heard by now. 'Or you could have read the notes.' He saw her tight smile, knew that Bridgette, more than anyone, would have hated things being played out on such a public stage—it was her workplace, after all. She opened the door. 'Come in.'

He was surprised to see how well she looked, or perhaps *surprised* wasn't the right word—he was in awe. Her hair swished behind her as she walked, all glossy and shiny as it had been that first night, and he could smell her perfume. She looked bright and breezy and not what he had expected.

Back perhaps to the woman he had met.

'I didn't want to read the notes,' Dominic said, walking through to the lounge. 'Though I heard that Harry had come home with you...' His voice trailed off as he saw Harry lying on the lounge, staring warily at him. 'Hi, there, Harry.'

Harry just stared.

'What happened to the nice smile that you used to give me when I came on the ward?' Dominic asked, but Harry did not react.

'Do you want a drink?' Bridgette offered, though perhaps it was more for herself. She wanted a moment or two in the kitchen alone, just to gather her thoughts before they had to do what she had been dreading since the night they had first met—officially say goodbye. 'Or some lunch perhaps?' She looked at the clock. 'A late lunch.'

'I won't have anything,' Dominic said. 'I'll have

something on the plane and there will be loads to eat tonight. A coffee would be great, though.' It had already been a very long day. 'You've changed the living room.'

'I've given Harry his own bedroom,' Bridgette said, 'and I quite like the idea of having a desk in here.' And she could breathe as his eyes scanned the room, because, yes, she'd changed the screensaver again. Now it was a photo of Harry and his mum, a nice photo, so that Harry could see Courtney often.

'It looks nice,' he said as Bridgette headed out to the kitchen and Dominic stood, more than a little awkward, nervous by what he had to say. He wasn't used to nerves in the least—he always had a level head. He said what was needed and rarely any more. He took off his jacket and looked for somewhere to hang it, settling on the back of Bridgette's study chair. Turning around he saw Harry smile, half-asleep, lying on the sofa. He gave Dominic the biggest grin and then closed his eyes.

'What are you smiling at?' Bridgette asked Dominic as she walked back in the room carrying two mugs and saw him standing there grinning.

'Harry,' Dominic answered, still smiling. 'That nephew of yours really does love routine.' He saw a little flutter of panic dart across her eyes, realised that she thought perhaps he was there to tell her something. He understood she had an overactive imagination where Harry was concerned. 'He smiles when I take my jacket off. I've just realised that now. Whenever I came onto the ward at night he watched me and frowned and then suddenly he gave me a smile. I could never work out why.'

'It's what you do.' Bridgette grinned, because she'd noticed it too. 'Before you wash your hands. I don't think I've ever seen you examine a patient with your jacket on. Funny that Harry noticed,' she mused. 'I guess when your world's chaotic you look for routine in any place you can find it.'

'Well, it doesn't look very chaotic to me. You've done great,' Dominic said. He waited while she put Harry down for his very first nap in his big-boy bed— Bridgette surprised that he didn't protest, just curled up and went straight to sleep. She gently closed the door. 'So,' he asked when she came back in, 'how did the meeting go?'

'You really didn't read the notes?' She was a little bit embarrassed and awkward that he might be here to question her *plans* to follow him to Sydney, because even though she hadn't given his name, if Dominic had read the notes, the indication would be clear. 'Because I was just bluffing…'

'Bluffing?' Dominic frowned. 'About what?'

'Getting a life.' Bridgette gave a wry smile. 'Moving to Sydney.'

'You said that at the meeting?'

'Oh, I said that and a whole lot more,' Bridgette admitted. 'I did what you suggested. I spent the time before the meeting trying to work out rules I could live with. I said that he had to attend daycare, but I had to be able to take him to a doctor if needed and to take him for any procedures if Courtney wasn't available. I said that Mum and Dad had to help more if Courtney wasn't around…that I was through looking out for Courtney, that I was only on Harry side.'

'You said all that?' He put down his coffee and took her hand. 'Well done. How did Courtney take it?'

'I didn't stay to find out,' she said. 'I just left the

meeting. I hope you don't mind, but I said that I'd been seeing someone, that he lived in Sydney—it just made it seem more real to them. It made them believe that I would leave if I told them I had somebody who wanted me to go with them.'

'You did.'

And she'd no doubt cry about it later—but not now. 'Thank you,' she said. 'For getting him squeezed onto the list.' He gave a frown. 'I know you must have…'

'Well, I thought it might buy another night before she dropped her act, and when you came out of the meeting…' He looked at her, didn't want to tell her how hard it had been to step aside, to not be in that room, not as a doctor but sitting beside her. 'I figured she might drop it a little quicker if you weren't there to sort it out for her.'

'Well, it worked. She fell apart when she had to actually make a decision and it all came out. It isn't drugs—it's alcohol. She's just been slowly falling apart since I kicked her out.'

'It would have happened wherever she was,' Dominic said. 'It was probably going on here…'

And she nodded because, yes, it had been a bit.

And she thought of Harry's birthday that should have been about cordial and cake but instead her sister had chosen to party on—and so too had Paul.

'I hate what she did,' Bridgette said. 'I just couldn't have her stay after that.'

'Of course you couldn't.' Dominic thought for a moment, knew he had to be very careful with what he said. Certainly he was less than impressed with Courtney, but even if people didn't like it at times, he was always honest. 'But I think it's something you have to move on from. She's clearly made a lot of mistakes, but if you're going to be angry with anyone—' he looked at Bridgette, who so deserved to be angry '—then I think it should be with him.'

'It was both of them.'

'He took advantage.'

'Oh, and you never have—' She didn't get to finish.

'Never,' Dominic said. 'Not once. My sexual résumé might not be impressive to you, but…' He shook his head. 'Nope, what he did was wrong, and however awful your sister has been, I bet she's been trying to douse an awful lot of guilt about her treatment of you.'

Bridgette nodded. 'She's gone to rehab. It's three months and Mum and Dad are paying. She came over last night with Dad and said she was terrified of letting everybody down…which she may well do, so I'm not getting my hopes up, but I've made a decision to be here for Harry.' She saw him glance at his watch.

'Sorry, I'm rattling on…'

'It's not that. I have to leave in an hour. I can't miss that plane.' He took a deep breath. Really, he was finding this incredibly difficult—she seemed fine, better than fine, as if she wasn't missing him at all.

Wouldn't miss him.

But he would miss her.

Which forced him to speak on.

'What you said about Sydney, about having someone who wanted you there, you weren't exaggerating, Bridgette.' He took her hand and her fingers curled around his. Inside her, those little wisps of hope uncurled too, and it was so wonderful to see him, to have him sitting beside her, to know this was hard for him. 'I want this to work too. I just can't not be there for Chris,' he said.

'I was very unfair to you—it was ridiculous that I couldn't even get away for a single weekend, and it is about to change. I spoke to my parents this morning so maybe I can get away now and then, maybe I could come up on days off, or some of them.' She stared at her fingers being squeezed by his, and she wished he would jump in, would say that was what he wanted, but he let her speak on. 'And who knows what might happen in the future? Courtney might get well—'

'You're not going to leave Harry,' Dominic cut in. 'You might be able to convince them, but you'll never convince me. You're not going anywhere while Harry's so little.'

'No.' She could feel tears trickling down at the back of her throat and nose. She'd been so determined not to cry, to do this with dignity, to let him go with grace. She could see the second hand on his watch rapidly moving around, gobbling up the little time that they had left. 'No, I'm not going anywhere. Well, not long term.'

'And I don't think the odd weekend is going to suffice.'

'No,' she said, because it wouldn't be enough.

And they could talk in the time they had left, but what was the point? Bridgette realised there was no solution to be had, so instead of tears she gave him a smile, not a false one, a real one. And she put herself first for once, was completely selfish and utterly indulgent and just a little bit wild, because as he went to speak she interrupted him.

'Have we got time for a quickie before you go?'

'We need to talk,' Dominic pointed out.

'I don't need anything,' she cut in. 'I know what I want, though.'

And he wasn't going to argue with that.

He didn't know what he had expected to find when he came over, how he'd expected her to be when he'd knocked at the door, but as always she'd amazed him. Then, as she opened the bedroom door, she amazed him all over again.

'Wow.' As he walked into her bedroom he let out a low whistle. 'You've got a carpet!'

'I know!'

'I'm impressed.' He looked at the shelves and politely didn't comment about five holes she had made in the wall—because he wouldn't know how to find a stud either.

'Just you wait.' She was at his shirt as she spoke. He pulled off her T-shirt and undid her bra and it slowed things down undressing each other, so they stripped off for themselves and then Bridgette peeled back the duvet.

'You get first feel…'

'Of what?' he asked, hands roaming her body, but she peeled off his hands and placed them on the bedding.

'Of my million-thread-count sheets. I was saving them for best…'

Which he was, Bridgette knew that, because he lay on the sheets and wriggled around and made appreciative noises, and then he pulled her in and kissed her.

'I want to feel them now,' she said.

So she lay on the sheets and wriggled around and made appreciative noises too.

And then he kissed her again.

'Don't let me fall asleep after,' Dominic said.

'After what?' She frowned, naked in his arms. 'If you really think you can just come here and have sex…'

She made him laugh and she loved making him

laugh. She loved the Dominic others so rarely saw. When it was just the two or them, the austere, remote man seemed to leave—and he understood her humour and matched it. He made her laugh too, turned those cold black eyes into puppy-dog ones. 'I don't want sex, Bridgette. I just want to hold you.'

'Oh, no.' They were laughing so much they would wake up Harry.

'I just want to lie next to you…' he crooned.

'No.'

He straddled her.

'I just want to talk,' he said.

'No talking,' she begged.

It was a whole new realm for Dominic, like swimming in the ocean after a lifetime doing laps in a pool.

He did not know that you could laugh so much on a Saturday afternoon, that she could laugh even now as she lost him.

As she loved him.

It was a different kiss from any they had tasted before, a different feeling from any they had ever felt.

He kissed her slowly and more tenderly and *he* let himself love her—smothered her, physically, mentally, buried her and pressed her against her very best sheets. He wrapped his arms under her and drove into her till she wanted to scream, and she pressed her mouth to his chest and held on for dear life. She didn't know what the future held and she couldn't control it anyway, so she lived in the moment, and what a lovely moment it was. And she could cry afterwards and not be embarrassed or sorry.

It was a wonderful afternoon, and nothing like the one he had intended, the most delicious surprise. His head was spinning that she could love him like that when she considered it over between them.

'I've made some decisions too.' He took a deep breath, dived out of the pool and into the ocean, where it was rough and choppy but exhilarating and wild. 'When I went to resign this week, when I told them I wouldn't be back, I was offered a job.' He looked at her grey eyes that were for the first time today wary. 'Here.'

She felt little wisps of hope rising again, then she moved to douse them. They were guilty wisps. Surely this was wrong.

'I'm going to ring on Monday and take it.'

'You want to work in Sydney, though. Your family's there, your friends, Chris. You always wanted to work there. It's your goal.'

'Goals change,' Dominic said.

'What about your brother?'

'I'm not going to say anything to him yet,' Dominic said. 'It's his birthday.'

He shook his head, because he couldn't do it to Chris this weekend. 'Look, the job doesn't start for a month and I'm taking the time off. I'm not working. You and I will spend some proper time together, do some of that talking you so readily avoid, and we'll see how I go with Harry…'

'You could have told me!'

'I tried,' Dominic said. 'You didn't want to discuss it—remember? I'll be back on Monday and we can talk properly then.' He looked at his watch. 'I'm going to have to get going soon. This is one plane I can't miss.'

She lay in bed and stared up at the ceiling, tried to take in what he was saying. A month…

A month to get to know Harry, to see how they went,

and then… She was happy, happier than she had ever felt possible, but it felt like a test. Then he turned around and maybe she should compromise too.

'I could ask Mum and Dad to come over.' She was torn. 'If you want me to come tonight…'

'I think Harry needs a couple of nights in his new bed, don't you?'

And she was so glad that he understood.

'I have to get back.' He smiled. 'Would it wake Harry if I had a shower?'

'Don't worry about that.' And she had a moment of panic, because Harry was being golden and sleeping now, but what about at two a.m. when he decided to wake up, what about when it was six p.m. and her mother hadn't picked him up from crèche? How would Dominic deal with those situations? She wasn't sure she was ready for this, not convinced she was up to exposing her heart just to have Dominic change his mind. 'I'll get you some towels.'

'Could you pass my trousers?' he asked as she climbed out of bed. 'Oh, and can you get out my phone?' He snapped his fingers as she trawled through his pockets, which was something Bridgette decided they would work on. Sexy Spaniard he may be, and in a rush for his brother's party perhaps, but she didn't answer to finger snaps. 'I can't find it and don't snap your fingers again,' she warned him. 'Hold on, here it is.' Except it wasn't his phone. Instead she pulled out a little black box.

'That's what I meant.' He grinned. 'So, aren't you going to open it?'

Bridgette was honestly confused. She opened the box and there was a ring. A ring that looked as if they were talking about a whole lot more than a month.

'I thought we were going to take some time…'

'We are,' Dominic said. 'To get to know all the stuff and to work things out, but, compatible or not, there's no arguing from me.' He pulled her over to the bed. 'I love you.' He looked at her and to this point he still didn't know. 'And I hope that you love me?'

She had to think for a moment, because she had held on so firmly to her heart that she hadn't allowed herself to go there. And now she did. She looked at the man who was certainly the only man who could have taken her to his home that first night. She really was lousy at one-night stands, because she knew deep down she had loved him even then.

'If I say it,' she said, 'you can't change your mind.'

'I won't.' That much he knew. She was funny and kind and terribly disorganised too—there was nothing he might have thought he needed on his list for the perfect wife, but she was everything that was now required.

'How do you know?' she asked.

'I'm not sure…' Dominic mused. 'Chemistry, I guess,' he said.

'And Chris?' she said as he pulled her back to bed and put his ring on her finger. She realised the magnitude of what he was giving up.

'He'll be fine.' Dominic had thought about it a lot and was sure, because of something Tony had said. He should have thanked Tony, not the other way around, for far better a full plate than an empty one. He didn't want to be like his father, hitting golf balls into the sky at weekends, a perfect girlfriend waiting at home, with not a single problem. 'I'll go up at least once a month and he can come here some weekends. If I'm working you might have to…' He looked at her and she nodded.

'Of course.'

'We'll get there,' he said. 'You're it and I know you'll do just fine without me, but better with me.' He looked at eyes that weren't so guarded, eyes that no longer reflected hurt, and it felt very nice to be with someone you knew, but not quite, someone you would happily spend a lifetime knowing some more. 'And I'm certainly better with you.'

'Hey!' There was a very loud shout from down the hall. 'Hey!' came the voice again.

'Oh, no.' Bridgette lay back on the pillow as Harry completely broke the moment. 'Those bloody grommets. It's as if he's suddenly found his voice.'

Harry had found his voice and he knew how to use it! 'Hey,' Harry shouted again from behind his closed door. It was a sort of mixture between 'Harry' and 'Hello' and 'Have you forgotten me?'

'I'll get him.' Bridgette peeled back the sheet, liking the big sparkle on her finger as she did so.

'If you say you love me, I'll go and get him,' Dominic said, and pulled on his trousers, deciding he had to be at least half-respectable as he walked in on the little guy.

'If you go and it doesn't make you change your mind—' Bridgette grinned, knowing what he would find '—I'll say it then.'

It was the longest walk of his life.

He'd just put a ring on a woman's finger. Shouldn't they be sipping champagne, booking a restaurant, hell, in some five-star hotel having sex, not getting up to a baby?

But with him and Bridgette it was all just a little bit back to front and he'd better get used to the idea.

He pushed open the door.

'Hey!' Angry eyes met him, and so did the smell. Angry eyes asked him how dared he take so long, leave him sitting in this new bed that he wasn't sure how to get out of?

'This isn't how it's supposed to be, Harry,' Dominic said, because surely it should be a sweet, cherubic baby sitting there smiling at him, but it was an angry Harry with a full nappy. The newly engaged Dominic had to change the first nappy in his life and, yes, it was shocking, a real baptism of fire!

'Think of all the cruises I won't be going on,' Dominic said as he tried to work out all the tabs, 'all the sheer irresponsibility I'm missing…'

'Hey!' Harry said, liking his clean bottom and new word.

'Hey,' Dominic answered

And then he picked him up.

A bare chest, a toddler who was still a baby and a mass of curls against his chin, and it *was* inevitable— he didn't just love Bridgette, he loved Harry too. For the second time in twenty minutes he handed over his heart and it was terrifying.

He would never tell, but he thought he was crying. Maybe he was because Harry's fat hands were patting his cheeks. He could never tell Bridgette that he was terrified too.

That the phone might ring.

That there might be a knock on the door.

That Courtney might come back.

That this little guy might have to be returned too soon.

'I'll make this work.' He looked into the little grey eyes that had always been wary and saw the trust in them now. 'I will make this work,' Dominic said again, and his commitment was as solid as the diamond he had placed on Bridgette's finger—his promise to Harry would cut glass if it had to, it was that strong. 'It will all be okay.'

He walked back into the bedroom with a sweet-smelling Harry and did a double-take as he saw his previously sexy fiancée in bright orange flannelette pyjama bottoms and a T-shirt.

'Don't want him having flashbacks about his aunt in years to come,' Bridgette said.

And it was hard, because she was more a mother than the one Harry had.

'I'm just going to wash my hands.'

He was so tidy and neat. As he handed over Harry and headed to the bedroom, she worked something out. 'That's why he smiled,' Bridgette said. 'When you took your jacket off, he knew that you were staying.'

She looked at her nephew, at smiling grey eyes that mirrored her own, and it was easy to say it as Dominic walked back in the room.

'I love you.'

EPILOGUE

BRIDGETTE never got tired of watching a new life come into the world. It had been a glorious morning and had been a wonderful straightforward birth. Kate was watching from the bed, and Michael, the father, was standing over Bridgette as she finished up the weights and measurements, popped on a hat, wrapped up their son and handed him over—the perfect miracle, really.

'We're going to move you back to your room soon,' Bridgette told the new parents. 'I'll come and check on you later, but Jasmine is going to take over from me for a little while.'

'That's right.' Kate looked up from her baby. 'You've got your scan this morning. I'm glad he arrived in time and you didn't have to dash off.'

'I wouldn't have left you,' Bridgette said. 'I'd already rung down and told them I might not be able to leave.' She looked at the little pink squashed face and smiled. 'You have a very considerate baby.'

'You'll have one of your own soon.'

'Not that soon.' Bridgette gave an impatient sigh, because she really couldn't wait. 'I'm only nineteen weeks.' And then she checked herself, because she sounded just like any impatient first-time mum, and then she laughed because that was exactly what she was. She gave a small wink. 'Nineteen weeks and counting!'

She would breathe when she got to twenty-four weeks, she decided, no, twenty-five, she corrected, thinking of the difference those extra few days had made to Francesca. Francesca had been discharged the day Dominic had started his new job—home on oxygen but doing brilliantly. It had been a nice way to start, Dominic had said.

As she walked down to the canteen where she was meeting Dominic, she wondered if he'd be able to get away. She really didn't mind if he couldn't. It was a routine scan, after all, and he'd end up asking the sonographer way too many questions. Still, even if she would be fine without him, she smiled when she saw him sitting at the far end of the canteen, sharing lunch with Harry, and she realised he was going to make the appointment—it was better with him there.

'Hi, Harry.' She received a lovely kiss that tasted of bananas, and asked about his busy morning, because along with building bricks he'd done a painting or two, or was it three? He really had come on in leaps and bounds. 'Any news from Courtney?' Bridgette asked Dominic.

'I was about to ask you the same,' Dominic said. 'She seems to be taking ages. I thought it started at eleven.'

Courtney had an interview this morning at the hospital. She was attending college, and now that she had been clean for well over a year, she was applying for a job on the drug and alcohol unit. But as much as Bridgette wanted her sister to get the job and to do well, she was a little bit torn, not quite sure that Courtney was ready for such a demanding role. Courtney lived in Bridgette's old flat, paid a minimal rent and had been working hard in every area of her life. Although Bridgette was unsure about this job, she was also worried how Courtney would take it if she was turned down when she had such high hopes.

'We're about to find out,' Dominic said, and she looked up as Courtney made her way over.

'How did you go?' Bridgette asked.

'I didn't get it,' Courtney said, which seemed contrary to her smile as she kissed her little boy. 'They don't think I'm quite ready to work with addicts yet. I need more time sorting out myself and they said that there was another course I should think about, but—' she gave a very wide smile '—they were very impressed with me. Apparently there is a position as a domestic. The patients do a lot of the cleaning work, but I would be in charge of the kitchen, sort of overseeing things.' She pulled a face. 'And I have to do the toilets and bathrooms. It's three days a week for now and some weekends, but they'll also pay me to do the course.' She gave a nervous swallow. 'Really, it's like a full-time job.'

'Oh, my!' Bridgette beamed. 'It sounds perfect.' Then laughed. 'Except I can't really imagine you keeping things clean.'

'She's such a bossy landlady, isn't she, Harry?' Courtney said, and Bridgette admitted that, yes, maybe at times she was. 'I have to go to the uniform room and then down to HR. I'd better get him back.'

'We'll take Harry back to daycare,' Dominic said, rather than offered, because Harry was still eating. 'That way he can finish his lunch.'

He was very firm with Courtney, didn't play games

with her, didn't bend to any to her whims, and he didn't let Bridgette bend too far either.

Courtney breezed off and Dominic rolled his eyes. 'She's doing great and everything, but she's still the most self-absorbed person that I've ever met.' He let out a wry laugh. 'She didn't even wish you luck for your scan.'

'That's Courtney.'

With Harry's lunch finished, they headed back to daycare but at the last minute, as he handed Harry over to Mary, it was Dominic who changed his mind. 'Should we bring him?'

'To the ultrasound?' Bridgette frowned at Mary. 'Won't it upset him?'

'It might be a wonderful way to get him used to the idea,' Mary said. 'After all he's going to be like a big brother.'

'I guess,' Bridgette said, because Harry was going to be a brother to this baby, even if not in the conventional way… And that just about summed them up entirely. It was as if Harry had three parents. Even if Courtney was doing brilliantly, it hadn't been the smoothest of rides, and it was an ongoing journey. As Dominic had once pointed out, Harry deserved the extra ration of love and he got it, over and over—from his mum, from his aunt and her husband, from his grandparents too, who made a far more regular fuss of him.

So as Dominic held Harry, Bridgette lay on the bed and the ultrasound started. 'Are we going to find out?' She still couldn't decide if she wanted to know the sex or wanted the surprise.

'I am,' Dominic said, studying the screen closely, and she felt sorry for the sonographer with this brusque

paediatrician in the room. 'Don't worry, I won't let on.'
He wouldn't; Bridgette knew that much. He was the
best in the world at keeping it all in. It had taken ages
to work him out and she was still doing it, would be
doing it for the rest of her life no doubt—but it was the
most pleasurable job in the world.

She heard the clicks and the measurements being
taken and felt the probe moving over her stomach. She
looked over to where Dominic and Harry were closely
observing the screen and then she laughed because there
he was doing somersaults, a little cousin for Harry, and
a nephew for Chris, who would be the most devoted
uncle in the world.

'Everything looks normal.' The sonographer smiled
and then she spoke to Dominic. 'Did you want to have
a look?'

She saw him hover, could almost hear the ten million
questions whizzing around that brilliant brain, knew
he wanted to take the probe and check and check again
that everything was perfect, that everything was just
so, but with supreme effort Dominic gave a small shake
of his head.

'"Normal" sounds pretty good,' he said, 'and it's not
as if we'll be sending it back.'

Already their family was perfect.

* * * * *

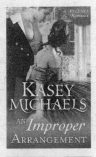

**Don't miss Sarah Morgan's
next Puffin Island story**

*Some Kind
of Wonderful*

Brittany Forrest has stayed away from Puffin Island
since her relationship with Zach Flynn went bad.
They were married for ten days and only just
managed not to kill each other by the
end of the honeymoon.

But, when a broken arm means she must return,
Brittany moves back to her Puffin Island home.
Only to discover that Zac is there as well.

Will a summer together help two lovers reunite or
will their stormy relationship crash on to the
rocks of Puffin Island?

Some Kind of Wonderful
COMING JULY 2015
Pre-order your copy today